90 MILES TO CUBA

by

linda carter-calhoun

Dedicated to my dad, David William Cobb, who taught me what it means to love unconditionally.

I miss you…

# Introduction

Elle was told some time ago by a very good friend; Laurie, that lobsters mate for life, having only one partner and no other. She shared that story with Bobby; they both loved the idea. As the years passed, she felt she needed to know the real truth about lobsters. This is what she found out:

"A female lobster can mate only just after she sheds her shell. Lobster society has evolved a complex, touching courtship ritual that protects the female when she is most vulnerable. When she is ready to molt, the female lobster approaches a male's den and wafts a sex 'perfume' called a pheromone in his direction. Unlike a female moth, whose sex pheromone may attract dozens of random suitors, the female lobster does the choosing. She usually seeks out the largest male in the neighborhood and stands outside his den, releasing her scent in a stream of urine from openings just below her antennae. He responds by fanning the water with his swimmerets, permeating his apartment with her perfume. He emerges from his den with his claws raised aggressively. She responds with a brief boxing match or by turning away. Either attitude seems to work to curb the male's aggression. The female raises her claws and places them on his head to let him know she is ready to mate. They enter the den, and some time after, from a few hours to several days later, the female molts. At this point the male could mate with her or eat her, but he invariably does the noble thing. He gently turns her limp body over onto her back with his walking legs and his mouth parts, being careful not to tear her soft flesh. They mate 'with a poignant gentleness that is almost human.' The male, who remains hard-shelled, inserts his first pair of swimmerets, which are rigid and grooved, and passes his sperm into a receptacle in the female's body. She stays in the safety of his den for about a week until her new shell hardens. By then the attraction has passed, and the couple part with hardly a backward glance."

So even though lobsters make tender lovers and then they part, elle and Bobby loved the initial story so much more that they decided to make it theirs.

Chapter 1 -- Her Quest


The dark and sinister halls of Abu Ghraib Prison have eyes
and ears at the beck and call of someone as powerful as he. Some
even say he is mystical and can walk through walls. That he takes a
keen interest in those who take a keen interest in him. Maybe--just
maybe--she had become one of them.

Her hope had always been to see and experience something
that would affect the rest of her life--something truly life changing,
but for the better *this time*. In those few days over there she did.

As she attempted to run down the dark, dank corridor of the
prison, she heard the heavy footsteps of someone running after her
and getting closer with every step. The whole evening felt surreal
to her. She knew that since she'd taken a few sips of her Dr.
Pepper, it was as if she had been drugged. *But how*, she thought, *or*

*more to the point, why?* It was a twist-off cap, and she'd just opened the bottle when she decided to save the rest until morning. She took a few sips, then put the cap back on. But who or even why would someone tamper with her soft drink? She knew one thing for sure, and that was that she had to get out. There was only one way to do that – the staircase. It was so dark, wet and slippery, she could only just manage to keep her footing under most normal conditions. But these were not normal conditions, and she could barely see the next step in front of her.

Her evening had started out as it had the past two nights, with her two roommates, with whom she shared the 8 x 10 prison cell, trying to unwind the only way 19-year-olds could. They were whooping it up until all hours of the late evening and the early morning with their friends--"friends with benefits," they liked to call it. She knew she had an early day tomorrow. She'd been working very hard on her research and felt for the first time that it was finally starting to pay off. She felt incredibly close to her target. Luckily, she had already made plans to watch movies with Bobby in the day room so she did not have to go through yet another night of moaning and groaning. She hoped that by the time their movies were over they all would be asleep and she could get some much-needed shuteye.

Before gathering her sweats and running shoes, she could not help but comment loudly about what she thought of all of this shit they seemed to continually do. She also knew that the problem right now, other than the noisy foursome, was that she could not simply watch movies and rest. She needed to let the day's research settle into the library of her mind. Her nature was that of someone who could soak in a lot of information and then draw a mental roadmap connecting all the pieces of the puzzle. But that required a moment of quietness. Iraq seldom offered a moment that was totally quiet. This was one of those times when it should be, but the young girls she bunked with were in high gear. While they were both nice, they tended to party as much as possible (as much as one could party without alcohol). Since they couldn't drink, they got high on sex. One was a young Air Force girl. She was pretty and a little quieter than her young Army battle buddy. The young Army E-4 was married, but her husband was not in Iraq. He was back home--he definitely was not the young man making her scream with pleasure at this moment. In fact, the young man with

3

his head between her legs was not the same man who was in that same spot two hours earlier, or from the night before. One thing was certain; the soldier's husband would be shocked if he knew just how much cock this young lady had swallowed within the last couple of months. But, as far as Elle was concerned, the young soldier could do whatever she wanted, if only she could do it more quietly.

So instead of trying to change into her sweats right there in the room before meeting Bobby in the "day room" to watch movies, she would have to drag all her shit to the ladies shower trailer to change clothes.

The day room was simply an area set aside for folks to sit, relax, and maybe watch a movie on the old television and donated DVD player. She felt certain she and Bobby would be the only ones down there. If only she could get there without having to go down those steps. No such luck though.

She hadn't gotten much rest since she and Bobby showed up at this place only three short days ago. No sooner as she had gotten there, she got into her total non-stop energizer bunny self She got on the ground running, as Bobby would say, most days not even stopping to have lunch. She knew what had to be done and she was ready, willing and able to do it. She had the tools available to her as she did in Cuba. Cuba, where she actually started this quest, the quest for Fadel al-Khalayleh, or better known to most people as Abu Musab al-Zarqawi--AMZ for short. She knew that in the dimmed recesses of the American military operations rooms dotted across Iraq, they called him "the Z-man." Intelligence specialists much like herself dedicated to studying him were referred to reverentially as "Zarqeologists."

She looked at the photos she had of him; only eight had been out there but now four new ones floated around. His features were soft, and his eyes were dark but strangely comforting. She wondered how this man could possibly be Washington's most wanted man in Iraq. Zarqawi celebrated his 38th birthday in October with a $25 million bounty on his head for a string of attacks against civilians and troops in Iraq. After more reading and researching this elusive creature, she soon found out just why his reward had been bumped up.

Of course, she knew the basics. Any news junkie knew these facts. They barely scratched the surface of what she would dig up during her quest. All the normal info was there - **Date of birth:** October 30, 1966; **Place of birth:** Zarqa, Jordan; **Height:** Unknown; **Weight:** Unknown; **Hair:** Dark; **Eyes:** Dark **Sex:** Male; **Complexion:** Olive; **Passport:** Jordanian Z264958; **Aliases:** Ahmad Fadil Al-Khalailah, Abu Ahmad, and Abu Muhammad, Sakr Abu Suwayd. *Kid stuff,* she thought. She delved deeper still.

His tribe, the Beni Hassan, straddled many borders in the modern Middle East. He grew up in poverty and squalor. When he was 17, he dropped out of school and began to drink heavily. Purportedly, he was jailed briefly in the 80s for sexual assault. Zarqawi is said to have a rivalry with Bin Laden, both of whom gained prominence in the "jihad" against Soviet forces in Afghanistan in the 1980s. Reports had shown that he traveled to Europe and started the al-Tawhid terrorist organization, a group dedicated to killing Jews and installing an Islamic regime in Jordan. After that, Zarqawi spent several years in Jordan and was detained on charges of conspiracy to overthrow the monarchy and establish an Islamic caliphate. After his release, he fled the country.

The next stop on his itinerary was his old stomping ground--Afghanistan. He was believed to have set up a training camp in the western city of Herat, near the border with Iran, and to have renewed his acquaintance with al-Qaeda. He was believed to have fled to Iraq in 2001 after losing a leg in a US missile strike on his Afghan base. In 2003, he was named as the brains behind a series of lethal bombings--from Casablanca in Morocco to Istanbul in Turkey. In addition, somewhere amongst all of his dirty dealings he somehow had the time to get married to his cousin on his mother's side and have four children. They supposedly still lived in the city of his birth, Zarqa. Three years ago he married his second wife, a 14 year old Palestinian, in Pakistan.

She was starting to think his life was spun in both legends and conflicting accusations. No doubt he had been involved in many violent acts of terror and he may or may not be guilty of all he was accused of. The gravest accusation that he was directly involved in, the planning of the September 11, 2001 attacks on the USA, had been refuted. Was AMZ the modern day "boogeyman"?

An example of the conflicting stories concerning Zarqawi was that he sometimes had a wooden leg and sometimes not.

Earlier reports indicated that he had lost his leg in a US missile strike, although the US military now believed he still had both. AMZ was not about to correct any misconceptions about himself and that was for certain. Then there were the reports that he was killed by a missile attack in Afghanistan. In all her research, she could not find a single source anywhere that claimed to have actually seen Zarqawi since late 2001 in Afghanistan. No one, on the record, had been able to independently verify that he actually even existed. He seemed to be everywhere and yet nowhere, plotting terrorist attacks in Britain, Spain and Jordan, while moving like a specter through Iraq's heart of darkness.

She was anxious to pick up where she had left off in Cuba. Even though many were uncertain of his existence, she felt confident in her research. She knew in her gut that she was not only in the same country as AMZ but in the same city, if not the same muhala; neighborhood. Only time would tell if she was to track him down or, worse yet, he to track her down. She knew that there were perhaps hundreds of "task forces" out in the DC area, and all parts of the globe for that matter, all looking for one of the most elusive and dangerous man in the world, but that did not stop

8

her relentless research. She felt that she had a different fish to fry--or catch being the better term--than AMZ. She had been tracking this Bedouin from Jordan as he moved easily from country to country as if he was invisible.

She was so close, so very close, that she could almost smell him, almost feel his hot breath on the back of her neck. This petty criminal who turned out to have ties to Osama bin Laden himself and Saddam Hussein. AMZ had a horrific history of terrorist acts and a reputation as a brutal, merciless killer. Countless people had died under his rule and his blade.

She'd thought a few times, while she was working with the detainees at Camp Delta in Cuba, that she was being followed or watched by someone. Sometimes her skin would crawl for no apparent reason. She "felt" someone who seemed to be barely there, invisible, just as she would turn around to look. Everyone at GTMO knew her devotion to this quest to get this man and it was not for the reward, regardless of the amount.

She wondered how quickly word might have already spread through the detention center where she and Bobby worked. Talk flew like wildfire amongst the detainees, specifically the Afghans.

9

The team she was on specifically dealt with these men and knew how much they seemed to know. No one knew how, but it was as if most, if not all, detainees knew the most current of events. She also wondered if any of the detainees knew she was the one who was hot on the tracks of AMZ. It worried her sometimes that that little piece of information was out there. She noticed at times while in the interrogation booth with these men that sometimes, just sometimes, she sensed that they knew her. It scared her because she knew that those guys still had connections "back home."

She recalled one particular interrogation with a certain high-level Afghan government official who had strong ties with al Qaeda, when all the electrical power completely died. It had been one of those thunderclouds-impending kind of days. As she, the interrogator, the linguist and one Mr. High Level Afghan Government Official sat in complete darkness for what seemed like hours but was realistically only seconds, she, the closest to the detainee, wondered whether that shackle on his ankles could stretch to the table where she sat. She could almost feel his breath to the right side of her cheek. She sat ever so quietly wishing she could just dissolve into the floor. Then out of the hot dark stillness of the room, she thought she felt his breath as he spoke in her direction. Because he spoke Pashto, his English was heavily accented. She was not 100% sure of what she heard, but it sounded something to the effect of "we know you."

Just as the word "you" floated in the heavy, hot, sticky Cuban air, the emergency lights kicked on. She'd been looking in his direction the whole time it was dark. The detainee sat to the right of her with the linguist behind him and the interrogator right in front. Mr. High Level Afghan Government Official stared right into her and winked, then quickly went back into interrogation mode. Chills ran down her spine, and all the baby fine hair on her arms stood straight up. He went back to the interrogation as if nothing had just happened. Every once in a while, she could tell he was checking her out with his periphery—the chills returned to slither down her back. She could not wait until that three-hour interrogation was up. She was scared and she badly needed to ask the interrogator and the linguist if they heard or even saw.

But here and now in this prison, as it was now known to everyone as Abu Ghraib Prison, regardless of the spelling, this vast walled fortress had distinct notoriety as the place where US

11

military police subjected Iraqi detainees to systematic sadistic abuse and degradation. The prison was located right outside of Baghdad. This place had been her home for the past three days and was to be her home for the next three months or so. Back in the day, this was the very place where Saddam Hussein used to execute and torture his opponents. It was currently being called Baghdad Central Detention Center, perhaps to rid itself of the awful stigma that was now and would forever be attached to that place.

Before the military, government and contractors moved in, what was now considered to be their living quarters used to be the actual prison cells where Saddam not only kept his prisoners but tortured them at will, right down to the hook that was still looming above on the ceiling in each of the cells. It hung there like some old witch's crooked finger, beckoning someone, anyone, to hang what he or she pleased there. And as Saddam would have it, he did that very thing more often than not.

She shook her head hard to physically bring herself back to the present. Back to what happened. Back to the pain and blood and the nightmare she was living. She grabbed her little shower bag, towel and change of clothes and hurried out to make her way to those stupid stairs. She had to get herself to the women's shower trailer before anyone woke up. She couldn't let anyone see her in this state. She started down the dark corridor, hearing footsteps coming faster and harder as she neared the stairs. Her poor heart was racing. She so desperately wanted to scream, but nothing would come out, and that strange tunnel vision and nausea she was experiencing was absolutely no help. She wondered why no one had looked out to see what the commotion was all about. Why didn't anyone come out of their "prison cells" to see what was going on? Was she hallucinating? Was what happened to her prior to this also a hallucination? Could the pain in her nether region be a hallucination? Could that certain someone coming after her also be a hallucination? She could not help but think that this was some very strange dream gone wrong. She realized just then that she had to depend solely on herself to get out of this place, regardless of the reality.

As she took the stairs two steps at a time, she could feel it giving way. The ground under her was no longer there. She realized, as one does when things like this happen, in slow motion,

13

that she had a couple of flights of stairs that she could and possibly would come thumping down on. How hard would her fall be? She had too much time to think what was going to happen to her and not enough time to react. All she knew was that her legs were almost perpendicular to her torso and getting higher with every second. Then it happened, her first big thump of many more thumps. Her elbow made the first contact; the boney joint hit straight on the wet concrete step with a crack, then the biggest blow, her head, and finally her back, making sounds of Rice Crispies--snap, crackle, pop--as she hit every single vertebra several steps later.

All she knew was that she was sinking in some black abyss. As the tunnel vision progressed, everything got dark all around her. She reached up towards the back of her head. She felt the warm wet stickiness she thought to be blood--HER blood--pouring out. It seemed to be too much blood. The whole right side of her hair was matted in a big tangled mess, and her clothes were soaked straight through to her skin in a combination of sweat and blood. She was one bloody mess. She knew her legs and sweat pants were covered in blood, and now her head was just pouring. Was she

14

hallucinating all of this? The pain in her every pore told a different story; this was real. Was this a drug-induced hallucination or real? She just was not sure.

Just before all the lights went out in her head, she made one last attempt to open her eyes. She wanted to try at least once more so she could have a better idea of exactly where she was. When she was finally able to adjust her eyes, she thought she saw an Arabic face floating right above her. He had the darkest eyes she had ever seen. Strangely enough, they were the most comforting eyes she had seen in a very long time. Something about him was incredibly familiar to her. It was as if she knew him, but not. As the realization came to her who this man actually was, she heard him whisper, "It is not our time. You will be back and we will continue where we have left off." With that comment just hanging there in the wet hot air, he seemed to disappear within the concrete walls much as he had appeared.

She lay there on the wet concrete landing; her almost lifeless body gave way to someone else, or was it? He scooped her up to carry her God only knew where. She could tell was that he was not a very large man, but he somehow felt very strong to her.

His steps were direct, as he seemed to know exactly where he was going to take her. He had the strong, measured steps of a soldier.

As she lay in his arms, he held her tightly against his chest. With her eyes closed, she thought at first she could hear what sounded like singing, or was it a faint humming sound? It was so faint, yet the tune was very familiar. She just could not pinpoint what it was. Was it time for Salaat? It was much too late for the Salaat-ul-Isha, the Night Prayer, and way too early for the Salaat-ul-Fajr; the Morning Prayer. What was that sound she heard? She could vaguely make out a word here and there. Words like Tripoli--*hmmm, Libya,* she thought. Was this guy from Libya? She then heard the word "fighting" and something of a battle. Her body trembled in his arms as she thought of exactly who this man was or could be. She wasn't quite sure if he was the one singing or if someone was with him and whether or not it was in English or a foreign language. She knew a little bit of a lot of languages. She just knew it was familiar. So much was going on in those few minutes.

With that, she was out. Her thought, or perhaps it was a dream that came to her in that moment, was that of her garden back

16

home. Was she dreaming all of this? Dream or not, in her mind she was no longer at the hellish prison. She was back in another moment that began her metamorphosis...

Her morning started out much like any other morning, except for that incredibly disturbing nightmare she had. It scared her to her very core. She knew how sometimes her dreams would come to fruition. Her mother said she had the gift, but still she hoped this was not one of those times. She had no time to think of things of that nature at this point because this was not any other morning. This was THE morning that would ultimately change her life forever.

As mornings go, this usually meant up at five, shower, change and on the road by six. That was the type of morning she had encountered all her working life, typical of the life of a government employee living in the DC metro area. That was all about to change for her. She was on her way to do something extraordinary, something she had dreamed about most of her life.

Two ex-husbands later, she was about to embark on a career change that had been long in the coming. She'd decided to get out of civil service. She'd been in the military intelligence field as a government analyst for over nineteen years. Now, she thought she would try defense contracting. She'd worked with contractors all her life. They always seemed to have the more interesting careers and at the best locations. Knowing how she was, she was not about to do anything half-ass. So before she up and quit her government position, she researched and found the largest and supposedly best defense contractor around. She considered herself a damn good intelligence analyst and believed that this company would benefit from having her on their team. Seriously, she was not one toot her own horn, but she was confident in her abilities and believed that she could make a difference. The bottom line was that, unlike many folks connected with the defense world, she actually cared about her job. So many folks liked the idea of being around the intelligence world because it was cool. She was in because it was all she ever knew, and she knew the world was not a happy-go-lucky place. There were bad people out there. Not bad like someone who robs liquor stores, but bad like someone who could rip the unborn children from the wombs of women while their husbands were forced to watch. The typical American heard about these things on the morning news and thought that because it

18

happened in some other country, it was horrible but ultimately didn't affect them. She knew better. She knew that the real monsters were out there and were really trying to take over the world--just like in the movies.

She felt that her job as a government analyst was not letting her get to where she wanted (needed) to be. She had heard that one company in particular had the contract she was looking for. She looked up their website and saw it—Lockhart Marion, job openings in Cuba. She actually had to read it aloud just to make sure she was not dreaming. For the past 20 years this civil servant had spent her professional life behind a computer terminal analyzing things that others experienced and wrote about, never actually experiencing it herself firsthand. That was about to change. She would be the one people would go to, and her words would be analyzed as they came firsthand from the terrorists and insurgents alike. The problem with being an analyst was that she was subjected to the thought processes of the investigators, agents, or interrogators speaking with the bad guys. Many times these questioners wrote their reports with their own spin to the information. She wanted to hear the monsters speak, form her own opinions, and then analyze what the bastards were really saying and thinking.

Amazingly, she applied for the position, and got it! She was going to the place that housed true evil. The media liked to portray GTMO as a travesty--a place where the bad guys were actually the Americans who tortured a bunch of misunderstood Afghan farmers. Well, the people who knew the reality of what happened in Afghanistan and Iraq (as well as other places throughout the world) knew that the folks spending their time behind bars in GTMO were anything but innocent. Simply picking up a history book would show that these "nice" folks came from a culture that thrived on violence. It was inherent to their culture. There were some truly disturbed minds in GTMO, and she was ready to use her skills to peel back the layers of their madness. Of course, she would have to be careful. Others like her had delved into the darkness and came back changed. True evil has a way of staining those around it. However, her trip to Cuba was important for other reasons as well.

As she packed her bags, she recalled a memory, or maybe it was a dream but one so real as to become a memory. Her dream was of going on a trip. Twenty-three years ago, she had traveled to Key West. That was the first time she saw a sign--THE sign. It was a big, concrete, buoy-shaped sign that said "Southernmost Point in the USA." She looked and looked at it, but what really caught her attention was that it also said "90 miles to Cuba." Her first thoughts were of Hemingway and mojito's. Although being in Key West also sparked such thoughts, there she stood looking at that damn sign and wondering. Wondering what it would be like to live in such a place. Little did she know 23 years later the dream would come true.

She had such thoughts every now and again, thoughts of living and loving in Cuba. Mostly those thoughts would pop into her head while hanging out in Key West. The last time she was there was the previous year. She was there for her high school reunion, during Hurricane Isabella. That was a story which involved her very first boyfriend's best friend, Michael. While in school, she felt that Michael hated her guts. She always felt such tension when the three of them were together. She could not wait to see if that tension was still there. She had not seen Michael for over 20 years. The events that transpired between the two of them during that hurricane really was a story all its own and one best mused about later.

Packed and ready to go, she waited for the taxi that would take her to her destiny. She looked around her house to see if she had gotten everything needed for this new life of hers. She didn't take much with her--clothes mostly. She decided that was best. Best to leave the past behind and start anew. The trip to Cuba was to last a year minimum. In that time she would not make any decisions concerning her home. She wanted to leave everything exactly the way it was, intact. She made sure that everything was in its place. That was the German side of her. Everything in its place; she recalled a saying, "a place for everything and everything in its place." That was her, through and through, everything just so. Everything in its box, all within the lines. The Mexican side would come out every now and again. Two ex-husbands got the opportunity to see her Mexican side all too often, to their respective dismay.

The taxi pulled up to the house. Unexpectedly, she felt an incredible sadness in her heart, the kind of sadness that feels as your guts are being ripped apart by hungry wolves. She'd felt this sadness before, once, when her dad passed away four years ago and another time before that, a long time before that. It was when she and her first husband Richard were still together, in Germany, their first tour together. Richard had been in the Army for over ten years when they first met. This was her first tour to Germany and Richard's second. Why unexpectedly would she feel such sadness right as she was to embark on her dream, the dream of a lifetime, her dream at long last? She thought for a few seconds and it struck her. She then realized why.

## Chapter 2 -- Husbands – Past & Present

She met her first husband almost twenty-three years ago. She was not a young girl but not yet a woman either. When they met in Miami, she had just broken yet another man's heart. She'd moved from Texas after the break-up to live with her family in Florida until she got herself settled in this new city. That was how she acted all those years ago. Love them, and leave them when or if they get a touch too close. Let no one person get too close, and if he had the misfortune of doing so and, God forbid, told her of his feelings towards her, that would be the last of him. At least that was the way it had been in her life. She never intended to hurt anyone. She liked having a good time and being with people. Moreover, like any young lady, she liked the idea of being in love. Still, she was not willing to fall so deeply in love that she would lose herself. Unfortunately, some of the men that she had let into

24

her life fell deeply for her--like this last guy in Texas. She had told him that she was not ready to give herself to anyone yet. She thought he would be mature enough to handle that kind of relationship. But, like most men, he could not and this led to heartache.

So here she was....brand new city, brand new life. Wow! Miami was not just another city! Miami had it all--culture, sunshine, music, and, of course, the beach! She loved the sun. Something about the sun just seemed to burn everything bad away. She thought getting some sun would make her feel better about herself, feel better about hurting yet another person. Hurt them before they hurt her was her motto. There he was under a very large palm tree. She could tell he had not been in Miami long or even anywhere with an actual summer. He was pale in comparison to everyone around him, including herself. He lay there reading Ernest Hemingway, "A Moveable Feast" she believed it to be. She was not particularly fond of Hemingway, but she did like this piece of work. Could it be because it was about Paris? Paris in the '20s where Hemingway and his first wife had lived happily on a few bucks a day and still had money for drinks, skiing in the Alps, and fishing trips to Spain. On every corner and at every café table were the most extraordinary people living wonderful lives and telling fantastic stories. That was the way she wanted to live her life. Richard loved Hemingway's way of writing based on one simple premise: "All you have to do is write one true sentence. Write the truest sentence you know." She liked that idea. She later found out that Hemingway was Richard's favorite author.

She thought of getting out into the sun and just bake her ass but her mother's words rang in her ears, "You're going to get cancer doing that," and of course, later on in her life, her mothers words rang true because in fact, she did get malignant melanoma. It happened when she was still married to her second husband, Tom, who decided with no hesitation whatsoever to go ahead and take his 30-day leave to skydive across America instead of staying with her through the trauma of surgery.

As she looked around the small stretch of beach, she opted for a section that had a little shade and a little bit of sun. Surely not just a tiny bit on her already cocoa brown body would hurt. She had to admit the man under the big palm tree reading the one and only Hemingway book she liked intrigued her. Could it be a sign?

26

She thought best not to appear too brazen by sitting too close, so she found a smaller palm tree close, but not too close, to this man. She turned on her radio and applied her sunblock. Boy, her mother would be proud--she hated when she actually listened to what her mother had to say.

As she lay in the sun thinking of her life, she wondered if she would ever be happy. Could she be happy? Was it in her to scrape up any happiness for herself? She thought what if that man under the big palm tree could make her happy? What a strange thought to have about a total stranger. She had to admit, there was something about him. One thing she noticed, he appeared to be completely comfortable. He was not straining his neck every time a half-naked woman walked by. In fact, he appeared as though he was the only one on the beach. He rather reminded her of a lion sunning himself on a rock shelf. Not arrogant, just assured that he was king of the jungle and that he was king of the jungle because it was simply supposed to be that way. Yep, this man was like that. And as far as she could tell, he did not even look her way when she applied oil to her tight little body. *Damn, the audacity of this man.* Wait a minute! That was it! This was a "real" man. That was the difference. It was evident that he had already proven himself in the world--unlike "what's his name" that she left in Texas. Honestly, the more she thought about this stranger, the hotter it seemed to get. At this point, she wasn't sure if it was the sun or the thought of the man reading Hemingway.

It was getting hot that early afternoon. It had been a hot summer but even as autumn neared, it remained just as hot. It was hot like only Miami could be. Hot with just a touch of something wicked on the sea breeze. It was also October and almost her birthday. She would be 24. She really was still innocent in the ways of the world. Sure, she'd had boyfriends and such, but she never felt real love, not the emotional kind and definitely not the physical kind. At 24 years of age, she was still a virgin. As a young Latina growing up in San Antonio, she grew up thinking that everything was a sin--especially sex. Therefore, she was still a virgin, but not so sure she was happy about that fact. She knew she had the kind of body that excited men. Truth be told, she felt certain that there were a few women who found her attractive as well. Once again, she cursed herself, for she had listened to her mother again, this time about "waiting for marriage."

28

As the sun beat down, small droplets of sweat started to form between her ample breasts. Oh yeah, she had extremely sexy breasts, and they were large and firm. Right now sweat was running between them. This was the time to cool things off! It was time for a dip in the ocean. Her nerves were in full tilt motion now; to the point that she seemed to trip on even the smallest grain of sand as she attempted to strut. She was nervous because the only way to get to that particular stretch of water was to pass in front of that intriguing man next to the big palm tree. She really was a shy woman. Would she be able to walk by and not trip? To ease her nerves just a bit, she decided to say just a little something to him.

"Can you watch my radio while I'm gone?" she asked.

He looked up at her and, with the calm and collected manner she'd expected he would have, said, "I'd be glad to! Hey, have you been to the refreshment bar yet? Would you like something to drink from the snack bar, before you take a dip in the ocean?"

Hmmm, now this was a little more than she had bargained for, and she was excited. Still, more than anything, she loved the quiet reserve he exuded. She now felt confident in her initial

29

assessment of this man. He was confident, and it showed in how he was able to look at her without staring at her breasts. Although she could sense that he was more than just a little interested. So, of course, she took him up on his offer of a drink. He did not bother asking what she would like. Was this arrogance, or was this just his way? Who knows, maybe he had noticed her and had been thinking of her while reading his book.

Returning with the beverages, he introduced himself as Richard. She felt totally at ease with this man, this stranger, for some reason. He came back with two Cokes instead of two icy "cold ones."

"I wasn't sure if you were of drinking age or not so I got us Cokes."

He was happy to hear that she indeed was of legal age and that her 24th birthday was just around the corner. They talked for hours and hours. Actually, he did all the talking. He told her that he was in the military, the Army to be exact, and that his field was in intelligence. She wasn't sure what that meant but was fascinated by everything he told her. She sat in awe of this "grown up."

She was still very shy around people, around men in

particular. She listened intently to him, captivated by his talk of his travels. "I just returned from Berlin where I was stationed for the past four years," he told her. The places he had been and the things he had done. She wondered about the intelligence business he talked about. She had no idea what that meant, but it sounded interesting. He had such a cool, aloof arrogance about him that you could probably lay an ice cube on him and it would never melt. She never knew anyone like him. The men--boys really--she dated were the typical alpha males. This one was different. He was an adult. He had a touch of gray in his hair, just on the temples. She thought it made him seem debonair. She had no idea how old Richard actually was but knew that he was older. He looked quite fit; the body of a long distance runner, she thought. She was glad that he was not a tall man. Her last boyfriend was too tall; she spent the past year with a crick in her neck, which was none too fun!

As the sun dipped down, she decided to leave before it got awkward. What if he did not ask to see her again? What if he had been bored to tears with her because of her lack of conversation? What if he didn't ask for her number? All these thoughts raced in her head. She felt panicky and thought that maybe she should just blurt out the number without him asking for it. She told herself not to do such a bold thing. Again, her mother's words buzzed in her head, "That's not what young ladies do."

She got up quickly. "Thanks so much for the Coke and conversation, Richard." She went back to her blanket and her stuff, to her radio. On the way back, she thought, *why? Why didn't he ask? Why doesn't he want to see me again?* Why did she even care? She was so caught up by her thoughts that she was completely oblivious to him standing next to her with paper and pen in hand. Apparently, he was as graceful with his movements as he was with his words--she had never heard him approach. Then again, her heart was still beating loudly in her chest. Just for a second she wondered if he could actually hear it! She felt certain he knew she was interested, but then in his quiet self-assured voice, he asked, "Would you give me your number so perhaps we could get together some other time?"

She smiled broadly and jotted down the number of her mother's house. For a second she wasn't quite sure if the number she wrote was correct. She'd only been living with her family for one week and who really ever calls themselves?

They parted ways with him saying those three infamous words, "I'll call you." She'd heard that line a time or two in her short dating life, so she was not about to hold her breath. She drove to her mother's house and before she even got out of the car her mother said, "Some strange man called looking for you. He wants you to call him back. His name is Richard or some such thing."

*Oh my God*, she thought. Her knees felt a little shaky when her mom handed her the note with the telephone number on it. She dialed the number and her life changed.

After a year and a half of courtship and an official "ok" from her dad, they married. They spent a few days in Key West before their wedding to pick out her trousseau she would take with them for their cruise to the Bahamas on their honeymoon. It was while they were in Key West that she saw that one sign for the very first time, THE sign. It was in the shape of a buoy, red, yellow, black, and white, which read "southern most point." It also said "90 miles to Cuba." For some reason, that particular part of the sign transfixed her. She had many strange emotions about this odd-looking sign. She felt that it was THE sign, HER sign, for some reason. She felt compelled to stare at that sign until it became too strange. Richard looked at her quizzically and said, "What the heck are you doing, babe? We're going to be late for our dinner reservations." It took Richard calling her to the car for her to leave that sign.

Their wedding was to take place in Miami in a chapel on the Air Force Base with the reception to follow at the Officers Club down the road. Richard had been only one of two Army officers assigned to the Air Force base. It was not the wedding or reception of her or Richard's dreams; it was her mother's wedding--traditional with the proper amount of bridesmaids and groomsmen, the proper white dress with the proper veil. All they really wanted was a simpler affair, perhaps at the beach where they first met, both barefoot, just like when they met.

The two of them spent the next eleven years together, working hard and playing harder, skiing in the French Alps, driving to Italy with no directions or Lire in their pockets, 'biking to beer gardens throughout Germany, shopping in Berlin back when "the wall" was still up. Although the times they shared were mostly good, it ended nevertheless. Not with a bang but with a whimper, much like it started. The marriage was a good one but because of Richard's work, she barely saw him. She needed and wanted him, but he was gone too often. Their sex life together was not bad, although because of her lack of experience, she wasn't sure if it was a good one either. She sometimes wondered if that was all there was to it. She did not have the experience to know the answers to all of her questions. She knew, perhaps just by instinct, that she wanted a different type of sex with her husband. He was a kind and gentle lover, but she wanted…needed more. Maybe not so much gentleness. So as it stood, their marriage hadn't stopped "growing" as much as it just stopped moving altogether. Many years after their divorce, he finally mustered up the courage to ask her, "Why did you leave me?"

Simply put, she said, "You never asked me to stay…"

Through the years, particularly during her second marriage, they both tried to make a go of it, but for whatever reason, it just was not meant to be. Perhaps they had the time they were supposed to have and quite possibly learn a thing or two from each other, then move on. Whatever the reason, it was apparent to everyone who knew them and even those who didn't know them well, that they continued to love and respect each other even though they were apart. Still, off and on, they both tried to make a go of it by making several trips back and forth while she was in Germany and Richard in Africa.

She and Richard had been divorced for over ten years by the time they decided to make a more serious go of it. Her first travel to visit Richard would be Ethiopia--Addis Ababa to be more exact. The name of the capital meant "new flower" but there was nothing new about this city or this country, nor "flowery." Ethiopia's elevation goes from 1,500 to 3,000 meters above sea level, which made sleeping difficult for the newcomer to this foreign country, and she was no exception. Preparing for the trip to Addis Ababa was not an altogether a fun experience. She had to go through a plethora of immunizations before leaving. The trip there from Germany had been a long one, and the change in temperature, dramatic. Luckily, she had just missed the monsoon season where she had heard that it could rain for days on end for months at a time. One thing she did not count on was that she would have such trouble sleeping. She knew about how the high elevation usually did a number with someone's sleep, but she did not realize that she would have this much of a terrible time of it. She may not have been ready for lack of sleep, but she was at least ready for the uneasy queasiness in her stomach when she ate the wrong type of food.

Going to Ethiopia was a revelation for her. Richard had gotten her a room at a posh hotel, and part of her felt guilty living this way when just outside the gates of this wonderful hotel was the poorest of poor countries she had ever seen. When she went to visit Richard at the Embassy, which was equally posh with a pool and tennis courts, she even had her own driver. The locals employed at the hotel actually had to learn how to shower and use a conventional toilet, but outside those gates was a different matter altogether. She witnessed more poverty than she could have ever thought possible, yet the people seemed to be happy in spite of the woes they suffered. She often wondered how these people could smile, having to live as they did. There were people in the States who committed suicide because they could not afford to move out of a trailer park. Here, there were people living in huts with a simple piece of tin as a roof--and the flies! They were everywhere! Regardless of their plight, she felt that she was offered a wonderful opportunity to see how things really were outside the confines of the inward-looking United States. While this trip was geographically stimulating, it was evident that she and Richard would probably never again be husband and wife.

Even as she was thinking about the finality of "them" and while she did not know it just yet, he would make another trip to Germany for his R&R, and she would be a bundle of nerves and excitement. By his last R&R, they both knew that it just wasn't meant to be. She and Richard were more like a pair of comfy shoes; nothing sexy or snazzy about the shoes but nevertheless, comfortable. While they definitely still loved each other, she realized that they felt the same way they had felt when they were first engaged. While this sounds wonderful, marriages and relationships should evolve and grow. Perhaps that was the problem here. They had the love, but they did not grow as a couple should. In spite of everything, love was something to be cherished, and they both felt that they had to give their love a chance. They made one more attempt after he was transferred to Mozambique. Richard planned a wonderful little get away to Pretoria, South Africa with a slight detour to the N'Kosi Sana Game Lodge to celebrate his "wife's" birthday in October. N'Kosi Sana Game Lodge is situated in the rolling hills of Groenfontein and offers marvelous views, the scenic Eland River, two dams fed by natural fountains, game in abundance and the best of it, it is only an hour's drive from Pretoria!

After being married for eleven years and knowing her for several years more, he was keenly aware of her "things to do before I die" list and he wanted so much to be a part of as many as he could. He knew that he could knock out, in no particular order, from her list, a few of them just with this trip alone: travel south of the equator, ride a horse, and go on a safari in Africa. While at the camp he could do those, but while in Pretoria he had planned one more from her list: jump out of an airplane.

Richard thought she would really like to stay at the Bush Camp where they could "rough it" and enjoy the wildlife in perfect seclusion. The Camp had the usual amenities, such as a pool with bar, hiking, as well as guided game walks, plus some horseback riding. They both had a wonderful time, but it was hardly the romantic getaway that either one of them anticipated or wanted. Even knowing this, Richard suggested that they still go on to

Pretoria afterwards because he knew that she would fall in love with the beautiful Jacaranda for all the purple blossom-bedecked trees which line its thoroughfares.

The Jacarandas are spectacular when they burst into brilliant lilac-blue blooms in late October; the sight sends rubbernecking drivers careening into each other. The flowering trees create washes of purple each season. They have the loveliest fern-like leaves, which seem to form a canopy above the handsome grey barked trunks and branches. Jacarandas come from Brazil, but they grow well there in Pretoria, Mexico, Central America, and South America and also in Australia. In particular, mass plantings of jacarandas along the street create a river of purple as well as a carpet underneath the trees when the flowers begin to fall. These large trees grow to 10 meters tall and up to 10 meters wide with a low, broad branching habit. As well as the commonly seen purple, there are also white-flowering and variegated foliage varieties. Richard knew the purple variety would captivate his former wife, as purple had always been her most favorite color.

Richard knew that she would love Pretoria, not only because of the beautiful purple trees, but because it was a lovely, quiet city with a long, involved and fascinating history. They had a wonderful time where they found open spaces that they could walk and mountain bike. Richard also took her to the Cullinan Diamond Mine. He knew that this would be one of her favorite places. He knew how much his former wife loved diamonds and the bigger the better as far as she was concerned.

After learning about this particular trip to the diamond mine, she couldn't help but do a little research about the place. She couldn't help it, it was her nature. She found out that this particular diamond mine was found by Frederick Wells, surface manager of the Premier Diamond Mining Company in Cullinan, Gauteng, South Africa. The largest rough gem-quality diamond ever found, at 3,106.75 carats, was cut into three large parts by Asscher Brothers of Amsterdam, and eventually into some 11 large gem-quality stones and a number of smaller fragments. The largest polished gem from the stone is named Cullinan I or the Great Star of Africa, and at 530.2 carats was the largest polished diamond in the world until the 1985 discovery of the Golden Jubilee diamond, also from the Premier mine. Cullinan I is now mounted in the head of the Sceptre with the Cross. The second largest gem from the

Cullinan stone, Cullinan II or the Lesser Star of Africa, at 317.4 carats, is the second largest polished diamond in the world and is also part of the British crown jewels, as it forms a part of the Imperial State Crown. Both gems are on display at the Tower of London, as parts of the British crown jewels.

Throughout the years, rumors spread of a second half of the Cullinan diamond, as certain signs point to the diamond being part of a larger crystal. Rumor had it that before Frederick Wells sold the diamond to Sir Thomas Cullinan, he broke off a piece which sized in at about 1500 to 2000 carats. If this were true, then the original Cullinan diamond would have weighed in at about 5000 carats.

After doing a tour of the diamond mine, they also took to the horse trail at the Vootrekker Monument, being very careful to check out the white rhinos that roamed there. The last activity for the pair was to do a tandem skydive at the Pretoria Skydiving Club, which is the largest in the country, number "2" on her list of "things to do."

Unfortunately, they both realized that there had been just too much distance and time between those R&Rs. It is sad, really, that the one thing that draws people together in the beginning ultimately drives them apart in the end. At least that had always been her experience. With Richard, it was his cool aloofness about everything, to include herself, that she was initially drawn to. She loved him with all her might but could not take what she felt was his indifference or perhaps ambivalence towards her in the end. They parted better friends than spouses. To her, and to Richard, they cherished the notion of having each other in their lives. Besides, they always had Key West...which actually lead her to where she was at this moment, waiting for a taxi that would take her to her destiny.

As the taxi honked its arrival, she was brought out of her reverie and back to her life--here and now. Back came the painful sadness in her heart. As she climbed into the taxi, she took one last look at her lovely little French country home with its Persian rugs, Austrian crystal chandeliers, which had special meaning all their own, and her beloved French antiques. "A place for everything and everything in its place," she said under her breath to no one in particular.

The taxi driver honked again, and just as she was about to

open her door, she heard the melodic voice of an elderly African American man call out to her: "Hello, Ma'am. Are you in there? Are you ready to go?" His warm voice caused her to smile, and she then opened the door. The man, who later introduced himself as Sam, walked up to her and said: "Howdy, Ma'am! Can I take those bags for you?"

She was completely charmed by this gentleman and said, "Would you please? But be warned, they are heavy!"

He laughed and grabbed the bags. "Holy cow! What do you have in here?"

"Just shoes and clothes," she laughed back.

He put her bags in the big Suburban and then opened the back door for her. She asked, "Do you mind if I sit up front with you? It just feels strange sitting back here in this big vehicle." It was obvious from the look on his face that he was not accustomed to folks being this nice and pleasant. During the drive to the airport, they made a little small talk, but mainly she sat in silence and thought about things.

The taxi sped away, away from her past and into her future. Her thoughts went back to Cuba, as her thoughts often did. *What*

44

*will I do there? Whom will I meet? How long will I stay?* So many

questions; not one answer. Not one yet! Enough time, though, to

think of the answers, to live out all the answers. *All the time in the*

*world,* she thought. As she neared Baltimore Washington

International (BWI) airport, her thoughts drifted to her second

husband--Tom. Thoughts of him must have caused a ripple of pain

to cross her face because the taxi driver actually asked if she was

alright. She quickly assured Sam that she was okay.

"I'm okay. I just have a lot on my mind." She wasn't sure

that Sam believed her, but he went back to driving and left her to

thoughts of Tom.

What a piece of work he was. She met him during her

separation with Richard. Actually, during the first day of her

newly-separated life. Brenda, a very close friend of hers, insisted

they go to a party to help bring her out of her depressed state.

That's where she met him. His name was Tom. Such a simple

name for such a complicated man, or at least that's what she

thought at the time. He was like no other she had met in the past;

so full of energy, so full of life and to her dismay, so full of

himself.

45

Tom seemed to breathe arrogance like others breathed in air. Arrogance was his oxygen, his drug of choice. His arrogance was intriguing, but there was more that interested her, to be sure. She could not stave off the physical attraction. Tom had the darkest brown eyes, which seemed to pierce right through her; his gaze, intense. Tom was indeed extremely intense, and he had the cutest southern accent she had ever heard. She loved southern accents. She thought about just jumping his bones right then and there, but again, her mother's nagging words rang in her head. Why she listened to that woman was beyond her. So, instead of just grabbing a hold of this man, she decided to get to know him a little bit longer before jumping into any sexual escapades with him.

Tom was different but somehow similar to her ex, Richard. They both had been in the intelligence field. Tom had that in-your-face arrogance; Richard had a quiet self-assured arrogance. Being with Richard was like being a character in a complicated novel. Being with Tom was like being in a comic book. While both the novel and the comic told a story, their stories were told in completely different ways. For one thing, she always wondered exactly what Richard was thinking--he was very economic with his

46

word usage, but there was little doubt that each short sentence was backed by a thick book of thoughts and emotion. Tom, on the other hand, told you exactly what he was thinking. He believed that everything he thought or said was important and that it should be shared. He would go so far as to draw diagrams to ensure people understood exactly what he was saying. Initially, this was somewhat cute. But she quickly realized that he was the kind of guy who did not simply want you to understand his way of thinking, he wanted you to conform to his way of thinking. People who did not agree with him were wrong, or even stupid.

She still recalled how he reacted when they first discussed whether she was married at the party. Tom laughed aloud when she answered his question. "I'm separated –one day now."  He wasn't sure whether to believe her or not, so he decided he didn't care. He did not to leave her side, not that night or ever again, for at least another eight years. What she initially thought was affection actually meant ownership to him. Unfortunately, their marriage lasted eight years. That is how long it took her to realize that the one thing that intrigues us in the beginning we learn to despise in the end. He, of course, realized it a lot sooner than she and made

47

special note to tell her just that very thing, in the end. She recalled one particular phone call she'd made to him after he had forgotten her birthday. She would never forget his words: "I really wanted to divorce you after the first year, but I didn't want to feel like a failure so I gutted it out with you for another seven years." After his characteristically cruel comment, she even surprised herself when she let out the biggest sigh…a sigh of relief that it was finally over! One thing was certain; she never regretted their divorce and never thought of trying to rekindle their relationship. She wished him well, and it was over.

The screeching arrival of her taxi at BWI brought her back from her thoughts of the past. Her taxi, she discovered, had almost run over a pedestrian. The look of shock on his face was one of surprise and one of recollection. He looked very familiar to her. The blue eyes—those bright blue eyes.

She thought that with all of her travels, everyone started to look familiar to her at some point. After checking in at the counter and walking to her gate, she saw him again, those blue eyes, those incredible blue eyes. Eyes like her father, whom she had not seen in over 40 years. Why was it that he seemed so familiar to her?

Was it just because she wanted him to be? Was it those piercing bright blue eyes? He too, she thought, seemed to recognize her as well. All of these years later, and she was still too shy to come up to someone and just talk. They both seemed to be walking to the same gate. Could this familiar-looking man be going to Cuba as well? Going to her destiny--their destiny? What a crazy thought to have.

Then he disappeared as quickly as he appeared. She thought that was probably for the best. With two failed marriages under her belt, it was probably for the best for her and for him. She realized that she was more than two hours early for her flight. She thought a shot or two of her favorite beverage—José Cuervo gold-chilled, no lime no salt, would be in order.

As she neared the airport bar, she noticed him again rushing past her, almost knocking her over. Later, she learned that his bumping into her was no accident. In fact, he was the kind of guy who seldom accidentally did anything! *He must be late for his flight,* she thought. *Probably not going to Cuba after all,* is what she surmised. As she got closer to the airport bar, she saw him take a seat, right where she was headed, the bar. He glanced at her and smiled. The bartender asked her what she would like. Before she could even utter a syllable, Mr. Blue Eyes blurted out, "José chilled for me, no lime, no salt, and -------for the young woman?" he waited for her to fill in the blank, but she was so surprised by his order that she just stood there with her mouth open.

She said, "Uhh, the same, please." She was so surprised, shocked really, by his order, that she decided to join this blue-eyed stranger for what it seemed, their favorite drink.

As he handed her the shot of Jose', their fingers touched ever so slightly. It felt like a little spark of electricity. It felt exquisite; it felt like...like magic. Did this magic mean something? Something special or did it have something to do with the sadness she had felt for the last four years? Actually longer than four years, she had to admit to herself. She'd felt this sadness during the whole course of her second marriage and even partway through her first. The longing for closeness; closeness with another individual that is built on total trust. The one question that haunted her thoughts was and will always remain, will she ever be able to trust again? Could she? Would she, could she ever have the intimacy that was built on total trust of another individual, another man? They sat and talked for what seemed like hours. He began the conversation with, "So do you come here often?" With this, they both began laughing! He then introduced himself, "Hi. My name is Robert, but no one calls me that but my mother. So I would be honored if you would call me Bobby." She began to introduce herself, but Bobby cut her off with a smile and said, "I already know your name. In fact, this is not our first time meeting." *Oh shit*, she thought, he has a southern accent...and then she smiled.

Finally, the recognition that she felt came to light. This blue-eyed stranger, Bobby, had been a former colleague of Tom's. They'd met some ten years earlier, but only once. After much talking by the both of them, and yes, even she talked and talked, he said farewell. They had just called his flight. He gave her a little kiss on her cheek, and she felt that same little spark of electricity, the magic, like when their fingers touched.

Then within a blink of an eye, she sat there and the sadness in her heart returned. She realized once again why it was there, the always-present sadness in her heart. She sat there for a while longer, thinking, just thinking. As she sat there in some kind of daydream, she had not even realized that her flight had been called. How long ago had it been called? They were calling her flight for the last time now. They had started the boarding more than a half an hour ago. Luckily, her gate was close by. Ironically, she realized that while they had talked for so long, they had never asked each other where they were going. Why hadn't she asked where Bobby was headed or would he would be back? They only talked of the past, nothing of the future. She made her way to the gate and to her seat.

Flying for her had always been a fun experience, especially the take-off. The second the wheels came off terra firma was always the best for her. She never fully understood why, at least not until now. She saw the take-off as a new beginning, and everyone knows that new beginnings are a good thing. Aren't they?

Her flight started at BWI, then on to Jacksonville, Florida. As the flight continued to Jacksonville, her thoughts wandered back to the blue-eyed stranger, Bobby. Who was he really? Where was he? Where was he off to? Why had this man made such an impact on her in such a short period of time? She purposely put him out of her mind. Who the hell was he to occupy so much of her thoughts? She tried to think of more...more realistic things.

She arrived in Jacksonville without much fanfare. She was only to stay for the evening before catching a flight out to Cuba, to her new beginning, her destiny. She ordered a small salad and a glass of wine and, of course, her favorite drink...a shot of José Cuervo--chilled no lime, no salt. Her thoughts instantly came back to him, to Bobby. Back to the blue-eyed stranger. Why couldn't she stop thinking of this man? Was she that lonely? Was she that desperate for closeness that she had to keep thinking of him, someone that she met ten years ago and then for just a moment at the airport? What was the strange and unusual hold he had on her mind? This time she went ahead and let her mind wander where it may. Her first thought was of those piercing bright blue eyes that looked right through her. That seemed to even know her. The real her, like no other man ever could or ever would, as it later came to be.

Even before realizing it, night had become day without as much as a wink of sleep. Or did she? All she knew was that her flight was to leave in two hours and she was not aware if she had even slept. She showered, changed, and packed as quickly as she could. The taxi would be there in less than 20 minutes. Thank God she thought to call the taxi ahead of time. She managed to get herself and everything else in order within 15 minutes...five minutes to spare.

The taxi was able to get on the naval base without any trouble. He took her to the terminal and unloaded what seemed to be hundreds of pounds of luggage. She had always been known to pack entirely too much. This time was no exception. As she sat there with all the others traveling to Cuba, to her destiny and to their own, she wondered which one of these people, if any, would have any impact on her life there. She looked around everywhere. She guessed what she really was looking for was that blue-eyed stranger. Why she thought he would be there was beyond even her thinking. He was not, of course. He was nowhere to be found. Sadness overtook her but was quickly brushed aside in an abrupt way by some other stranger. This man would not quit talking--to anyone who would give him one itty-bitty second. He too had piercing blue eyes, but his eyes held danger and were clouded with dishonesty. She tried to look away, pretending to be occupied by reading the novel on her lap. He still would not stop talking. Finally, he sensed her discomfort, so he excused himself. As she boarded the plane and looked to find her seat, she noticed "he" was to sit right next to her during the whole damn flight to Cuba. For 2 ½ hours the man would not stop talking. God only knows about what. He just went on and on and on. She hoped with all of her heart that he would have nothing more to do with her…her destiny especially, but the incredible sick feeling in the pit of her stomach said otherwise.

She wanted so desperately to have the time to think of the blue-eyed stranger, of Bobby. She even thought she saw him on the plane in the first class section, but she knew she'd been mistaken. This man sitting next to her would not stop talking. Only when the flight thankfully ended did he shut up. She should have listened to her mother's voice that time, "Don't talk or make eye contact with strangers."

The closer she got to Cuba, to her destiny, the more scared she became. She did not understand why. This should have been the happiest time of her life, but there she was, shaking like a leaf. Was it because of all the dreams she'd been having for the last 23 years? What if the dreams were to come to fruition? What if it was anti-climatic? What if nothing really came of it, nothing significant? Could she stand to know that "this is as good as it gets" was to become a reality for her? Was she afraid of her future or of just change itself?

As she was about to deboard the plane and step into the hot pulsing air of Cuba, she noticed how incredibly sweet the air smelled. She could not get past the sweet smell of Cuba. That surprised her because, as she could see as she got closer to the door, Cuba was a desert. More like Arizona than the tropical island she thought it would be. All of a sudden, the sadness came back. She stood there, not knowing whether to climb down the stairs or quickly go back in the plane. The decision was to be made for her as others pushed to get out.

The sickeningly sweet smell of the near by sugar cane fields of Cuba took her back in time, back to so many years ago during her first marriage, to Richard. Back to Europe, back to Germany, that country that used to hold such promise for her and her new husband. The smell of Germany was not sweet. It had the smell of old...the smell of so many antique stores she had visited during all those years there. She loved Germany. She thought no other country was for her. She was, after all, half German. Little did she know how much more important Cuba would be for her.

Everyone who got off the plane were herded to the ferry and then herded to different cars that would take all of them to their own private destinies and to her own. She, like all the others, including the "talker" on her flight, did the usual in-processing, which included getting rental cars, housing, phone, cable, internet, etc...It would not be until the next day that she would see where she was to work, what she was to do and the people she would spend a good portion of the day and evening.

She could barely sleep as she wandered around her little two-bedroom townhouse filled with all the prerequisite furniture from "housing." Not necessarily the best of things but not bad either. She had a small fence in the backyard. The backyard was truly in a sad state, pitiful really. No grass, no flowers, no plants, no life. She hoped that was not a bad omen. She then realized that this garden did not look nearly as pathetic as hers did back home.

She set her alarm for 5:00am, out of habit more than anything. She had done this for so many years; she just did not know what else to do. Almost for a second there she forgot where she was. She thought for sure, there for a split second, that she was back in DC. She had to reset the alarm for a much later time. She did not need to be at work until 8:00am and she only lived five minutes away. She didn't know what to do with all of that extra time.

She thought of the time she had to be at work, 8am, minus the time it took to get there, 10 minutes max, minus the time it took her to get ready, 50 minutes. She set her alarm for 7:00am. What in the world would she do with those 2 extra hours? She could take up jogging again. It had been years since she'd laced up running shoes. After being there one day, she knew that it was hotter than hell, even at five in the morning. She would try to stay up later than normal and hopefully stay asleep a little longer in the morning. Unfortunately for her, she'd had insomnia for the past 23 years now. At the most, she would get 4 hours of interrupted sleep. This would be difficult. Hopefully she would be able to change the hours she worked, once she started.

In her youth, she'd not been a morning person. The best part of any day had been in the wee hours of the morning; 2ish was when she felt the most alive. As she got older and with working in DC for all of those years, she tried to get to bed early, but she usually got to sleep no earlier than 1:00am and woke up at 5:00, with or without the alarm clock. This place....this Cuba....was going to be very different, she thought.

She finally was able to start work after the security personnel checked and re-checked her security clearances. Clearances she'd had for the past 20 years. She got to the special security office promptly at 8am. As usual with things of this nature, it was hurry up and wait. So she hurried and waited. Finally the special security officer came, did his thing and she was on her way. After receiving verification of her clearance and access, she finally found out what exactly she would be doing. She was going to be working at the detention center there on the base, working with possible terrorists by doing the necessary research and interrogations to separate Taliban/Al Qaeda members from the actual dirt farmers.

She loved the work. She absolutely loved it. Before she knew it, 13 hours would pass each and every day. She had a special pet project, a quest that she would work on her during her off hours. After working for about a month, she happened to hear one of the detainees, with help from an interpreter, talk about an individual they called AMZ. She found the acronym so strange that she was compelled to leave as quickly as the interrogation was over and rush back to her desk to start what would become endless days and nights of research on this man, who was believed to have set up a training camp in the western city of Herat, near the border with Iran, and to have renewed his acquaintance with al-Qaeda. She read and re-read the dossier she had created to try to find something, hell, anything, that would lead her to his direction.

Being here in Cuba and working with the detainees, she had never felt so needed or felt so much like she was actually contributing to something of importance, professionally speaking. She met many people there and learned many new things. The people were friendly. One of the people she was to work with was the "talker" on the plane. True enough, he was friendly but he just would not, or perhaps could not, stop talking. She found out his name. The blue-eyed "talker" was named Harris. Those blue eyes were dangerous and filled with deceit, she thought.

Someone was always having a BBQ or a party. Everyone

was like family and she was welcomed almost immediately. At one particular BBQ given by the senior civilian in country, Mr. Ramirez, in walked the "blue-eyed stranger," Bobby, to her utter amazement and joy. She was so excited, surprised and shocked all rolled in to one that she about peed her panties. He looked all around the yard, looking for a familiar face in a crowd of strangers. Then he saw her. His smile broadened as he approached her. She felt as if she was in a coma. She could not move or talk, even if she wanted to, which she did, to walk towards him as fast as she could. Why did he have this effect on her? She never remembered feeling quite so frightened and excited at the same time.

He came up, hugged her hard, and kissed her gently on the cheek. He took her by the shoulders, looked into her eyes, and said, "You look good enough to eat!" That alarmed her. She wasn't the touchy-feely type, not even with her family, nor had anyone had ever talked to her in such a way. She then felt that crazy yet familiar electricity again.

There were hundreds of people there. It was a hail & farewell for those who were about to leave and those who just arrived. Yet with all the people around them, they were in their own little world. She found out that the blue-eyed stranger was to work with her, HER! Well, not exactly with her, but at the detainee camp nevertheless. Again, she felt ecstatic and scared at the same time. Why was it that he could stir two opposite emotions in her at the very same time? She was definitely scared, too scared to get close, to trust this blue-eyed stranger who somehow was able to stir one emotion right after each other and sometimes at the same time within her.

It was way past dark when Bobby suggested going to the local tikki bar to talk some more. They both thanked the host and left.

As they walked back to their respective cars, Bobby asked her again, "Want to join me at the tikki bar for a while longer?"

She looked at him and wondered what he really wanted. "Sure thing, I'll follow you there or we can take one car, if you like."

They sat side by side at the bar. She could feel the heat of his body next to her. She wondered if he was always this hot. Bobby looked at her. "What are you smiling about, and most importantly, what are you thinking about?"

Bobby ordered their favorite drink, "Jose' chilled, no lime, no salt please." There they sat, side by side, just doing the normal "getting to know you" chit-chat before realizing that it had started to rain and rain hard. They quickly kissed and ran to their cars and promised to see each other again very soon.

For her and Bobby, days turned into weeks that turned into months. They fell in love, the old fashion kind built solidly on friendship and trust--most importantly, trust. Trust she had not felt for anyone in over 23 years. She let herself become so vulnerable with Bobby. She let her protective "lobster shell" down and let him in her heart and soul. At this point, he had the ability to destroy her, if he wished to do so.

For them, Cuba was an ideal place, their ideal place. They talked of moving in together but knew it was against the rules for two unmarried contractors of the opposite sex to do such a thing. So they kept things as they were, he at his place and she in hers. They spent all day working together, him an experienced interrogator and she, the best damn analyst around. They spent their nights being in love and spending as many waking hours that they could. After several months of being head over heels in love, they decided why not just get married? They decided to make it legal and took off for Jamaica to make it official. It was a beautiful wedding, set at dawn; as the sun rose to bring in a new day, so did their lives together.

Their wedding day was full of fun and sun. After the morning's ceremony, they spent the rest of the day renting vespas and buzzing all around the island. They ate the most exotic of foods and drank the fruitiest of beverages. They even stopped at a tattoo parlor and got matching tattoos, a little sun on the left side of their hipbone. As day turned to night, they decided it was time to make it official. They started with a bubble bath in the large soaking tub in their suite. This was to be their first time--first time as a married couple and their first time, period. It was indeed the old fashion kind of love for them. She'd wanted to make 100% sure she was right about him without having sex interfere with her heart or her groin.

She leaned her head back and nibbled on his ear. She could feel just how much he enjoyed this. She felt him behind her, growing more and more with each little nip of the ear. She decided to hold off a bit longer, make him want her all that much more.

64

They soaked in the bubbles a bit longer, but the anticipation grew too much for her, so she hinted, and not too subtly, to Bobby, "A nice little massage would be wonderful right about now, perhaps with oils." As he took her hints, he lightly touched her back. He looked in wonder and amazement at her body art and lightly traced each one first with his finger and then with his tongue. Bobby could not help but question her concerning all of this wonderful artwork. "Hey, baby doll, would you explain what all of it means? Maybe not now, but perhaps later on?"

He wondered what had prompted this little lady to get such art. From the complex tattoo on her lower back, he traced the little purple morning glories and vines in the center of her back that had extended down to the crack of her butt. *Hmm,* he thought, *interesting,* to the sides of her waist. Then to the right side of her. Last was a bunch of butterflies and to the left a phoenix rising. He wondered what this all meant. He had never been this close to a woman with this type of art before. He found it a little unsettling but yet erotic.

As he lightly touched her back, he heard a soft purring sound. *She must really like this,* he thought. He then moved to her front where he took each of his hands and cupped each breast. For such a small woman, she really was endowed. Thank goodness he had large hands. He thought them to be at least a 34D. One more curious thing about this intriguing woman was that her left nipple was pierced, not with a hoop but with a steel bar. He definitely wondered to himself if that could be a sign that she was into pain, a little S&M for this little lady, perhaps, or was it a different statement all together she was trying to make?

The tattoos on her back all held the significance of new beginnings in one way or another. He thought perhaps that there had been many changes for her since the last time they saw each other that one time in Germany when she was with her then-husband. He could tell by the soft purring sounds she was making that it was definitely time to climb out of the tub…perhaps that massage she had not so subtly hinted to earlier would be in order. He didn't have any oils, but he did have regular hand lotion. Perhaps that would work.

As he held her by her tiny waist, he prompted her to stand right before him, not even six inches from his face. With that, he could see almost her entire body. For a woman of 47, she did not look half-bad. In fact, to him she looked pretty damn good. A few scars here and there, like most of us, but hers came from cancer, malignant melanoma, he believed she said. The first scar was on the back of her thigh, and it was a doozy. It went from one side of her thigh to the other, cutting across the muscle instead of along the course of it. It was a terrible surgeon who had done that to her leg, the legs of an athlete even all the years later.

Long had it been that she had done anything athletic but normal household chores, but one would never notice it from her legs--the sweep of her hamstring to the tiny diamond shape of her calves. Her tummy looked pretty tempting and with it being this close to his face, flat as could be, having had no children showed on her. The only thing that remotely showed her age was her skin tone. Although he didn't care about that in the least and probably would have never noticed if she hadn't said how dissatisfied she was about how her skin had lost some of its elasticity. She must have lost a lot of weight quickly for it not to bounce back a bit more. He didn't care. All he cared was that this wonderful creature wanted to be with him and him alone and married him to prove how much.

As she stood there, very unashamed, he turned her around to "inspect" her artwork... she loved that he did that. No one had ever taken the time to look to see what she had done, much less ask for the meanings of all of them. From the big white rose on her wrist, to the six little white roses around her belly button, to the other six white roses around her ankle. He could not help think all of this meant something. Would she tell him? He had already asked her the meaning behind it all. What about the first one she'd done so many years ago, the tiny itty-bitty butterfly that could only be seen if completely naked like she was now. It was small. Even in a tiny g-string, its presence would not be detected. Bobby had to know the meaning of all of this artwork. He looked up at her quizzically. She could tell he wanted to know more about her and not just jump right into bed. He had to know more about her.

She started to describe all of the artwork one by one, "All 13 of the white roses were a tribute to my first husband. He was the only one who ever sent me white roses; 13, always 13 white roses for all occasions, most of which I knew would mean that he would be going away on business again, which was often. I never thought that I would ever receive another white rose from anyone

68

but Richard. I wanted to make sure that I would always have them permanently, so I had them inked on so I could always treasure them, even though we are never to be."

Bobby then lightly touched the artwork on her lower back. "What about these?" She hesitated to make any remarks concerning that or the little baby butterfly close to her nether regions. What was he to make about that, about her not saying anything about those? He wondered if he should prompt her. She had a very sad look in her eye, as she knew that was what he wanted to know next.

She readily agreed to talk about the phoenix rising. Instead of ashes, it rose from the purple morning glories; purple being her favorite color, was not really a tribute so much as a reminder of her second husband.

That man was difficult and not always nice to her. She felt when he told her yes, that he had filed for divorce, without even telling her it was all over, she felt that it was she, the phoenix rising out of something that was very difficult and made it through. The butterflies were in the truest sense of meanings, new beginnings. The new beginnings they referred to were her new life without him, without any man. The morning glories were for her dad. How he loved the early mornings with his coffee and cigarette, and how he loved his yard. He would work on that yard every single weekend, without fail. He would sit there after his work when the yard was done early Saturday morning and be proud of his yard.

That was it, all of the artwork, and with that, he scooped up his little bride and got out of the tub. He dried her and then himself. He led her to the bed and said, "You are going to get the best damn massage of your life, so lie down and get ready."

She happily agreed, "It better be a good one. It's been ages since I had a good one. She flung herself on the big king-size bed as Bobby got the lotion. She boldly looked him over. She definitely liked what she saw: nice chest, furry but not too much. As she looked lower down, she was a bit intimidated. She thought, never in a million years was that going to fit. You see, not all little women are little "all over" but she was indeed. She had spent all of her grown-up female years doing her "exercises" and the fact that she never had children…well, one could only say that there might be some difficulty in managing that feat but she was ready, willing and able.

He instructed her to lie on her stomach. He would do the back first, then build up to the front. She loved his strong powerful hands. He sure didn't spare the deep penetrating motions either. She loved that. She hated a wimpy little massage. Sure, she loved the light touches as well but that is what that is supposed to be. A wimpy massage without any real oomph just wasn't worth it to her. Half an hour later, she was getting sleepy. This was doing the trick, but at the same time she was really worked up, and by the looks of it, so was Bobby. He flipped her over and started to massage her breasts, then delicately made little circles around each nipple. Bobby thought her dark brown nipples looked exactly like the head of a pencil, the eraser part, the exact same size and shape. He wanted to just nibble at them all night long…goodness, how that felt good. She purred lightly and that brought him to come in a little closer and give her small little kisses on her face. All over her face, very gently. She kept her eyes closed so she could truly appreciate the feeling he was giving her. He was such a gentle man, yet he had a take-charge attitude with her body.

She could not take any more of this. She felt the need to

have him. Have him in her mouth. Just a little, a little taste was all. As she sat up, she felt the need to take charge of the situation. She playfully pushed him back on the bed and knelt in between his legs. She lightly touched, explored really, all of him. She started with soft kisses everywhere. Then the licking; she licked everywhere, and when his moaning became loud and louder still, she started to lick up his tummy, around his belly button and then up to his nipples.

She teased him unmercifully. Little licks and then nips at each nipple. Back and forth, then worked her way back down his stomach, past his belly button and down to where the source of all of her pleasure would be, his cock. She took it firmly in her small hands. She could not get her hand all around it. Again, she thought of the logistics of it actually fitting.

She decided to lick just here and there, then slowly up and down the whole length of it until she realized that she had the whole thing in her mouth licking and sucking like mad. Bobby could not help but moan loudly and plead with her, "Babe, I love it, suck harder, I want you…yes, yes. That's fantastic!"

Just when she thought he would cum, she stopped…and

started with the little licks here and there. She could tell she was driving him crazy. He wanted to just take her head and shove it down on his cock, but he knew how women hated when men did that, so he held back and took it…took all of her teasing until it was just too much for him.

He sat up, took her by the shoulders, and plopped her on the bed so they could be face to face. He had to see her while he made love to her. He wanted to know that he was truly making her happy in a way she had never been before. There was no gentleness about this. This was to be a little on the rough side, and he believed in his heart that is the way she wanted it. The next time…the next time would be gentle and patient but not this time, not now. He grabbed her by her hips, tilted them up a bit, and tried to get inside her.

Boy, this woman was not joking when she had mentioned how small she was. He started to wonder if there was going to be a "fit" issue. Instead of trying to force himself in, he tried something a bit smaller for starters. He tried one of his fingers, and to be truthful, that was even difficult, but he made it in. He could tell this woman had done her kegals and did them religiously. He could

73

feel her tighten, relax, tighten, relax movement. Oh god, if he could just be in her right now, but he had to be patient. He had to make sure she was ready to take him, all of him, and if that meant more foreplay, so be it.

He took his time with her…slowly teasing her this time. Going in and out with his finger, it wasn't easy but he did it. She had such control that it just totally blew his mind. At the point where he thought she couldn't take any more, he pulled out and tried again to penetrate her with his cock. He made several attempts at sliding in but couldn't quite get there, so he decided to just lie on her with his cock in between her legs…let her get used to the size being that close. Slowly he could tell that this was working. He felt her wetness and decided to see if it was going to work. He first put in the head, and that in itself was an amazing feeling. Tightened muscle all around him. He felt he was splitting her apart. She asked him if all of him was in. She had not realized that there was yet more to come, a lot more! He told her, "Oh no, there's more…" She groaned, but in pleasure and in pain. He asked her if he should stop.

"No, Bobby. Keep going. I think I can take all of you now."

As he pushed through her, her walls stretched with every movement. He felt as if he was in a warm, wet, fitted glove, one made only for him. As he lay there on top of her, all of him inside, he decided not to make any movements just yet. He wanted to relish the feeling, the warmth and strength of her. He felt he would almost cum by just being in her without moving. He could feel her rhythm, her heartbeat and her muscle control. He thought that she would actually cut him in two with that strength. It scared him and excited him at the same time, as most of her did. She just had that effect on him, in and out of bed. She could feel the mounting pressure of what she thought to be him getting ready to cum, so she stopped with her flexing. Best to let him be in her...she felt the stretching of her whole body like she had never before. Although there was pain, there was also an exquisite pleasure in this.

They lay there, just lay there and began to kiss, deep penetrating kisses. Tongues exploring tongues, teeth, and gums...then she bit him. Bit his bottom lip. It hurt yet it sent a little bolt of electricity up his spine. He felt strange, just how much he really enjoyed this little bit of pain. His thoughts came back to her nipple piercing. He wondered if that is what that felt like to get pierced. Years later, he would experience a piercing firsthand.

When he thought she was ready for him to move, he slowly slid out a little. It felt like the walls were caving back in, and he just wasn't sure if he would be "allowed" back in, so he pushed back in a bit....This feeling, this amazing feeling was almost too much for him. He wanted to cum at that moment, but first, he wanted to pleasure her. So knowing instinctively how she liked it, he decided to take action into his own hands. He started to thrust in and out with such force he thought for sure he was going to split her in two. However, she was now like a wild animal, they both were. They could not contain themselves any longer. She met each and every thrust, back and forth, with such force. She loved it, so he went harder and faster. He looked at her face. He could tell it was about to happen as he saw the flush of red go from her breasts to her neck and then to her face. She was loudly saying, "Oh Bobby, oh Bobby." Screams of delight he had never heard before, but while she was cumming, she was silent, not one sound, not one little peep came from her. It was almost like a little death for her...Then as the wave of orgasm was over, he heard her gasp....it was his turn now and all it took was one more stroke and he was there, making noises like he had never made before.

When it was over, he stayed on her and in her. Little did he know that was when she usually got up to pee and wash up. This time, she did not move, she just held him and he held her, still inside her. Bobby, still trapped within her walls, the muscle not letting go even as he got softer and softer. After a while he tried to pull out but he couldn't. She looked up at him and asked, "Do you want me to set you free?" He had not even realized that she had purposely been holding him in with her muscle. He smiled, thought about it and said, "You know, I'm pretty happy in here so I don't mind if I stay a while longer, if you don't mind." His matter of fact response made her laugh. He sounded so very serious about it all. "I just love being so deep inside of you. I want to be so deep inside that it hurts."

Bobby really had to admit to himself that he truly liked being inside where it was safe, cozy, warm, and wet. After several minutes of basking in the afterglow, they both went to the bathroom. They decided to take a nice long hot shower. The shower actually had a little bench in there that brought all sorts of ideas to both of their minds. They slyly looked at each other and in

77

unison said, "Why not, ready for another go round?"

When they finally returned from the wedding and honeymoon, they decided to move into her little townhouse instead of his. They worked on their little garden together during the weekends. With care and love, it changed from having no life at all to almost an oasis, which is rare in that part of Cuba. They both worked hard, usually 13 or 14 hours a day. That did not change even after they married. They were both very passionate about their jobs, thank God. They understood each other that way and luckily, unlike most marriages, were able to talk about the day's work together.

At the end of the day, it would be Bobby coming into her office and saying, "Hey, baby doll, its martini time." That usually meant that it was around 9:00pm, a long, long day but very exciting for her.

For the first time in her professional life, she was actually doing what she was trained to do. Totally hands on, actually talking, analyzing, and researching people, most of whom were actual terrorists, al Qaeda. Not from what others wrote about them, but them firsthand, right in front of her, not even one meter away.

It was all new and different for her. However, after the workday, she and Bobby would then leave to go to their little oasis. Bobby would either make his infamous "dirty martini" with gin for her and vodka for him, with extra olives, stuffed of course, with jalapenos. Bobby was the one who introduced her to martinis. Martinis always seemed too sophisticated and grown up for her, but she loved them now. Not as much as she loved dear Jose' though.

Or some evenings they would have their favorite drink—Jose' chilled, no lime, no salt. They would take their drinks outdoors to their little patio and turn on Jimmy Buffett.

They both loved the Jimmy Buffett mentality and hoped one day they would be able to live that way. Here in Cuba they felt they were able to feel that to some small extent. They would talk for hours on end about work, the garden, their life together and everything else under the sun. They loved being together morning, noon, and night. Everyone knew that, everyone could see that. They were in their own little world. A world only built for two. As the days passed, their work and their love just got better and better until one day…

Chapter 3 -- The Beginning of the End

The whole team was to meet for a breakfast meeting with the general in charge of the detainee camp. This was where their happy world would start to unravel a bit. The general had asked for volunteers to deploy to Iraq. She'd been trying for years to go to Kuwait or Iraq but was never selected. Those jobs at the time were slotted for military and contractors only, and she was a government employee at the time. That was one of the reasons she decided to take the contractor route, not for the money but for the different and exciting jobs that were offered. She shot her arm up and said that she wanted to be one of the first to go. Bobby looked at her as if she had lost her mind. Why would she, why would anyone, want to leave the comfort of home to live and work in a country torn apart by war, a place where you would have to tempt fate every single day and night. He could not help himself though; he too shot his arm up. The general smiled broadly. He told everyone there to send in a request to their supervisors and four would be selected.

As they left breakfast, they walked in silence for the first time in their relatively short lives together. She finally broke the silence and asked, "Are you mad at me?" He hugged her hard. She still felt that familiar electricity. He had tears welling up in his eyes. He said, "Of course not. I'm just scared for you...for us." She told him that she had been trying to get there for a long while. He knew that, they had discussed it a time or two. Bobby understood how important it was for her to go. He could not help but understand. She knew that he did not want to go. Bobby tried to explain, "I never had any desire to go there, but honey I am just so scared for you. I love you so very much, but I know you want to go, need to go."

She looked sadly at him and said, "You don't need to go along with me. I'll be fine. You need to stay here and continue the great work you started. I'll be back in no time, I promise!"

Bobby looked at her with the saddest of eyes and responded, "Hun, let's drop the subject for now or at least until we know for sure if we are even selected. Ok?"

In the meantime, their idyllic life went on as usual. They decided to have another of their infamous BBQs at their home. Everyone was there, including Harris. The three of them all became friends, or so they initially thought. Harris always came to their BBQs and parties. She and Harris worked on the same team, Central Asia team. To anyone who knew the three of them, they appeared to be friends, but something inside told her not to trust him, not totally anyway. He, on the other hand, had confided in her about most things, personal things. Things like his relationship problems with his wife, his bad financial standing, and just whatever had popped into his mind.

One thing he did not confide to her was about his feelings for a very young co-worker on their team. She was indeed very young. She was a 19-year-old soldier, a girl by the name of Jess. At first, she noticed Harris looking and chatting with the young Hispanic soldier. When Jess first got to Cuba, her first assignment, she was full of life and optimism but as the days passed, she looked more and more sad, confused and even scared. Elle assumed that being away from her family for the first time could be taking their toll on the young interrogator.

It wasn't until one evening when she was working late again, to Bobby's dismay, that she actually witnessed something strange. Harris pulled up a chair next to Jess and started to speak to her in Spanish. She wondered why Spanish but then thought it seemed ok, but the longer the conversation went on, the more a look of panic washed over Jess' fine exotic features. Jess' eyes seemed to have the look of a poor rabbit caught in a trap. After about thirty minutes of talking, Harris got up and went back to his desk.

Jess got up, tears welling in her eyes and said, "I don't need this shit!"

Elle was not sure what to do next. She asked her teammate, an analysts like her, if he thought she should go after Jess. He said, "Please find out what is wrong, go after her."

As she traveled all around Camp Delta, she realized just how scary this place looked in the dead of night. After looking and looking, she wasn't sure where Jess had taken off to. There were so many places one could actually go on this remote part of the base. She looked everywhere for her without much luck. As she looked and looked around the camp, she had the sense that she was being watched and followed. The hair on the back of her neck stood straight out. After wandering around this remote part of the detention camp, she decided to get back to the office. She knew all too well when someone was following her; this was not the first time since she had started working there.

She told her teammate that she couldn't find her. As she searched for Jess she ran past Bobby. He looked alarmed but didn't say anything. Finally, he came back to her office with his familiar comment, "It's martini time."

She quickly typed out an email to Jess, "Do you need to talk to someone, to a woman, to me?" She and Bobby were headed back to their little oasis to talk about what had happened.

As she and Bobby walked to their car, she stopped in her tracks and said, "Do you feel that Bobby? Do you see anything in the brush over there?"

Bobby looked cautiously around. "I don't see anything. What's wrong? Is there something you aren't telling me?"

She told him that she thought she was being watched again. Bobby didn't like the sound of that one little bit. The more involved she became with her research on this AMZ character, the

85

more often she had the sense that someone was watching her or that she was being followed. Could she just be getting spooked by what she was reading about this man, or possibly just paranoid? Bobby didn't know the answer and he really did not want to. All he knew was that he would make sure to keep a close eye on her when he could.

When they finally got to their little oasis, drinks in hand, she blurted out, "Harris is coming on to that young girl in my office, and I don't know if I should do something or say something to someone. What do you think?"

Bobby couldn't believe his ears, that this man, this older grown man would be doing anything wrong. Bobby said, "Let's see if Jess even wants our help before we do anything. It could be something totally different than what we think it could be."

That night they tried to put it all behind them and just let things happen, but the look on her face would not allow it. The next day she opened her email to find a short reply from Jess. All it said was, "Yes, please meet me at the gym tomorrow and please bring Bobby."

*What a strange request*, she thought. "Please bring
86

Bobby..." She went over to his office to let him know that tomorrow she wanted to meet both of them at the base gym. She understood the gym part because she was going to start to train her using free weights, but she was taken aback at the second part of the request. She was unable to make any contact with Jess that morning or afternoon because she worked the night shift, as well as Harris.

Jess' partner, Scott, came in early and whispered in her ear, "Harris has been harassing Jess, following her around base and he asked her to go to Jamaica with him. That's why Jess looked so upset last night. What should we do?"

Apparently, her looks of sadness, confusion and fear were not about being far from home but from the ongoing sexual harassment from Harris. She was shocked because Harris was easily in his late 50's, and here she was just 19. She was also shocked because Harris had confided in her about almost everything in his life, even the breakdown of his marriage, but not this, never anything like this. She was so appalled at this that she just stood there listening to Jess' partner about everything Harris had done to her since her arrival.

87

She went to Bobby's office, repeated what Scott had told her and said, "What now?" Bobby grabbed her hand and walked directly to their supervisor's office. "What do we do if someone is being sexually harassed by one of the contractors?"

The supervisor dropped what he was doing and asked, "What is going on here? Who is harassing and most importantly, who is being harassed?"

Bobby said that he didn't want to give any details until they talked to the young woman to see if she wanted to take it further.

The next morning, Saturday, the four met at the gym as planned. Jess asked her partner to come with her. She was that frightened of being alone. When they got to the gym, all had started to do their own particular work out. She decided not to say anything because she figured Jess wanted to ease into the reason why all four were really there. She and Jess went through many different exercises with the free weights, not really talking of anything but that. It was almost surreal.

After they worked out for about an hour, they all went outside, and she started to tell her story. The words spilled out of Jess as she reiterated what her partner had revealed the day before and added a few things that not even her partner had known: stalking her, the trip to Jamaica he had asked her to go on with him. Jess had asked to be there to get a woman's perspective about what to do and if, in fact, what she was experiencing was sexual harassment. She wanted Bobby there for his prior military background. Bobby had been prior military, a counterintelligence special agent in the army. She needed to find out the right course of action to take. Who did she need to talk to and with whom to see? The comment in the email all made sense now. All four of them talked for about an hour. She was ready to do what needed to be done to make sure none of this happened to her again or anyone else.

In the meantime, she and Bobby were told they were not selected to go to Iraq. Her heart dropped, but she could see the happiness in Bobby's eyes. They had selected four others who had been in Cuba longer. Bobby sighed in relief. She was saddened and a little hurt that she was not selected.

She looked at Bobby with little teardrops rolling down her cheeks. "Why didn't they select me? I was the first one who volunteered to go. I wanted to go to really make a contribution, not for the extra cash like the others said their reason was." Bobby looked at his lovely bride and squeezed her hard. He knew she wanted, needed really, so much to find out why she was not selected.

She knew she had an impeccable resume with a wide variety of experience. Bobby was more than relaxed and happy that four others were selected so they could go on with their very happy lives. He was concerned, of course, about her, because he knew how much she wanted to go. He knew the reasons she wanted to go versus the others and, of course, his own reason for volunteering. She believed Harris had said it best: "Yes, I'm a contractor, much like a mercenary. I go where the money is, to the highest bidder!" He said that to anyone who would listen, even his military boss. She'd assumed that perhaps the others selected to go wanted to go for the same reasons she did but had heard different. She knew that they just wanted the extra money they would get while deployed there.

As any seemingly idyllic life, the days passed quickly. It seemed that days turned into weeks and weeks to months with barely a blink of an eye. Life was going on like that for them, normal with the occasional speed bump here and there. The speed bump of the week for them and for Jess was the sexual harassment situation. Jess did what she thought best to end it once and for all. With the help from her and Bobby and the support of her partner, Jess took the necessary steps. A meeting was held with all the appropriate people: the military supervisor, Jess, her team partner, her and Bobby, Harris, his team partner, the non-commissioned officer in charge. They were all there to tell their versions of what had gone on. By the end of the meeting, everyone could tell where it was going to go. It seemed what would happen was to happen to Jess and it would appear to be a punitive action against her and her team partner.

She could be wrong; she'd been wrong in the past but, honestly, not that often. She felt in her gut, which was usually right, that something bad would happen--to her, to Jess and to God only knew whom else.

It wasn't until the next day that they all found out the outcome of that late night meeting. As she had felt in her gut, Jess and her team partner were both to be reassigned to other sections, leaving the guilty party, Harris, to continue his merry way, unfettered or bothered in any way. She felt so bad for Jess but knew nothing she could do would matter. What was done was done. Not even the contractor, Lockhart Marion, would do anything to Harris. How could one of the world's largest defense contractors just sweep it under the rug like everyone else seemed to be doing, just sweep the damn mess under the rug?

She decided to go on with her wonderful life with Bobby and put this all behind them. There was only one problem though. She still had to work with Harris. How difficult would it be for her to work with this man now? How difficult, knowing what he had done to the poor young girl? She told herself that she could put all of this mess behind her and she did. Luckily for her, Harris was to go on holiday in the next couple of days. No awkward feelings towards each other or unnecessary tension in the work place, she hoped and prayed. During those two weeks with Harris away on holiday to visit his wife, she and Bobby got some good and some bad news--good news for her but bad news for Bobby. The four who originally were scheduled to go to Iraq decided not to go at the last minute. She and Bobby got the call from their temporary boss that if they still wanted to go, they could. She was elated and

Bobby, well Bobby was upset about the whole ordeal.

Before Bobby could say anything, she started to jump around the room dancing and bellowing, "We are going to Iraq, woohoo, we are going to Iraq!" Bobby looked at her as if she had gone mad. He knew that was no place for either of them to be. Crazy shit was happening over there, especially to contractors. That fateful call came on, of all days, the day of their first anniversary. Her only wish was not to have gotten this particular call on that day. Of all days, why that one? Nevertheless, there just wasn't a way to plan fate as much as she would have liked to.

She assured Bobby that she could and would go without him. That she would not think badly of him if he chose to stay behind. She said it, and she meant it with her every fiber. For Bobby, there was no other choice but to go with his lovely bride. "Baby doll, you know I would never tell you what to do or not do, but this place isn't for us. There is crazy shit going down over there right now. I cannot let you go without me there. I may not be able to keep you out of harm's way 100% of the time, but at least I will be close by in case anything does happen to you or to me."

So they answered that fateful call with a resounding "yes,

we still want to go." Their next two weeks were a blur of activity for both of them. Getting ready to go to war was something she had never done before. Luckily, Bobby had been there, done that and helped ease her stresses concerning what and when to do all the things needed to be done to be ready and totally prepared. She loved this man like no other. He was the only person in her entire world who understood her and could calm her. No one ever could do that. For sure, the exes tried, but none succeeded. Could it be the total sense of trust that she had for him? Trust that she would have never thought possible? Whatever it was, she loved him for it. She realized that Bobby was indeed her soulmate, her lobster love. All her life she searched and searched for her true love. Who knew that a woman in her mid-40s would find this kind of all-consuming love? As you know, lobsters mate for their entire lives, and she finally felt she had found her very own lobster. She wondered if Bobby knew the story of lobsters. She decided she should tell him so he would know exactly how she felt about him. Bobby sat and thought about this little story of hers. He thought of speaking, responding, but instead looked at his lobster lovingly.

One week left before going off to yet another one of their

many adventures. She believed that this particular adventure would change her life, their lives, forever. Little did she know just how life-changing it would be. Harris returned to work only a few days before she and Bobby left for Iraq. Luckily, with all the preparations needed for this trip she would not have to see him too often. She still felt there would be this terrible awkwardness between the two of them. After all, they had once been friends. She had been his confidante.

The next day she was at work bright and early as usual. They only had eight more days left, and it was the beginning of the weekend. Weekends were usually about puttering around the house and the garden and then a BBQ or party. Sunday was to be a farewell BBQ for her and Bobby. It was going to be held at the beach, one of their favorite places in the world other than their little garden.

This would be the first time she would see Harris away from the office since the whole incident. When they arrived, the BBQ was in full swing. She and Bobby always showed up fashionably late. As they neared the parking area, she could see Harris' truck. For some reason she was a bit scared but did not know why. Like most times when something scared her, she would confront it head on. She walked right up to Harris and asked about his trip home. He looked at her as if she was from Mars with possibly two heads and just walked past her, not saying a word. She was shocked yet not altogether surprised. She was sure he blamed her for everything that had transpired. At this time, she had not even realized just how much he did blame her. She attempted to talk to Harris once more. He acted the same yet again. She was hurt and very pissed off. She told Bobby that she was going to take a walk on the beach to clear her head. She surely did not need this eating at her just five days before their departure.

While she walked on the beach, little did she know that Bobby had cornered Harris to find out what this was all about. "Hey man, what the hell are you doing to my wife? Why are you being a pain in the ass to her? She has done nothing but be nice to you. If you are pissed off about what happened, at what YOU initiated, then you have no one to be pissed off but yourself!"

Harris glared at Bobby and said, "Look, Bobby, my wife served me divorce papers the day I left, and that bitch is going to leave me in financial ruin for a very, very long time to come."

Harris, of course, blamed Bobby's wife for all of his woes. He hated Harris for his unjustified feelings. Bobby knew he couldn't do anything here and now, at least not with witnesses. Bobby decided best to leave Harris standing there alone before she came back. He knew her "Mexican side" would surface. He hated when she got that way. He knew that it rarely happened but when it did, everyone really should take cover and quick, especially the person that it would be directed at. God save Harris, or maybe not. For such a small woman, most people, men and women alike, were more than a little intimidated by her, scared really.

As she strolled back, she had noticed what was going on and did not like it one bit. She could see how Harris seemed annoyed. Why would he be annoyed at her? She knew in her heart of hearts he blamed her for all that was going wrong in his poor pathetic life. She had heard through the grapevine what had gone on with Harris and his soon to be ex-wife. She had overheard Harris on the phone to his soon to be ex one morning at work. Lots of anger, lots of yelling, lots of promises and lots of lies. She herself had heard this type of bullshit before, firsthand. She heard the promises of "trust me, I won't try to screw you. Leave all of this to me to care of."

It had always been her experience that any time anyone said, "trust me," one should run, not walk and not listen to another word from that person! Nevertheless, she had to find the underlying cause of all of this before her and Bobby left for Iraq. She and Bobby had heard earlier that day at the BBQ that Harris was to join them in Iraq. She was scared about that possibility and had hoped it was just the rumor mill. Although she did not really believe that Harris would actually harm her, if a mortar would be incoming and if Harris was within close proximity, she thought he would use her small body as a shield. She wondered if Harris even had an idea that he was to go along with her and Bobby. She didn't care if he did or not, all she knew was that this needed to be taken care of once and for all and soon! They were all to leave in five short days.

She tried to talk to Harris one more time. Seeing this, Bobby rushed over. He knew how she would get. He stood silently by her side, ready to do whatever it took to take care of his wife. If anything, she knew how to take care of herself, but nonetheless, he was at the ready. As she attempted to speak to Harris, he tried to walk away—yet again. Stupid, stupid man! Bobby warned Harris to stay and listen unless he wanted to unleash some real drama here and now, at the BBQ and in front of everyone. She knew how Harris hated drama or loud "white" women. He told her one day the reason he liked her was because she was a quiet, respectable Hispanic woman. No, this man Harris didn't know her very well at all. Harris reluctantly stayed there, looking bored and bothered. As she tried to talk, Harris would not even look at her. For the first time since she'd known Harris, he had nothing to say. She asked Harris why he was acting the way he was towards her, snubbing her, shunning her, embarrassing her in front of their team. Of course, Harris lied and said he did not realize that was what he had been doing to her.

"Harris, you know goddamn well what you have been doing and how you have been acting towards me. Look, if we are ever going to make it back from over there in one piece, you need to straighten out your shit with me. Get it out all in the open!"

Harris finally looked at her. He had no idea what she was talking about.

"Harris, the three of us are to leave in five days," she said.

99

Again, he looked at her as if she had two heads. "What the hell are you talking about, woman?"

Bobby piped in, "Man, the three of us, plus the military team, were selected to go. We leave this Friday." Apparently, no one told Harris of this news. She told him that their temporary boss told her and Bobby last Thursday.

After the initial shock, Harris said to the both of them, "Ok, ok. I have been acting a little hinky lately. It's my bitch of a soon-to-be-ex-wife that has gotten me this way. Everything is good between the three of us. Ok? Are we good?" Harris said his goodbyes and said he had to get busy.

Of the people she and Bobby told of Harris going to Iraq with them, their comments were varied but carried a consistent theme. "What? They're sending Harris over there? That man shouldn't go over there. He should be on suicide watch for god sakes, not going to Iraq."

"No way are they going to send Harris to Iraq. That man has personal issues at home he needs to take care of."

She and Bobby said their goodbyes to all of their friends and colleagues at the BBQ. They both stood for a long while and, almost as if performed, said in unison, "Oh God, isn't Cuba beautiful?" The both looked at each other and laughed. They really were much alike, the two of them, the pair of them. As they drove off in their little black convertible punch buggy, they both took one last look at the beach and at their friends like it was the last time they would ever see any of them, waved, and went on home to have some alone time. Soon they would be spending every evening apart. They would work all day together but their nights would be different. The military doesn't allow for that type of arrangement, married or not. Although she and Bobby were told that they were going to be housed with the other civilian contractors and not with the military, they still figured they should be prepared for the worst.

The next few days seemed to fly by. The powers of attorney appointments, the Last Will and Testament appointment, shots, physicals and everything else that went along with being deployed. This was all new and different for her. For Bobby, it was another of many deployments he'd been on. She was glad for that. She relied on him heavily to help her be totally prepared for this adventure. Being in the military for 19 years, he'd seen more than his share. He was glad they would be going together. He could help her prepare. He knew that she could take care of herself and had done many things on her own in her lifetime, but this was different.

This was a first. A first time he would show her what had to be done. This time he was the teacher and she was the student, the "grasshoppa." He knew she liked being in charge, being the teacher. He had accepted that part of her personality. Sometimes she was a tough taskmaster, but that might be to her benefit over there. Iraq was not a place for pussies. Moreover, she, this tiny woman, was no pussy.

They went back to their little oasis and enjoyed their tiny garden. They sat out on the patio enjoying their beverages and, as always, Jimmy Buffett on the CD player. Perfect—just perfect was what their life together seemed to be--all that was to change. They just didn't know how.

They loved their lives together. Jobs they loved, their little townhouse, and each other more than either one could ever express. They, of course, had an idea what they were getting into over there. They both felt that it would be an opportunity of a lifetime. An experience and adventure they would never forget.

How little did they realize how terribly wrong it would all go? Had

they known, would they have still volunteered? Would they do

anything differently had they stayed? Was all of this inevitable?

Too late to think or worry about any of that right now. Right now

was to be enjoyed. As day turned to night, the weather cooled just

a bit, not enough for a jacket but enough to feel a slight whisper of

a breeze in the air. As she talked of their lives together and the

things that she thought they might like to do when they got back,

she noticed the look in Bobby's eyes. She knew that look all too

well but wanted to talk to him about the future, their future.

"Bobby, what do you think about having the whole yard

landscaped by professionals and then maybe having a pool put in?"

Bobby, with thoughts other than landscaping and pools,

responded the only way he could when he felt as he did at that

moment, "Sure thing, hun!"

Bobby had that familiar stirring in his groin. How he loved

this woman. How he craved her, wanted her, needed her, to be in

her. He had never felt this way with any one woman. Sure he'd felt

that red hot passion for women, many women--too many women,

in fact. However, along with that, he felt a deep respect, a deep connection, a sense of belonging to her and only her, a sense of belonging to another person wholly and with every cell in his body.

They of course, he felt, were what true love was all about. She had told him about the cute story of "lobster love" and what it meant. He had never heard such a story in his life. *Hmm,* he pondered, *do lobsters really mate for life? They only have the one mate, forever?* What a strange idea that was to him, not being able to be with any others, not wanting to. He never thought that a possibility, at least, not until she came into his life. They both finally found their "lobster love" in each other.

The both of them were very similar in many ways--too many ways sometimes. It was eerie how they both could finish each other's words, sentences and even thoughts. He supposed that was probably why they accepted their pasts and trusted each other so much. No one else did. Neither of their ex-spouses did. In the beginning, they vowed to each other to disclose all. All the lies, the affairs, everything and let the chips fall where they may. If either felt that they could not stomach such truths, then they needed to say something at the moment. It felt good to him to finally come clean. It was a first for him, to tell all to someone. Every little thing, good or bad, he had done in his past, his life before her.

She felt equally good. She knew she had lied to her exes a time or two. Lied about the affairs, lied about who she really was on the inside. She had always played a character with men. Give them what they wanted; what they expected her to be. She was for the first time…completely herself. It felt good. Clean for the first time, it seemed. She was not a bad woman or bad wife, but she had been less than truthful about a few things in her life and in her marriages. There was only one thing that she would not talk about. She could not talk about and never would, not even on her dying day, not even to Bobby.

They spent their Sunday evening much like most other evenings, in each other's arms enjoying the warmth of the afterglow. It seemed to her that when she met him she had won some type of lotto! Perfect love. How did she get so goddamn lucky, she asked herself repeatedly.

As the hours turned into days, their departure date grew nearer and nearer, only one day now. The team was to go to a meeting that night but Harris assured both of them that it would not be necessary and that he would go for them all. He could take whatever notes needed. He would see them first thing in the morning to depart Cuba for Iraq. They would have one layover in the DC area.

This was to be the first time Bobby was to see where and how she lived in her own home. He always wondered what it would be like, how it would look. He wondered if her Mexican side took over in the decorating: full of color, full of life, or would it be the German side: neat, orderly, "a place for everything and everything in its place." He recalled her saying that to him before they moved in together.

In Cuba the decorating was sparse at best. Neither of them brought over much. They had the benefit of getting furniture from the base, so there really wasn't much for him to go by as far as the type of decorating he would expect. He wondered about the outside as well. She'd told him as they were working on their own little oasis that she had never done this type of thing before. She loved a beautiful garden but never had much luck. He wondered if she ever had such ideas about him. What would his house look like? He figured that she would assume that he lived much like other unmarried men—like bears in caves. She would be right in that respect. He never really cared one way or the other when it came to decorating or furniture for that matter. As long as it was functional, were his thoughts on decorating.

Bobby had become increasingly concerned about how Harris had been acting these past four days. Almost like before all the drama, the sexual harassment, almost like normal. Yet Bobby knew that nothing about Harris was really normal. Nevertheless, this was to be their last night together in Cuba. Bobby wanted it to be special for her because she was special to him. Bobby thought a nice big juicy steak on the grill – very, very rare for both of them. A generous stuffed-jacket potato, as she called a baked potato, with all the fixings and of course, her olive oil grilled asparagus and a big tossed salad on the side with the best margaritas he could make, to boot. His woman was indeed different in so many ways, he thought to himself. From the phrases or words she used for everyday things to the unbelievable way she could put away the groceries. The woman could eat and drink unbelievable amounts of food and alcohol.

Well, if Bobby was to pull this feast off, he needed to get his rear in gear. He smiled at her and said, "March upstairs to the warm bubble bath I prepared. I even set up the bathroom with those fragrant candles you like so much and a nice chilled class of white zin. I also have that crazy foreign music you like, one of your favorites on the CD player as well."

Bobby wasn't familiar with this music, but she seemed to love it. Bobby thought it must be something French. She loved all things French for some reason. As he prepared their meal, he felt he had been transferred to some small Parisian cafe. He too was starting to enjoy this particular music. Strange thought because he just about hated most things French, but since his wife seemed to like it, he thought, *what the hell.*

As she jumped into the warm bubbles, he could hear her voice singing to the music. Strange, not because she truly was tone deaf--she was--but that she was singing in perfect French. Her enunciation was impeccable. How did she know French, much less what he thought to be a Parisian dialect? He never recalled ever hearing her even remotely speak another language besides the occasional swear word in Spanish or in German. She, much like

108

him, did not learn languages easily, or so he thought. It was not their forte!

As he prepared their feast, her singing mesmerized him. Not only was it French, but it didn't sound like her at all. He could only remember hearing her sing along to tunes on the radio, and his loved one was sadly tone deaf, but this was not the voice of someone tone deaf. Perfect tone and perfect pitch—this was not his lovely wife singing, he thought, but who else could it be?

He was so caught up in his thoughts that he almost forgot what he was doing. Apparently, he had been standing there listening for a better part of a half an hour. All he heard now was the tub draining. He had to get hopping and quick; she was on her way down. Luckily, they both loved their steak raw. Everything was coming together perfectly, strangely enough. All that was left to do was sauté some button mushrooms in garlic and oil. She loved that on her steak. That woman of his could eat those buttons by the fistfuls.

As she sprinted down the stairs, he looked up and was completely transfixed. He could not take his eyes off her, his bride, his wife, his best friend. She wasn't what one would call classically beautiful, but she did have an exotic sensuality about her and she was pretty darn cute to boot. She was the sexiest woman he had ever met. He could not wait to see this woman, his wife, at 60 and beyond. He prayed daily to the gods above that brought her into his life, and Bobby was not the praying kind.

She leaped down the stairs in her little Hawaiian shorts and tight little white tank top…sans bra. She did that for him and he knew it. He loved and adored her body. From her heart-shaped ass up to her large teardrop-shaped breasts. What a remarkable sight. It was a full size woman's body on only 58 inches. This woman had more energy than women half her age. He thought, where did all her energy come from? She was always on the go, even when she was sitting still, which was not too often. He often joked and called her the "energizer bunny."

The mushrooms started to pop, and neither of them realized it. They just stood there staring at each other. God, how they loved each other. How lucky they were to have found each other. If they only knew what was to become of them….over there. One of the little buttons' pop caught Bobby on the face, and only then did they realize they had just been standing there gazing at each other.

Their gaze broke with an uncontrollable laughter they shared together, together they loved and laughed. He hugged her as they giggled in each other's arms.

## Chapter 4 -- Harris

As Harris packed for his trip with those two idiots, his heart raced. He felt like he was going to keel over from a heart attack. He had really let himself go over the years--high blood pressure and higher cholesterol. He ate and ate and ate, never limiting himself on anything. Harris wondered what he would look like if he also drank. Thank God for his father's alcoholism to keep him on the straight and narrow on that respect. He knew that at some point he would have to lose some of the 75 pounds he had gained over the years, but when, he just didn't know. It was an effort just to walk to his truck in the carport every morning. One day, he thought, one day he would get healthy.

What had happened to his life? He tried to think of happier times, but he couldn't think of any. He really couldn't even pinpoint one place or even one time that he would consider happy.

He wondered if he had always been this miserable. He thought of his last 30 years working for the government. How law enforcement left no room to have a family. He assumed that was why he got married so late in life and then to have a kid even later so. Not even his family made him happy. Of course he loved his "little man" but was he really happy, had he ever been? Could he ever be? He guessed the reason why he hated those two so much was because they always seemed so goddamn happy and in love. They epitomized what he didn't have, never really ever had, true love.

How long ago, if ever, did anyone look at him the way they looked at each other? He `knew his hatred was based out of his jealousy of what they had. It looked almost seamless, their love for each other. Jealousy, he knew it, but also that little problem she brought into light. Why did she have to ruin everything? It was none of her business, his little innocent remarks and looks towards a co-worker of theirs. Why did she have to stick her nose into his business? Of course, it was nothing but a minor flirtation with a girl half his age. Who was he kidding, a third of his age. He supposed some would think him a dirty old man. He didn't think his feelings for her were dirty, and he definitely didn't feel old around her. She seemed in awe of him. She listened intently to his old war stories, taking in his every word, trying to learn from him, the master. And when he followed her as she drove to the PX or even to go get some dinner, he never saw anything wrong with that. Nor his innocent invitation for her to join him in Jamaica. He just wanted to be her friend and, well, much much more if she would only be willing.

Well at least that's the way he saw it, anyway. It was something so harmless that got blown out of proportion all because "she" had to butt in. Harris had like her before all of this happened. When he first met her, Harris thought of her as a "good Mexican," not like those white women who talked loud and cursed. She was quiet and knew who the boss was. Hell, he liked her and Bobby both. He wanted very much to have what they had, one day. Maybe if he could take that away from them somehow....would that make him feel better? Harris thought that they needed to be stripped down naked and displayed for the frauds they were taken down a peg or two.

The "power couple," as everyone referred to them, needed

to feel what it was like to be where he was--alone and lonely. He would definitely think of a way to take them down, *bring them down to earth with the rest of us mere mortals*. As he continued to pack in auto-pilot, he plotted and planned and planned and plotted their demise--not their physical demise, perhaps just their professional demise, but he didn't want to limit himself. He would keep that option open if the opportunity presented itself. Just as he thought he should give up, it came to him. The perfect idea! This will teach those two shits a lesson they will never forget; something that would affect the rest of their lives. He would also make sure it would only take a few days, but those few days would be days they would never forget.

## Chapter 5 -- In Love

She and Bobby sat under the Cuban sky -- simply stuffed. Bobby had made the most wonderful meal. She ate every last morsel. He was surprised just how much his wife could eat. He loved to watch her enjoying every single bite as if it would be her last. She made love the same way, like it would be the last time. So intense sometimes that he would nearly cry, but he never did. He could hear her harassing him unmercifully if he had.

She sat there, almost lying down in the lawn chair. She could barely move enough to unbutton her shorts but she had to. They both knew the only solution to this dilemma came in the form of two words….Jose Cuervo! Surprisingly, she bounced off the lawn chair and came back with a full bottle. He knew right off that no good would come of that. A bottle of Jose—chilled, the cool sea breeze, two shot glasses and a woman who could drink all women and most men under the table, even Bobby. She knew she could drink Bobby under the table and he knew it also, but she let him think differently, made him feel good, so why not.

She asked, "Just one shot?" He knew no matter how he answered, there would be more drinking than just one measly shot; he knew it and so did she. Just as they were about to toast, the phone rang. It was strange because they rarely got calls. A look of alarm came over her face as if she could only think it would be something bad. Bobby decided to answer instead of letting the machine do it. It was Harris letting them know that they didn't need to go to the meeting that evening. There was just no need.

"Just enjoy your last evening in Cuba," Harris said. "Trust me; I'll take care of everything for all of us."

Bobby hung up and looked strangely surprised.

As he reiterated the phone call to her, she began to tremble ever so slightly. She felt a cold chill race down her spine. She had no idea why she was behaving like this. Her heart felt so heavy with doom and gloom for absolutely no reason at all. She tried to snap out of it so as to not ruin their last night there in their beloved Cuba. She knocked back her first tequila quick instead of their usual sipping.

Bobby couldn't understand her feelings concerning the phone call. Harris had been pleasant, hell more than pleasant, downright happy. It had been a while since Bobby saw that from him. He didn't want interrupt their last evening in country. *Pretty darn considerate*, Bobby thought to himself. And besides, Harris said he would call with any information he had gotten at the meeting. Knowing this, they decided not to get too hammered. You never know if something very important about their trip could change and they needed to be sober to take it all in.

True to his word, Harris called and told them that they were to be picked up at 6am sharp! "Don't be late," he said, "We have to meet up with the military team to catch the first ferry out to make our connecting flight." This time Bobby sensed something as well. Harris sounded friendly enough, but there was that nagging feeling neither of them could get rid of.

They decided it best to go on and head for bed. No wild passionate love-making this evening. Besides, there was still time for that before getting over there. She set the alarm for 5am. They packed clothes, ironed and got ready to go. They would now have a little extra time in the morning to sit down and enjoy a cup of coffee and, of course, her caffeine of choice: Dr. Pepper. As they lay there, Bobby rubbing her back as usual--boy had he spoiled her with that rubbing. What in the world would this poor woman do without him rubbing her back, he thought? How would she ever be able to sleep? They both lay there unable to sleep. Both worried something was afoot. Both were scared to say anything for fear of unnecessarily upsetting the other. Both of them felt it. They just didn't know what "it" was. Was evil too strong of a word? She didn't think so. As the minutes turned to hours, they realized they were only two hours out before the alarm clock rang. No sleep for either.

# Chapter 6 -- The Trip to Hell

They decided to get up anyway. They could sleep on the plane to Jacksonville or better yet, the plane trip from Jacksonville to BWI, to her home, the place she really had not missed as much as she thought she would or should. As they took their separate turns in the tiny bathroom, an observer would think of it as a ballet; perfectly choreographed--one coming and the other going and the other going as the other came--like they had done this very thing for years.

Of course Bobby was done before her. It took her forever to get an outfit "just right," even if it was an outfit she'd be sitting eight hours in. That is who she was. She had such attention to detail. It boggled the mind. Some would say anal retentive or even obsessive compulsive. Bobby loved to mess with her about that, all her little peculiarities. All it took was for him to move something, anything in the house, just a hair differently, and she would still take a second to "fix" it back to the way it was, even if she didn't know he had done anything. "A place for everything and everything in its place." Her mantra. God, he couldn't wait to see her little house.

They sat quietly in the dining room drinking their caffeine of choice when outside came a light knock on the door. They stared at each other. It was only 5am. She stood up to get the door and saw Harris walking back towards the van. She called out to him, but he just climbed back in the van and proceeded to leave. She started running towards the van. What in the hell was going on here, she wondered. Bobby came out to see his wife running after a white van. The van wouldn't stop so Bobby peeled out and ran in front of it. Risky, yes, but he just wasn't sure how the hell to stop that madman. Finally Harris stopped the van. He genuinely looked shocked. As Harris stopped and got out of the van, Bobby tore into him. Harris was totally nonplussed and said to Bobby and now to her, "I told you two 5am sharp. We can't wait around on you two to primp and pamper yourselves; we're off to war for god sakes!" he shouted at them. She and Bobby stared at each other in shock.

Harris would not look at either one of them. She and Bobby just weren't sure what to do next. Risk going back inside and get their bags together and Harris drives off, or she could stay and Bobby get all their bags but feared for some reason that Harris would surely try to hurt her, or he could stay and she could get the bags. No, that wasn't the right answer either. They were all too big and bulky for her to struggle with. Neither she nor Bobby knew what to do next. Harris had a savage, wild look about him. It had even scared him a bit...that look, the look of a predator. Finally she yelled in the van that she was going to call the police. That seemed to pull Harris out of the trance he was in to some degree. Bobby moved out of the way as Harris pulled in the drive way for the second time. They both ran and grabbed their bags and locked the door. Boy, they never expected to have this type of morning. They weren't sure what to expect when they got back outside or even the rest of their adventure. Harris sat there stiff behind the wheel. She and Bobby tried talking to him but got nothing...dead silence. They didn't know what to do next. What would have happened if they woke up with the alarm clock? They both felt sure he said 6am sharp, don't be late. What was going on? Neither could guess

122

what he had planned for the both of them over there, but rest assured he did have something planned, you could count on it.

The three of them sat in silence. The team sat there stone quiet. She and Bobby had no idea what to do next, so they followed Harris' lead. Get out of the van, grab your bags and start walking towards the ferry. They saw the others, the military team of three, waved at them and then sat down. They all looked at her and Bobby strangely, or maybe she was a little paranoid from this morning's drama.

The military team asked why she and Bobby were running late, and Harris piped in, "I had to practically wake them up and pull them out of bed myself." The soldiers just looked at Bobby with winks and nods. She, on the other hand, glared at Harris. It would do no good to argue or disagree, so the pair just sat there...wondering, *what's in store for us next?*

"We haven't even gotten to Iraq yet and this is how it starts," she whispered to Bobby. Surely it couldn't get any worse than this, or at least that's what they hoped.

After a few minutes, Harris got up and walked away. She and Bobby made a vow to each other that whatever was to happen, they would stick together. They would not leave each other's side. No matter what! They had no idea what he would or could do and weren't about to take any chances in finding out. He strode back to the group, all puffed out chest and arrogance written all over his face. A look of smugness washed over his features. She wondered why he was so smug. *What is he planning?* These answers she wanted to hear, but at the same time, she was very much afraid to hear. What did he have in store for her...for the both of them? And why? Why her and her Bobby? Bobby never did anything to him. And her, well, she knew why he directed this towards her. Because of what she had witnessed and was asked to report. But surely he couldn't be doing these things because of that; could he? He couldn't blame her for something she had no control over. Or could he?

As both teams sat in silence, everyone with their own thoughts, in came the General who had started all of this mess. He wanted to see his volunteers off and give them a "coin" for this act of bravery and dedication to their country. He shook everyone's hand and then left as quickly as he came. One thing she and Bobby noticed was that Harris decided that he didn't want to be part of their team, the civilian team, any longer. He ignored them and stayed with the military team. They both wondered if this is the way it was going to be over there. This would not be a good start.

Finally Harris, who simply by age decided that he was going to be in charge, called the military team to a meeting right there in the airport. The only way she and Bobby even knew what was going on was that all of a sudden the other three were missing. They looked around and found them in a separate room, talking. She and Bobby came in and sat down to find out what was going on. Harris looked upset that he was found but continued to talk. He said that when they got to Jacksonville Naval Air Station, they would then take a taxi to the Jacksonville International airport where they would catch a connecting flight to BWI.

Harris proceeded to tell the teams that they were all going to be staying at the airport hotel right next to BWI, then meet the next morning at 6am for a 6pm flight. She thought this was incredibly strange as they both had already told Harris that she and Bobby were going to stay at her house a half hour away and that they had an appointment with an attorney that morning would meet him and the rest of the team at 3pm at the international check-in counter. This was all discussed and decided beforehand, but Harris looked at her like he had no idea and told them both that was totally out of the question. They were both to come with the rest of the team as he had just discussed.

Bobby got up close and personal with Harris and informed him that arrangements had already been made and that they would see them at three the next afternoon. Harris turned a bright red. It appeared he would have a heart attack any second now. As she and Bobby returned to their seats, they both heard Harris whispering something to the military team, "See, I told you guys these two were going to be trouble. They won't be there when you really need them. They will just go off on their own. Stick by me. You can trust me." At that point she and Bobby had no idea what to do so they sat there feeling defeated. All they could do was do their jobs and watch after each other to make sure that neither of them would ever be alone with Harris.

It was almost time for them to board the plane to Jacksonville. They all sat in silence. The four of them, Harris and the three soldiers, looked over at her and Bobby. She wondered what in the hell were they thinking. What had Harris told them that she and Bobby hadn't heard? She and Bobby had always gotten along very well with the military team. They had all worked together, went to the same parties and BBQs. Why were they acting so strange now?

At long last their flight was called. Everyone started boarding. It was strange how the four of them were able to sit all together, yet she and Bobby sat as far as physically possible one could sit, in a plane. Probably for the best, she supposed. As she and Bobby took their seats and got settled, Harris looked over at the two of them with such disdain, such hatred. That look sent a chill down to her bones. What did he have in store for them?

Surprisingly, instead of talking with Bobby, she fell asleep straight away. She only awoke when she heard the pilot say they should be in Jacksonville within the next ten minutes. She must have fell into quite a deep sleep because she had the strangest of dreams. Dreams of them actually being over there, and it wasn't pretty. She didn't want to tell Bobby any of it, but he could tell by her look, something was wrong. He asked what was up, but she said nothing.

"Just surprised I fell asleep so hard and so quickly," was

the lie she told him. She hated lying to this man. She never had, at least, until now. But for some reason something told her not to tell him. Not yet, anyway. She had to think on this some more. It felt so very real. Could it be what was to happen? Could she predict the future? She had in the past had dreams that seemed to come true. As far back as she could remember she could do that. Could this be one of those times? She hoped not. If so, the future looked incredibly bleak for her and Bobby.

Bobby looked at her quizzically. Wondering....wondering what was the matter with his lady. She looked so upset, scared really. Maybe it was just a bad dream. But if it was that she would have told him. She told him everything, even her worst of dreams, or at least that's what he had thought.

As they disembarked, she couldn't get her thoughts past that dream. It was like she was now walking into some type of dream. Everything around her, including herself, seemed surreal. Was this really happening, she asked herself silently. Was it? Was this part of the dream and she was actually back in Cuba? Or worst yet, back in her little French country home, having never gone to Cuba or met her true love? All of this kind of thinking was starting to freak her out. She decided, from that second forward, she would not think of anything but going to Iraq, no thinking of dreams, period!

As the teams waited for their luggage to come off the conveyer belt, she and Bobby looked at each other. They knew they were both thinking the same thing. *What next?* She and Bobby got their luggage around the same time, so they waited on the rest of their team so they could catch the bus that was to take the two teams to the international airport 45 minutes away. As they sat and waited for the team and, of course, Harris, she had the need to go to the ladies room. She wasn't sure if that was a good idea right now. She remembered how he acted this morning by trying to leave them. Would he do that again? But it was at least 45 more minutes at minimum if they left this minute, and they were nowhere near being ready to leave this minute. She couldn't wait. She told Bobby she just had to go. Bobby told her, "No worries, babydoll."

"He won't try anything stupid in front of others," he assured her. She sure as hell hoped he was right.

# Chapter 7 -- The Dream

As she walked quickly to the ladies room, she kept looking over her shoulder. She wasn't sure why, but well, she knew why. That stupid dream. She told herself not to think! Not to think about that dream, but here she was, dwelling on the damn dream. She was scared for her husband. Frightened for them both. Before she realized it, she was actually running to the ladies room. She wondered if anyone thought she was a lunatic. *Well, can't worry too much about that. Get in there, do your business and get back to Bobby.* As she sat on the toilet, the dream came rushing back to her. She seriously thought she was losing her mind. She couldn't stop the damn dream no matter what. There it was in technicolor, for god sakes! Ok... maybe this was a sign. Maybe she just had to let it all play out in her mind. Maybe there was an answer as to what to do if that dream came true. As she sat there, she heard the comings and goings of what seemed like millions of women. Primping and preparing to meet family or friends at the airport. And others like her were just trying to get from point A to point B. She decided if there was a sign to be shown to her, it wouldn't happen while she was sitting on the pot. She finished up, washed her hands and ran back. There Bobby sat, alone. The other team, including Harris, left them both there in Jacksonville.

"Geez, what now," she said to Bobby. Bobby had a gleam in his eye. Harris thought neither of them had a clue as to what to do next. Luckily Bobby had gotten all the information prior to leaving Cuba. He knew where to go and how to get there. Thank God for Bobby, her savior. The "other team," as they would now forever be called, walked right by Bobby even after he tried to talk to them. Harris had really done the both of them in, even with the other team.

Bobby told her to get the small bags, and he grabbed the larger ones. She loved when he had a plan. "Follow me; we're going to take an alternate route and beat them to BWI."

They were moving so quickly that she completely forgot about the dream. She was thankful for that and for Bobby taking the lead on this. She loved to see him this way. A man with a plan…a man in action…a man ready and able to take care of the situation at hand! As they arrived at the counter, Bobby talked to the ground crew about changing flights. The dream popped back into her thoughts. She told herself, *not now, not now. I don't have time to think or listen to you right now.* Boy, if anyone could read her mind, they'd think her to be a lunatic at this point. Thank God Bobby came back to let her know that the flight was now boarding. *Thank God,* she thought and with that, they were in line to board. She would have the time to let her thoughts take her where they may. A few times Bobby gave her some strange looks, but she couldn't tell him, not yet. Not until the dream evolved in her waking mind. Maybe she could find a solution.

Bobby looked at her as they settled into their seats. "Tired, baby doll?"

She said, "Dead tired, sweetie."

With that, she had permission to let her mind go and wouldn't have to answer any questions from Bobby. Not right now, anyway. She felt like she was going into another dream state as the thought of the dream took over her mind. Was she really asleep? She couldn't tell, she felt wide awake but yet not.

As Bobby watched her sleep he wondered what was bothering his darling wife. She had been acting strange since waking up in Jacksonville. He wondered if she was keeping something from him. They knew each other so well, he could almost tell her every thought, and his thought was that something was up with her. What could it be? His guess: whatever she dreamed about was really getting to her. He knew that she could have some powerful dreams and sometimes, just sometimes, stuff in them would come true. He hoped for their sakes this wasn't the reason. She looked too shook up for his comfort. She looked fitful as she sat next to him, head on his shoulder. The worry lines were getting deeper on her forehead, and her nose was all scrunched up. Should he wake her? He couldn't decide. What if there really wasn't a bad dream? What if she was just dead tired, like she said? He decided to let her sleep. He kept a close eye on her though, just in case. His woman could just drop to sleep in seconds sometimes. Sometimes he could rub her back for hours on end and she would lay awake, thinking God only knows what.

He wondered how much he really knew her. How much did

she hold back? They both made promises to tell all, but he had the feeling that she didn't, wouldn't, couldn't for some reason. He felt that she trusted him 100% but there was still something he felt he didn't know about his woman. Sometimes she had the saddest look in her eyes when she thought he wasn't looking. Sometimes he could hear her crying in the middle of the night. He was never sure if he should get up and see if she was ok or if she would be too embarrassed. He tried that once, got up to see if she was ok. The look of embarrassment washed over her tear-soaked face. He didn't know what to do. She said she was ok, that it was just a bad dream. He accepted that answer and went back to bed when she urged him to do so. That is when he found out about her dreams, that next morning.... about how some of them came true. It was a little eerie but also very interesting. He always wondered how her mind worked, and getting to know even a little bit at a time was good with him. So he sat there looking at her sleeping and wondered why she looked so panicked early on but now she seemed so relaxed, so serene. So incredibly at peace. So very happy right now. He understood the deal with Harris was upsetting, but nothing the two of them couldn't handle on their own.

Bobby wondered if they should call their company, Lockhart Marion, like his wife wanted them to. But what to tell them? That Harris was acting weird? Everyone at work knew that, surely that news had been passed to the high-ups at HQ. If they tried to talk to the company while they were in Maryland between flights, that they, the company, would look at him and his wife as having serious issues and probably would tell them to not go. She had mentioned making an appointment with them sometime in the morning before departing that evening. They even told Harris that they were not going to be able to meet at 6am for a 6pm flight. They said they had an appointment that day. That just made him come unglued even further. He yelled at them both and said, "The company wants us all together at all times!"

Bobby wasn't sure how much of that was true but he felt, as his wife did, that going to the company in person just had to be done before going over there with him. Without realizing it, they were landing in North Carolina. Time had passed quickly. He watched his woman "sleep" the whole time, not wanting to take an eye off of her....just in case.

She slowly opened her eyes and looked up at him. *What a beautiful sight,* she thought to herself. Those blue eyes, how they penetrated her soul. How she loved those eyes looking down at her. For some reason, she felt pretty good. She didn't have any solutions to the dream. In fact, she wasn't able to come back to that damn dream, try as she might. She actually had a lovely dream of them in her garden. It looked so much different than it did now, the way she left it. Before Cuba, she was never any good with outdoor work.

Her expertise had been on the inside, the interior decorating process. The breaking down of a room into several pieces and putting it all together; from floor to ceiling. The yard, well that was a different story altogether. She looked out at that yard daily…just staring at it not knowing what the hell to do with it. The new housing development she had moved into didn't come with landscaping. It was up to her to do with it what she may. Unfortunately for her, she had no idea. The idea of hiring someone to make her yard feel her own just didn't suit her. She felt she had to be the one to make it her own. So, day after day, she would stare at it from her deck or, if it was raining, from her screened in porch, wondering. There were easily 50 scrawny pine trees out there. She loved pine trees, but these skinny ones did nothing for her. Oh, and the "monkey grass," as the locals called it. Little tufts of grass about three feet high by now, made it look more like swamp than anything else. For some reason she thought she should just leave it and go to Cuba and see what happened while she was away. She had the next door neighbor mowing the front lawn. Nothing else could be done to that sad lawn either. Keep it mowed was about all she could do. So she left it. Left the yard looking pitiful; perhaps there was a reason why?

As she rubbed her eyes, she thought back to this last dream. It was definitely her house. She could see the bright yellow siding and the emerald green shudders, but the yard, this yard was not hers. This yard was like a Garden of Eden. How funny that thought was, that her garden looked just like one would think the Garden of Eden to look like and the actual country it was located was Mesopotamia. The Garden of Eden would have been located at the one place they were headed to, Iraq. Her dream garden had little trellises, arbors, a white gazebo with a little white metal picket fence around it with lots and lots of white flowers. All her favorites where there: white roses, Casablanca lilies, gardenias, and lily of the valley, camellia's, clematis; even some white pansies, all of them with their own beautiful scent. It looked like a beautiful moon garden. And on a different part of the garden, lots and lots of beautiful climbing vines, all the ones she loved and saw in other people's gardens: bougainvillea, clematis, jasmine, morning glories, and honeysuckle. And the flowers were everywhere and they were all blooming, all colors of the rainbow. She thought of them as a big box of crayolas. Every color one could think of and every shape of flower, right in her own back yard. She even had deep purple and white butterfly bushes with tons of butterflies fluttering around them. That was the strangest dream she'd ever had. Strange because it was beautiful and it looked like her yard.

There was one thing about her garden that was a little off, but in dream world everything seems ok. There was an old woman walking in her garden. Could that be her walking around some fifty years from now? She looked like she belonged there, and she looked very familiar to her. The old woman was walking towards the pool and tikki bar. She couldn't believe it; there was a pool. She had a swimming pool and tikki bar in her backyard! She had always wanted a pool, even as a young child but never could afford one. But there it was, not large but not small either. No diving board but a beautiful waterfall. It looked like it was put there by nature. It was not your standard-looking pool. This one had natural-looking rock for a deck and one side of the pool just flowed in, like the entrance of a real beach. On one side was a nice hot tub for soaking after a long day and the other side was a sunken tikki bar with stools in the water for sitting. She loved this dream. She didn't want to wake up. She wondered if this was the future or just a beautiful dream.

She woke up and saw Bobby looking down at her. Elle couldn't keep her little dog lips from grinning and she smiled from ear to ear. She wanted to tell him about every detail of this dream. She wanted him to see how pitiful her yard really looked. This dream would then make a big impact on him as it had done her.

Bobby looked at her and wondered. Wow, this was like a 180-degree difference from the last time she woke up. He wondered what she'd been dreaming about. He decided not to ask her. She would tell him if she wanted and when she was ready. She told Bobby she had a dream but wanted to wait to tell him after they got to her house and specifically wanted to tell him about it while sitting in the backyard. He thought that a bit strange, but he had long since stopped asking her why she said the things she did. She was more on the strange side as it was, and he loved that about her. She probably thought him a little strange as well. That was probably the reason they got along so famously. They were both a bit "off." As they sat there waiting to land, Bobby told her the next part of the plan. They were to switch planes in North Carolina to get to BWI a full two hours before the other team. The only question in their minds were, *do we go straight to the company and tell them what is going on or do we wait for the other team?* What was the right thing to do? They decided when they landed in North Carolina to call the company and try to set up the appointment. That would be better than just popping in on them the day of their flight to Iraq, as they'd intended. She called and called and called and left many messages but never actually got through to anyone. They decided they'd wait for the other team. That would be the right thing to do, even though they were not shown that courtesy themselves. They hopped on the plane in North Carolina and made their way to BWI in no time. They decided to have some dinner and a drink to calm their nerves. They weren't sure what was going to happen next.

As they sat in the bar at BWI, she thought back to the times that she would take her first husband, Richard, to the airport on one of his many business trips. He was gone more than he was home back in those days. In the beginning it wasn't too bad. Being recently married, she wasn't used to having a man around the house too much anyway. Every time he came back, though, was like a honeymoon all over again. She supposed that was probably one reason that they stayed married as long as they did. Would it have ended sooner if he had been one of those husbands who never left to go on business trips? She would never know the answer to that. But as the years went on she grew tired of the constant trips here and there without her. Sure, he was a generous, giving man and always brought her gifts from all sorts of exotic places, but nothing would take the place of having him close. She wanted that so badly from him, for him to be really close. It seemed to her that he wouldn't or couldn't do it. It always felt as he had an arm's length between their hearts. Without fail, though, she would be at the airport saying goodbye once again, the deep sadness entering her heart once more. She never knew where he went or how long he would be gone. He would just come home "when he was done."

Her first husband had been in the Army when they first met at the beach but soon retired and went to work for one of those agencies with the initials. There wasn't much he could say about what he did or where he did it, but he seemed to love it. Sometimes he seemed to love it more than her. At least that's how she felt at the time. She always knew when he was going to leave and go on a long trip. He would always bring her such wonderful expensive gifts: beautiful white rose, a bakers dozen, right before having to leave. She loved him for the thoughtfulness of the gifts he picked out, but she wished he would sometimes just bring her a handful of daisies or was able to call her while he was gone. Only after it was too late for them both did he show a glimmer of what she knew he could be, down deep, a loving, caring husband able to show how deeply he felt. He of course, was the one to take her to the airport after their divorce. She was going back to Germany, back to where they had lived and loved. She'd hoped she would find the love she once experienced there.

Only as they called for her flight to board did he say, "Don't go, stay with me." She wept, for that was the exact thing Richard had told her in barely a whisper so many years ago as he put her on the train to Czechoslovakia. She told him that it was too late and kissed his cheek and never looked back and boarded her flight. Why hadn't he said that a month ago, a week ago, last night, for god sakes, an hour go? Why wait till it was too late? What would have happened if she'd stayed? Would it have been the same?

Her first month in Germany was tough for her. She had loved him so much, and this country reminded her of him. He called her weekly and they talked for hours. This is what she'd missed during their marriage, this kind of closeness with him. And once, on her birthday, after she'd left, she got flowers delivered to her place of business. It was handfuls and handfuls of white daisies. The sight of them made her cry with happiness that he had actually listened to her and sadness because it was too late, she had already met her soon-to-be second husband but even that little fact didn't stop her from loving this man who tried so hard but tried just a little too late. Little did she know at that point that they

143

would have an opportunity to make it work for the both of them again after her second divorce.

She wasn't sure how long she'd been thinking back on those days with Richard but was brought back to the present by the waitress asking what they wanted to drink. In unison, they both said, "Jose chilled, no lime, no salt."

They looked at each other and smiled. They were quite the pair. So there they sat, having dinner and the beverage of choice for the both of them. Waiting for the next drama to appear in the form of Harris. What would this fool do next, they both thought. They decided to just play it out. Just see what happens and then go to their company the next morning. It was a Saturday but someone was always there. They would find someone, and someone would find the person they needed to talk to, and that would be the program manager.

He was new to the company, and hopefully that would be their saving grace. She had just talked to the program manager about a week before leaving Cuba. It was a job interview for the team lead position for her office. The interview had gone well. It lasted well over an hour, and it seemed that they had similar managerial styles. He seemed to like what he heard, and she felt good about applying for that position. She knew everyone on her team liked her, respected her and went to her specifically with questions to everything, even though she hadn't been there that long. She was a natural leader, and her program manager could see that. They'd never met but were looking forward to meeting him upon her return from Iraq, as she had told him during the interview.

She would talk to him; she would take the lead to say what they thought about Harris. She had at least spoken with him and she felt good about what he thought of her. They waited and waited, not sure whether to just take a rental car to her house or continue to wait. They both ordered another drink, non-alcoholic this time. They still had to drive to her house which was about a 30-45 minute drive. So there they sat and waited and waited. Finally they heard the arrival of the other team's flight. They both knew that they were going to be driving to her house that evening. Bobby had already mentioned that little bit of news to Harris.

Harris of course came unglued again and did the "company wants us all together the whole time" spiel. Bobby had told Harris

145

that they had appointments that day and would meet the team at

3pm for their 6pm flight. That was not going to be an issue tonight,

Bobby hoped anyway. They only stayed to let Harris know that

they made it ok though they'd been left in Jacksonville. It was the

right thing to do. She and Bobby stood there waiting on the other

team.

Down the ramp they came. Bobby called over to them.

Harris was nowhere in sight. Bobby talked to one of the soldiers to

let him know what was up. The soldier looked shocked by their

presence. He was told that they had changed their minds about

going to Iraq and decided to just go home for a quick vacation. She

and Bobby looked at each other in disbelief. They assured the

soldier that they were in fact going and that they had been the first

two to volunteer. Nothing was stopping them from going and

finishing up the mission there.

They walked with the rest of the soldiers to pick up their

bags. They were told that they were to stay at the hotel near the

airport and be back at the airport in a matter of 5 hours; it was 1:00

in the morning when the flight finally came in. She asked the

soldier why in the world would they all needed to be there that

146

early for a 6pm flight. They all looked exasperated and said, "Harris wants it that way."

They said he had taken control of the team and that she and Bobby were to be left alone and not talked to. As far as Harris was concerned, he considered her and Bobby deserters. They assured the team that they were going and nothing was stopping them. They felt the need to keep telling them that; that they were all one team. That they would all work together over there.

Finally, as they all stood there, Harris strolled up and looked at every single one of them with hatred, but he knew that he could still control the soldiers, so he talked to them and said it was time to get moving. He told them to pick up their stuff and they would take a taxi to the hotel. She told them all that they had a rental car and could drive them to the hotel.

Harris, without looking at her, said, "None of us needs a rental car. The hotel is right down the road." Bobby mentioned again that they were driving to her house and that they could drive them to the hotel.

Harris was about to lose it again when he realized that he had an audience this time, the soldiers, his team. He tried to be polite and said, "The company wants us to stay together, and that means you two also."

She told Harris that she and Bobby had an appointment with the company in the morning and they would mention it to them at that time. A look of shock washed over his already beet-red face as he finally responded, again not looking directly at her, "Well, uhhh, they cancelled that appointment. I forgot to tell you. I got a call earlier and they cancelled that appointment you had with them."

She and Bobby just looked at Harris with utter disbelief. How could this man just bald-face lie right to their faces and in front of witnesses? The pair looked at Harris, and he knew they knew he was lying. All Bobby would say was, "We are leaving. If anyone wants a ride, come on."

The soldiers were all about to come with her and Bobby when Harris said, "Men, we have a taxi waiting". So all the soldiers followed Harris to the taxi stand, and she and Bobby went their own way.

"See you here at the airport at 6am sharp. Don't be late!" was the last thing they heard from Harris as they sped away in their rental car. Strange, they had heard him say those exact words just 24 hours earlier.

With that, they were on the way home…her home and soon to be their home. She was very worried about what Bobby would think of her home. She hoped he would love it as much as she did and would make it his own, especially the yard. As they past Annapolis and drove across the Bay Bridge, she was reminded how beautiful the water looked from up there. How the stars and moon twinkled in the water. She loved it there. Sure, she hated the commuting and the yucky winters, but this time of year was wonderful. She felt confident he would love the way she decorated the inside of the house. She was a little afraid for him to see the sad-looking yard. Sadder than the little yard they fixed up together in Cuba. More than a sight worse, in fact. She thanked God that at least it was nighttime and he wouldn't be able to see the extent of the terribleness, at least not until morning. Sooner or later he would see it and hopefully come up with a plan. It was usually her who came up with plans. She loved it but she had no plan for this, not for this yard. She loved the fact he had a plan in place with the whole Harris fiasco. But as she recalled the wonderful dream of the

Garden of Eden, she realized she had a plan too.

As he drove to the little house, she noticed a familiar car in her driveway. It was her very best friend's car. She had given her a key so she could check up on the place from time to time. She wondered out loud, "What in the heck is Maria doing here at this hour?"

Bobby just looked at her and wondered the same thing. She knew that Maria and her boyfriend had their terrible ups and downs and wondered why she just didn't cut bait; he was bringing her down. Everyone told her that, and she would appear to listen but then go back to him. Bobby knew one thing for sure, he had other plans for his little woman, and it sure didn't involve friends being over, that's for sure.

As they got out of the car, they decided to just leave everything as was. They would unpack first thing in the morning. They walked into the little house and Bobby was shocked and amazed. How wonderful it looked, even in the dark. He smelled furniture wax, the old fashioned kind, bees wax. The type they use on antiques. She flipped on a few lights so he could see the rest of the house. As he walked through the house, she walked back to the bedrooms. First, the master bedroom, no one there. Then to the guest bedroom, and there she was, Maria, fast asleep. She wondered if she should wake her. She was afraid if she didn't she would get spooked if she heard any movement later on.

She sat on the bed and whispered to Maria, "Are you ok? Is everything ok?"

Maria opened her eyes and then closed them and opened them again quickly like she thought she was dreaming. After finally coming to, she smiled and said welcome home. She had gotten the message that she had left for her at work. She'd gotten Maria a job at Lockhart Marion. Maria was so worried about the messages that they had left, she thought best to come straight over, dust a little bit and make the little house feel lived in.

What Maria neglected to tell her that evening was that she had gotten into a big fight with her boyfriend. He had locked her out of their condo again, and she had no place to stay. She'd been living there for a couple of days now. Of course, that little part of the drama didn't unfold until daylight. One thing for sure with Maria and her boyfriend, regardless of who, what, when and where, bets could be placed that there would be big drama when they were together. This time was no different.

As she talked to Maria, Bobby walked through the little house. For him this was a dream come true. Not so much because her home was beautiful, but because he was able to get a much better understanding of who she was. She really should have been an interior designer. She had a gift, he could see it. He couldn't wait to see the yard once it got light outside.

He wasn't sure what was going on with her best friend, but he knew he was tired. He came back towards the voices and there they were, both of them sitting on the bed chatting away as if it was mid-afternoon. He thought how strange it was that they looked so much alike, so much like sisters. Bobby cleared his throat, and she made the introductions.

"Maria, this is Bobby, Bobby, Maria. She is my best friend in the entire world and couldn't be any closer unless she was my own sister. I've known Maria since she was a baby, a newborn really. I use to babysit her way back when."

Bobby laughed. They both wondered why he was laughing. The sheer embarrassment of it all made the colour of merlot go from Bobby's ear, neck and then his face. Bobby had a look of embarrassment.

He apologized and said, "It's weird because I was JUST thinking that same thing. That you two look like sisters."

Bobby said that he was beat and asked where he should lie down. She excused herself and told Maria she would be right back. She apologized to Bobby and assured him that everything would be ok, she was going to talk to Maria about Harris and see what she thought they should do. Bobby thought that was not a bad idea. She showed Bobby where everything was and told him to make himself totally at home because, after all, it was his home now too. As she rejoined Maria on the bed, she heard the shower go on. Good, all settled in now, she could get back to what was going on with Maria and her boyfriend. They talked for hours and hours about everything: Bobby, Harris and that whole ordeal and everything else under the sun. She never realized that it was already daylight; she'd had no sleep whatsoever.

Maria was in a dilemma again. Her boyfriend had locked the door and wouldn't let her in. She needed help. She needed them to help her get into the condo and at least get her clothes out. She knew that she and Bobby had to leave in about nine hours but needed their help and didn't have anyone else to turn to. She promised Maria that they would do their best to help her out with the limited time they had left in country and that she could stay at their house. She told Maria that she needed at least a couple of hours of sleep so she could function correctly. The two "sisters" hugged each other and said good night.

She crept into the bedroom and found Bobby sleeping on her big king-size bed. He looked so peaceful and content. She quickly jumped in the shower and washed up, then slid into the bed next to him. He automatically pulled her little body close, spooning, never missing a beat of his snoring either.

Bobby wasn't sure exactly what woke him up but there he was, wide awake, and it was only 8:00 in the morning. It had been a long, long night so he was really surprised at how rested he felt. He thought that perhaps it was this California deluxe king-size pillowtop bed. What a big bed for such a little woman. In fact, as he looked around last night he'd noticed that all her furniture seemed to be either overstuffed or just plain big, super sized as it were. As he started to get out of bed, he realized that his wife had his arm pinned down. She looked so peaceful he didn't want to wake her, so he moved ever so slowly. He tried to slide his arm away, but he just couldn't do it. She had her little paws around his arm like a pillow. That was strange, he thought, she had never slept like that before. He wondered why. It was as if she was scared and holding on for dear life. He tried to see the expression on her face. He could always tell if she was having a good dream or one of those bad ones he's heard about. He couldn't see her face because her hair was all over the place. She looked like a wild animal, a wild exotic animal. *Hmmm,* he thought. He started to get "ideas." Ideas perhaps he shouldn't be having since there was company in the house. At least he thought there was still company in the house. He could have sworn he heard the other toilet flush a bit earlier.

He wondered if he should just go back to sleep, stay there with her as long as they could. Soon enough they'd possibly be sleeping apart for the next three months. They still weren't sure about that arrangement. They were told before they left Cuba that had already been arranged, that they would be housed with the other contractors and not with the military folks. No further information was provided. As Bobby tried to get comfy again, the tingly feeling when a part of the body "falls asleep" started to take over his whole arm. This was going to be tough, he thought, tough to get up and tough to get back to sleep. He actually would like to get up and look around the little house in the daylight and to see the yard.

He looked around the master bedroom. *Nice, very nice,* he thought. Dark olive green walls and very pale olive ceiling and the reverse in the adjoining bathroom. Dark olive velvet drapes over pale olive sheers. She had the most beautiful hand carved wood furnishings in this room. The darkest of wood and the carvings were very intricate. Beautiful, everything in this room was beautiful and meticulously done. He wondered how much time it took her to do each room. He knew it took her simply hours to place the salt and pepper shakers "just so." That thought made him smile. He loved all her little idiosyncrasies.

The chandelier hanging above caught his eye. The colors of the little crystals matched perfectly to the linens on the bed. How did she find all of these things? Everything seemed to go so perfectly together, yet they were not "sets." They were from different places, different periods of time, but it all worked incredibly well together.

He felt a pair of eyes staring up at him. She smiled at him and said, "What are you doing?"

He smiled slyly and said, "Oh nothing, just hanging out."

Then out of the blue she jumped up and threw on her sweats and t-shirt. He was shocked to see her move so quickly. Bobby asked her what the heck was going on. She had forgotten to tell him that she was going to help Maria today; they were going to help her. As she slowed down and put her socks and shoes on, she told Bobby the story. He was disappointed but ready to help. If this Maria person was as close as family, as she seemed to be, he wanted to help. They both quickly finished dressing.

While she looked around to see if Maria was wandering around the house, Bobby took his time looking at every little thing. She had nice things, things that she picked out herself and took the time doing it as well. He could see that. He could see the care in which she picked out every single item. While Bobby was looking around, she wondered where the heck Maria was. Possibly out front smoking a cigarette.

She found Maria outside looking tired and sad. She felt bad for her "sister." She'd told her on several occasions about this fellow. She wouldn't listen then, but maybe, just maybe, she would

listen to her now. She knew that Maria didn't need any preaching

today. Not now and possibly not ever. After all, Maria was a

grown up. She tried hard not to treat her like she was 13, the age

Maria was when she took off for Germany. Maybe they would

have a good long talk when she and Bobby returned from Iraq, in

three short months. That should give Maria a good amount of time

alone with her thoughts as to the right thing to do. For now they

had to get busy.

She told Bobby that they were going to go to the condo to

see if she could get in. If they could, they would bring back some

of her clothes so she could stay here until she figured out what to

do next. Bobby asked if she wanted him to go with. They both said

no at the same time. They took off in Maria's car and screeched

around the corner.

Bobby continued looking around. He thought, *I'm going*

*outside finally to see what that's all about.* Outside the front door,

he was a bit surprised at the sparseness of the front yard. Not a

tree, not a bush, not one flower. *Wow*, he said to himself, *this is*

*sad.* He walked around to the side of the house--same thing, nothing. He walked around shaking his head in disbelief. He thought, *OK, she probably put her all into the backyard.* As he came past the side of the house, he just stared wide-eyed with mouth open. He was in shock. He could not believe what he saw back there. He thought for a second that this must be someone else's back yard. This was even more pitiful than her backyard in Cuba, and that was pitiful!

As he approached the back of the house, the next-door neighbor yelled over, "It's pitiful, isn't it?"

Bobby saw a young man talking to him from next door, standing on his deck against the fence. The man said, "Hi, my name is John. I'm the one who's been mowing the lawn. Haven't done anything to her backyard, but I figured you guessed that already."

Bobby introduced himself. They chatted and chatted about everything. They got along very well. John mentioned to Bobby that she would come out every day, stand right over there, pointing to the deck, and just look out at her yard. "I asked her several times if she wanted help with the landscaping, but she always said no. Said she wanted to do it herself, said she needed inspiration. As you can see, inspiration hasn't hit her yet," John said with a smile. "She needed to feel one with the garden."

John wasn't so sure about all of that mumbo jumbo but he said ok. Like clockwork she would come out, stand on the deck for a good hour and then walk back in the house shaking her head, much like he saw Bobby doing about an hour ago.

They continued to chat, and soon he heard the squealing of tires. John said that would be Maria coming into the neighborhood. He knew how she drove, apparently, because there they came screeching around the corner. Bobby said his good-byes and said that they would talk again soon. "In about three months, to be exact," he said. Bobby told John that they were on their way to Iraq. John said he would continue to mow the yard while they were away and wished them both well.

At the car, he could see that Maria had been crying. Time was slipping away from them. They had to be at the airport in less than three hours. Bobby asked his wife what was wrong. She told him that they couldn't get into the condo and that apparently her boyfriend had broken a key in the lock, and no one could open the door. No one knew where her boyfriend was. Bobby asked what they wanted him to do. Maria told Bobby that she knew this guy who knew a guy who could "get into the place" but would have to buy another lock. Unfortunately for Maria, her boyfriend had apparently also made off with all her money. He'd taken her ATM card and knew the password. In other words, she was in a world of hurts. There was much to do and not enough time to do it all.

They decided to split up and divide the work that needed to be done. They were good like that. Figure out what to do and get it done. While she took Maria to get some food for the house, Bobby went back to the condo and talked to the friend of the friend. He bought a doorknob and locks, and the friend of the friend was getting ready to put them on when she and Maria made it back to the condo. Maria ran in, grabbed a bunch of clothes and waited until the friend of the friend was done putting on her new lock.

As Maria grabbed some of her things, Elle she sat there feeling bad for her "sister." She had gotten the little condo on the water for Maria right after she secured her the job at Lockhart Marion. She knew that Maria wanted to bring her boyfriend with her when it was time to leave Texas, so she found him a job as well. Everything was set for them, a place to live and two jobs to make sure they could do well. But here she was, Maria, gathering what belongings she could hold in her arms instead of kicking his ass to the curb. She knew best to keep her nose out of Maria's business, but it pained her to see her used in this manner. Through the course of those two characters' lives, she had helped out many times and in many ways and not just financially, even though that was the biggest of ways. She had even paid for them to move up from Texas. That was a pretty penny, but she felt it was worth it, even though the boyfriend came with whole package. She knew that Maria would have an opportunity of a lifetime, professionally speaking, here in the DC area. After all, she was now working for the largest defense contractor out there.

But with the good you get the bad, and that bad was Rickie, the boyfriend. He simply didn't want to work. He wanted to be taken care of. For some reason, Maria accepted that in him. She knew when you hate someone you think you are harming them, when actually hatred is a curved blade and the harm that we do to others, we also do to ourselves. She heard that somewhere and knew it was true, but she still couldn't stop feeling that about him.

After all that was done, she and Bobby rushed back to the

house, showered and repacked and got ready to leave for the airport. No time for anything. No time to go to the company and talk to them. They both hoped that Maria would pass on what had been going on with Harris, but with her own drama, that could be iffy at best. As they waited on Maria for a little while longer, they both wondered what the hell was going on with their lives. It had been a whirlwind of activity since they first found out about Iraq.

They were just about to leave when Maria pulled up in her Mustang. She looked like they felt, bone tired. She asked Maria if she needed anything else, told her to turn off all the utilities at the condo and turn on whatever utilities she needed at the house; they would cover that as well as the mortgage. Now if Maria would play her cards right, no rent and no utilities to pay; she could pocket at least $3,500. Only if her boyfriend was out of the picture, was the only stipulation that she and Bobby put on it. They sure as hell weren't going off to war to help Maria just so her boyfriend could live in the lap of luxury and not have to work a lick on top of it as well. Maria said he had taken her phone and she didn't have any money until payday. Bobby took out a hundred and handed it to Maria before hugging her goodbye. He wished her well and got behind the wheel of the rental car. She gave Maria a hug and slipped her some more money so she could get another cell phone. As they drove away, she noticed that Marie had look of someone that lost their most favorite beloved teddy bear. How sad Maria looked. She hoped staying here at her home would make her feel better. It would give her a chance to think things out and realize that this guy was bad news. She'd been out of her condo for four days and not once did he try to find her. It was as if he couldn't give a damn where she wound up.

As they left the housing development they sat there with their own thoughts. Bobby sure as heck didn't think this was the way he was going to spend his last day alone with the woman he loved. She too thought this was not how she wanted to spend their time together, but when a friend needs you, especially a friend as close as family, you need to help. They had enough time to get to the airport and turn the car in but not enough time to be alone together. They both had things they wanted to talk about but neither thought this was really the time to do it, so they sat in silence for the first time in their relationship.

As Bobby pulled up to the airport, he decided to let her out with their entire luggage, and then he would turn in the rental car and take the shuttle bus back to where she stood. As Bobby drove off, she wondered if she should go ahead and drag the stuff inside to get it checked in. She found a little buggy to put all the bags on and stood in line. She noticed in the front of the line was none other than Harris and the other team. As she stood in line, Bobby made his way back. They both wondered what would happen this day, and worst yet, what would happen to them over there. As the other team finished checking in, she and Bobby were only behind them by one person. They would be there approximately the same time.

After checking in, she and Bobby made their way through security and found a very pissed off Harris yelling at security personnel at the top of his lungs. He looked near to having a heart attack right there, his face all puffy and red. He was making quite the spectacle of himself. The military team were mortified by his behavior and left him there to take care of the situation he had started. She and Bobby passed Harris and went on to the gate to wait. Realizing that they had over three hours before boarding, they decided to have one last beverage for the road. The waitress came over, and automatically and in unison they ordered the same drink, José chilled, no lime, no salt. As they waited for their drinks, the military team came over and sat with them. They ordered an early dinner and drinks. All five of them were enjoying their last time of freedom, at least for the next three months.

After about an hour of "smoking and joking," Harris finally made an appearance. Apparently Harris and the security people at the airport continued to have it out. He looked around and apparently didn't like what he saw. It was *those* two and they were with *his* team. He wasn't sure what to do. He surely didn't want to do anything that would alienate his team, which he came pretty close to doing back there at security. It wasn't his fault; it was the fault of security. Those bastards wanted to take away his buck knife and Harris knew that just wasn't right. Anyway, his team left him so he knew he didn't want to say anything to these two that would push them further away. He needed these guys to carry out the plan he had in store for them over there.

He casually strolled away and sat at the gate to wait for boarding. He continued to plot his revenge, going over every angle meticulously to make sure it was foolproof, make sure his tracks were covered on all bases. Working for law enforcement for 30 years would be a benefit to him in this case.

As she and Bobby joked around with the other team, they had almost forgotten the tension that had been around them for what seemed forever. They knew these military guys liked and respected them. Maybe Harris wouldn't do anything. Maybe they were just being paranoid or maybe, just maybe, they just had a heightened self-awareness. Whatever it was, they were both going to be on their toes.

As their flight was finally called, the sense of gloom and doom swept over them. *Why did it have to be this way,* she thought. They both sat there having a wonderful time and thinking about the adventure they were about to embark upon. She couldn't wait to get started working. She'd been thinking of doing this very thing for ages now, and she finally had the opportunity to show her years of knowledge, experience and her well-honed skills. She could take what she'd learned in Cuba and apply it here. She knew that she and Bobby were a team to be reckoned with. Terrorists/insurgents look out!

She and Bobby worked so well together and were able to

talk over every angle because they had both sides of the job down pat; he as an interrogator and she an analyst. They were ready to go headfirst into work. If only they could get there without incident from Harris, but they feared he wasn't going to let that happen. Bobby was scared for her. He knew Harris' grudge was directed more at his wife than at himself. He was on the periphery of it all. He might get caught in the aftershock of what he felt Harris had planned for her, and that scared him to his very core. Bobby would not let anything happen to her. Not to his wife, not to his little baby doll. He made himself a promise to do whatever, and he meant WHATEVER it took, he would do it--even murder to protect her! He tried to push that out of his mind, but he knew he would do what it took to make sure she was safe and sound, even in a war torn country like Iraq. It was a terrible thing to go to this country ripped apart with war and then have to worry about a fellow American; he too was the enemy.

The pair waited in line for their seats to be called. Thank goodness Harris and the other team had already boarded. Hopefully they wouldn't have to be too close to Harris. That way they could at least have those six hours it took to get to Germany to be alone and try not to worry. He wondered if this would be the time she would tell him of the first dream she had, the one that spooked her so bad. He decided not to ask her. Let her make the move; when she was ready she would tell him. Finally their seats were called, and luckily they sat very close to business class, and the other team was at the very back of the plane. It seemed strange to the both of them that the other team was as far away as two teams could be on a plane. She wondered if that was planned or coincidence. It didn't matter to her, she just thanked God that they could have at least six hours of peace and quiet, and she would be able to tell him about both dreams.

First she wanted to think of the more wonderful dream, the beautiful one about the garden--the Garden of Eden dream. At least Bobby now had an idea of how sad her yard was. That would make him really appreciate this dream that much more. Later on, after a drink or two, she would tell him of the other dream. She was scared to say out loud what the dream was about for fear that it would make it come true, but he had to know. She had to tell him so he could be prepared, just in case. If it did come true and he was ready, he could possibly try to stop it before it happened.

As she told Bobby of the wonderful dream she had about her garden, their garden now, he sat in wide-eyed amazement. He found it hard to believe that sad little yard could be turned into the Garden of Eden with just the two of them. *That would take nothing short of a miracle,* he thought. He watched as she became more and more animated. He had really never seen her quite this excited before. Sure, she was excited about their little garden in Cuba, but this was different. It was as if she had died and gone to her own private Garden of Eden on cloud 9. Her eyes were so bright and lively, and her hands and arms gesturing all the movements they would have to make to make that little dream of hers a reality, their reality.

Bobby wondered where in the world they would have the time to do all of the things she wanted to do to that sad little yard. At the most, they only had two weeks holiday after they returned from Iraq before having to head back to Cuba. It was their time to "decompress" as everyone called it. He sure as hell didn't think they could accomplish this feat alone in just two weeks, not the way she described it in such vivid detail, the things that had to be done and the things that needed to be bought. Maybe they could enlist the help of their neighbor John? No, she probably wouldn't go for that idea. She was adamant about doing it on their own, just the two of them. Well, Bobby sure as hell wasn't going to spoil this dream. Not him, not now and not ever. They would work and work on that garden until it was done, even if it took both of them to their last dying breath morning, noon, and night to do it; right down to the very last of her details. Bobby thought, *boy this woman sure can dream in vivid detail and color. It really is a wonder she isn't bone tired when she wakes up each morning.*

As she finished telling Bobby her dream, she realized how out of breath she was. She really had to remember to breathe when talking about this dream. The garden dream just excited her so, she couldn't help herself. She didn't say anything about the old woman in the dream. She thought he would really think she was off her rocker if she spilled that little detail; best to leave that part of the dream to herself. As she let the idea of this Garden of Eden soak into Bobby's head, she considered the best way to bring up the other dream. She just couldn't throw it all out there. It was just too scary to do that.

She could tell that he was thinking about this other dream,

the bad one. Sure, he stayed focused, captivated even, by the garden dream, but he really needed to hear what the other dream was, the one that had upset her so. Well, no other way than just to spill it. She saw the flight attendant coming their way and flagged her down. This was going to take a stiff drink. Bobby ordered for them both. Unfortunately, it wasn't chilled but what the heck, they were in the middle of the Atlantic Ocean for god sakes.

Whatever that particular dream was, it sure as hell spooked his wife. As she spoke in tones that were barely whispered, Bobby couldn't help but get panicky all inside. Could this really happen? Would he really do that? Could he convince the other team to do that? He hoped that this time she could be wrong, way wrong. This was just too scary for even him to fathom. As they both sat there, not knowing what to say, the flight attendant asked if they needed another drink. They both said "please."

Bobby didn't move and didn't say a word. What should he do? He should do something, shouldn't he? Why was this happening to them? Why them? They hadn't hurt anyone. They loved each other. How could anyone do this to them because of that? They loved each other so unconditionally. Well, Bobby knew for certain something had to happen and happen to him before anyone did anything to her, his bride. Ok, he had to think of a plan and then a plan B, just in case. He could call their company, but they would only think that he had totally lost it even before getting over there to Iraq.

She watched Bobby's face. She wasn't sure if telling him the whole dream was the right thing to do. What if it was just that, a dream? She hoped that he wasn't already of thinking of a plan and a plan B for goodness sake because that would only mean one thing. He was ready to jump into action, and if he was, then what? What if it was just a dream? She felt bad now. But somehow in her heart she knew this felt too real to be just a dream. She knew when something was a dream and when it was a dream that would come true. It usually felt different.

They sat there with their now 5th shot of Jose. They looked at each other as they ordered their 6th. They would have to stop right now or they wouldn't be able to get off the plane in Germany. All of that and no dinner, not good; he knew that, and so did she. They were compelled, for some reason, to keep drinking though. They both agreed that the 6th would be the last drink, but they would now have to wait for breakfast before they could get something to eat. She thought she might have stowed some goodies in her carry-on luggage. She felt pretty sure it was all junk food, but that would be better than nothing. She wondered how long it was since they last ate. How many hours ago was it? Oh yes, she remember now, at BWI with the other team. She wondered if any of them knew what was in store, what Harris would make them do, what Harris would make specifically one of them to do. She hoped not because that would mean they really could do such things. After all, they all sat and ate, drank and talked together like friends, and if they knew the plans Harris had....how could they sit there with her and Bobby like everything was ok?

Bobby was now getting very hungry. He hoped that that his wife had packed something good. She always carried snacks with her, and he hoped this would not be the exception. As she opened her carry on, she pulled out cookies--Nutterbutters, candy--several varieties, and chewing gum. Bobby slid down in his seat. Not exactly what he was hoping for. Then out of the blue, she shifted a few more items and pulled out two huge ham and cheese

174

sandwiches. He looked at her in amazement. This woman thought of everything, and she was always taking care of him. He beamed at her and she smiled her crooked little half smile.

Bobby said, "That deserves a big ole' kiss." As she positioned her little pursed lips in his directions, complete with her eyes shut, he took advantage of her moment of vulnerability and gave her the biggest kiss right smack dab in her ear. The sound was deafening for her, but she knew she had that coming. She had always done that to Bobby, and she supposed it was time for her own comeuppance! As she opened up the Saranwrap on the sandwich and passed it to Bobby, she thought she might just try to get some sleep. That scared her a bit, but all of a sudden for some strange reason she just got so tired. *It was probably Jose's idea,* she thought with a little smirk. She offered him both sandwiches and said she was tired. He was very concerned for her. He knew it scared her to fall asleep because she never knew what she would dream. She assured Bobby that she would be ok and if he stayed awake, just to look over every once and while to make sure she wasn't having a bad dream.

Bobby knew, of course, he would not take his eyes off her.

175

He hoped he wouldn't get sleepy now with food in his stomach and, of course, 6 shots of Jose. She looked so peaceful, like she was having the sleep of a child. He was glad. He didn't like when she had those dreams. She said she had them quite frequently when she was younger, but as she got older they started to taper off. In fact, it had been quite a while since her last bad one, that is, until the other night. As he watched her even breathing his thoughts went back to the first time they met. It was in Germany, she was with her then-husband and he with his ex. As soon as they met he had felt that he'd known her all his life. There was something so familiar about her. Maybe in a previous life, if he believed that kinda thing.

He recalled that first time, the introduction. They shook hands briefly and he felt the slightest bit of electricity. She sure had a strong grip for a little person, was the second thing he noticed. They were both married then. He'd wondered if she felt as he did, trapped and unhappy. She had the appearance of being happy, but there seemed to be a strange sadness in her eyes. He wondered why in the heck she occupied so much of his thinking. He liked it though; he liked thinking about her, and he liked it a lot! He wondered if the four of them would become friends or if he would ever see her again. He'd hoped so, but one never knows in the military.

Little did Bobby know that they would be together nine years later, happy and very much in love. With that thought in his mind, he too drifted off to sleep. It had been a very long day for the both of them. As they slept, Harris walked by, supposedly to use the bathroom. He stood there looking at them, staring down at them while they and everyone else slept. He wasn't sure how he would convince the other team to do what he wanted them to do. He might have to just scrap that part of his plan. He could take care of this little one on his own, he thought. As Bobby stirred, Harris moved quickly back to his seat. He wondered to himself if either of those two idiots suspected that he was up to something. Could they even imagine the plans he had in store for them, for her in particular? He thought not or at least hoped not. It was best that the both of them be caught completely off guard.

The two snuggled together, each with their own dreams and thoughts. Strange, but she had the strangest feeling that someone was staring at her while she was sleeping, not Bobby, and it gave her the creeps. Or was it part of a dream she was having? She couldn't tell, but she was so comfy snuggling up with Bobby that she didn't want to move or wake up.

As they both sat there all entangled, he could faintly hear the flight attendant letting them know that they were a half an hour away from landing. How strange that was, because Bobby felt like he had just dozed off for a second or two. He had the weirdest dream that someone was watching them both while they slept. What kinda weird dreams was he having? He usually never dreamed, but he did then and he didn't like it too much. Not too much at all.

It wasn't until the flight attendants starting coming around with the warm wet cloths when they finally decided to wake up a little. They looked at each other and smiled. Then at that precise second, they were brought back to where they were and what might or might not happen to them over there. They were about 15 minutes out before landing in Germany. They both wished they could stay here in Germany for a day or two just to visit, but the layover was to be only one hour; not enough time to do anything but wander the airport. As the plane landed, Bobby thought maybe a call back to the company might be in order. He talked it over with her, but they both didn't know what to say. They hoped that Maria had passed on what they told her.

They made a pact. The dream she had would not, could not come true. It was just too "out there," even for Harris. So now they would just concentrate on doing a great job over there, do their time, which was three months, and get back home, back to Cuba.

After they landed, they all wandered around the terminal; some ate, some shopped but she and Bobby decided to just sit and talk. They talked about the first thing that needed to be done with the garden in Maryland. Bobby knew their work was going to be cut out for them. He told her that he really didn't think they could do everything she wanted right away, not in two weeks time. She made a little frown and said, "Ok, as much as we can do in two weeks then."

He hated to disappoint her, so he promised that they would slave away for as long as they could in those two weeks. He promised her that they would try to get it all done, even if it took them 20 hours a day! That plan made her little crooked half smile appear. He loved when that happened.

179

As they talked and talked about what they would start on first, Harris stared and plotted his own demented plans. *Why do they have to look so goddamn happy all the time? It just isn't natural. Don't they know they're going to war, and Iraq is no place for happiness?* Harris had a burning sensation in the pit of his stomach as he watched those two. Hatred, he hated them both. He knew that was a strong emotion, but what the hell, it's what he felt in the burning pit of his stomach. He knew what he had to do to quell that burn. It had started already, back in Cuba but they hadn't seen anything yet. If he could get her alone, that's when the burn in the pit of his stomach would disappear. He wondered if perhaps he shouldn't get his team involved with this plan. He thought that probably was the wisest thing to do. No witness, not the other team and certainly not Bobby. He hated him so. Bobby had everything he'd ever wanted. Not the little woman in particular, although she wasn't that bad, he thought, but the idea of her. The way she looked at Bobby turned Harris' stomach. No woman ever looked at him that way. And the way he looked at her, equally sickening. Harris recalled having that look for another woman, but she put an end to all of that. Harris thought he had finally found the love that she and Bobby shared, but she had to bust that all up. Why did she have to stick her damn nose into his business? Why did she have to write that letter about his so-called sexual harassment? Well he would take care of that and of her soon, real soon.

She and Bobby wondered if they should make another attempt at talking to Harris. What would be the harm in it? Maybe the other team could see that they were at least trying to get along with this lunatic. So they got up and crossed the long room towards were they had been standing.

Bobby spoke first, "Hey, Harris, were you able to sleep at all on the flight?" Small talk really, nothing significant, but it would be a start. Harris looked Bobby over and then walked away, per usual. They all looked at each other, no one really knowing what to say. The other team thought best just to follow the old man. They simply didn't know what else to do. She and Bobby sat back down and decided not to worry about it and just do their time.

The flight was finally called and everyone got back on the plane. This part of the trip would take them to Cyprus for a quick layover, not getting off the plane, then onward to Kuwait where they would wait for a military flight out to Iraq.

As they all got off in Kuwait, she felt the dry hot air. It was 11:00 at night and still mighty hot. The team went to where all their bags were and started to put them in a big pile. They were to stay here until sometime in the early morning. Everyone grabbed their bags and found a place to crash for the night, which meant a couple of seats in the military terminal to lie across. As she and Bobby got settled in one aisle, the other team decided--well, Harris decided--that they all needed to get some coffee at the all-night mess hall, called the "grab and go."

For the first time Harris looked at the pair and actually spoke *at* them. It really was more of an order than a question. "Hey, watch all the stuff while we get some coffee?" he said to neither one of the pair in particular.

Bobby said, "Sure thing." He had hoped that maybe this might be the ice breaker. Since they were in the Middle East things would get better. He was wrong and would find out soon enough just how wrong he was.

As Harris and the other team took off for the grab and go, she and Bobby sat there amongst all the duffel bags. They wondered if perhaps this could be a turning point for the positive.

"Well, he did speak to us," she said to Bobby.

"Barked is actually more accurate," Bobby replied. They both thought that it might be at least a good start. She and Bobby started to discuss a plan. Perhaps they should try to get closer to the other team. Three military guys, two of them in the Army and one Marine. Of the three, all of them were reservists with other full time jobs back home. The Marine was the most experienced. He was not only an experienced interrogator but also a police officer, NYPD to be exact. He wasn't a very big man, but he was strong. His heritage was Lebanese and he definitely had the features that went along with that. He could pass for any number of other ethnicities.

She and Bobby decided that if anything happened to him on this trip she should stick close to the Marine for safety. Bobby told her that he would discuss this idea with the Marine. Bobby felt comfortable he would be ok with it. The other two Army guys were young and appeared even to her, scared, very scared at even being here in Kuwait. Bobby told her that if worst came to worst on the convoy from the airport in Baghdad to the prison about 40 miles down the road, he would grab one of the inexperienced guys' weapons, only if worst came to worst. They discussed other things, more pleasant things. Without even realizing it, the other team had come back. No one let them know they were back; they were just milling around behind them, and it wasn't until she had to go use the "porta john" did she see them.

Bobby thought it would be a good idea to go to that same all-night grab and go to get some cold drinks. It seemed like days since they had all of those tequilas on the plane. She and Bobby got up and walked right up to Harris and informed him, as he did to them 2 hours prior, that they would be getting some soft drinks. With that Harris stood up, chest all puffed out, and informed them that she and Bobby couldn't leave at this point and had to stand fast. Loosely translated, can't leave, stay where you are. That made Bobby fume, but he wasn't going to explode right then and there, not with witnesses. They both just went back to where their bags were; not knowing exactly what to say. They just sat there in shock by his remark.

As the night turned to morning, their flight was called. All of them had fallen asleep here and there, over, under, and on top of anything they could find to get comfortable. Of course, the pair was entangled with each other; hugging like they were never going to see each other again. They woke up slowly, looking at each other and smiling. Smiling until reality smacked them in the face, and that smack came in the form of Harris, who told the others to pick up their gear and to go to the flight line. Nothing was said to her or Bobby. They were invisible to Harris. She and Bobby jumped up and gathered their gear and started to rush after the other team. Soon they were all on the flight line waiting on the C130 to take them to Iraq.

This was her first flight on such a plane. She had never seen much less been on any type of military aircraft. She was the first one to board this big plane. How strange not to have a bunch of windows to look out and to be sitting side by side along the length of the plane instead of across it facing the front. They sat on some type of netting. She could only imagine how noisy this trip was going to be. They handed out earplugs before everyone got on. What an experience she was about to have. She was a little excited and a little scared. To be flying over Baghdad in this big military plane. Luckily she had Bobby right by her side to calm her nerves.

The flight took about two and half hours. It flew by for her. She couldn't stop looking around and wondering what was going on outside the plane. The plane often seem to go wildly to the right and then to the left. She wondered if they were avoiding getting shot at. Having no windows was not good for her; her imagination ran rampant with wild war scenarios. She wanted to look at the scenery. *Well,* she thought, *I'll be there soon enough and get my fill of the scenery.*

As they got off the plane, she, being the last person off, looked out and smiled….but as she continued to look she realized what a rainy cold, cloudy day it was. Baghdad had a strange sweet smell…not sweet like sugar canes, like Cuba, but more of sweet fresh rain smell. But there was nothing fresh about this place. This place was hell, and she would soon find out what kind of hell it was going to be. She and Bobby grabbed their bags and waited for the others. Someone was to pick them up via convoy to head out to the prison.

As the experienced Marine set his bags down, he looked at all of them and counted, "1, 2, 3, 4, 5…6. Ok, all here." With that, he went to one of the large tents, the military PAX terminal, and made the call to find out where the convoy was at.

He came back with eyes as big as plates. That scared her a little too much, a Marine shaken up this badly. Bobby finally asked, "What's wrong, gunny?"

Gunnery Sergeant Malouff replied, "I think we're going to have to be here overnight." He slowly and quietly whispered to all of them, "They got hit this morning. The prison was hit hard--50 killed." They all stared at each other, everyone with their own mixed feelings.

Harris strolled over and said to anyone who would listen to him, "Ok, I'm in charge here. I will make the call to the admin people at the prison and see what in the hell is going on. We should have had someone waiting to pick us up when we touched down."

As he was about to arrogantly stroll off, the gunny stopped him in his tracks. "Look, sir, we are not going to be picked up today."

With that little bit of news, Harris' face turned even a deeper shade of red than normal. He appeared about to pop a vein. "What in the hell kind of system do we have here? They are to be here, now, not tomorrow but right this goddamn minute. Who the fuck do they think they are dealing with here?" With that loud outburst not only did she and Bobby stare, but finally the other team did too. The look of shock took over all of their faces. The gunny pulled Harris over to the side and told him what had happened. A sense of embarrassment washed over Harris' face, sheer and utter embarrassment. For all intents and purposes, Harris' "I'm in charge" façade disappeared. She and Bobby could tell by the look on the other three faces that they were starting to have their own doubts about Harris, finally.

Harris could see the look as well. He tried to cover his arrogant behavior with talk of being motivated and wanting to start work as soon as possible so we can "get these mother fuckers." Harris believed that gung-ho attitude would win the men over; he could care less what those other two idiots thought of him. He had his plan for her…had his plan all figured out and it was not about to go down the toilet, not now, not when he was this close.

So they all went into what was called the "transient" tent, a tent for those much like this group who had to stay over for a period of time. The entire tent was filled with row after row after row of cots and the odd chair here and there. As darkness fell she realized that it had been several hours since she had last used the ladies room. Boy oh boy, did she have to pee and pee bad. She was to have a little shock of her life as there were no bathrooms, per se, only porta johns. She told Bobby that she had to find a place to go, so he put their bags on two of the cots as he walked his little wife to her first porta john experience.

As they trampled through the mud and rocks, they held hands. This seemed to be the worst experience in their entire new lives together, yet they were happy because they were together. They had that much going for them. They finally found the porta johns and in she went, holding her nose as she opened the door. She closed the door behind her, but before it could actually shut closed, she quickly opened it. Bobby, knowing these types of things, handed her the baby wipes without her having to say a word. She smiled at him. He knew everything, she thought.

As she sat there in the dark little room, she wondered what in the hell were they getting into. The news from earlier still rang in her ears. "They got hit hard." She wondered if Bobby or even the others were as scared as she was now. She could tell something

189

was up. Everyone appeared to look calm and collected, but there was a strange quality to their eyes. It was as if fear grabbed them by the throats and wouldn't let go. The look was panic in their eyes, but they all tried to play it off. The only one who looked what you could call normal was Harris.

Harris, with his stupid arrogant stroll and puffed-out chest, the look of a peacock. The look in his eyes was nothing less than pure evil, especially when he looked at her. Oh, the things he would say and do to her. That thought made him smile ever so slightly. He would take great pleasure in ruining her life as she had ruined his: personally, professionally and most of all, financially...and if that didn't work, he had other ideas for her. She wasn't a bad looking woman, he thought to himself. He always did like Hispanic women, even though this one had a mouth on her. And the thought of harming only her would do double the job because he knew what this would do to Bobby. Hurt Bobby without directly hurting him. The plan was a good one. He knew he was to get on to it as quickly as he could. He started this little plan early on, first with the soldiers--planting little ideas about the two of them. Disinformation is what it was called. He knew,

190

though, that once they all got to the prison, he had to move quickly, before anyone got to really know either one of them; before they could work their "power couple" magic on everyone. As he thought of all the delicious things he had in store for that little woman, he noticed off in the distance that those two were talking to the team, his team! The sight of all five of them together laughing and joking was going to stop, and it was going to stop now! This was not the way it was supposed to happen. The other team was supposed to hate those two by now. Harris had fed them enough disinformation on her and Bobby to ensure that, but low and behold, there they all were, having a good ole time.

Harris marched up to all of them and told the other team that it was time to go to chow. Gunny looked over at Harris and asked, "Who's going to watch all of our stuff?" Before the words were barely out of his mouth, Harris replied, pointing to her and Bobby, "Those two. They don't have anything better to do!"

Little did Harris realize that he had just sealed his fate with the military folks with that blatantly cruel and uncalled-for remark. They all looked at Harris with a mixture of disgust and shock. Almost in unison, the other team all volunteered to stay with the bags.

Gunny said, "She and Bobby really should go get some chow first. They stayed with the bags the last two times. I'll stay here with the bags."

It finally hit Harris smack dab in the face what had just transpired. He had to do some fancy footwork to get past this. What was he thinking? He couldn't afford another fuck up like this one. He still needed their help. *Well, not all of their help, just the gunny's,* he thought. He would be the perfect man for the mission he had planned for that little Mexican woman. Harris knew that this particular Marine was one tough son-of-a-bitch and Harris felt secure in the fact that the gunny would do exactly as he was told. With that, Harris tried to regain some sense of loyalty from his men. "No, I meant that I would stay while those two go get chow, uuuh while all of you go to get some food. That's what I meant."

They all eyed each other, unconvinced by Harris' words but decided to let it drop.

She and Bobby grabbed their jackets and headed off to the bus stop with the other team. At first they all stood there not saying a word to each other, no one really knowing what to say. Then

Bobby just blurted out, "Was that just weird or what?" with the funniest face he could make. Actually, more of an imitation of what Harris looked like when he was mad was more like it.

All five of them laughed at Bobby's attempt to puff out his chest and cheeks. The laughter must have broken what silent barrier had been between them all. They all seemed to relax, and everyone was verbally pinging all over the place and talking a mile a minute all at the same time. This was such a good feeling, she thought to herself. This is the way a team should be, not divided like Harris wanted them all to be.

They all climbed on the bus for the five-minute ride to the chow hall at Camp Stryker, all five of them chatting away like long lost friends. It was a quick trip and before they knew it, there they were. The chow hall wasn't fancy or anything, just the standard ultra pedestrian food which usually consisted of lots and lots of meat and potatoes. The food was plentiful and not too bad tasting either. They all ate their fill. She worried if she continued this type of eating she would come home bigger than a house after their three month deployment.

After they finished their meals, Bobby pulled the gunny

over for a private conversation. She watched them. They looked so serious, and at one time she caught the gunny looking straight at her, looked back at Bobby and then back at her. She wondered what in the hell was Bobby doing. As they got up to rejoin the team, Bobby shook hands with the gunny and then gave the man a big bear hug. *How strange,* she thought. She had never seen Bobby do this with anyone. Bobby wasn't really a touchy-feely kinda guy, except with her, of course. They walked back talking like old friends. She could see a faint hint of red-rimmed eyes on Bobby, as if he had been crying; but why would he be crying?

As they got ready to board the bus, she thought it would be a great idea to go back and grab some food for Harris. She knew it would be late and the chow hall possibly closed by the time they got back. She told the guys that she would catch the next bus and that she would go back to get some food for Harris; they all thought that was a good idea.

Bobby said, "Go ahead and go without us, we'll catch the next bus. Let Harris know that we'll be bringing some food back for him." They all waved goodbye, and she and Bobby went back inside the chow hall. They brought back a good amount of food for

Harris, which included a couple of different desserts.

The look on Bobby's face was one of deep sadness. It almost made her practically go into comma-like mode and stopped her right in her tracks. She wanted to ask him about the conversation with the gunny but for some reason, she thought better of it. *He would tell me, if he wanted me to know,* she thought silently to herself. Bobby caught her staring at him so he took that cue to liven up his mood. He didn't want her to know how scared and worried he was about the trip to the prison tomorrow. He didn't want her to know that he had talked to the gunny about her, about taking care of her if anything was to happen to him. The gunny had gladly and proudly agreed with Bobby.

"It would be my honor, sir, to take care of your pride and joy," he'd said. Bobby felt a great sense of relief over this, but the idea that something could go wrong sickened him. He tried to be upbeat for her, but it was a hard task to carry out. He wanted take her back home and work on that little garden like she had talked and talked so much about. He didn't want to be in this god-forsaken hellhole with no idea of what was to happen from one second to the next, but this is what his wife wanted. She wanted to experience this; she wanted to make a difference. For Bobby, he just wanted to be with her, plain and simple!

After grabbing much food for Harris, they waited outside for the bus to get back. It was hard to believe they were actually in Baghdad; it looked more like your average military base, with the occasional distant sounds of gunfire. As the bus rolled to a stop before them, everything seemed to stand still for a mere second when a sound--something like *whoomph!*--followed by the highest pitch whistling sound, directly above them. They tried to look up, but it was dark, and then a resonating BOOM! rang in their ears. At that moment, everything seemed to break loose. It seemed to her that no one knew what to do or where to go.

Everyone hit the ground, and with barely a bat of an eye, Bobby pushed her to the ground and lay on top of her. He could feel her heart beating faster than a race horse. All he could do in this position was to gently stroke her hair. He hoped that was enough to make her feel as protected as she possibly could at this moment. As he lay on her, he wondered if there was more he should have done, something he should have said to her to convince her that they shouldn't have come here. Why didn't he push it more? Why didn't he just say no to her? He knew all too well the answer to that, but the thought still crossed his mind from time to time.

Bobby realized that all was clear. There was nothing to worry about, at least not for now. He got up and then helped his mate to her feet. He looked at her tear-stained face covered in mud and couldn't help but hold her tight in his arms. She looked so small and helpless standing there with the oversized flak vest and Kevlar on. Strands of her hair had come loose from the braid she'd made earlier that day. She looked like a small, scared young child. He didn't know what to do or say to make the tears stop. They just rolled down her cheeks effortlessly. Maybe a quick light-hearted joke would make a good segue at this point.

He gave her a serious look. "A horse walks into a bar and the bartender says why the long face?" She couldn't help herself; she loved that joke. She knew how silly it was, but she loved it nevertheless, and he knew it, even after hearing it more than a thousand times.

She dusted herself off, grabbed all the packaged-up food for Harris and jumped on the bus. Everyone else got on with their business as well. As they sat side by side, she stared out the window. It seemed as if she were a hundred miles away. Bobby could still see the tears rolling down her cheeks. He just didn't know what to do or say. Would she be ok here these next three months? They hadn't even made it to Abu Gharib yet, and that place was getting hit every single day. Would she be able to deal with what could be in store for the both of them? She was a tough broad, but she had never been in this type of environment. He knew that war could change people; his hope was that it wouldn't change her for the worst. He hoped that the sheer shock of what just happened would make whatever was to happen next not as traumatic.

When she and Bobby finally got to PAX terminal with Harris' smashed up yet edible food, she looked up at Bobby and told him to please not mention what had happened. Bobby looked at her quizzically. Surely she knew that the other team would know what had just happened. Everyone would have heard it.

"Don't tell them I was crying. I don't want them to think I'm a pussy and can't deal with being here."

Bobby hugged her. "Of course not and YOU, my dear, are

no pussy," he said to her with all the sincerity in his heart. He really believed this. This was one tough broad he was married to and he knew it. They walked back with all the semi-crushed styrofoam boxes filled with food for Harris. At the entrance of the big transient tent; Bobby stopped, turned her around, inspected her face and wiped what little tears were left. "Good to go," he announced. She smiled up at him. She loved this man so much she could barely contain herself.

As they opened the door with all the food for Harris, they immediately noticed something different in the setup of the cots and the other team. It appeared that they had separated themselves from her and Bobby. She looked over at the four of them; the guilt on their faces said it all. Well, not all of them; all but Harris, who had the most arrogant and smug look on his heavily jowl pig like beet-red face.

All Bobby said was, "Harris, we brought you food, here ya go."

Harris turned away and said, "I've eaten already. I had an MRE while you two lollygagged around."

Bobby wasn't sure what to do next, so he just stood there

holding all the cartons of food until the gunny came over and took

all the food from him and told Bobby, "Well at least we have some

breakfast."

# Chapter 8 -- The Gunny

The gunny tried to smile but could see how upset the two of them were. *Slapped in the face yet again,* the gunny thought. He didn't understand why Harris had such a hard-on for those two. She and Bobby seemed like such nice people. They were always professional at work and seemed to be so in love with each other. They were very friendly, and everyone seemed to like them. He'd heard the phrase "power couple" a few times when anyone would talk about them. He could see what they meant. Apart as individuals, they were good at what they did professionally, but together they were fantastic. And she sure was a cutie. *If only she wasn't married*, he thought. He wasn't sure how old she was, but he'd heard rumors that she was a lot older than she appeared. It didn't matter to him. He liked what he saw: small package but had a lot of spunk! He loved Hispanic women, their exotic look, dark almond-shaped eyes. He'd heard that she had some nice artwork on her back but he had never seen it. He wished he could have had the opportunity, but he could tell the way she looked at Bobby that would never happen. He silently cursed his bad luck on that front.

Nevertheless, he still couldn't figure out what Harris' problem was with the two of them. Bobby seemed like a pretty upstanding guy. Whatever it was, he didn't want any part of it. He really appreciated when Bobby asked him to take care of her if anything were to go down. The thought of Bobby trusting him with her said a lot for how Bobby looked at him. He obviously respected and appreciated his expertise and experience. The gunny would make sure if anything did happen, he wouldn't let Bobby down. Heck, this little lady was small enough to throw on his back and run at the same time and shoot his M16, if it came down to that. That thought made him smile and tear up at the same time. The gunny said to himself, *what in the hell is going on with me, tearing up like a school girl?* This was not how he was trained, not how Marines are trained to be, but somehow the sight of her made his heart all soft and mushy inside.

He remembered the first time he saw her. It was on her

first day of work in Cuba. She must have been the smallest full grown woman he had ever seen. His guess was that she was about 58 inches tall, if that, and maybe a hundred pounds soaking wet. He had thought less than one hundred pounds until he saw the rack on that little woman. "Wow," was all he could say to himself and then, "oooh my GOD!" He had hoped he wasn't openly gawking at her, but he just couldn't help himself. He didn't think she knew or even realized just how adorable she was. Sure, she was confident but she didn't have that air of someone who knew she looked good. He liked that about her. She was a little on the shy side, and he like that too. He thought to himself, there really wasn't anything he didn't like about her, well except for the fact that she was married. He cursed himself for not asking her out right then and there, when they were first introduced. But he wasn't that way by nature; he liked things to progress slowly. Well, he did realize something and it had been too late, that things sure did progress; progressed without him. She and Bobby hooked up, and that was the end for everyone else.

Bobby was a good looking man and a good person also, so he didn't feel too bad. He at least knew that she would be in good hands. Still, he cursed his own bad luck. Gunny finally snapped out of his reverie by the look on Bobby's face. Bobby was staring at the gunny with eyebrows up in a "what in the hell are you doing staring at my wife that way" kinda face. All the gunny could do was wave at Bobby and turn away. Sure enough, the gunny was staring and staring hard. His thoughts had been back when he first laid eyes on her. *Kinda funny,* the gunny thought, *busted right here in front of her husband.*

As she and Bobby went back to where they had originally laid their bags down, they realized that the two cots they had picked for themselves were now gone and what was left were two folding chairs. She thought, *how in the hell are we going to sleep sitting on two folding chairs?* Bobby saw the question in her mind and answered her before she could ask out loud.

Bobby marched over to Harris and asked, "Ok Harris, where the hell are our cots that we set aside?"

"What cots?" was all Harris replied and, with that, he strolled out of the tent, leaving Bobby teeming with anger. Bobby and the other team got together and hunted down extra cots but couldn't find one single one left. The tent was packed.

The gunny handed over his cot for her and told Bobby, "Man, I can sleep on the floor. We're used to that anyway." Bobby thanked him and thought that maybe he could use the two chairs to position himself on to catch a couple of winks, but she wouldn't hear of it. The two other military guys volunteered their cots, but Bobby didn't want to take theirs; so they handed over Harris' cot. That made Bobby smile.

"We'll just tell him that someone else took it," the other team said. Bobby also noticed how Harris had surrounded himself with all three soldiers and moved away from where they all were initially. She and Bobby looked at each other and said, "Fine, whatever," out loud to each other. That made them chuckle a bit. They still could do it. They still were able to read each other's thoughts.

As they all got ready to rest for the evening, she pulled out a little notebook she had bought for work, but something inside her told her to start writing everything, everything that had gone on from when she had met Harris up until this point and to continue to write until she was safely back in Cuba. She couldn't understand why her gut told her to do that but she was always mindful of her

205

gut feelings. It hadn't led her astray yet. She pulled her little cot as close to Bobby's as she could. Well, this wasn't home on the king-size pillow top mattress but it would have to do in a pinch. It would have to do, she thought. It was a lot better than being separated, which could have been a real possibility had the powers that be chosen only one of them to go. Luckily it didn't quite go down that way.

Bobby sat and wondered what his babydoll was up to with the little notebook and pen. He remembered buying her the notebook with the little daisy on the front. For some reason, he thought this was for work. It was strange for her not to share with Bobby what she was doing. He was so accustomed to her telling him everything she did or thought. He liked it that way. *Well, if she wants me to know, she'll tell me,* he thought to himself.

She started to write in such a feverish pace that she didn't even think to tell Bobby what she was doing. She couldn't write the words down fast enough. She would tell him in a second, she thought. When she got to the point of where they were right this second, then she would tell him. He would think her paranoid, but what the heck. It felt like the right thing to do; write absolutely everything that had gone on.

The two of them didn't hear Harris come back in the tent, and God only knows where he had been all this time, but this was not the first time he seemed to just disappear for hours at a time. She wondered if Harris knew anyone out in these parts. It seemed he knew quite a few people. Maybe he was out doing whatever it was that Harris did, which, to her, meant harassing poor innocent young girls. Hopefully that type of behavior wouldn't fly here in this combat zone, not like it did in Cuba anyway.

Everyone in the big transient tent seemed to wake up around the same time, around 6am, probably out of habit, as no one had set an alarm. She was still snoozing when Bobby sat up in his cot. She'd stayed up very late writing in the little notebook. He would ask her today what was going on. He looked over to the other team but the team wasn't there. He started to panic a bit and decided to wake her. She woke up with such a start that she about fell off the cot. She immediately looked over to where the other team and Harris had been the night before.

"Where did they go? Did they leave us here?"

Bobby knew that the other guys wouldn't just leave them

without saying anything. Of course, Harris would, but not the other guys and especially not the gunny, not after the talk they had yesterday. Bobby told her that he thought that they were probably at chow. "You know how Harris likes to shovel down the food," he said.

They gathered their belongings and tried to clean up as best they could without the benefit of a shower. As they sat there with all the belonging, Bobby couldn't help but look at his beautiful wife. Even without makeup or hair done she was still a beautiful woman--correction, a cute woman, as his wife would correct him. He was just about to tell her this when in strolled Harris, looking, as usual, arrogant and full of himself. This time something was a bit off, though. He smiled broadly at the both of them. He looked like the cat that swallowed the whole canary pie, Bobby thought.

As Harris strolled up to the pair, "the pair of idiots" he thought to himself, he chatted with them and gave them the update as to when they would leave. For the first time since this trip began Harris tried to act like they were part of the team. She wondered what in the hell was going on with him. Why this change of heart? This man had something up his sneaky sleeve, and she could feel it. And she sure didn't like the way he was eyeballing her right in front of Bobby too. It was more of a leer, as he looked from one tit to the other. He was talking to her but in his head, she thought, was thinking something entirely different. Bobby had walked over to the gunny to talk to him before Harris' blatant leering started. From the outside, anyone that might walk by would see what looked like the two of them having a conversation--nothing more, nothing less.

Harris made sure he was not facing anyone. He wasn't going to get caught this time doing anything wrong. As he talked to her of how they would get to the prison and what they would do once they got there, he kept his eyes directly on her tits, from the right one to the left one. Not *too bad, not too bad at all. I could do some strange crazy things with those*, he thought as his mouth began to water.

She thought for a second that he had actually licked his lips. That was the last straw for her. She called Bobby over with a loud bark. If anything, she thought that would startle the hell out of Harris. Harris wondered what this woman was going to do next.

Bobby walked over quickly and said, "Yeah, babydoll,

what's up?"

"Just wanted to let you know that Harris is telling me about the trip to the prison and what our duties are once we get there."

With that, Harris calmed down. He wondered why she just didn't bust him on that move, especially the last one where he licked his lips. Could it be that she actually enjoyed that? That she liked to be looked at that way? Or was there something up her sneaky little sleeve?

As the gunny called everyone together, he let them know what was going to happen and that everyone needed to prepare for the convoy to the prison. Bobby kept his eyes peeled on Harris. There was something up and he knew it, he could feel it. His wife would have never just barked like that for nothing. He wondered why she didn't say what she wanted to say. Did Harris do something to her, say something to her? Bobby wondered if he was going to get the opportunity to ask her what that was all about, or would they be sequestered with these guys for the rest of the day?

As everyone picked up their gear and walked outside to wait for the convoy, Bobby whispered over to her, "What happened? Did he do something to you? Say something to you?

Let me know what's going on, ok?"

"I'll tell you when we're alone."

As they all stood waiting, getting more fidgety by the second, the next thing anyone could see or hear was the arrival of five hummvees and five deuce and a halfs. From inside the cab area of one of the deuce and a halfs came this soldier that looked to be about 100 years old. He probably was nowhere near that age, but being here for a time takes its toll. He stood in the middle of the team and asked if they were from GTMO. With a resounding yes from everyone, he started to brief them as to how the convoy would take place. This trip was not only to pick up the six of them but to get supplies such as water, soft drinks and other essentials for the prison. They would travel in the back of the deuce and a half, which was nothing more than a very large truck. They would be totally uncovered from the elements as well as from any harm.

Bobby could tell by her eyes that she was petrified. In fact, everyone there looked that way with the exception of himself, the gunny and, of course, Harris. Even if Harris was petrified, he would never show it to anyone, and especially not to this audience. The old soldier informed them that the bags would border the outside part of the bed of the truck and the civilians were to be in the middle. The three soldiers would be kneeling with M16s at the ready. As they took turns throwing all the duffel bags up to the bed of the truck, it was her turn to climb up there. She was so small that she could not even reach the bottom step up to the truck bed. The gunny, who was already up on the bed, grabbed both her arms as Bobby lifted her by the legs.

Gunny looked down at her and said, "Don't be scared, I gotcha. I'm not going to let you go." With one quick pull, she was up and almost over. Then the rest of them climbed in, all relatively easier than she did, except for Harris. That big belly of his made it difficult to climb, but he wouldn't take anyone's help. He made it after a couple of tries.

For as cold and wet as it was yesterday when they'd arrived, it was the complete opposite today: hot, very very hot and strangely humid. It looked as though Harris would have a heart attack, his face even redder and more swollen than it normally was, and he was sweating profusely. He was literally dripping sweat from everywhere. He looked as if he was standing under a shower. The sight of Harris definitely grossed her out to no end, the sweat just pouring out of him. She thought back to him licking his lips and shuddered. Oh god, the thought of him doing that could just make her spew. She tried to push that thought out of her mind and think of more pleasant things, like this trip to the prison; the same trip that was just hit the morning before. As everyone got settled, the gunny motioned for her to sit right behind him. She looked over at Bobby and he nodded. Bobby stayed close to one of the inexperienced soldiers. He'd said he would grab the weapon if the guy got too scared and he was sitting close enough to make that happen, if the shit came down. Harris, of course, decided to do his own thing and kneel at the back end of the truck alone and without a weapon. The last soldier was sitting to the left of him and looked every bit scared as she felt. In fact, both of the soldiers looked very scared.

She was glad to be sitting next to the gunny, as he looked as confident as they come, prepping his weapon and surveying the area. She said, "If anything happens, I'm jumping on your back and staying that way till it's all over."

He smiled. "That's the plan," he said as he winked at Bobby. She looked back and forth to the both of them and

213

wondered what in the heck was going on. Did they plan this already? It seemed to her that they had discussed this before. It didn't matter to her, she felt safe and sound with these two guys watching after her.

Before they took off, the old soldier came back and said, "Everyone ready?" Everyone nodded, affirmative, then he went on to explain what had gone wrong with yesterday's convoy.

"Ok. This is what happened. As we drove under an overpass, they got us, so as we're going down the road, look up before we pass the overpass and see if you see anyone up there. If you do, yell out." As he spoke, the strangest thing started to happen. The old soldier's nose started to bleed. She took that as a very bad sign and hoped that this time she was wrong. Apparently the old soldier could see their confusion and perhaps felt the blood rolling out of his nose. He wiped it with his hand and then wiped it off on his uniform and calmly continued telling them what was going to happen next.

As they started to drive away, she could see just how nervous the other two soldiers were. They fiddled and fiddled again with their M16s. They were visibly shaking as they knelt there. As she sat slumped over with her oversized flak vest on and Kevlar on her head, she felt she looked like a human turtle. She couldn't stand up if she had to; she hoped that she wouldn't have to do it in a hurry. As they drove for about ten minutes, she sensed that an overpass was nearing. She picked up her head and looked behind her. She had been facing the back of the truck, so if there was an overpass she guessed it was nearing because the two soldiers really started to shake. As she turned around, she saw the first of six more overpasses. Luckily she saw no one lurking above them. *Thank God,* she said to herself. As they drove past the seventh overpass, she let out a big sigh--almost there. The sight of the prison sent shivers down her spine. How bleak and dry and barren it looked. She wondered why all the people were standing right outside of the prison. There seemed to be hundreds of them just standing there. She thought perhaps it was "visiting day" or something. It wasn't until later that she realized that these people were there every day, every single day, waiting to see if their relatives would be released.

They drove a few more minutes until they were thoroughly inside the prison complex: Abu Ghraib, soon to be infamous and a household name to the entire world. It was only the middle of April 2004 but hotter than hell. Even she was sweating, and she hardly ever did that. As they threw down all the bags, she recognized someone she had known…someone from her past. He looked up at her and smiled. She quickly turned away and caught Bobby's eye. He was looking at what had just gone on between the two and wondered who the hell was this guy? Did his wife know this man? It sure appeared that way to Bobby. There was something a little too familiar with the way he looked at her. She grabbed a bag and threw it down and kept doing so until all the bags were unloaded. Now it was her turn to jump out. Bobby at her side, the gunny down on the ground below her, and next to the gunny…this man, this stranger to Bobby standing right there ready to help her get down as well. *What in the hell is going on here,* he thought. As Bobby held her from behind and slowly lowered her down, the gunny grabbed her legs and set her down. Before Bobby could do anything else, this stranger was upon her, talking to her in an all-too familiar way. She motioned him to leave but he stayed at her side. Bobby finally jumped down and introduced himself to this man.

The man almost dismissed him until Bobby said, "Are you bothering my wife?"

The stranger took a big step back. He said, "Hi, I'm SFC Garcia. I wasn't bothering your wife. She looked upset, and I asked her if she needed any help. I can see she doesn't. Welcome to Abu Ghraib. I'm the noncommissioned officer in charge, NCOIC, here. I'll be giving a briefing to you guys as soon as you catch your breath." And with that, he was off helping to get the supplies out of the other deuce and a half.

Bobby looked at her and waited to see if she had anything to say. She looked up at him and said nothing. She just started to grab bags and hand them to the next person in line. What was going on? Who was this man, this SFC Garcia? How did he know his wife? Had she ever told him anything about this guy? He racked his brain trying to go back through all of their "getting to know each other" talks. Nothing came to mind, nothing of a Garcia in her past that he could think of. Not one little thing. Why was she hiding this from him? Was he an old boyfriend, an old boss or coworker? The name just didn't ring clear to Bobby. This was going to be a long, long three months as this rate. At least they

217

were told because they were contractors, they could be housed together. At least they had that going for them. At least that's what they were told before leaving Cuba.

As she grabbed bag after bag and passed them along, she wondered, *what in the hell is he doing here?* Why did he have to be here? She knew she couldn't do three months with this man here and to make it worse was Bobby's insistent questions. She didn't want to talk about it. Couldn't he see that? She wanted to put it out of her mind. She HAD put it out of her mind for almost 20 years or so. These three months were going to drag on. It wasn't bad enough with having to deal with Harris, now she had Garcia there as well. Why did life have to play such cruel jokes?

As the six of them gathered in the room of where headquarters was to be, SFC Garcia started to speak. "I am SFC Garcia, I am the NCOIC here. I'm in charge here at the prison. I will be the one telling you where you will be living, what you will be doing, while you are here. I will start that by saying that all the men will be staying over here and the one female will stay in G-block with the rest of the females."

Bobby said, "Sarge, name is Bobby. I'm a contractor, and

so is my wife. We were told that we would be housed with the other contractors here, so if you can just tell us where they are located, we can get settled in."

SFC Garcia's demeanor changed dramatically. He said, "Who's in charge of these contractors?"

Harris jumped up and said, "I'm the boss, I'm their supervisor."

She and Bobby stared at him and wondered what in the hell was he talking about. No one at the company said that he was in charge or that he was, of all things, their supervisor. They knew there was some mistake. What company would put a man who sexually harassed a young soldier in charge of anyone, much less two seasoned analysts? It didn't make sense to her or Bobby. They would get to the bottom of this, but there were more pressing matters, such as where the two of them were going to be housed. Before they left Cuba, they were told by the team lead that the company had made arrangements with the company that was already on the ground. He even showed them the email that said as much. They'd said nothing of having to be housed with the military.

SFC Garcia took Harris aside and talked for several minutes in relative privacy. During this conversation, Harris felt it was the perfect time to set things straight with the two of them and with Sgt Garcia.

No sooner than the team's arrival in Abu Ghraib, Harris informed SFC Garcia that he was the boss, the senior person on the ground. He was their supervisor and they were to do what he told them to do, not Garcia.

"There is only one boss here," Harris told her and Bobby and that they were not allowed to talk to the other contractors or the military with any concerns, questions, comments or issues. The pair had broached the subject of sharing a room, but Harris said that he personally didn't think that was fair, not that their company thought so, but he personally thought it was unfair. His own personal opinion was that they should not associate/house with the other contractors. He said he made all the decisions for them as to whom to talk with and whom not to, including the military. What Harris didn't know was that they had already spoken with the military, Chief Barney, prior to the above talk with Harris, since Harris had not been giving them the time of day. Bobby asked about housing, and Chief Warrant Officer 3 Barney said he could and would arrange "conjugal" visits. He said it was the policy of the military for men/women not to share quarters. They asked if he thought it was ok to talk with the other contractors on the ground. Chief Barney said the military had their rules but didn't see a problem if they made arrangements, since they were not military, with the other contractor that was on the ground already. He said these types of things were insignificant, and if they could make other arrangements he didn't have a problem with it. As far as he was concerned, they had a clean slate with the military and he looked forward to working with them.

When they both came back, it was announced that there would be no accommodations for husbands and wives to be housed together and that the military did not and would not stand for them to be housed together.

The SFC said, "Like I said, you will be over there with the other men and she will be over in G-block with the other women."

She and Bobby looked over at Harris to see if he was going to do anything about this. Harris stood in silence saying nothing and looking at no one in particular. If Harris was claiming to be their boss he should have spoken up. He should have let the military know that the three of them were to be housed with the other contractors. Instead, when the briefing was done, Harris stopped them both and started to bark out orders.

"You over there, grab a cot and get your stuff unpacked, and you, up in G-block, now!"

Bobby wasn't going to stand for this man talking to him that way, much less the way Harris was talking to his wife. "Look Harris, no one told us you're in charge, much less our boss, for god sakes. We will get to the bottom of this and pronto. We were told that you take our timecards and that is it. But if you want to play boss, then get this situation straightened out."

Harris smirked at Bobby and said, "Do what you're told. Unpack and meet back here for chow!"

They stood there stunned. They had no idea what to do next. They had talked to the Chief earlier and he'd said that everything would be ok. But from the sound of this tyrant, they decided the next best thing was to just get settled and try to email the company later, first to talk about this housing business and then most importantly this "I'm your supervisor, I'm the boss" nonsense. As she grabbed her bags and started to walk towards G-block, SFC Garcia walked out.

"Stop, hold on, I'll help you." Apparently he had no idea Bobby was standing right behind him with her other bag. Out of the corner of his eye, Sgt Garcia saw Bobby and turned and said, "Bob, get to your room, I'll take care of this! I'm in charge here and you'll do what I say, end of story!"

Bobby fumed as the words sizzled in the air around him. Who the hell did this asshole think he was? Sure, he may be in charge of this prison to some extent, but he wasn't in charge of him or his wife. He wasn't going to stand for this, not for one second. "Sgt, that is my wife you seem to be a little too interested in. I'm going to help her with her bags and get them in her room. If you have a problem with that, please, by all means, voice it, and I will voice the interest you seem to have concerning my wife, and from what I can see with the wedding band on your left hand, that just isn't an interest you should be having."

The Sgt sneered at Bobby and whispered under his breath, "I'm not done with you or with her for that matter. She and I have unfinished business to tend to!"

223

As the Sgt stalked off, Bobby grabbed both of the bags that were left and rushed up next to her. From what he could see of her face as she ducked her head, tears started to well up in her eyes. "What's wrong? What's going on here? What is the connection the two of you have? Is it bad? Have you told me about him before?" The questions kept coming out all at one time. Bobby wanted the answers but was scared to hear what the answers might be. Something was terribly wrong with this whole thing. His eyes pleaded for an explanation. She just kept her head bowed down as she walked towards G-block. He didn't know what else to do but follow and hope that when she was ready, she would tell him what was going on. There was just so much going on this first day, first with Harris, then with this Sgt Garcia person, then with the housing situation and then back with Harris. How in the hell were they going to get through all of this?

As she climbed the steep wet steps of G–block, she looked around and just wanted to die. She had never seen such a place. The place had some bad jou jou attached to it and she could feel it. She felt it as she walked down the corridor and for sure upstairs to G-Block. It clung to her skin like flies on shit. She finally found her room number on the right side of the jail cell door; she opened it and looked inside. Even in the evening, it was damn hot and the little A/C they had didn't improve matters one bit. She tried to act and look brave as she peered in the darkness of her "bedroom." The one thing that caught her eye, and even in the dark she saw it, gleamed brightly through the dark. Dead centre of the room on the ceiling was a big bright shiny hook. Her skin crawled just looking at it. Bobby touched her shoulder as she about jumped up there on that very hook. He asked her if she was ok. She simply didn't know how to answer that question. Not right now, not this minute. She turned around and saw his bright blue eyes and felt comfort from them. She knew she could do this, she knew she would be alright because he was with her. She got her strength from him, from those eyes.

In she walked. She didn't have to move too far inside the little jail cell to realize she had just bumped into a cot, her cot, less than half a meter from the door. How in the hell was she going to be able to live like this for three months? Anyone could walk right into the jail cell; there were no locks. It appeared that the remainder of the room was taken by her two cellmates. They, her new cellmates, divided three quarters of the space between the two of them; the last quarter of the room was her cot and nothing else. This is where she was to live for the next three months. There was nowhere to put her bags, much less unpack any of it.

Bobby, sensing the situation, said to her, "Don't worry, honey; I'll talk to the officer in charge. You shouldn't have to live like this; sharing a room with lower enlisted. You're a senior intelligence analyst, for god sakes. There has got to be something done. No one should have to live with their bed right at the opening of the door. I'll be good to go where they have me, but you should at least get a place that has enough room to at least put your bags. I'll take care of it. Ok?"

She piled her bags on top of the cot. There was barely room to turn around, much less unpack. They left the tiny room and started back down the stairs.

Bobby worried about these stairs. They were concrete but had been so worn down that they were slick, and wet on top of that as well. Anyone walking down here could take a bad fall on these if they weren't extremely careful. She accompanied Bobby to get him all settled in his room. She hoped that his was a helluva sight

226

better than her new place. She hated that she'd made him come here to this place, to this mess, to this hellhole. They could have continued being happy in Cuba if she wasn't so persistent about coming here. She'd thought that if she could just get to the country where AMZ was doing a lot of his terrorizing, maybe she might have a better chance at catching that bastard. It was that and the opportunity to be there, be where it was all going on, a chance to be a part of history, a chance to make a real difference. But she'd dragged poor Bobby into this mess as well; for that she felt like a piece of poo. It wasn't bad enough to put their happiness on hold and for her to be discomforted, but he too would have to suffer in this for three months as well.

Bobby looked back to see where she was at....she was really walking slowly. He wondered what she was thinking about right now; he wondered if it was about that Garcia guy. He finally stopped to wait on her. Her little square face had such a sadness to it. He had seen the sadness before in her eyes, but this time the sadness took over her whole body. She smiled her crooked half smile, but her eyes didn't light up like they normally did. The spark was not as bright, almost like a little light in her eyes had

227

dimmed. It was not completely turned off but not as bright either. He had seen this look in her eyes before, every now and again when she didn't know he was there, but not to this extent. This look was more dramatic. This was not the babydoll he knew and loved. This woman seemed lost, so lost in her thoughts and in her sadness. If she would only talk to him, let him know how he could help. He would kill for this woman, if need be.

As she walked slowly behind Bobby, she wondered what in the hell was going to happen on this trip. There was such a bad vibe around this whole place. It just couldn't be any worse; first with Harris, then with the housing issue and now with Garcia, and it didn't help matters that all of that was wrapped up in the Iraqi war. Good God, how bad could a girl's luck get?

*First things first,* she thought. *Harris, hmmm, that man has mental demons the size of Texas and guilt and so much other crap. He is layering it upon himself. He never sees his role in anything because he cannot look at himself introspectively.* She thought it was because he was afraid of what he would encounter there. His karma was already in full swing. If Harris took a serious interest in bettering himself from the soul inside out, then maybe, just maybe, he would be able to look at himself unflinchingly. *But he hates himself, as much as he seems to love himself.* She really was surprised that he had not died of cancer from all the imploding self-hatred.

She shook her head a couple of times to get the thought of him and his sickness out of her mind. Focus, she had to stay focused. She thought if she could just send out an email to the company to let them know how irrational (i.e. crazy) he was acting since the whole harassment incident, they would understand. She knew just the person to talk to: the new program manager, the one who interviewed her just two weeks prior. That telephonic interview went very well, and she never said that lightly. She always felt she did worse at interviews than she usually did, but not this time. This time she felt she aced the interview. It seemed to her that they were on the same wavelength, same management style. She felt confident that she would be at least in the running for the team lead position. Everyone on her team went to her for answers or if anyone needed anything. She was the "go to" person, she always had been.

Ok, so that was settled, email the program manager and let

him know what was going on and let him know about the housing

situation. She and Bobby were not promised that they would sleep

together, but they were promised that they would be housed with

the other contractors from that other company. Those two issues

would be settled. Now, what to do with Garcia, how was she going

to handle that situation? She wondered if she should just tell

Bobby everything. Tell him what happened so many years ago, a

lifetime ago. Bad memories she had put way behind her;

practically forgotten. She never tried to mislead or hide this part of

her life. She truly forgot about the whole incident. It took her

several years to get to that point. Well not get over it but to put it

out of her mind, to pretend that it never happened.

She knew that every now and again those memories would

slip back in, and she found herself drowning in a sea of sadness,

more sadness than when her dad passed away. She had to

physically pull herself out of it, and most of the time it worked.

She felt herself sinking into it, and this time she just wasn't sure

she could climb back out. She never would have thought in a

million years that she would see this man again and especially not

now, not here, in the middle of a war.

230

As she and Bobby neared HQ, Harris and Sgt Garcia came out. They looked thick as thieves as they laughed and joked. *Oh God,* she thought, *they are in cahoots. These three months will be very difficult now.* It would be pure hell, and she knew it. It was bad enough that Harris hated their guts for reasons beyond her, other than that harassment situation, but now Sgt Garcia appeared to be on his side. Now she and Bobby had to deal with two lunatics. This would be an insane three months. She didn't care, though, she had a mission to do here, and she was going to do it regardless of who hated whom and who wanted to hurt whom. She stopped in mid-thought. Where did that come from? "Who wanted to hurt whom?" Why would she say or even think something like that, even to herself?

Sgt Garcia and Harris sneered at her as they passed by, that's all, just sneered. He hadn't seen her for a very long time. She hadn't changed a bit, still the exotic little beauty he remembered her to be. How he loved her back then. He would have done anything for her, if only she would have let him. He thought back to the time he was stationed in Munich, to the time he had first met her. It had been a long time since he let himself have these thoughts. He tried very hard to push them out of his mind for over 20 years now. This time he would let the thoughts flood every single cell of his memory. First, though, he had to get rid of Harris. He wanted to be alone with all the thoughts, the thoughts of her and their time together in Germany. As he talked to Harris, he had to make up some excuse to get rid of this character. He wasn't a bad guy, Garcia thought, but boy could this guy talk. Harris talked till Garcia's ears went numb, He about talked his ear off, and what was the deal with his hatred for the two of them? Garcia wondered if it was more of a hatred of her husband and not so much her. Garcia knew that he definitely hated that bastard. What did she see in him? What was she doing with this gringo? Maybe he could get some answers from this Harris guy. He felt confident whatever he asked him, he would deliver the goods, the answers.

Harris started to wonder what was going on with Sgt. Garcia. He caught what had transpired when they first got there. Some words were exchanged between Bobby and the sarge. He also noticed how she didn't want to have anything to do with Garcia. He wondered what in the hell kind of skeletons were in her closet. This was going to be interesting. He could definitely use this to his benefit. This wasn't going to take long at all, not long at all. These two would be destroyed sooner than he anticipated, all with a little help from Garcia. He knew Garcia hated Bobby's guts. Could that stem out of jealousy? Was it because Garcia had had something going on with her way back when? Harris could easily manipulate this soldier. It wouldn't even be that difficult. He would have a "partner in crime" at least. He'd left Cuba thinking that the gunny was going to be his partner, but he noticed how gunny was warming up to that little Mexican woman. But this was a far better plan, someone not from where they were stationed. This could have not been better planned if he had planned it up himself. Maybe he and the sarge could have their way with her first, and then destroy the both of them...financially. He knew how to get to a woman and that was always through the pocket book, but first, a little degradation was in order and he was just the man to do it.

Harris also thought that Garcia could get into a little action like that. He felt a strange bond with this stranger for some reason. He would continue to play the Sgt like a fiddle and learn as much as he could about him as quickly as he could. He sure didn't want those two to get a chance to prove themselves to any of these people. That would not work to his benefit. He wanted them to be unknown quantities here in Iraq which would make his plan more believable. Everyone was more apt to believe all the "wonderful" stories he would tell, EVERYONE!

As she and Bobby got to HQ, they held hands tightly. He was scared for her; he didn't know why, but he was. He felt heaviness in the air that was so stifling that he could barely breathe. Everyone was there, Harris, Garcia; of course they got there AFTER their little chat outside about God only knows what; gunny, the other two soldiers that came with them and, of course, Bobby and his lady love. Garcia started to brief the group by stating that everyone should be settled in and ready for work tomorrow at 0800 hours sharp. As Garcia said this, he looked over at her and that bastard, her husband, and said, "That's 8am for you civilians."

Bobby wanted so much just to punch this guy's lights out. The nerve of him talking to him and his wife in such a condescending tone. He had already been brainwashed by Harris, and it didn't help that there was something between him and his wife. What it was, he just wasn't sure or if he would ever be sure what it was. With that, everyone was dismissed to go to chow or to go to the internet café. If anyone wanted to go they would be leaving in five minutes. On the way to the chow hall was the internet café right up next to it, so they could do both. Bobby knew that she wanted to type that email before anything else so he thought that they could peel off from the group; then after she sent the email, go have a bite to eat.

She and Bobby decided not to go anywhere but to just stay in place since they were to meet right back here in less than five minutes. Everyone else grouped up and formed their own clicks, the pair, the military guys and the two assholes, she thought.

"Perfect, just perfect," she said to Bobby. He looked at her and said nothing. He wanted to let her talk when and if she was ready to. He just held her hand and hoped some news would be forthcoming. When everyone was finally ready, they were told to make sure they had their flak vests and Kevlar helmets. They were told that within this prison compound you were to wear it if you went past certain areas of the prison; past the showers you had to have your gear on, no exceptions. Everyone had their gear on and was ready, everyone, that is, but Harris. He told the Sgt that he didn't need it, he would be fine. Bobby rolled his eyes and thought that Harris had to be the stupidest civilian he had even seen or heard.

Sgt Garcia just couldn't believe how stupid this civilian was. After talking with Harris and finding out that he had worked with the Justice Department for over 30 years, one would think he would know a thing or two about what it was like being in a war zone. Garcia wondered if it wasn't so much stupidity as just plain ole arrogance. That Garcia could understand; that he could respect, but unfortunately, Garcia couldn't let Harris fuck up the way the prison was run, how he ran the prison, to be more precise. So Garcia just glanced over at Harris, without saying a word and motioned him to his room; he didn't want to embarrass the man in front of his underlings. Thank God Harris had picked up the nonverbals and turned around and went back to his room to grab his gear. As they all stood there, Garcia decided to introduce everyone to the warrant officer in charge so as to take the focus off of Harris' stupidity.

A warrant officer is an officer appointed by the Secretary of the Army, based upon a sound level of technical and tactical competence. The warrant officer is the highly specialized expert and trainer who, by gaining progressive levels of expertise and leadership, operates, maintains, administers, and managers the Army's equipment, support activities, or technical systems for an entire career. The warrant officer is a single-track specialty officer. In walked Chief Warrant 5 Barney, with all the cool, calm, collected demeanor of someone who had been here for years. The "chief," as everyone called him, had a kind face. He had a lot of power here at the prison, but he didn't flaunt it, not like Garcia did.

Chief Barney had already met the pair just hours before. They seemed to be a fine couple and dedicated too. The chief could see why they were called the "power couple." It seemed that their reputation had preceded them. They were very sought after for their expertise and tenacity. The chief liked what he saw and heard about the pair. And towards the end of the conversation they'd had earlier, the chief winked at Bobby and said, "Just let me know when the two of you need a conjugal visit; I'll disappear for an evening or two." She blushed a deep red, and Bobby shook his hand and smiled.

Bobby was glad that they had the chance to talk to the Chief about the housing situation. Later, Bobby would talk to the chief again to thank him concerning the housing, perhaps tomorrow after they get settled in at work. The chief continued to make his rounds as everyone waited on Harris.

"And this is supposed to be our supervisor, OUR boss? Jesus Christ, this guy is making us civilians look bad, real bad," Bobby said to her.

She nodded and stood there with her own thoughts, how to fix this mess. She felt good about the email she was going to type. The company would see what they had done by letting Harris go on this trip. The company would figure out how, first of all, they screwed up by not firing him, especially with the "zero tolerance policy on sexual harassment" but somehow and for some reason swept that incident under the rug. Apparently no one at work had talked to Lockhart Marion about Harris' behavior, or surely they would have never sent him in the first place, not with all the personal shit he was going through and would continue to go through with the divorce proceedings and the rest of the bullshit that goes along with that. As the chief strode towards the chow

238

hall, they all stood there…waiting, waiting on Harris. Finally when they were about to leave without him, he came back looking as though he had seen the most ungodly of apparition a ghost. Garcia asked what the hell happened that it took this long. Garcia knew that Harris' room was just down the hall.

Harris was all out of breath and, looking like he was about to pass out, sat down and tried to calm his racing heart. Garcia yelled to no one in particular to get the man some water. One of the soldiers ran and grabbed a bottle. Harris chugged the whole bottle and was finally able to speak. "Sgt Garcia, I think I saw someone malingering outside. I thought I saw a shadow at first, but then when I went to my room to get my gear, poked my head out the window and wasn't 100% sure, so as I'm walking back here, I saw the shadow again, this time when I looked out the window, I saw the shadow moving. So I ran out the door and starting chasing this bastard, but this guy was fast. He wasn't very big, but he sure as hell was fast. As the shadow got close to the floodlight, he turned around and that stopped me in my tracks." Harris took a deep breath, he had the feeling that no one here was going to believe this story, but he had to get it out. He could have been imagining all of this, but he knew what he saw. "Like I said, he turned around. Sgt, the man looked exactly like Zarqawi!"

The Sgt stared at Harris with shock, disbelief and, well, amusement. All the others stood there, mouths open, wondering if this old man was bullshitting everyone to deflect his earlier faux pas or if he was actually telling the truth.

One thing was for sure, and that was that she wasn't shocked, not one little bit, and she hated to admit it, but she believed Harris. She hadn't said anything earlier, but when they came in hours before, as she poked her head up as they were entering the prison compound, she thought she saw him in the throngs of people. She felt he looked right at her, almost like he knew she would be on that particular convoy. She'd turned away for a second and looked back but he was gone. Part of her wanted to believe it, and the other part was too scared. She stood there with the others not saying a word. She wasn't about to back up this asshole's story. Not now, not ever. She was even kinda scared to tell Bobby. He knew how obsessed she'd become with her quest to find him. He would have thought maybe that she not necessarily made up the story as much as she wanted to believe him to be there so much that she thought she saw him. Could Harris be trying to make a fool of her? Surely he knew of her quest from when they were back in Cuba. Did he want to make fun of her in front of everyone? Was that his game plan, to mock her? She thought that maybe this time, Harris could be serious. Why would he be so out of breath and on the verge of a heart attack if he didn't believe in what he was saying?

Sgt Garcia said, "Ok, Harris, enough of the bullshit, we're late for chow."

They all started marching out into the darkness, motioning at points of interest along the way. Garcia pointed to the showers, men's and women's trailers, two for the men and one for women. He also stated that the men's shower was hit last week while he was in the other one. Garcia acquired a strange facial tick around his left eye as he talked about this. They all had heard the rumint, rumor intelligence, that little episode last week changed Garcia for the worst.

As they got closer to the chow hall, Garcia pointed towards the internet café that was bumped up right next to the chow hall. "Only 30 minutes allowed," Garcia bellowed.

The two of them peeled off. They would eat later, after they told the company about Harris. As it turned out, once you got to the café you had to sign in and wait for them to call your name. Garcia was right concerning the time allowable. Thirty minutes didn't seem long, she thought, but it would have to do. They decided to take a two-prong approach; they both put their names down. Whoever was called would start writing the email, and the other would check their joint account to see if anything from back home had come in.

"Bobby, next," they called. Bobby jumped up and started towards the rows and rows of computers with little numbers next to each one. He wondered how they kept track of the time. He thought half an hour was more than enough time. He asked her if she would like to actually draft the email, and she eagerly agreed. She was really good at these things. As she started to type, the words wanted to come out faster than she could type, and since she could type close to 90 words a minute, that said something. She thought about making it a little less detailed and just going right to the highlights. She didn't want to sound like a possessed lunatic to the company, just the facts, do not delude with personal opinions,

242

at least not now. She would wait for the company to ask for more info, and then she would provide it by the boatload!

While she typed the email, Bobby checked their email account. They had gotten something from Maria, something strange. He waited for her to finish up before telling her of this news. He didn't want to interrupt her thought process for something that might not be that important; the email back to the company was of the utmost importance to the two of them.

As she ended the email, she read it and re-read it again. She wanted to make sure it conveyed the right things. The right details and the right "sound." She really didn't want to come off as some panicky, complaining bitch. She wanted the company to know the seriousness of what was going on without being a big spaz. She thought it had the right things said in the right tone, so she hit the send button. She looked at the screen as the letters of the alphabet disappeared into the big computer sky, hopefully coming to rest in the inbox of the program manager's computer. She walked over to where Bobby was sitting, looked over his shoulder and read. Maria said something about "talk" around the Lockhart Marion corporate office, something about the two of them. Maria didn't know exactly what the talk was about because people would stop talking as she neared. Everyone knew that she had gotten Maria the job there and that they were closer than sisters. Maria ended her email with "watch your backs."

"Oh my god, what now?" she said out loud to Bobby.

Bobby agreed, "What now?"

That was all the mail they had, and that was more than enough to chew on for the night. Bobby asked her if she was hungry. She knew she had to eat but wasn't the slightest bit hungry. It had been a long-ass day for the both of them, and she knew that Bobby needed to eat so she said, "Sure thing."

She surprised herself as she inhaled every single morsel of her dinner. She hadn't realized just how hungry she really was, and her hunger started with the smell of the food. As she stood in line she looked the food over. It was cafeteria style so she could see several entrees at one glance. All of it looked really appetizing, so appetizing she had a difficult time deciding. She finally selected the roasted chicken, mac and cheese and a vegetable medley. Then came the dessert; what good choices, too many choices. She decided that a couple of peanut butter cookies would suffice.

Bobby picked hamburger, mac and cheese and big salad with a big piece of chocolate cake.

"They sure aren't stingy with the servings here," she said. He was eating like there was no tomorrow; they both were. There was no conversation going on, just munching. When they finally devoured their meals they looked at each other and said, "José!" They both laughed and shrugged. The thought of having a little bit of José right about now was very appealing to the both of them, but as everyone knows, no alcohol is allowed in a war zone. They got up and walked towards the exit door, holding hands, of course.

She looked up at Bobby and said those four words that all men hate to hear, "We need to talk." Bobby was not all men though; he loved to hear that. He loved to hear anything and everything she had to say. She went on to say, "But not here, not right now. There are things that I want to tell you. I never purposely kept anything from you. I promise I didn't."

Bobby squeezed her little hand and said, "I know babydoll, I know. When you are ready; know that when you are ready, I will be waiting." They went back to their respective rooms, he to the new wing of the prison that was built entirely of plywood and she to G-block, the oldest part of the prison. Bobby had insisted that he walk with her down the hall and up those scary steep stairs, but she said she couldn't be safer anywhere else in the world; she was in a prison for goodness sakes. As she walked down the hallway and past the many doors on the left and the right, she had the distinct feeling that someone was following her but not from inside where she was, but just outside. She felt the familiar shudder that she'd had many times in Cuba and a few times since she'd been in this country. She looked behind her and saw nothing, but within her periphery she thought she caught a shadow. If this shadow was a man, he wasn't a very large one, not that that made any difference at this point, but it was an observation of hers. It was a habit of hers to look, to search to find every little detail, and those details were observations and she was good at it. If she said she observed something, people stopped, listened and believed it to be true based solely on what she said.

It was hard to believe that they had been in Iraq for only two days now: a day and half sitting at the PAX terminal waiting for their convoy and the other half day here at the prison. She wondered if this deployment was going to feel like "dog years"

246

and if so, this was going to be the longest three months of all of

their lives.

## Chapter 9 -- Garcia

As SFC Garcia sat back on his bunk, he let his mind wander back to Munich, back to the time they first met, back when he was still a young buck barely out of high school. "Young, dumb and full of cum," so went the saying. It almost took an act of God to get Harris off his back. Sure, he thought the guy was an upstanding kinda guy, but good Lord, he let no one get a word in edgewise. And on top of it all, he really didn't talk about much, just old war stories mostly, his time working for Justice Department and all his deployments. Garcia would agree with anyone who said that Harris talked a lot of shit; that much was true. As he settled himself a little bit better on his bunk so he could let his mind and his hand wander freely. You just never knew where your memories might take you, and it had been a long eleven months here in this godforsaken hellhole without the benefit of female company. Sure there were women here, but he never could settle for some stray piece. He spent his life looking for her or at least someone that looked and acted just like her. He recalled how bad he had it for her back then, and strangely enough, those same feelings came flooding back.

The hows and whys she still had this control over him was a mystery to him. He didn't even want to try to explain or understand it. All he knew and all he cared about was that she was back in his life, husband or no husband. True, he was married, not happily so, but that was how it had been since the first day he got married. Not miserable but not altogether happy either.

He wondered if she had changed. She had changed a bit physically, but was it possible that she got better looking with age? She had to be getting close to her mid-40s by now. He had always loved older women, but when he met her, he really had no idea how much older she was. All he did know was that it was love at first sight, for him.

He knew that she had remarried but did she love him? Was she happy? He knew he could make her very happy if she would only let him. He would see how it went tomorrow. Today wasn't good, she had been traveling for God only knows how long, and she had just gone through the trauma of the convoy from Baghdad PAX terminal to the prison. Even the toughest of soldiers hated that half-hour trip. He was so glad that she wasn't on the convoy that got hit the day before. This must mean something, some type of omen. Maybe it was a sign that they were meant to be together? So what if his wife of 20 years was kicked to the curb now; he never really loved her the same way, never loved anyone the same way.

He wondered if she ever thought of their last time together, how special it was for him, for them both. She was his first and you never forget the first one. He never really understood why she was so mad at him after that. Why she refused to talk to him, to see him. He tried several times to call, but she would just hang up. A few times her husband actually picked up the phone and, having the arrogance or maybe ignorance of youth, he asked for her. He didn't care what her husband said or thought. Always, he would say no, she's not here. There had been a time when he was welcomed in their home, when they both had welcomed his phone calls, but not any longer and he couldn't understand why. Was it

250

because her husband found out about them? Could that be what happened? She stopped talking to him right after they made love. She probably was just confused about her feelings for him, probably loved him too much and had to make herself withdraw from him. He was too much for her; she felt as strongly about him as he did her; probably more so, that was it, he felt confident about that.

But for all his confidence, he still felt abandoned by her. He used to spend morning, noon and night with her. They worked together during the day, and he would come over for dinner with or without her husband there and, to be honest, he was mostly not there. Her husband Richard had one of those jobs where he was always gone, and she never knew when he would return. That made it a really sweet deal for him. They could spend just about 24 hours together; he even slept over sometimes, and that was also cool with her husband. That was one thing that Garcia just didn't get. Why would it be ok with her husband with him spending all this time with his wife when they were obviously in love? Maybe Richard couldn't see how much they loved each other …that man had to be crazy. How could he not see how much his wife loved him?

He noticed her pulling away more and more as the days went by after she got the new job where her husband worked. He didn't get that quality time with her during the day like he had grown used to and missed her so much. He tried to call her at work, but she always said she was really busy and she would call him later; she never did. Initially the new job took her away from him for just those eight hours, but she would still make time for him in the evenings when they would spend time talking about their day. He never made a move on her, even though he could tell she wanted him and wanted him badly. He wanted to wait, wanted it to be special for the both of them. But before he could fully realize it, he was spending less and less time with her to the point of not being able to see her for weeks at a time. He started to think that maybe she stopped seeing him because she felt more than he did. He thought that maybe if he just came over and made his move, maybe that was what she wanted, to be shown just how much he loved her with the physical aspect of love. He had never been with a woman but knew he wanted her to be the first. Ok, he had a plan of action to get her back to the way she used to be, the way they used to be: like a couple.

Tonight was the night, he felt it, but he was so nervous about doing this, worried about doing everything he was supposed to do. He read all the books and looked over his magazines so he knew where everything was at. First things first, though, he needed a drink, a nice strong tall drink of anything, just to calm his nerves. He unscrewed the bottle of Jack Daniels, the bottle he'd kept for the guys when they wanted to watch movies. He took a big swig straight from the bottle. That sent a bolt of shivers throughout his body and a burning in his gut. *Good*, he thought. This would do the job. He sat down and had one more swig, a short one this time. Before he realized it, he had finished half the bottle. He was a little tempted not to go because he wasn't sure he could actually drive to her place in his present condition. There wasn't anything that was going to stop him from his mission tonight; that much he knew. It was Friday night and he felt confident that Richard was on another one of his business trips. He felt that everything was perfect. He knew she would be so happy to see him; it had been almost a month since they last spoke.

## Chapter 10 -- Overwhelming sadness

As she sat on her cot, she finally let herself think of Garcia.
Why in the hell did the powers that be have this happen? Why?
She looked up to the sky and cried, *why, why, why me?* How was
this going to end? As she lay there in the jail cell that she shared
with two young soldiers, each one having her own "fun" for the
evening, she realized that they just didn't care who heard what. All
she knew was that one of the "couples" was rolling around on the
floor, and she knew this because she saw two sets of feet rolling
from under the hanging sheets they used as "walls." That was their
privacy, no matter how thin or short the "walls" were, it was good
enough for the both of them. At least the other couple had the
decency to keep the noise level down to just a few grunts and
moans here and there. This was the last thing she needed to hear
while thinking about Garcia and how to fix this bullshit in her life.

She let her mind go where it seemed it wanted to go, to him, to Garcia, to that time in her life. She remembered when they first met. It was her first job in civil service, in Munich, Germany when she was married to Richard. They had only been married for two years at that point, still in the honeymoon stage of their marriage. In she walked with the confidence of someone who owned the place. Of course it was all a ruse; she had been scared shitless. She hated being the new person, the feeling of floundering for at least a month until you learned the ropes. There he was; a specialist in the army and what was called a 71Lima, which translated into civilian terms as "administrative assistant," more or less. He knew the ropes inside and out, all the forms and publications she would need to learn. She was to be the executive secretary to the commander, pretty high profile for her first civil service job. She had been in banking for the past seven years, but she felt confident that she could do this job once she learned the Army lingo. And he was there to help her along with anything she needed. They were to work side by side to make sure the commander was taken care of. Garcia was a nice enough young guy, not attractive but not ugly either. He had what you would say was your typical Hispanic features. She never went for that look herself. She preferred "gringos" to Mexicans; her mother had told her the horror stories about how they were with their women. She made sure she steered clear of them growing up. She didn't want to be treated as a doormat like her mother had said. She and Garcia were going to spend the next six months together for eight hours a day. It was only to be six months because this particular job was only open for that period while the secretary went on maternity leave, and after that she would have to find another job. She didn't worry about that right now; she had other issues to worry about, like what a DF was. So many forms, so many regulations; everyday seemed to be a blur of information--information overload.

She felt comfortable around Garcia. He was more like the little brother she never had. Richard seemed to like him as well. He was invited over to dinner almost every night and Richard said it was ok for him to come by while he was away on business as well. It was nice for his wife to have company while he was away. She stayed alone most of their marriage. Before you knew it, she and Garcia were inseparable, like brother and sister. Richard trusted this young man, he surely didn't see him as any type of threat, and besides, he trusted his wife and he knew the type of men she preferred: much older, established in their careers and white.

As the weeks turned to months, her time there was coming to the end and possibly the end of their time together, at least their day times. It was almost time for the other secretary to come back from maternity leave. She started to notice how clingy Garcia was becoming. She had already secured another job where her husband worked which was practically across the street from Garcia. She told him that they would still spend a lot of time together; he was still welcome at dinnertime. She promised nothing would change much, just the daytime part of the day. On her last day, the whole office took her to a local German restaurant. She got some wonderful gifts from the commander and his staff. Garcia presented her with a medium-size box and whispered to her to open it later, at home, after dinner while he was there. She looked at him quizzically but did what he said. No telling what kinda gag gift he bought for her. Friday was her last day of work, and that night he would come over as usual, for dinner. Richard was gone per usual.

This evening she just didn't feel like cooking. She told him that they could order pizza if he was hungry. He said, "Naw, let's play some cards, I'm not hungry either." She had taught him to play Gin Rummy and he was getting really good. He told her that he wanted to make it "interesting."

"Why the hell not?" she responded. "What do you have in mind?"

"Ok, what kinda liquor do you have?"

She got up, checked the liquor cabinet and said, "Not much; just tequila and not the good kind either. This is the one we use to make margaritas. It isn't top-shelf stuff."

"Cool, that'll do the job. Do you have any lemons or salt?"

She looked around and didn't have a single lemon, nothing but green seedless grapes, her favorite fruit. "Nope, no lemons," she told him.

"No worries, we'll play hand for hand, and whoever loses a hand has to down a shot; not in a glass either, straight out of the bottle. How does that sound?"

"I'm game!"

So off they started. This poor kid had no idea who he was

up against. She could drink all women and a lot of men under the table. This amateur would be no problem for her. As the game progressed, she had a shot, he had a shot, she, he, she, she, she, he, he, she, he, back and forth almost one for one. It seemed to be a tie. The only thing that wasn't a tie was that he was totally wasted while she had a happy little buzz going. As he stood up to go to the bathroom, he started to sway. She asked if he needed anything to eat to soak up some of the alcohol, and as he staggered towards the direction of the bathroom, he said, "Yes, something, anything."

She looked in the fridge and cursed herself for not buying some groceries or even calling in for pizza, but it was too late now for pizza. She found some cheddar cheese and bread. *Well, better than nothing,* she said to herself. She made Garcia two thick cheese sandwiches and hoped that would be enough. She pulled out the two pounds of green seedless grapes for herself. She realized that wasn't much, but she really still wasn't hungry. The grapes just looked good. He came out looking more sober than he did going in. Garcia patted her back as he passed her and aimed himself towards the sandwiches. "Mmmmmm, perfect," he mumbled.

"So, do you concede? Do you admit that you lost to yours truly?" she asked, taunting him to another game.

"Ooooh, hell no I don't. We are so far from finished. We still have half a bottle left. As he ate his cheese sandwiches and she her green grapes. The strangest look came over his face. She wasn't quite sure if it was more of a drunken stupor or something else. Something she would have never thought of when thinking of him. He had the look in his eyes like he was looking at her naked. He just looked her up and down. *Eeeewwww*, she thought to herself. He was more like a little brother than anything thing else, much less a lover. She hoped that she was wrong about that look in his eyes. She hoped it was a drunken stupor, prayed that it was a drunken stupor look. And as she was about to slip on a sweater to cover anything he may or may have not been looking at, he said, "Ok, let's go. I'm going to kick your ass this time!"

And so they went back and forth, he winning, she winning, back and forth, both winning and losing about the same amount. She could tell that all this rot gut tequila was starting to take its toll on her. It had gotten to the point were the liquid would just slide down her face; some went in the mouth and some down her chin,

260

down to her neck, down to her t-shirt. She wondered how far "out there" he was now. She really was in no shape to judge his condition. With the bottle emptied, they both declared a fair and square tie. She got up to use the bathroom when he grabbed her hand as she walked by. His touch startled her. She couldn't ever recall, even after all of these months, him actually touching her in any way. No hug, no friendly kiss on the cheek, no pat on the back, nothing. She wasn't too surprised, some people just aren't touchy-feely people, and that was cool with her.

She looked down at his hand grasping hers and said, "Yes? I gotta pee. Be right back, ok?"

He let go and off she wandered to the bathroom. After sitting there on the toilet for a minute or two, she heard something, someone in her bedroom. Could that be Richard back from his business trip? She hoped so, but it didn't sound like him. But then again, she really was too drunk to know who or what was happening on the other side of the door. After peeing and washing her hands, she took a look at herself in the bathroom mirror. Wow, she looked rough. A half a bottle of rot gut tequila would do that to a person, she supposed. She kept looking at herself and noticing little things, like the dribble of tequila down her chin that went down her throat and almost soaked the top half of her white t-shirt. She had not realized that you could see right through the t-shirt and right through her bra to her left tit. *Oh my god. That is what he was fixated on. No wonder. Well, he is a young kid, he can't help himself.*

She opened her top drawer and pulled out a dark colored t-shirt and found a bra that would match. As she stood facing away from the door, she took off the wet t-shirt and bra and took the warm wash cloth to wash off the tequila that had soaked her left side. As she reached down to grab her bra, she didn't realize that the bedroom door had been opened. In he walked, and he put his arms around her and put both of his hands on each of her breasts and slowly licked and sucked the back of her neck. For just a second she let the feeling of the tequila and his wonderful touches continue. Then it hit her! *This isn't Richard! Richard is away on business.*

She quickly turned around and grabbed her chest. "Get out; get the hell out of my house."

He stared at her like she had given him a blow the

balls,with an expression of surprise and hurt, and he tried to talk to her but she just kept yelling. So he left, stumbling down the stairs and out to his car in his drunken and lust-filled condition.

Oh, how she hated herself. What in the hell was she thinking? Why didn't she see him as a man and not a little brother? How stupid could she be? "Goddamn stupid," she said to herself out loud. As she put her clothes on, she paced the bedroom wondering what she had done to lead him on. Did she do something wrong? Did she lead him on? She didn't think so. How in the world could he look at her in that way? She surely never thought of him as anything but a brother. She knew that Richard saw him more as a son.

She wondered if it was wise to tell Richard what had gone on tonight. Would he be upset with her? Would he think she did something to lead him on? She wanted to be honest, but she was scared that he would blame her. Because she was the adult, he was the "kid brother."

She walked back to the front door, locked it and decided to crash. She was still pretty drunk. At the time, she didn't even wonder if he was ok or if he crashed his car or what, and she didn't even care at that point. All she could think was, *what was he thinking? I'm old, he's young.*

She passed out on the bed, fully clothed. At some point in the evening, she heard a knock on the door. She wasn't sure if it was real or a dream, but the knock kept getting louder and louder. She sat up in bed, and the room started to spin. She hated that feeling and tried to open her eyes and focus on one thing. There was the alarm clock on the dresser, she concentrated on that and was able to get up and walk towards the door. She hadn't even stopped to think that it might be Garcia, she just unlocked the door and walked back to the bed like she was in a trance. Luckily for her, it was Richard.

As Richard followed her back to the bedroom, he wondered what in the hell was wrong with her. In the living room he saw an empty bottle of tequila, a bunch of grapes, a half-eaten sandwich and a deck of cards. *Oh, Garcia must be here and passed out in the guest bedroom.* He had never seen his wife quite so out of it, not like this, before. *Interesting, to say the least,* Richard thought.

He poked his head in the guest bedroom. "Hmm, this is strange. Where the heck is Garcia?" Richard said to no one in particular. Well, no worries, tomorrow was Saturday and Richard didn't have to go into work until a little later than normal. His wife flung herself on top of all the covers fully clothed. She was a tiny woman, and Richard was able to move her here and there to help her out of her clothes. At first she protested but then let him remove every last bit. He then picked her up off the bed, folded the covers down and placed her little body down, covered her and then took a long hot shower.

Richard sat straight up in the bed. It was full on daylight outside. At some point he must have shut the alarm off and went back to sleep. Richard saw his poor wife half hanging on the bed, half hanging off, but he didn't have time to do anything about it, so he just threw some clothes on and ran out the door. He had a briefing to give in less than a half hour. He grabbed a pair of jeans and polo shirt, and he was outta there. He hadn't even noticed the spew that was on the side of the bed where his wife was. It was perfectly shaped green seedless grapes, not even digested, in a pool of gastric juices--no food, except for the grapes. If anyone were to analyze that particular spew, they would see that she hadn't eaten anything for quite a while and had nothing in her but the tequila and those sad little grapes.

As she attempted to move parts of her body, she thought to herself, *This just isn't going to happen today. I am not going to be able to move any part of my body and that is all there is to it.* The phone rang loudly from the living room. It made the sound of one of those large steel balls that swing into the sides of buildings to bring them crashing down, only louder. How could it be possible that her fingernails hurt…her hair follicles throbbed. The phone rang insistently. *Oh god, who would call at this ungodly hour of--* She looked around for the clock but couldn't find it. It wasn't where she had left it yesterday. Yesterday before Garcia came over…*oh no, oh noooooo!*

It all came back to her like a runaway train; there was just no stopping it. Little by little everything was coming back slowly and not so slowly. The damn phone was still ringing. God, why didn't they just give up? Was it Garcia? Wait, where was Richard? Shouldn't he be here? She vaguely remembered unlocking the door for him. Or was it him that she unlocked the door for? She looked down at her naked body. "Oh my god, what have I done?" She looked around for signs of Richard; she saw nothing, not a thing to make her believe he had even been home. The phone, the damn phone wouldn't stop ringing. She finally decided that she would attempt to stand up. She was having the worst morning. She started to question the content of that tequila bottle. She had never had a morning like this in her life. She swung her legs around to the side of the bed, pushed the covers over and put her feet on the floor. As she placed her feet down she heard and felt a very weird yet somehow familiar "squish." She looked down to see goo and green grapes between her toes. With that little visual, she leapt from the gooey mess and ran to the bathroom to relinquish the rest of the grapes that had been lodged in her belly. Out they came--gastric juices and more green grapes. It would be a long long time for her to be able to eat another green seedless grape, many years later--or tequila for that matter.

The phone rang off and on throughout the whole day. She couldn't bear to answer it. She didn't know what to say or what to do. She still wasn't sure what to do about all of this. She racked her brain, did she lead him on…did she do something or say something to let him think that it was ok to do what he did? Or was it just the alcohol? She knew that alcohol allowed you to do the things you wanted to do anyway but made it easier to do. She hated herself for what happened. Why did he have to ruin everything? She was happy, she loved Richard. She didn't want any complications. She didn't see Garcia like that. Even now, afterwards, it felt dirty; it felt like incest to her.

After cleaning up the gooey mess on the floor, spewing more--actually dry heaving was more like it, washing the bed linens, showering and blow-drying her hair, she took her little handheld mirror to check out the back of her hair. She really liked when it spiked out, and she had to make sure the back did it as well as the front. As she looked in the mirror, what she thought she saw shocked the hell out of her. That couldn't be what she thought it was, could it? She turned on the other bathroom light to make sure it wasn't a shadow she saw back there. *Oh God, what in the hell do I do now?* Her mind wouldn't/couldn't stop racing. *What do I do, what do I say, how do I handle this?* She still had no idea if Richard had come home last night. Had he seen the monstrosity on the back of her neck and now had he left her? Was he mad and just staying at the office?

It was almost five in the evening, and she still had no idea

268

what to do next. Should she call Richard at the office? Should she just pick up the phone when it rang again? She had never had such complications in her life before. As the thought of whether she should answer the phone rolled around in her head, it rang again. She decided to answer it and if it was Garcia, she would pretend nothing happened. She wouldn't mention it. If he brought it up, she would deal with it then and there. If it was Richard, well, she would deal with that too, as best she could. She picked up the phone and said hello.

A sigh of relief escaped her mouth when Richard asked her if she was ok. He had tried to call over and over. He was so worried when the phone kept ringing and ringing that he was going to call the emergency room and have an ambulance stop over. He wanted to let her know that he had to work late tonight; something came up. He told her if she was able to keep anything down that she should go ahead have dinner without him. It would probably be about ten by the time he could get home. She said ok. She was partially glad, as she would have time to think things through, and she was partially sad for the same reason. She hung up with mixed feelings much like how she answered the phone in the first place.

*Ok. Nothing resolved with Richard. Not yet, anyway.*

As she went to the kitchen to look for some broth, the phone rang again. She hurried to answer it. She thought maybe it was Richard again to say he would be home on time after all and that she should order something from take–out, and he would pick up before coming home. She answered with "Hi baby! What's up?"

The sound of her voice when she said those words made Garcia warm inside. He was so glad that she greeted him this way. He was afraid she would be mad at him for not calling all day long. He knew that she had raised her voice at him last night, but that was because she wanted him so badly, and she was embarrassed about those feelings because she didn't know how he felt towards her. At least that's what Garcia thought; scratch that--that is what Garcia knew for fact. It was a plan; he would come over tonight to finally let her know how much he loved her and wanted her and needed her. She would feel relieved to hear such good news, he thought. There shouldn't be anything to be embarrassed about, not now, not ever. But first, a shot of something strong to prepare him for what he was about to do. He had never told anyone, not even

270

his mother; that he loved them. This was going to be special. He would not only tell her, but he would show her. He knew that is what she wanted anyway. He felt it; he could feel her longing for him, but somehow she stayed in control. She wouldn't have to be in control tonight; he would just take control of the situation, and she could just lie back and enjoy.

Garcia cooed in what he thought to be his sexiest voice, "Hi baby, back atcha."

She nearly dropped the phone on the floor. Oh god, why did she have to answer the phone that way and why did it have to be him at this particular time? Why couldn't it have been Richard like she thought it was? She had no idea what to do at this point: hang up or say something, anything. She responded with what she hoped to be a cool, aloof *"hello."*

As Garcia went on and on and on about God only knows what, her mind wandered off. She said the usual yeah and oh really, so he thought she was listening. But then he said something that made her actually choke on her saliva as she tried to swallow; she stopped in her tracks.

"I'll be over in an hour, and I won't take no for an answer!"

And with that, he hung up the phone. Well she just wasn't up for

that. In fact, wouldn't stand for it; someone barking orders at her

like that. Who the hell did this kid think he was? This kid telling

her what was what! No way was she going to sit there and wait for

this fool because he said he wouldn't take no for an answer.

She grabbed her coat and her bag and took off, for who

knew how long.

As she drove her black RX7 down the autobahn for parts

unknown, she wondered how did this all happen and how could

she just avoid this person for the rest of her life, or at least until it

was time for her and Richard to PCS from Germany. She decided

to pull over to a lake she had passed more than a hundred times, to

stop and just be alone. She got out and sat on the hood of the car

and stared at the water. She thought about what had happened the

other night--correction, last night. It seemed like it was months

ago but was about 24 hours ago, just last night. She wondered if

she did anything to make him believe that was what she wanted.

Then out of the blue, it hit her; her going-away present from him

was still in the back seat of her car.

She jumped up and grabbed the flat little box. Part of her was curious about what it could be and a big part of her was scared, and she didn't know why. As she tore into the wrapping and ribbon and bow and pulled the box apart, she saw the prettiest deep purple color. She wondered how in the world he knew that was her favorite color. Then she saw it, the whole thing, and in her shock, she let it slip from her fingers and into the grass. She looked down at it as if it was poison. She backed away and just kept staring at this little purple piece of lace. Why would Garcia think it would be ok to buy her such a gift, such a personal gift, a gift her husband hadn't even bought her? It was the smallest, laciest g-string she had ever seen. And what made him think she wore this type of thing? Well of course she did, by the way, but why buy this for her? He was like a little brother she'd never had, not a man buying his lover lingerie.

Before she realized it, she had backed herself up against a tree. She wanted to just run and leave this place. She didn't know how long she stayed there at the lake staring down at what now was a blur of purple, but it had gotten dark. She thought it best to leave. Hopefully he would have come and gone by the time she

273

made it back home, or at least Richard would be there.

As she pulled slowly into the parking lot, her eyes darted back and forth and front and back looking for his car. She didn't see it anywhere. She sighed a sigh of pure relief. *Thank God,* she said to herself. As she walked up the stairwell to their second-floor apartment, she felt eyes on her. She looked around and didn't see anyone. She quickly opened the door and yelled out to Richard, who came out of the bedroom looking very worried, if not downright scared. He came to her and hugged her tight. She asked him what was wrong, and all he could say was, "I thought I lost you." She looked up at him and saw a glimmer of tears welling up in his eyes. She couldn't understand what was going on. Why would he have this reaction? She finally just asked him what was going on.

Richard finally told her that Garcia had come over and looking for her and said he had told her he was coming by. Richard knew it wasn't like her to just up and take off, especially when her good friend Garcia said he was going to stop by. He thought that something bad had happened to her. Kidnapped or a car accident, something. Oh God, what should she say, how should she react

274

now? All she could do was to tell Richard the truth, tell him what had happened the other night and how weird Garcia had been acting towards her lately. Down deep though, she knew that Richard would find him and kill him. Richard who had ok'd the visits, the dinners and all those times alone with his wife feel stupid; made stupid by some young punk.

She was not about to let that happen to Richard, no way no how. So she told a half truth. She decided that she would just say that he was acting weird towards her, and she preferred to not have to bother with his immature behavior. She hoped that was a good enough explanation without causing unnecessary concern, but strong enough for Richard to know that she didn't want him anywhere near her again.

As the days turned to weeks, she realized that she was more than capable of avoiding Garcia. The phone calls at work, her boss took. The phone calls and visits to the house, Richard took care of. She was thankful that the building she now worked at would not allow him in. Garcia didn't have the proper clearance to gain access. She made sure she varied her arrival and departures so he never really knew when she would come in or leave her office. She

275

was pissed that she had to live like this, but she felt it was better than the alternative. *He'll get over me and concentrate all his efforts elsewhere,* she thought.

It had now been over a month since she had left that little piece of purple lace in the grass and drove off, and she couldn't have been happier. The days were filled with fulfilling and interesting work, and her nights were spent with Richard. When he was away on business, she would stay home reading and watching TV alone or sometimes with a new friend from work. She had learned her lesson with Garcia, and before asking her male colleague to come over, both she and Richard felt very confident that her friend was gay. What a relief to be able to chit chat and spend time with a man and NEVER have to worry about anything happening.

One day Richard came down to her office to let her know that he had to leave quickly for an emergency business trip, and he wasn't sure when he would be back. It was just the nature of his business, and she understood. She went next door to see if her friend Rick wanted to come over tonight and do nails. To her dismay, he too was away on business, but he would be back the very next day. Time alone, time to just sit and do nothing; she loved the idea. It had been a while since she was totally alone. She always seemed to have something going on in her life. As she pulled in her parking lot, she thought she saw Garcia's car parked there. Surely after all this time he wouldn't still be lurking about, would he? She was afraid to get too close to the car to find out for sure, so she literally ran up the two flights of stairs and unlocked her apartment. It was sheer relief to be indoors away from anything that might harm her. She knew her thoughts were on the dramatic side, but she always felt that she was being watched or followed. She thought maybe she was a tad paranoid. She didn't care, it made her hypersensitive to her surroundings, and there wasn't anything wrong with that, the way the world was nowadays.

After a wonderful dinner of steak and a big salad, she thought, *first things first,* fill the tub with nice warm bubbly water, pour a glass of wine, put on some wonderful Parisian music and strip down and soak. It was almost ten at night by the time she actually got out of the tub all pruney. She wrapped the towel around her head and threw on her terrycloth rob and strode to the bedroom to get her most non-sexy PJ's she had: sweatpants, t-shirt

277

and big soft socks. It was a Friday night and way too early for bed, so she found a movie to throw in the VCR.

Her favorite movies were horror, and the one she picked out was a good one. As the scariest part of the movie was just about to happen, there was a loud knock on the door. Her eyes got as big as saucers, and she eyeballed the door from where she sat on the couch. She didn't hear anything for about a minute, and just as she thought that maybe she must have been hearing things, there was another knock.

This time though, it was Richard's knock. Three taps, pause, then one more. It was their signal since he knew she couldn't reach up to the little peephole in the door. She wondered why he was home but didn't care, because he was home. The weekend wouldn't be a loss after all. She jumped up and over the couch and turned the three locks on the door, pulling it all the way open. She almost passed out dead in her tracks as she stood face to face with Garcia. She didn't know what to say. She could smell alcohol on his breath several meters away. She wanted to snap the door shut, but she had opened it just a little too wide. He smiled at her and she could tell he was totally shit-faced drunk. That thought scared her to her core. What would he do? What would he say? She just stared blankly at him, waiting to react to whatever he decided to do.

"Can I come in?"

"I prefer that you don't," she said.

He strode in the house as if he was deaf to her words and sat himself down on the couch like he owned the place. He patted a place on the couch very close to himself and said, "Join me. You know you want to." His bravado was almost too much to bear. She left the door ajar just a little bit in case she had to run out of there quick-like.

She stood there in the living room and finally had the courage to say, "What the hell do you want? Why are you here?"

"Oh you know why I'm here. Don't play dumb. You know you want it, that's why you kept that little going-away gift I gave you. You wanted me to see you in it. Stop being so coy." He stood up with a cat-like reaction and stood next to her now. He tried to kiss her on the lips, pushing his tongue into her mouth. She was so scared and tried to move away, but he had her pinned up against the back of the couch.

He said to her, "Come on, you know why I'm here. I know what you want."

He grabbed her arm, twisting it as he motioned her into the bedroom. She pleaded with him to talk about this. That it didn't have to be this way. He could care less what she said, he knew what she wanted and he was going to give it to her, right here, right now, like it or not.

She looked at him dead-on and said, "If you don't leave, I will call the police."

"I will tell everyone that you wanted to do it." Garcia laughed. "No one will believe you; everyone knows that we're the best of friends. People will say you wanted me as much as I want you and then you had a change of mind because of your husband. So tell them anything you want, everyone has seen us, EVERYONE."

The next hour was a blur to her. She tried to disconnect her body and her mind. Don't let him in your mind, don't let him do it. She fought and fought, but he was too strong for her. She couldn't scream with his hand on her mouth. He pulled the belt off his pants and yanked her around until she was on her tummy. He tied one of her hands to one of the head board posts and grabbed what looked like a scarf that she had probably worn earlier that day at work and tied her other arm. The arm that was tied to the post with his belt started to sting, the leather cutting into her flesh. He took what appeared to be a pair of panties that were also lying on the bed with the rest of her outfit, and crammed it in her mouth. She felt she was going to pass out, but she tried to keep it together. She should have just let herself pass out, but she kept fighting and fighting it. She wasn't going to let this happen to her; she couldn't let it happen to her. Richard was the only one she had ever been with, and now this disgusting thing was going on. She didn't know what else to do to make him stop. So she lay there, her sweatpants stripped down to her ankles and her t-shirt almost ripped off but not completely. He only bothered to raise it up to her face so he wouldn't be able to see her eyes, those deep brown almond-shaped eyes filled with tears.

As he pushed himself into her most private spot, she managed to disconnect with what was going on. She felt herself rise up to the ceiling. She could actually look down and see what was going on. She didn't feel pain, she just didn't feel. He

281

wouldn't stop; he just kept pumping and pumping, going from one hole to the next until finally he stopped.

As he grabbed his shirt from the floor to wipe himself off, he looked down at her and wondered if she had enjoyed it as much as he did. He thought of asking her, but he was just too tired, and all the alcohol was starting to wear off, which was making him very sleepy. He decided best to just gather his things and give her time to think of all of this, to think of him and the wonderful life that they could have together without Richard. He undid his belt from her wrist and simply walked out the door. She lay there for God only knows how long. She was afraid to move, afraid he might come back for seconds.

When there was nothing left but silence, she took the panties out of her mouth with her free hand and then untied the other one. She tried to stand up but was having problems doing so. She ached everywhere; every single place on her body throbbed. She managed to make it to the bathroom and took a look at herself. She stared at her image in the mirror. What she saw almost made her scream out loud, but instead, a single teardrop rolled slowly down her cheek. She had blood and semen everywhere below the waist, in the front and in the back. She hoped that a pregnancy wouldn't be the result of what she knew to be an act of anger. She climbed into the tub and turned on the shower to the hottest setting it had. She opened the linen closet and grabbed the little hard bristled scrub brush she used to clean all the tiles in the bathroom. She stood there and scrubbed and scrubbed till her private area was raw, and then she simply collapsed in the tub. She sat slumped over while the boiling hot water poured over her, and she wept for her innocence. Not the innocence of a child turning into a woman but the innocence of the belief that all people were good and if you didn't harm anyone no harm would come to you.

Until this happened, she had always felt protected and comfortable around people. She thought she could trust her own judgment when it came to others. Now, instead of feeling that most people were good, she now felt that everyone had the capacity to be evil—she now felt that she would never completely trust anyone again. As she sat there, her skin starting to blister, she started to think back through her life about everyone she had known or met-- were they really her friends, or were they also hiding sinister or dark thoughts? Regardless, her view of the world would never again be that of an optimist.

It was to be more than three weeks before Richard came back home, but before he did, she already knew the outcome of that terrible evening; she was pregnant. There was only one option in her mind as to what to do next. She couldn't keep this baby, not the way it had been conceived. She knew in her heart if she did that she would blame the baby and might not love it the way a good mother should. Before Richard returned, she made an appointment at a local clinic. The news wasn't good—in the state of Bavaria where she and Richard lived, one could not get an abortion for any reason, not even rape. The state of Bavaria was mostly Catholic, and that was not an option. Under her breath, in a very quiet tone, the nurse suggested that such a doctor could be found, but he was in Czechoslovakia, in a small city not necessarily known for the doctors but more known for their fine crystal. The town was Karlovy Vary; it was actually a small town nearby.

As she walked back to their apartment, she had to think of how this was to going to happen. She didn't want to wait too long. She thought about getting there and what could be her excuse to go to, of all places, Karlovy Vary. After talking to some folks at work about this town, she found out that it was the most known town for crystal and their spas. *Perfect,* she thought. She would tell Richard that she wanted to travel there to buy crystal and perhaps to take a few days to enjoy the spas there. She couldn't tell him what had happened. She knew that he would find him and kill him. He would ruin his career in the process, and she would not let that happen. She would never breathe a word of any part of this to anyone ever; through all the years she lived, she never did. She kept the deep sadness within her till she died.

Richard had been back for almost a week and a half, and she still hadn't let him know of her "crystal shopping trip." She would do it tonight. There was no more time to wait. She usually arrived home before Richard and either prepared a simple meal or ordered in. She wasn't much of a cook; it wasn't that she didn't know how, she simply didn't enjoy doing it. While she was making a big salad and going through the dialogue she was to have with her husband, in he walked. His first words were, as they had always been for the few years that they had been married, "Lucy, I'm home." For some reason, this remark always made her smile,

285

at least until now. She had just too much bottled up emotion to know how to react most of the time nowadays, and on top of all of that, to be pregnant as well.

She came to him, gave him a quick hug and said, "Go change babyness, supper is almost ready, and I really want to talk to you about a shopping trip I have planned." That was so smooth, it scared her, that she could lie so effortlessly. Hopefully this was not to become a habit; she vowed to herself that it would not.

As she talked of Czechoslovakia and the things she could buy and that she could also take a few days off to enjoy the spas, Richard was more than excited for her, but something was wrong. Something seemed so different about her, yet he couldn't put his finger on it. At work, Richard was considered the best at being able to know what a person was really thinking or feeling. Colleagues always said that it was almost as if he took an empathy pill, he was that in sync with whomever it was he was working on. But now, here with his wife, he just couldn't tell. But he knew something was amiss. She acted like she was totally excited about this trip, yet…it was an act. He wouldn't ask her, he would let her tell him when the time came. He felt confident that she would.

The day came when it was time for her to go on her first trip without him, and she was scared. She still didn't know the language and, two, scared about what was to happen to her. Richard made sure to write down all the pertinent questions she might need to ask and where she would need to change trains to get to her final destination. As he drove her to the train station, he had the gnawing feeling that something was going to go very wrong with his young wife. He wanted to stop her from going but knew that would not be the right thing to do. She would think he was babying her, and she hated that, although she loved the idea of being taken care of. He thought that maybe he could just go with her on this shopping trip so he could at least protect her from what he sensed was something very bad. He could not bear for something to happen to her, not now, not ever. As he parked her car, he walked slowly by her side instead of his usual fast-paced walk. He held her hand, trying against all odds to think of a way to stop her before putting her on that train.

As they approached the correct train track, tears appeared to be welling up in his eyes. She wondered why he looked so sad. Why did he look like he was on the verge of tears? She had never

287

seen him upset, much less crying. Could it be that he would miss her so? Or was it something deeper, something more accurate? She thought that couldn't be possible. No one knew, not her friends from work, not that asshole Garcia whom she hadn't seen since that terrible night--thank God for small favors--no one...no one but her.

As they called for her train to board, Richard grabbed his wife and hugged her tightly. He whispered something in her ear, but she wasn't sure. She thought he said, "Don't go, don't leave," but she just wasn't sure and she didn't want to, couldn't find out. She knew what she had to do, but did he? Did he know what she was about to do? It wasn't possible. Could his colleagues be right about him--how he could sense, feel what the other person was thinking and feeling? She hoped not, at least not on this one occasion.

Richard climbed up on the train with her and helped her find a little space for her small bag. This was by far the first time he had known her to pack so light. What was going on? He had to know, but he couldn't bring himself to ask the question directly.

With her planted in a little cabin alone, he walked out the

door and back onto the platform, looking at his wife through the window. She had such incredible sadness in those dark brown eyes. He wanted to break down right there and take her off that train. Would she think he had lost his mind? Would she hate him for doing that, or did she want him to stop her...but stop her from what? Shopping? No, he was just overreacting. His last trip lasted longer than he had hoped, and he could not call her the whole time he was gone. That was when he first noticed something wasn't quite right with her. The day he got back. Did something happen to her during that time? Did she need him and he wasn't there, again, because of his work? He hated himself for having that type of job where she couldn't get a hold of him. She understood, though, and accepted this kinda life. He knew a lot of women, much less a young bride, wouldn't be up for that type of marriage, but she loved him and understood. For that, he loved her more, even though he had a difficult time showing her. It was hard for him to do; it had always been. It was who he was...the way he was. That was what made him so good at what he did. He could turn off the emotions with just a thought and the next moment; empathize with what a person was feeling.

289

As the train pulled away from the tracks, she saw Richard still standing there, walking along with the train as it moved. She had never seen him quite like this before, and that made her afraid. When there wasn't any more platform for him to walk on, he finally stopped. He waved, and she saw for the first time a tear roll down his cheek as he turned to walk away. Why didn't she just tell him and have him help her with all of this? But she simply didn't want to jeopardize a wonderful and flourishing career. She knew that he would really go places, even after he retired from the military, and that one little fact, that one terrible evening would ensure he would not.

So here she was, all alone and about to go somewhere totally foreign to her to do this terrible thing. If this type of trauma doesn't make one stronger, she sure as hell didn't know what would. As the train lulled to a stop, she checked out her schedule that Richard had prepared for her. He left nothing to chance when it came to thorough directions or instructions. *Ok,* she thought, *just a quick stop here in Augsburg.* "Do not get off the train here," was what he instructed her to do--or not do, in this case. Next in store for her was a longer ride, all the way to Frankfurt. She knew that she could probably catch a few winks before getting there and changing trains. She had not slept or ate much since she found out. She was always sick to her stomach and always tired. This was so not her; she had always had a voracious appetite. Everyone warned her that it would catch up with her as she got older. She never paid them any mind and ate as she pleased, which often included a pint of ice cream almost nightly. Right now she would barf at the idea of having ice cream, but she sure wanted some fried scallops. That was the only craving her little body wanted, but where to get those pesky little scallops in the middle of Germany?

She'd never thought that her first pregnancy would turn out like this. She dreamed of being pampered and of getting the most chic of maternity outfits one could find, searching for the cutest antique furniture for the little one, of her and Richard picking out name after name until they BOTH found the perfect name for the perfect baby. But instead of that, she was hiding in baggy clothes and throwing up all day and nauseous all night, on her way to a foreign country to God only knows what.

With the steady hum of the train, she fell fast asleep; perhaps she would dream of far away places and distant music or even a little Garden of Eden she hoped to have one day or even living and working in Cuba. She had not forgotten THE sign she and Richard saw in Key West. That wonderful sign still held such fascination for her. *Maybe one day,* she thought as she drifted off...

She woke with such a start that she nearly fell off her seat. All she could hear was *"folgender Anschlag, Frankfurt."* While she was sleeping she'd heard different cities being called: Stuttgart, Heidelberg, Darmstadt, but she knew she didn't have to do anything while the train came to a stop, dropped off and picked up passengers. But this was it, her stop and she wasn't even prepared. She started to get up, straighten out her jacket and grab her little bag. She consulted the instructions Richard had prepared for her. He, himself, had taken this route to this point many times and knew from the very second her small foot hit the platform how many steps to the next train track it would be. She looked down at the map and looked at her watch. His timing was impeccable, to the minute. She walked towards the main train station and off that particular track, turned to the left and continued to walk past three tracks and stopped at the fourth, turned left and walked towards the centre of the track. He instructed that was where she was to wait for the next thirty minutes, unless the train was late. If it was late, she was to look up at the board and it would show the arrival time. She knew that "*minuten*" meant minutes, and of course, the numbers looked the same. She had several minutes to spare if she needed to go pee or get a bite to eat, per Richard's instructions.

As she got to the exact point she needed to at the exact time she needed to be there, she wondered, *What now?* Should she risk it and leave to grab something to eat? She was ok doing that, as it was all spelled out in the instructions if she chose that route. She just wasn't sure she was hungry. She was still feeling extremely queasy every single minute of every single day. She knew that she had lost at least ten pounds in the past 2 months. That surely wasn't good for anyone but especially for a woman as small as she was. The thought of having a bite to eat, then to have to run on the train and try to find the bathroom just wasn't an idea she wanted to actually take on. So she sat…and waited…for fate to help give a hand to what would happen next.

Funny thing was that during this whole "shopping" trip she felt as though someone might be following her. She knew how dumb that sounded, but she didn't care, she still felt it. She thought she might pull out her book and start reading, but her mind was too occupied with what was to happen in the next few days. She had scheduled, in her mind, the order of business. First day, get settled in pension; bed and breakfast and relax. Next morning do all the shopping needed for the shopping trip she was supposed to be on; the next day was THE day, the day that would change her life, hopefully for the better. Then the next couple of days she would take to rest in the room and not have to worry about anything but recuperating, with no questions asked of her. Then the final day back home. She thought that Richard said he would be gone on another trip by the time she returned but to make sure to leave all the stuff she bought out, so he could take a look at all the wonderful finds his wife had found for them.

The train arrived at the exact minute it was supposed to. She was always amazed by the punctuality of the Germans, her people. She knew that was where she got a lot of her good qualities. Quietly she picked up her bag and climbed up the stairs to the proper compartment. She was glad that Richard had secured her a place to sleep overnight on the train. She didn't think she could sit up all night till she got to Czechoslovakia. She got on and turned to the left and counted the compartments as she walked. When she finally got to her cabin she slid open the door only to find a kind-looking old woman. She thought maybe she had mixed up the numbers because Richard had told her that he reserved the whole cabin just for her. The little old woman smiled kindly at her and started speaking to her in German. *"Gekommen, sitzen Sie hier mit mir, den ich mit Ihnen sprechen möchte. ich verletze Sie nicht, daß ich hier bin, Ihnen zu helfen, mit Ihnen während dieser schrecklichen Zeit in Ihrem Leben zu sein. ich bin Ihr Führer. ich bin dort für Sie im Ende."*

She sat down on the opposite side from the friendly old woman and tried to tell her *"ich verstehe nicht."* She was very limited in what she could actually say to the old woman, but this one small phrase seemed to work, at least for a little while. Then quite suddenly, quicker than she would have thought an old woman could move, she was sitting right next to her and holding her hand. The smile was gone, and what replaced that beautiful smile was a look of such extreme sadness. The old woman just kept patting her hand over and over again and repeating something over and over again. It was barely a whisper. She tried hard to make out any of words, but all she could hear; thought she could hear was, "*Sie sind O.K., das Sie stark sind.*" Well, she was able to understand the OK part of it, but that was it. She thought about writing it down so she could ask Richard about this when she got back, but she thought best just to sit and try to relax. Out of the blue she just started crying. She didn't know why; well, she knew why, but she didn't know why now? Why right here, right this minute? The old woman just kept patting her hand, trying to comfort her. Strangely, she felt for the very first time that she could just totally let loose of all the emotions she had bottled up for the past two months with this old woman and so she finally did. She cried and cried for over an hour, all the while the old woman repeated the same phrase over and over.

Before she even realized it, she had fallen in a deep sleep, and when she finally woke up, she was alone. She poked her head out the glass sliding door and looked left and right, no sign of the old woman. She decided to just take a small stroll to the bathroom; *damn it, the bathroom was empty,* she said to herself. When she returned to her cabin, she saw a small wrapped box. Funny, she didn't notice it when she got up to look for the old woman. It was wrapped in the prettiest and deepest purple wrapping paper she had ever seen. There was a small note right next to the box. She wasn't sure what to do. Open it or leave it there just in case the old woman came back? She read the note over and over, trying to make out any of the words. The handwriting was so small and perfect that she had thought at first that it was typed. All it said was, "*für Sie holt es Ihnen Glück*" She thought best not to touch it and just let it sit there across from her. She looked it over and wondered, wondered who was that woman, where did she go and was this little package for her? She had not even realized how long she had actually dozed off. She looked at her watch and realized that several hours had actually passed. She couldn't believe it, she just couldn't believe it! How in the world does someone just doze off and wake up five hours later, especially since she wasn't sleepy in the first place and especially on the shoulder of a stranger, a little old woman.

As the little purple box sat there across from her, taunting her, beckoning her, she said "What the hell!" She hurriedly grabbed the little box like a child that sneaks a cookie from the cookie jar without mom's permission. She ripped open the pretty paper and found the nicest piece of white lace. It was about an inch wide and about six inches long. She didn't know what to make of any of this. What did it all mean? Was this some type of sign? What kind of sign?

She looked out the window and noticed that it had gotten dark. She guessed it might be time to get ready for a little shut-eye, even though she just wasn't tired. She knew that she was to arrive the next morning and wanted to make sure that she was refreshed. As she opened her little carry-on bag, she decided to grab the little box with the pretty paper and stuff it in the side pocket. The little piece of lace, she decided to keep that with her. Maybe it's some type of good luck charm? She didn't know or care; she loved the little piece of lace and loved the old woman who gave it to her; she didn't know why but she did.

With her pj's on, and the shade pulled down and the lights turned off, she surprisingly dozed off once more. The sleep came quickly and was filled with the strangest of dreams. It was of the old woman. This time it was just a little different. This time the whole thing was in English. It was the strangest dream she ever had. She heard the old woman say "come, sit here with me. I would like to talk with you. I won't hurt you. I am here to help you. To be with you during this terrible time in your life. I am your guide. I will be there in the end." And as the dream progressed as it had done in real life, she sat there with the old woman holding her hand and telling her that "you will be ok. You are strong." The only part that was a little different was where she fell asleep for those five hours. In the dream it was mere seconds and she woke to find the old woman gone. Even the part of not noticing the little pretty purple box was in the dream, with the little attached note. It still looked typed but it was in English; it said, "For you. It will bring you luck."

Well she was right about the idea of the lace; it was supposed to be a good luck charm, a kind of strange good luck charm, but she loved it and the old woman who gave it to her. She continued to dream about the old woman but in different locations. One location was what she thought might be her backyard. This yard was very beautiful and filled with all sorts of flowers. The garden she would dream about when she and Bobby left Cuba for Iraq. She walked in the garden with the old woman and they chatted while she puttered around. And another time when she was a few years older. This time she was kneeling over the toilet throwing up. The old woman was standing over her holding back her hair with one hand and rubbing her back with the other and saying it would be ok. That was the strangest part of the little dreams that she had. She dreamt off and on, but mostly about the old woman. Another time, the old woman was sitting on the edge of the bed and Bobby was sitting on a chair close to the fireplace, by Elle's side. The old woman was talking to her while she lay there resting. Bobby didn't seem to pay the old woman any mind and kept to his reading, although he did get up once to check to see if Elle was ok. He had thought he heard an old woman talking but paid no never mind and went back to his reading.

For some reason, she woke up and it was a bright sunny day. She thought about last night's dream and wondered about the old woman. How very strange that whole incident and dream turned out to be. She wondered if it was a premonition. She also wondered about the part about throwing up and why the woman was there at that time. Well, none of this mattered right now. All she knew was that she had better start getting ready for the day.

This was the beginning of what would be a very strange week for her. She hoped all would go well. She had gotten the name of the doctor from the nurse in the clinic she had gone to. It was all very whispered talks and hushed tones. She didn't know what to think of that but thanked the nurse. She had also asked the nurse if she would do her a favor and call to make the appointment. The nurse agreed but told her she would have to do that after her shift was over. She promised to call her at home with the details. Luckily for her, the nurse spoke English and seemed to be very understanding about the whole ordeal or at least the part she knew of.

As the train rolled into Karlovy Vary, Czechoslovakia she realized how ready she was to get this mess over with. She would start anew. She would not trust anyone ever again. She now believed--correction, knew--that all people had the potential to be evil. EVERYONE! Before the train came to a halt, she consulted her notes once more. This part of the trip Richard wasn't 100% sure of but he did the best with what little information he had. Richard had told her that there are always taxis in the front of the train station and all she had to do was hand the driver the handwritten address, and he would take her exactly where she would be staying. The hotel would be able to supply her with the directions to get to the shopping district of the town. Richard had made the reservations for her, and he found out that there was someone there who spoke very good English.

She walked past the train and into the main terminal and out the doors to the taxi stand where she flagged down the next available taxi, handed him the note and off she went. Less than ten minutes later, she was there in the front of a beautiful old pension, bed and breakfast. There were other more fancy hotels but she liked the quaintness of this better. She paid the taxi cab driver and asked him if he could return the next morning at 7am sharp. She didn't know where the clinic was but showed him the address. He looked up at her and frowned, said he would be there. She wondered what in the hell was that all about. Why the strange frown. She didn't know the city that well, but from the looks of it, it was very nice; kind of modern for such an old city. She waved goodbye and walked into the pension, Pension Kucera. As she stood there while the taxi pulled off, she noticed that this little guest house, this pension, was located in the centre of the spa area, in a place the history of which dated back to 1715. The original name of the pension was "At the Three Moors."

At the reception area, she gave her name. To her surprise, the man behind the counter spoke perfect English and welcomed her to his and his wife's pension. If she needed anything, absolutely anything, please let him or his wife know. She had told him that she needed a few directions and perhaps a timeframe for how long it would take to go to this certain part of the city. She would come back down as soon as she freshened up. He walked her up the stairs and opened the door to the most beautiful little room she had ever seen. It looked like it had come straight from a fairy tale book. She thanked him and attempted to tip him, but he refused, walked away and closed the door behind him. She just stood there staring at the little room. She had been in grand hotels that oozed money before, but this was different, this was better, at least to her. She loved the little room and wanted to stay just there and nowhere else. She didn't want to do anything else but lie on the most comfy-looking bed she had ever seen. There was a big fluffy white down comforter on the bed. It felt like a cloud, even softer than anything she had ever felt; even softer than any of her cashmere sweaters. But she knew she had things to do this very first day, lots to accomplish to make the story complete. It wouldn't work well if she were to come home empty–handed, and she really didn't think she would be up for a lot of activity after it was all over. She needed that time to rest, and this was the perfect place for it.

After getting unpacked and a quick touch-up to her face and hair, she walked down the flight of stairs back to the reception area. Before asking the owner the needed questions, she asked if she might just walk around the pension and grounds. He, of course, agreed cheerfully. As she wandered around, she noticed that near the guesthouse, there were a covered thermal pool, a golf course and tennis courts, a sauna, a museum, a theatre and other cultural facilities and services (massages, hair-dresser, sale of souvenirs, etc.). She later found out that they did spa treatments in specialized spa houses close to the guesthouse, "according to the requirements of our guests," so said the owner. She had also found out that before this current owner, in 1909, an owner named Chief Building Councillor Strüdel pulled the 150-year old house down and a new Art Nouveau styled house was built up on the site. The construction was performed by Bedrich Ohmann, a well known architect of Prague, the builder of the Castle Colonnade.

The proprietor was still there smiling all the while. He called for his wife so she could meet the nice American lady who would be staying with them for a week. Everyone made introductions and asked if she needed anything right now. She asked for directions to the shopping district and was glad to find out that it was within walking distance. Then she asked about the neighborhood she was to go to tomorrow. Both radiant smiles turned to frowns. The very exact expression the taxi cab driver gave her.

"What is wrong? Is it too far away to go?"

The husband/wife team looked at each other and then at her, not knowing exactly what to tell her.

She waited for what seemed to be several minutes. She couldn't take the suspense any longer and asked them again. Maybe she pronounced the name of the neighborhood incorrectly. She showed the couple the address. Something about that address really upset people. The wife excused herself and disappeared in the back somewhere. She finally asked the man again, "Is there anything wrong?"

He motioned for her to take a seat in the small living room. He sat very close to her and spoke in the same hushed tones that the nurse had done at the clinic. She was starting to get spooked by all of this but couldn't let anything deter her from her visit tomorrow.

He finally looked up at her and said, "Miss, you don't want to go to that neighborhood. There is nothing for you there. Nothing. " She pleaded with her eyes to tell her more of this neighborhood. He continued, "That is what you call the bad side of the street, I think you Americans call it. It is where there are women who walk the streets looking for dates, if you know what I mean, miss. That is no place for a respectable woman. They too have doctors there that take care of accidents." He said that last word in such a confusing tone that she wasn't sure if he meant like an emergency doctor or the type of doctor she needed to see. It didn't matter to her. She didn't know what else to do or where else to go.

She looked at him with determination and conviction. "How far is it from here?"

He looked shocked that she still wanted information about

306

such a place but answered her, "Only about forty-five minute drive, miss. Shall we call you a taxi?"

She thought about that for a second and then took him up on the offer. "Yes, please for tomorrow for 7am."

He walked away with his head bowed down and went to the back to talk to his wife and to make the call.

She decided she just wasn't going to think of any of this and just go out today and do her shopping. She didn't want to think of this talk for one second. As she strolled out to the street, she flagged down a taxi, and asked him if he could take her down to the shopping district. She wasn't sure what to buy this warm sunny day. She'd told Richard that she was coming here to get crystal but what type? Glasses, chandeliers; maybe both. She knew she would be able to mail back the chandeliers and maybe the glasses so she wouldn't have to carry around a bunch of heavy items. The streets of modern-day Karlovy Vary were shabby at best, but she could still see vivid reminders of days gone by. The glory days appeared to be long over. There seemed to be a few superficial changes that the Communists made; they spent little new investment in the town, and it appeared that the buildings were literally crumbling

307

behind their beautiful facades which were mostly decorated with stucco. But she thought the town was beautiful. The architecture was beautiful. Everything was beautiful here…but her. She felt like a used-up piece of dog meat.

She needed to get her mind off of what was to happen to her tomorrow and also the conversation she'd had with the owner of the pension, so she kept walking, just aimlessly walking. She had heard of a few museums in the area and thought she should give those a try. As she walked through the town, she saw the Spires of the Byzantine-style Orthodox Church, St. Peter and Paul, that had once been visited by Czar Peter the Great. The museum she found first was called the *Krajské Museum*. She walked in, paid the small fee and strolled around, not really looking at anything, just strolling. She usually loved going to museums and art galleries, but for some reason--a reason she knew in her heart-- she just couldn't get into it so she left. Back in the shopping district, she entered the first crystal shop she came to: La Bootik Perl & Co. She immediately found the wine glasses she wanted to buy, ordered a set of twelve and moved on to the next store. This one had the most beautiful Swarovski chandeliers. She couldn't take her eyes off of any of them. They were breathtaking. Little prisms of light flickered everywhere; all the colors of the rainbow could be seen. She wanted them all but settled on just one, a perfect chandelier for their dining room. It was an eighteen-bulb chandelier and it was incredibly "cute." This was a word she used often for things that she really wanted. For her, that would mean it was the epitome of the perfect whatever it was she was talking about. She hoped that Richard would love it as much as she did.

For just a moment she forgot her troubles but was then reminded by the queasiness that started in her still-flat tummy. She realized that she had not eaten in over a day and a half so she hurried on with her purchase so she could grab just a small bite to eat. She had been told not to eat or drink anything past 9pm this evening. As she passed on her address to the owner of the shop, she thought she saw the old woman out of the corner of her eye. She quickly turned around but saw no one. Just her imagination running wild, she thought. As she walked out the door, she needed to take a deep breath to calm her unsettled tummy. She looked around and was amazed once again at the beauty this city held. She had to admit, before this trip she didn't know a whole lot about this town other than the German name for it was Karlsbad and for its most famous Bohemian spa.

The town was named for the bohemian king and German and holy Roman Emperor Charles (Karl) IV who allegedly found the springs in 1358. The owner was very forthcoming when it came to information about his lovely pension. She later would learn that the owner of this very pension would have a grandson whom she would meet much later on in Iraq, on her second tour there, of all places.

With all her shopping done, she decided to find a small café and get a sandwich and maybe some warm milk, if possible. She found a corner café and took a seat outside in the sun. This café looked as if it belonged in a movie. It had all the fixings: red and white checkered tablecloth, small empty bottle of vino for a vase and a big store front window with a red awning. As she looked in the window to see the layout of the actual café, she could see straight across the street from where she was sitting. That same old woman was there on the other side of the sidewalk. She quickly turned to look but couldn't see her, so see turned her head back to the store front window. Nothing; nothing in the reflection from the glass. She started to really think she was losing her mind, so she thought best just to look at the menu.

She was happy to see that it was in German. Since she was able to read most German menus, ordering would be a breeze. For some reason, she just didn't feel up to it. She was very upset about these sightings of the old woman. Maybe she was just tired. She sure felt tired all the time and she wanted to sleep all the time as well. She had taken a couple of weeks off of work to be able to recuperate from this ordeal, and she would need every single day of it.

She decided to just get up and go back to her room to rest for the trauma of tomorrow. She thought she would try to walk back to the pension instead of flagging down a taxi. As she walked back, the wind started to pick up a bit. Just then a chill ran down her spine. It felt as though very cold hands had been placed on both of her shoulders in some type of death grip. She kept walking faster and faster. She needed to get inside and out of the cold. She finally decided to flag down a taxi to take her the rest of the way. As she climbed into the taxi she looked at the mirror to see that it was the same taxi cab driver who had dropped her off this morning. He too recognized her at that same instant. The smile of recognition in his eyes turned to what appeared to be that of worry. He said something to her but she didn't understand. She decided to just not do anything but sit and look down; no eye contact. She felt spooked as it was. When the taxi came to a halt, she gave the driver the fare, but as she reached over to put the money in his hand, he held hers in his and looked her dead on in the eyes.

"Don't do it, miss. Don't go there. I cannot take you to this place."

She yanked her hand away and left him all the money, which was beyond the amount owed, but she didn't care. She just had to get out of there and back to the comfort of her room.

As she climbed the steps to her pension, she felt compelled to turn around but did not. She was afraid of what she might see if she did, so she literally ran up the stairs, past the reception, up a flight of stairs and straight into her room. She closed and locked the door quickly and leaned against the door, just standing there and shaking like a leaf. Why was she so frightened? Ok, sure a couple of folks had warned her of this neighborhood that she was going to visit tomorrow, but this guy was a doctor for god sakes.

He was a man of medicine, dedicated to saving lives, and she felt that everything would be ok. Really, what could go wrong?

A warm soapy bath was in order. She took out her pj's and toiletries, filled the tub and waited. She looked around the room to see if there was perhaps a radio that she could find a nice radio station to turn to. Nothing, no radio, no TV. This place was for total relaxation with no outside interruptions. She thought the idea of using the spas would be great but wasn't sure it that would be possible after her procedure. She would ask the doctor what he thought.

When the tub was full, she slipped in and moved some of the bubbles over. The water felt great on her chilled skin. Soon she would get in the zone of relaxation and push all the negative vibes out of her mind and body. She was ready for what was going to happen. The nurse had told her what was to happen, what she would hear and how it would feel, to a certain extent. She came prepared; she was not going to be deterred by anyone. After a nice long soak, she toweled off and put on her pj's. She thought about writing down the exact address and phone number to where she was going tomorrow just in case the owners didn't see her come back. She thought that might be a little paranoid, but all the talk had spooked her a little too much. She would leave it on the reception desk when she left in the morning.

As soon as she laid her head on the pillow she was out. She had a mixture of weird images, not dreams really, just images. For some reason she woke up refreshed promptly at 6am. She just took a quick shower to calm down her hair and brushed her teeth. She didn't do anything else. She slipped on a nice pair of sweat pants and sweat shirt with a clean t-shirt underneath. She didn't think she could actually put on slacks and blouse as she had first thought. The outfit was nice and clean, and she didn't want to stand out too much amongst the locals. She looked around the room to see if she had everything she needed. She sure was thirsty. She wanted her morning Dr. Pepper in the worst way but was told no eating and no drinking at least twelve hours before the procedure. She grabbed her purse, opened it and made sure she had the $500.00 needed and also some Tylenol just in case she was headachy later on.

She took one last look in and closed the door, walked down to the lobby and left the address and phone number of where she would be for at least five hours. The owner didn't look up; he just

314

took the card and turned away. She sat in the lobby for about a half hour when a taxi cab pulled up. She got up, grabbed her purse and looked back. The owner looked over at her and quickly turned around, not saying a single word. She hopped in the back seat of the cab and handed the address to the taxi cab driver. He eyed her from his rearview mirror, smirked, gave her back the address and sped off. Oh how she wished she would be there already and get away from this sleazy cab driver. He was giving her the creeps. As the minutes past, she could see the difference in scenery. What an ungodly difference a fifteen minute drive made. It was dark and seedy-looking. She didn't see any of the women who walked the streets looking for dates, as the owner of the pension had mentioned.

The taxi cab came to a screeching halt, which almost threw her into the front seat. She looked up at him and realized that he was smiling at her, or was it a smirk? Either way, she didn't care; she gave him the money and jumped out of the cab. He sped off and left her standing right there in the middle of nowhere. Well, somewhere, but not anywhere she knew. She looked at all the buildings. They were old, worn-down and dirty. She didn't see a

315

clinic anywhere. She walked a little bit and looked for numbers on the doors. Finally she saw a very small sign that looked about as grungy as anything she had ever seen. She tried to open the door, but it seemed to be locked so she hit the buzzer.

Someone on the other side said, "What do you want?" in English. She was taken aback by such a gruff greeting. She gave her name and told the rude person that she had an appointment; she was buzzed in. She had not noticed which floor he was on but hoped that he would have a "shingle" hanging outside the door like in the U.S. No such luck, just a piece of paper taped to the door. She was scared, very scared, but didn't know what else to do but go in and hope for the best.

The floors were sticky and blackened by dirt and grime. As she opened the door, she quickly scanned the room for any sense of professionalism. There was none. There wasn't even a reception area, only an old desk, an operating table and a few medical instruments. No nurse, no anesthesiologist; just this grimy-looking doctor; at least she hoped he was a doctor, standing there looking her up and down.

With the same gruff attitude he had on the speaker, he said,

"Before you take off all of your clothes and get on the table, my fee is 500 U.S. dollars. It is to be paid before this procedure." She started to tremble as she opened her purse and handed him the wad of bills. She wanted to cry, she wanted to run screaming from this terrible place, but she had nowhere to go, no one to take care of this problem. So she stayed.

She asked if he had at least a dressing gown to cover with or a sheet. He looked her up and down and told her, "I've seen it all before. You have nothing to hide from me, I am doctor."

She slowly approached the table and found that it was covered with a somewhat clean sheet. She decided that she would just take it off the table and use it to cover herself. He looked at her and just shook his head. At least he had the decency to turn around while she undressed. At the desk he counted his money, shoved it in his pocket and then came towards her. He told her to relax and put her feet in the stirrups. He slipped on his surgical gloves without washing his hands. She lay back and tried to take herself out of her body and float away like she had done the time this all had happened, but it just didn't work, try as she might. She couldn't tell exactly what he was doing. All she knew was that he

317

was rough with her and did not even try to attempt to be gentle.

He spread her legs wide and pushed something inside of her. It was made of metal and very cold. Then she felt something compared to a sharp twitch inside her, coming from the walls of her uterus. It was almost a scraping feeling but caused waves of cramps like she had never had. She lay there with tears streaming down her face but making sure not to say anything. She was so very cold and scared, but she let him do what he needed or wanted to do. It was like he was yanking all the flesh from her insides, and the cramping was horrendous. She tried very hard not to move as the waves of cramps hit. She didn't want him to mess up anything on the inside. She was a young woman and still thought she had time to have kids later on, maybe in her 30's. He then took a vacuum-like tool and stuck that inside her as well. He flipped a switch, and the shrrrrrrrrrr sound it made was deafening. She felt that her insides were being sucked out now. She didn't think she could take another second of it and was ready to jump off the table and run, if she could.

Just when she thought she would pass out from the sheer pain, the shrrrrring sound stopped, and he yanked out the hose from inside of her.

He stood up and took off his bloody gloves. He told her to just lay there for a little while; he had forgotten something. She lay there shaking and crying and crying and shaking. She couldn't control either one. When he returned, she looked up to see that he had a big wad of gauze. She sure as hell didn't know anything about this part. The nurse had not mentioned any of this and, in particular, the wad of gauze. She could only imagine where that was going. She hoped that he would just use it as a "pad" of sorts, to take the place of a Kotex or something. She was craning her neck up so much that he had to tell her to lie back down. He took the wad and stuffed every bit of it inside of her. He asked her if she had worn panties, and if so she needed to put them on. He was done and she could go ahead and leave. No medication for pain, no waiting to see how she would react; just leave.

He went to another room as she tried to get herself up from the table, from this nightmare. She made her way to her clothes neatly folded on the floor. She slipped on her panties. At this point, she thought she was going to pass out but steadied herself on the table. There would be nothing that would make her happier than to leave this ugly place, and she couldn't dress fast enough. When she had all of her belongings, she walked unsteadily to the door; tears still ran uncontrollably down her cheeks. She made her way down the stairs and to the street. Surprisingly, a taxi was waiting right there. She hoped that the doctor had called the taxi for her and that he wasn't waiting on another passenger. She poked her head towards the driver and asked if he was available; he nodded yes. She didn't know why she didn't instantly notice the old woman in the back seat, but there she was smiling a very sad smile at her.

She was so happy to see this woman. Just to have a familiar face was all she wanted at this point. The taxi cab driver looked back at her with sad eyes and started to drive. The old woman took her hand and said *"Sie sind gut, es sein rüber jetzt"* over and over in such a soothing tone that she couldn't help but lay her head upon the old woman's shoulder and fall gently asleep.

Chapter 11 -- First Day of Work

With a loud scream, she woke up and realized that she had almost fallen off her cot. She looked around and realized that she was in her jail cell bedroom in Abu G, Iraq. She thought how spartan her living quarters were and how, at times, it seemed quite appealing. The simplicity with which she had to break down her life and daily habits…if even the least bit spiritual at all would always serve as a reminder of how small daily details can give the pleasure of peacefulness.

She realized that her roommates were "going to town" with their friends. One of the couples was getting a tad rough and screamed a little too loud but didn't stop their activities. She decided to get up and take a walk while the couples finished off. She couldn't believe they were all still going at it. How long had she dozed off and dreamed about that time in her life, that terrible point where everything changed for her, the time when she realized that she couldn't trust a soul, no one--that was, until Bobby. She found new hope and true love with him. She knew that down deep she never trusted her second husband or loved him for that matter. Trust hadn't come back to her until Bobby, and with trust came love. She took the long walk to the porta jons, and that was when she decided that she had to tell Bobby something of this Garcia fellow. But she didn't want to tell him everything. She wanted and had to keep some of this to herself forever, the part that was so incredibly disgusting, even to her.

It wasn't that she didn't trust him, she did to the utmost. It was that this part of her she never wanted to share, with no one, not even Bobby. She would tell him later on this morning, perhaps before work. She still had a lot going on work-wise trying to track AMZ down. The longer she stayed in this place, the closer she felt to him, which was eerily comforting to her.

At this hour of the morning, the Iraqi air was still and quiet, surprisingly quiet. It was so peaceful here for a change. She walked slowly down the corridor and thought she heard the faintest of footsteps behind her. They did not seem threatening in the least, just another person having to pee in the middle of the night, or morning as it were. She started to think about the research she would do later on this morning. She also wanted to remind herself to check the email to see what the company thought of the email she had sent the day before. Hopefully they would pull Harris out of this place before he could do anything else.

As she neared the porta jons, she felt the need to look behind her. Just as she thought, some guy still in his uniform needing to pee just like her. No sooner than she sat on the toilet, it hit her about the soldier behind her. She thought the guy with the uniform was also wearing a red and white Jordanian yashmak with ekal. She felt compelled to poke her head out the door just a tad, but here she was with her sweatpants down to her ankles. So instead she tried to hurry herself up so she could check this out again, just to make certain. Before she was through peeing, she heard someone incredibly close to the little room she was occupying. It sounded like someone was actually circling the porta jon she was in. She sat very still and tried to control her fear, but she could feel her heart racing a mile a minute, thumping so hard it felt it would jump straight out of her rib cage.

Then all of a sudden, whoever it was circling, stopped dead in his tracks right in front of her door. Oh god, she was scared shitless; *no pun intended,* she thought to herself. She didn't know what to do--fling the door open and hope to hit someone smack dab in the face or wait to see if they leave and god only knew how long she would have to be in there if she chose that as an option. She tried to look through the little rivets in the door, no luck. She held onto the little plastic circular lock for dear life, hoping against hope that whoever it was would leave.

Then quite suddenly she heard a voice. If she was not mistaken, it was Harris. She could hear him but not words, not understanding the words. He was talking to the other person, the one standing right in front of her door. All she could hear was mumbling. What was Harris doing out there especially at this hour of the night? Had he been lurking around waiting for her to come out so he could do something hateful? Well, someone else was there with him. Surely he wouldn't do anything to her with witnesses around. But then again, it sounded like they were talking like they were familiar with each other.

She could take the suspense no longer and just yelled out

the door at the both of them, *"Obtenez l'enfer parti de ma porte ou je vais crier!"* With that, it got quiet and she could hear two sets of footsteps walking briskly away from her and towards the prison. She wasn't sure if this was a good thing or not but decided to go ahead and make a run for it.

She would push her door open hard and fast, just in case someone was still standing there. Hopefully that would catch whoever it was offguard. Then she was going to run like she never ran before! She sat there, listening...listening to every single sound out there. When she was finally satisfied that no one could be there, she pushed the door open hard and fast and pretty much flung herself out of there and down the hall before she realized that there were two military police standing there in the hall way. They continued running towards her and asked if she was ok, but she just kept running like her life depended on it. As far as she was concerned, it did.

As she sprinted the long hallway, she took a quick look back, only to realize that she was being chased by the two military policemen, MPs. They almost fell on top of her as she came to a dead halt. All three were out of breath. They asked her if she was ok, and she told them what she had seen and heard. They looked at each other quizzically. They had no idea what she was talking about. They had been standing in the hallway for a good half hour or so. They told her that they were on their way to start their shift but waiting for the third MP to show up. She looked at them like they were speaking a foreign language; she just didn't understand what was going on. She thanked them for their concern, but she was probably just dreaming or something.

She walked slowly away down the stretch of the corridor till she got to her block. She looked to the left and to the right. She still felt some type of presence with her, and it wasn't a good feeling; nothing to the left and nothing to the right. Before she climbed the very steep stairs up to her cell room, she stopped at the community fridge and grabbed her Dr. Pepper, took several sips and screwed the cap back on. She mumbled to herself, "Boy, I am losing control. I am going mad, I am simply going mad."

As the word "mad" came out of her mouth the second time, she thought she heard something like labored breathing. It felt so very close to her. She could almost feel it on her neck. She thought instead of doing the obvious, like yelling or running, she would

326

just walk along like nothing was the least bit wrong. Perhaps it would just go away or at least show itself to her. She was tired of all of this hiding behind the shadows bullshit. Of course she didn't feel this brave twenty minutes ago when she was trapped in the porta jon, but oh well. The breathing was hot and definitely labored, like a person who was out of shape and had been running! *Hmm, so that is where they went to so quickly.* They probably took the other door in and split up, each one going in a different direction, and now one of them was near her. She decided to just stand there in the semi darkness and ask a simple question.

"What do you want?" That was all she could think of asking: short, sweet and to the point. For just a second she thought she heard something, some kind of movement to her left. She waited. As she looked in darkness of the cell block that had the only light coming from the floor below, she thought she caught a glimpse of something there in the corner. She walked towards the darkness. She was tired of what she thought was running away from situations. She had been creeped out since she started her quest for AMZ. Her mind was starting to pay for all her long hours of work on him. If it was him in the shadows, so be it!

Before walking any closer to the darkness, she was positive about only one thing, and that was that she didn't want to leave a very large, what she liked to call, an energy mark here in this place. She knew that everyone left an energy mark everywhere they went in life, but if you make an impact, a most traumatic impact especially, you leave the biggest mark of all. She didn't want to leave the biggest one here in this cell block at Abu Ghraib. She walked closer and could feel the hair on her arms shoot straight up; still nothing but darkness. She didn't know what to make of this, so she just pressed on and continued down the corridor to her room. Before going inside, she turned completely around and stood there, looking at all four corners of this cell block. At the edge of the railing, she looked to the floor below. Nothing, a big fat nothing! She was almost disappointed instead of glad that she wasn't being hunted down.

As she slowly and quietly stepped into her little jail cell, she thanked God that the crazy shenanigans that had been going on in here had finally stopped. It was almost 5:30am; only about an hour left before her alarm went off. She thought that maybe she should just get up and shower and get on with her first day of

328

work, but she had no way to let Bobby know that she had gone on without him. And they were all to meet in the front of HQ as a team. "HA!" she said to herself. Instead, she laid her head back down on her favorite little pillow and started her peaceful descent into the most relaxing sleep she had ever had. She had the sleep of a child; unfettered, undisturbed and uncomplicated, just peaceful sleep. Unlike most other nights, she had no dreams she could remember when she awoke exactly one hour later without the help of her alarm clock, just deep peaceful sleep for an hour straight.

As she walked out of her little cell to take her shower, she looked at her little bag to make sure she had everything she needed: towel, soap, shampoo, blow dryer, deodorant; yup, she had everything. She walked out the door and looked to the left and to the right; just to make sure. It was hard to believe she had such drama only an hour ago. It felt like she had slept all night long instead of getting into all sorts of craziness half the early morning. She started to doubt that any of it actually happened. It was just too weird how refreshed she felt at this hour of the morning. As she came out of the cell, she paid special attention to all the little dark shadows that seemed to overtake the area at night. She wanted to

329

see the lay of the land, just in case. Ok, nothing to trip on or stumble over in any of the corners. She took special care looking in the one corner in particular, the one in which she had felt the presence of someone less than an hour ago. Not a thing there, just emptiness. It was the corner closest to that incredibly steep staircase. She hated coming up and down those damn stairs. She just knew that no good had happened there before and probably would happen again, just hopefully not to her.

As she strolled down the corridor towards the women's shower trailer, she continued to get the lay of the land. "One never knows", she said out loud to no one in particular. Today was going to be a great day, she thought. She felt refreshed and ready to make a serious impact at work, her first day at work at Abu Ghraib. She was also excited to see what her company had to say about Harris. She knew that the news would be good; how could it not? Everyone could see the craziness taking over in that man. She showered her three-minute combat shower, as they're called, blow-dried a lot of the moisture out of her hair but not completely. It was only 6:30 in the morning and had gotten up to 85 degrees. Other than a little moisturizer and lip gloss, she went sans makeup; much too hot to bother with the "war paint." She wasn't really the kinda woman who liked to go around with a "mask" on unless it was for a night on the town, and it had been forever since she'd done that.

She headed back to her little cell, passing Bobby as he was headed to the showers. They stopped, kissed and a quick hug before going about their business. She told him that she was going to get quickly dressed and head over to the internet café, and he should meet her there when he was done, then they could come back to meet the others at 8:00 sharp. He balked at the idea and told her that he couldn't bear to be away from her any more than he absolutely had to. She smiled, gave him a quick kiss on the cheek and said that she would be back here in precisely 20 minutes. He rushed by her and said that wouldn't be a problem.

She quickly dressed and went downstairs to wait for Bobby. As she sat there reading her notes from the day before, she saw a shadowy figure above her book. She wasn't the least bit scared, so why did her skin begin to crawl? She looked up and saw him standing so close above her that his leg was actually touching her knee. She was stuck there sitting on this bench with out any place to move away from him. He just looked down at her and smiled.

"We are meant to be, Layla; accept it, I have." She knew that no one ever used that nickname but Richard and the thought of him using it, even mockingly, was an insult to her, much like his presence.

"Look Garcia, leave me the hell alone. I don't have anything to say to you. The days of me pretending to be nice to you are long gone, much like you should be right now."

She was usually much cleverer with the words, but for some reason she really didn't know how to handle this situation or the emotions she was now feeling for this man. As she stood up to leave, he attempted to press his body against hers. At that point, any passerby who didn't know what was going on would have thought that something good was happening between these two, just as Bobby initially did when he opened the door and saw the two of them nearly joined together. Garcia jumped away, all the while looking very sheepish, and she blushed a deep shade of red as if she had got caught doing something bad. Bobby didn't know what to say or do. It looked like his wife was pressed up against this stranger. Well not a stranger to her, obviously, but definitely a stranger to Bobby.

She didn't know what to say or do at that point. She could see the questions forming in Bobby's mind right about now, and she sensed he thought there was more between the two of them than really was. She grabbed Bobby's balled-up fist and led him out of the prison towards the internet café.

He finally asked, "What the hell was going on back there?"

He sounded pissed, but he had no reason to be. She wanted to explain everything, to tell him everything. She decided to tell him just enough. She didn't want to share her disgusting shame with anyone, not even Bobby. She decided to just tell him the basics of the story. Tell how they met, that he wanted to be more than colleagues but she was married and that was that. She never told him that the so-called doctor in Czechoslovakia had butchered her insides so badly that she couldn't have any children. That would be too much for him to put his arms around; that was just too much truth there to swallow for some.

She told the story to Bobby; he sensed there was more, a helluva lot more than that. He decided not to press, for now. In time she would trust him enough to tell the whole story. For now, he knew this guy was bugging his wife and that had to stop right here and now. Initially Bobby was a little scared that there was some mutual attraction from each of them, but as she told the story to him, he could see that it was definitely just one-sided. Bobby wanted to know more; he could see and feel the pain behind his wife's lovely brown eyes. What happened? What did he do to her? He could tell it was not good. He felt it in his own heart, as if it had happened to him directly.

As she and Bobby neared the internet café, they decided to take one machine this time, read their mail and hightail it back to HQ so they wouldn't be late. It wouldn't look very professional to be late on the first day of work. She logged in and saw that the company didn't write them back.

"How odd," she said to Bobby.

"Well, they have to decide how to first fix their mess, I guess, before emailing back," Bobby replied. He told her that they probably finally realized that the sexual harassment of the young Army girl being swept under the rug wasn't such a hot idea after all. Surely, by the time they get off work, there would be news. So they logged off and held hands all the way back to HQ.

The other team made their way out to the meeting point. Everyone exchanged good morning pleasantries, everyone, that is, but Harris. For Harris was nowhere to be found. Even the asshole Garcia was there. True, it wasn't 8:00 yet, but Harris was really cutting it close. He had five minutes to hightail it out here. Bobby said he would run back to his room to check to see what was going on, since they shared a room.

Bobby went back and, low and behold, Harris lay there on his cot like a beached whale. This little sight made Bobby smirk more than just a little. *Classic, so classic,* was all he could think of Harris. One thing was strange, though, Harris had on all his clothes, and his boots close by were covered in mud. *Strange, something about this picture is very strange.*

Bobby yelled, "Harris, get your ass up. You're late and we are all waiting for you in front of HQ."

Back with the group, he reported exactly what he saw. This pretty much pissed off the ole sarge, and that too made Bobby smirk. In fact, his wife was smirking herself.

Garcia said to everyone, "We will leave in five minutes, so if there's anything last minute you need to do, do it!" Everyone

335

stood in place, everyone ready but Harris. And five minutes later, there was Harris with his t-shirt hanging out of his pants and his boots not even laced up. He was a disgrace, and for some reason, he didn't feel that he needed to shower, shave or change. He'd worn those same clothes for the past four days; four days without showering. *Disgusting,* she thought, *totally disgusting.*

At the chow hall, Garcia gave them the chance to check mail or grab some breakfast. The power couple, having checked their mail, decided on a nice big breakfast. Harris slid in to check his mail, again with that smug look on his face. The couple looked at each other and said, "Something is up!" right at the same time.

All during breakfast they were laughing and cooing with each other like teenagers in love, and Garcia hated every second of it. He waited for them to sit down first. He didn't want to sit with them but wanted to sit close enough to watch them, to see how they act together, to see if they were in love. At first he'd thought they weren't and, of course, with the episode from this morning, he could see that husband of hers thought that something was going on between them. Garcia liked that idea a lot. Garcia decided right then and there to make sure he did that often, just to keep the ole man wondering and questioning their love. *Hey, it might even break them up, and I would have a chance,* he thought to himself.

After about 45 minutes, the group set off for their actual job site and to be introduced to the people they would spend the next three months with. Everyone was divided into teams. She and Bobby worked well together and enjoyed it immensely, but the powers that be decided to split the pair up. Within their respective first hour of work, they sat in on an interrogation and started working on whatever was needed for both of their teams. Harris, on the other hand, spent the day on the unclassified computer emailing God only knew. He did no work to speak of. He was assigned to a team like the rest but spent no time with that team. He did a lot of bullshitting with the guys in charge, as if he was one of them, instead of a worker bee like her and Bobby. The couple didn't care, they were here to work and work they did.

While Harris left precisely at 4:30pm, she and Bobby kept going. They both had much to do and not that much time to do it in. At 7:30 or so, she looked over at Bobby as he was pouring over a huge book. He wasn't crazy about the research part, but he did it well. She could see how tired his normally bright blue eyes were.

She came over to him and said, "Come on, baby doll, its martini time." The look of excitement lit his eyes for only a second, then he realized that there would be no martinis here, not in Abu Ghraib, and especially not in a war zone, that was for sure.

The pair decided to grab some chow to go, eat in and watch a movie in the day room instead of joining the hundreds of men and women at the chow hall this evening. Just a little quiet alone time would be refreshing, they both thought. After grabbing some snacks to go from the chow hall, Bobby walked with her towards the day room which was just downstairs from her jail cell.

"Meetcha back here in 10," she said as she climbed those stupid stairs.

"Ok, later, baby doll."

As she neared her door, she heard the sounds of yet more hanky panky in the room. "Geez-us Christ," she said out loud. "You have got to be fucking kidding me here." She said it loud so both her roommates could hear over the moaning and groaning. She grabbed her sweat pants, t-shirt, socks and running shoes and left them to do what seemed to be the only thing they knew how to do. She walked briskly down the stairs and almost fell but was able

338

to grab the rail in the nick of time.

Bobby was already sitting there on the couch trying to figure out the portable DVD player and TV combination. He looked up and realized how pissed off she looked. She hadn't told him that this crap had been going on morning, noon, and night since she moved in with the two of them. She even forgot to tell him about the incident at the porta jon as well. There was just too much stuff occupying her mind these past couple of days. She told Bobby that she was going over to the women's shower trailer to change into her sweats and she would be right back. He asked if she wanted company for the walk over there, but she told him that wouldn't be necessary.

When she returned, she and Bobby sat close together on the big old ratty couch and watched a couple of movies while feeding each other snacks off and on. Although it had been a very long hard day at work, they both felt extremely good about what they'd accomplished. A good contribution, they felt. As the second movie neared the end, she told Bobby that she was pooped and would try to sleep if only there was some peace and quiet upstairs. He told her that he would bring his cot over to the hallway of the day room and watch over her so she could try to get some sleep on the ratty couch. She loved the idea but thought it best just to suck it up and go back to her noisy jail cell. They hugged tight and parted, she to climb up those creepy stairs as Bobby walked down the hall to the left.

Half way up those stairs, she thought best to stay there on the couch. She knew she didn't see the two friends "with benefits" depart. Since there was only one way out of there, she would have had to see them leave. She had her little favorite pillow and a comforter and was just about to cocoon herself in, but before doing so, she got up quick for one last big swallow of her leftover Dr. Pepper from the fridge. She jumped back on the couch and started the cocooning all over. She drifted off to sleep so quickly she thought she had to have been drugged because she never just dozed off quick like that.

She did feel a bit weird when she finished off the Dr. Pepper but tried to push it from her mind. All she knew was that while she was passed out she had the worst dreams--dreams like the time back in Germany. She tried to wake herself up but couldn't. All she could see was Garcia on top of her, prying her

340

clothes off. She tried to scream, but he had his hand pushed so tightly across her mouth, no one would have been able to hear a peep. This nightmare she was having--Garcia was done with her and up and left her there half dressed. She felt like she was in a never-ending nightmare. Then next thing she knew, she was climbing those awful steps up to her room, swollen, bruised and bleeding. Was it a dream or was this really happening? She felt so weird, like she had been drugged, but how and why? She got to the door of her jail cell and all was dark and quiet inside for a change. She just wanted to grab her comforter and flop on the bed, exhausted. All she knew was she wanted so desperately to wake up from this totally freaky state she was in.

Chapter 12 -- The Shock of Their Lives

As they approached the café the next morning, out walked
Harris looking incredibly smug and surprisingly already awake,
much like a cat who had swallow a canary pie. As he strolled past
the couple, he didn't look at them or talk to them. He pushed his
way through as if they didn't exist.

Bobby said, "Now that is even stranger than ever. There is
something wrong, isn't there? Can you feel it too?"

She really didn't know what to think, especially after last
night. She felt violated, but what could she say? She wasn't sure
what happened, if anything. She didn't know if she should say
something to Bobby or not. Or if she did, would he wonder why
she was dreaming of this Garcia guy and especially about
something like them having sex? No, she blocked it out of her
mind like it was just a nightmare and nothing more.

Bobby looked over to his little baby doll and wondered what was wrong. She looked so tired, and she had the strangest…what looked like a bruise across her mouth. He thought and thought about what they did last night and couldn't recall anything that may have caused anything like that. Unless she slipped on those godforsaken steps last night. She seemed awfully quiet too. Maybe she was just too hot. She wasn't used to heat like when she was younger. Too many years in Germany, he supposed. He understood how his wife was, never complain, never explain. She never wanted anyone to think she couldn't cut the mustard here in Iraq. So if something went wrong or if she felt ill, she would undoubtedly keep it to herself. He wondered if this was one of those times.

They put both of their names on the list; she was called first to check their email account. What she read from the company was nothing short of unfuckingbelievable!!! She read and re-read the email. She couldn't believe what she was reading. Could this be right? The email had come through company channels that started with their program manager, Banister, via the clerk at Cuba's email address then to Harris, and CC'd her and Bobby, and then the

Human Resource Chief. The email was dated the previous evening. Harris had checked his email that evening and that very morning. After the three of them left the internet cafe', Bobby asked Harris about this particular email. Harris denied ever getting or seeing the email. She had mentioned several times of the content, i.e. she and Bobby were to get out of the country ASAP and they were not to return to Cuba because their area clearance there had been suspended and to report to company HQ as quickly as they could, of course, without any guidance or plane tickets to do it. She told Harris that she would and could show Harris that particular email since they were still standing in front of the internet café. Without so much as a look her way; Harris refused. He continued to stare at Bobby and told him that he would check his mail later on for this supposed email.

Here Harris claimed that he was supposed to be the team lead, their boss, their supervisor, and yet when his team was being told to leave country, he responds with, "I'll check my mail later!" They asked him if they should go to work or go back to HQ. He said he didn't give a damn what they did. It didn't make a difference to him. So, without any guidance from their supposed team lead, they decided to go to work. The military didn't say anything to them. Harris had said it was the military's decision for the pair to leave, not further defined as to whether "they" meant Cuba or Iraq. Then in Harris' next breath, he said he personally thought they were not fit to stay. Harris said he wanted the pair gone because he felt that they, she and Bobby, had an adversarial relationship with him.

Bobby responded with, "No, we do not have an adversarial relationship. I just don't like you, but I can and will work with you."

Harris then stated he wanted them both to leave because they didn't like him. She and Bobby continued to ask for answers. Number one, the reason why they were being asked to leave Iraq; Harris refused to give them an answer. Then the pair asked him what he had said to the customer about them; Harris said it wasn't his place to say. Harris flat out refused to answer. He then said that they were to wait until corporate told him what to say, which never happened.

Not knowing what else to do, the pair asked Harris to please set up a meeting with the military so they could at least find out what was going on; he refused. He said he had his reasons and that he told the customer, both in Cuba and here in Iraq, that the reason they needed to leave was because she and Bobby didn't have a good personal relationship with him, because they didn't like him and he simply could not work with people who didn't like him. Those were the exact words Harris said to her and Bobby.

As the tears ran down her face, she asked him point blank, "Did you get us fired? Did you?" This was the first and only time Harris looked at her.

What he did next, she wished he had never done. He smiled as sweetly as he could and said, "I have no idea what you are talking about," and started to walk away from the both of them. She ran after him trying to get him to tell her something...anything. She was really crying hard now, really sobbing and pleading and talking, telling him how he had ruined their life financially.

"How are we supposed to pay our bills? We're going to lose our house, our car, everything we worked so hard for." She knew she was starting to sound like a rambling idiot but she couldn't stop, she just couldn't stop herself. Why had he done this

346

to them? She couldn't believe he did this. All she could see was the stupid smirk on his big fat red face and she hated him more than anyone she had ever hated, even more than Garcia. What they both didn't know was that Harris had been emailing the company before they even left Cuba, almost twice a day with lies of how they weren't doing this or that. All lies, but the company bought it, and they bought it because it was easier to believe him. Harris had 30 years with the Justice Department. All she and Bobby knew was that there was no justice here.

They wondered the real reason that the company had taken Harris' word for everything. In Harris' past, there were several red flags as far as his loyalty, sincerity and professionalism. Bobby thought of all the things that Harris had done in just the short four months that they knew him. Three big things stood out in both of their minds:

- 1) mercenary: "I will go to the highest bidder at a moment's notice -- all I'm about and all this Cuba job is because I'm a mercenary. I took the highest paying job that was offered." (i.e. with Lockhart Marion, Harris was told by the hiring manager that analyst's jobs paid more than interrogator jobs, and even

347

though Harris didn't have analyst training or even experience as an analyst, he still got the analyst job. Harris appeared to have no loyalty to the company or to his Iraqi team. Harris even told his co-workers, civilian and military alike, and even the self-appointed SSR and the military customer down to his immediate military supervisor, that all he was was a mercenary.

- 2) Harris also padded his timecards. She remembered a fellow co-worker in Cuba who worked the night shift with Harris said that Harris was claiming 10 hours but never seemed to be at work more than eight per day. Harris also instructed his Iraqi team, she and Bobby to do the same, stating that "there's always research you can do to get your 12 hours." The requirement for 12 hours a day, 6 days a week was not there. The night shift, mostly other contractors, came in at 4pm and there was simply not enough room for all of them. She and Bobby stayed one evening until 5:30pm and were overtaken with the night shift employees. They were both told by the customer at 4:15pm that they should think about leaving. They told him that they both had some reading/research to do and would find a corner somewhere to finish up. On their first day of work, she had already been given a task to start on. She and

Bobby thought that since their company told them to work 12 hours that they should make every attempt to, but there simply wasn't the room. While she and Bobby worked with their IZ counterparts, Harris stayed on the computer for the first 4-5 hrs of that day. Harris had been gone prior to 4pm (duty day started at 7am). They claimed 10.5 hrs for that day. There was no other place to conduct research there in IZ besides the internet cafe, but you could only use those computers for a maximum of 30 minutes.

- 3) And lastly, Harris was reported for sexual harassment of a young (just turned 19) female soldier. She was told by her military supervisor to write a statement (as did others) concerning what she saw that had taken place between Harris and the soldier. She had witnessed on a daily basis Harris staring at the soldier instead of working. One particular evening he came up to the soldier and sat at her desk and talked to her for over 30 minutes in Spanish. The more he talked, the more upset she appeared. Finally at the end of his conversation she got up and left the room, upset. She went to look for the soldier to see if she was ok but could not find her. So she emailed her to see if she wanted to talk. She and Bobby, the soldier and her analyst, who was also a company analyst, talked of what was going on. The soldier told her that Harris had been harassing her, but she was afraid to say anything. Harris had even asked her to go to Jamaica with him. Bobby told her that maybe she should talk to the chaplain or at least EEO personnel. Everyone involved in this had a meeting one evening to get everything out in the open. The results were that the soldier would be moved to another section, as well as the contractor analyst. Harris was allowed to stay undisrupted. Harris had later said that he had no ill will towards her but that she needed to mind her own business and for her not to poke her nose into things that didn't concern her. All of this happened prior to Harris going home on vacation to visit his wife and child in the south. When Harris returned, his attitude and demeanor had changed even more towards her. Harris was more angry and agitated. She knew that he took those feelings out on her. When she tried to talk to him the day of his return and days after, Harris would ignore/shun her or gave her one word answers and then he would go to everyone in the room and greet and talk with each of them at length. She later found out, in a special room in Cuba where you could conduct your top secret research, that Harris and his wife were having problems. Harris had mentioned this fact to her earlier, before leaving for vacation, that he and his wife were having problems. Harris came in that room to make a personal long-distance call to his wife. In this small room was it difficult not to hear. Harris was having a heated argument with his wife, telling her she needed to waiting for the divorce until he could come home the very next month, even though he knew that he would be Iraq the very next month. His wife had apparently served him divorce papers, his words, at the departure gate as he was boarding the plane to get back to Cuba.

And even though their company had all this information, they decided it was best to go with the word of that man to decide the fate of her and Bobby. And much later on, she and Bobby found out through a friend in Cuba that eventually, upon Harris' return, they made him the Team Lead, the very position she had applied for and with whom she had completed a very successful interview.

So that early evening, the pair sat outside in the dark warm air, confused and a whole lot scared. Why did this have to happen to her...to them? Neither of them had ever been fired from a job.

Bobby tried to put a positive spin on things for her. Bobby kept telling her that they didn't know for sure that they were fired. "Maybe they want us there so we can tell them what is going on over here with Harris? You don't know, babydoll, you just don't know," he said while rubbing her back.

She looked up at him with big brown sad eyes, tears welling up in them, trying hard to believe him but knowing better. She saw that look on Harris' face; she knew. She knew he'd won. He got his revenge, but for some reason, she thought that there was still more to come. If there was, then something had to happen this very night because they were due to leave the next morning at 6am sharp.

One thing that lay heavily on both of their minds right that second was that they had to figure how to get out of Abu Ghraib Prison, a freaking Iraqi prison in the middle of a war, all on their own, without the help of their company or even the military. Luckily for her and Bobby, Chief Barney liked them both and had managed to get them on a convoy the very next day that would get them to the PAX terminal in Baghdad 20 miles down the road with some other soldiers that were leaving. With the Chief's help, they got as far as Baghdad airport, but from there on they had to get back home all on their own, somehow, some way. Luckily for the both of them, they were seasoned travelers and knew their way around the military system. They were able to find what is called a space available flight here and there. They made it to Kuwait in three hours but took a day and half to make it to the next leg of their trip, Spain. The Kuwait to Spain part of the trip took over eight hours, then had a six hour layover, then to Dover, Delaware in nine hours, and then finally back home to Maryland in fifty minutes flat. It was very strange how their own company Lockhart Marion made sure that they made it all the way to that Iraqi prison but then just left them there to figure out how to come back home. Anyone less tough or not as strong would have folded and probably would have wound up dead or worse.

All she heard the next morning at the convoy meeting area was that Garcia must have flipped out and went absent without leave, AWOL. At least that is what everyone that was on the convoy that morning had been saying. There was simply no trace of him or any of his belongings.

Also, there was bigger news than that, and it was how the

military police, MPs, had found Harris that very night. The MPs found Harris beat the hell out of and stripped naked and also tied by his neck hanging over the door jam. The rumors were flying fast and furious as to what exactly happened, suicide or some deviant sexual escapade gone wrong. There was even speculation concerning one of the detainees paying him back for something he had done to them. No one really knew and to be totally honest, no one really cared. Also, that same night there had been a jail break. Sheer lunacy had taken over the warm Baghdad night. She knew that it was a full moon that was red, and that had always meant danger and that infact karma can really be a bitch!

## Chapter 13 -- The Beginning of the End

When they got to their little house on the Eastern Shore of Maryland, they both breathed their first sigh of relief that they made it out of that godforsaken country alive and together, neither worse for the wear. Bobby could see that she was still shook up from their last night there. He wasn't sure what exactly transpired while he was taking care of the Garcia issue. She hadn't told him the particulars of that yet. Bobby felt good about what he had done and knew that when push came to shove, he would have not done anything differently. They both made a pact that what had happened over there would never be known. They would both go to their graves with that information, never to be mentioned even amongst themselves.

The first thing they did after pulling up to their little house was to look around for Maria. The last they heard, less than two weeks before, she was living quite comfortably here in their house, but there just wasn't a single sign of her, and the house smelled as if it had not been occupied in some time. They knew that she must be ok because if she wasn't, she would have been there. So they gathered all their bags and took nice long showers and crashed so they would be ready to tell the real story to the company. The only thing they knew, from a handwritten note from Maria, was that they needed to be at the company HQ "first thing in the morning," whatever that meant. They climbed in bed, snuggled for a few minutes and then were both off to sleep. For her, the sleep was restless. She tossed and turned, trying to escape the dream. Regardless of how she lay down, the dream kept coming back to her, but it wasn't a dream. These things really did happen; it happened only three short days ago.

It was like a 35mm film going on in her head. The night before their early departure seemed so surreal. Neither could tell what was real or what was imagined. She thought back to the night before. She thought someone had put something in her drink, and after she passed out she was raped. She wasn't 100% sure, but she felt that what had happened to her really was a nightmare, but it had more real qualities than not. She couldn't find any proof of it, not like the first time in Germany when it had happened to her. She decided to tell Bobby what she thought happened. She knew what he would do if he ever laid eyes on Garcia again, and she was more than ok with that. She felt confident he could take care of the situation without any witnesses if need be.

As she started to tell Bobby what she felt had happened the night before, she could see red starting to creep up from his neck to his face. She noticed his hands were now balled-up fists. He waited till he heard the whole story. He looked at his wife's face, hugged her tight and told her that it might be best to go up to her room. He would be back in about two or three hours. He told her that there was nothing to worry about and that he would meet her back in the Day Room no later than 9pm sharp.

The look in Bobby's eyes scared her to the core. She wanted to plead with him, to tell him not to go but to stay with her, but part of her wanted Garcia out of here; correction, out of their lives once and for all. She had faith that Bobby would do that very little thing and without anyone knowing any the wiser. She knew that is why he told her that he would be back in 2 to 3 hours; he

357

wanted it to be dark outside. What he did or how he did it would never be explained to her, not then and not ever. He would live with what he did till the day he died.

As this dream, nightmare really; progressed, it shifted to her leaving her room and walking towards those steep slippery steps and the feeling that someone was after her. She could feel her heart beating faster and faster. She tried to wake herself up but the "film" in her head kept going. She was now dreaming and actually feeling the sting of pain when she slipped on the stairs and her crack when her elbow hit. She felt herself wincing as if it was happening to her all over again. Then she heard the voice, that voice whispering in her ear, "You'll be back."

What did he mean and was it really who she thought it was? Could it be the man she had been searching for all of these years talking to her as she lay helpless on the floor of this prison? Then as she was about to pass out, she felt the arms of a stranger pick her body off the floor and quickly take her out of one of the doors, her vision blurry even in the dream. Who were these two men? She knew or at least she felt that they were two distinct different men within seconds of each other. Who were they? Did she ever know? And what happened to her after that? She just wasn't sure. Maybe the dream would continue and tell her what her waking life didn't. Was there a reason the outcome was hazy in her head?

All she knew was that she had to gather everything and take a shower and hope against hope that Garcia didn't come back and didn't do anything bad to Bobby. She gathered everything up and tried to make it up the stairs to her room. She had no idea how much time had passed. Was it minutes or hours? Her legs were wobbly as over-cooked pasta; she attempted to raise one leg then the next. What had he given her? How did he give it to her? Oh god, she realized that she had been sipping on a Dr. Pepper during the good part of the evening. How stupid could one grown-up woman be? She could have kicked herself if she wasn't so scared and in such pain. She got all the way up the stairs with only a couple of slip-ups on the stairs but nothing too dramatic. She opened the cell door to find her two roommates and their boyfriends all asleep. She grabbed her little shower bag and made her way down the stairs. As she left the room, she felt a presence so close to her. She could almost feel the hot breath of someone, so she moved as quickly as she could towards those goddamn steep stairs. For some reason, it was always worse going down than coming up. She stood for a second before trying to make her way down the stairs.

She said out loud, "Who is it? Please leave me alone. I'm not going to say anything to anyone, so just please leave me alone." Whoever it was that was following her didn't stop; her words meant nothing to him. He just kept getting closer and closer still. She stood at the top of the stairs and started to make her way down, but both her legs gave out. She could see her legs rise almost above her head. The first body part to hit was her right elbow. It banged on the concrete with such impact she thought it just disintegrated.

Chapter 14 -- Lockhart Marion

The power couple arrived at company HQ, 8am sharp, dressed as any professional should be, in suits with briefcase in hand. They were told to sit and wait until the others were ready for them. They sat in silence, holding hands and hoping against all hope that they would be listened to. As the minutes dragged on to hours, they were told, three hours later, that "they" were ready to meet. The Human Resource Chief, three other Lockhart Marion employees and she and Bobby were in attendance.

The HR Chief did all the talking. He told the pair that their services were no longer needed nor wanted in Iraq, or Cuba for that matter. As she sat there in stunned silence, Bobby asked why. After about 15 minutes of hemming and hawing, the HR Chief said "conduct and behavior." He went on to say that the senior government employee in Cuba said he wanted the pair removed.

She and Bobby had had a good relationship with him in the past and he'd even said they had done great work there in Cuba. The pair also had good relations with everyone, to include the military customer.

The HR Chief intimated that the military supervisors were not satisfied. When she asked the HR Chief more directly about the military customers not liking their work, the HR Chief refused to answer. Then he said not to put words in his mouth. The HR Chief stood up and said, "We are done here." During the whole course of this meeting, which lasted no more than 30 minutes, the HR Chief kept saying, "I don't want to argue, don't put things in my mouth." He would not answer questions about how they were going to get reimbursed or the reasons why they were let go. She told the HR Chief that they were not arguing, they just wanted to try to find out reasons. The whole time the pair was there, they were treated as criminals and in a very demeaning, dismissive manner. They'd never had anything negative said about them. They were treated as one employee, not two. Both of them were fired for the same reason, conduct and behavior?

The HR Chief would not further identify

"conduct/behavior." He told them to get off the premises. The sad pair were treated as common criminals. The HR Chief then told her that she was fired as of that day, 28 April 2004, but Bobby would have to catch a flight on Monday to Jacksonville, Florida to leave for Cuba on Tuesday. Bobby would then return both of their military equipment (TA50) and pack their household goods and car and return the following Saturday; then he would be fired, even though they were two separate employees with two separate shipments and had to sign for different things. She signed for the house and registered the car. Bobby signed for the phone, internet and cable; he was the one instructed to go back, not the both of them; only one employee to take care of both of their responsibilities.

They asked the HR Chief about different timecard/pay issues and that they needed to know how were going to get their timecards and how it was going to be charged and their expense vouchers, etc. He told them to leave. He would not answer. Bobby said that they both needed to fill out an expense report and did not have forms. The HR Chief would get them. They were also told by the HR Chief that the company would make all arrangements for

363

Bobby to return to Cuba, to include hotel arrangements that would be paid. Later on, they found out that they were not. The couple had to go out of pocket for this expense. When the HR Chief went to get the proper vouchers, she asked if it would be alright to talk Maria, who of course, worked there. When she found out that Maria wasn't in that day, she asked to talk to her boss, Martin. Martin had also been the former guy in charge of the Cuba contract.

Martin, who had known the both of them, came down and took the pair into a small conference room. He said he had no idea what was going on. He looked really shocked.

"Ask the HR Chief about the reasons why you two were let go."

The both of them said that he wouldn't answer. Martin again looked surprised. He also said he had been treated shitty due to "others" and that he was pulled off the Cuba contract, and no one told him anything concerning Cuba any longer. During their discussion with Martin, there was a loud knock at the door, and someone told the pair they had to leave the premises. The HR Chief said that she and Bobby had one minute to get out of there.

Martin apologized and said he didn't know anything. They both thanked him for seeing them and thanked him for taking care of Maria while they were gone. They were then given the appropriate expense report forms from the HR Chief. She asked if they could just fill them out there in the lobby and turn them in right then and there. The HR Chief instructed them that they needed to get off the premises. including the parking lot, or he would have them removed. There were now two other individuals standing right behind him. So they turned and walked out in shock and disbelief.

Upon Bobby's arrival in Cuba, he was met at the airport by two police escorts, taken to a room and detained while everyone else went through. Bobby was then escorted by two more military police. The company clerk was also at the ferry. The new Senior Site Rep, SSR, was also on the ferry. The two military police stayed within arms length of Bobby on the ferry to the other side of the island. The SSR drove Bobby to their quarters with a police escort following closely behind. Bobby was then told that he was to get out of the country sooner vs. later. Their household goods were going to be picked up the very next day. What usually took at minimum one full week was going to be accomplished in less than

365

24 hours. When Bobby inquired about the police escort, he was told because of the "confrontation" at company HQ.

The SSR left Bobby at their little house, and the police escort left. Bobby was told it was ok to take care of all issues needed to get out of the country. The company clerk made arrangements to have Bobby on a flight back to BWI either the day after they picked up their furniture or earlier, if possible. The sheer embarrassment of this treatment could not even fully be expressed. The two of them had been treated as criminals--worse than. They did nothing to receive this type of treatment. The company and others involved had fired them for unjustified reasons.

As they drove back in silence, each one in their own thoughts, neither knowing the right thing to do or say to the other, they decided to just sit and get home. They'd decide what to do once they got in their little house; then they would know. The hour and a half back home seemed to drag on forever, but when they finally got there, they both smiled just a little. When they got back to their house, she ran to her computer and opened up her email to find that a friend from Cuba had written and told her that everyone there in Cuba had been told by their company that "they" were going to make an example of them, her and Bobby. The Cuba contract had had serious personnel problems in the past, and this was one way to keep everyone in line, by showing all the employees there in Cuba that you don't even have to do anything wrong and that you can and will get fired. They, the employees in Cuba, were also told not to speak to or write or have any communications with "those two." With that news, she just sat there, numb, not knowing what to do or say.

As it turned out, on 28 April 2004, the very day she was fired, "60 Minutes II" broadcast photos of abuses at Abu Ghraib, which had taken place in late 2003. It was a pity that no one would ever know, see or hear of the abuses that she had been through those few days over there.

Chapter 15 -- Extended "Vacation"

The weekend was brutal for the two. They didn't know what to do with themselves. She was beside herself with grief. Bobby spent day and night on the computer job hunting. She lay in bed, never even getting out of her PJ's, crying all day and all night, not even to stop to eat. That picture of the two of them as far apart, emotionally and physically, as they had ever been was indeed a sad one. Bobby tried and tried to get her out, even out of the bedroom much less the house. The hours turned to days, and the days turned to weeks. No one wanted them. It was if they were poison to the intelligence community. Once sought after by everyone, but not now, and to her it seemed, not ever. She wouldn't even get out of bed. She just lay there, questions running through her mind. Questions of why she was even here. Why was she wasting oxygen, wasting valuable oxygen that a productive person could use. She felt indifferent towards everything and everyone, even to herself.

And with all that was going on with the pair, life decided to throw yet another curve ball their way. Maria and her boyfriend had asked if it was ok to move in with the two of them. Apparently their condo had burnt to the ground and they had nowhere to go. So being the soft-hearted couple they were, they said "of course." Even though there was absolutely no money coming in, the pair assumed that Maria and her boyfriend would pay their own way while there with them and that meant at minimum, pay for their food and drinks and maybe just clean up here and there.

Bobby thought that was a good move because at least that got his babydoll out of the bed, even though it wasn't until *just* before the two of them got off of work. She would at least try to prepare some dinner for them all. What little money the two had put away for a rainy day was just about spent.

After three weeks of the foursome living under one roof, she went off the deep end. For the first time in her life, she needed to be taken care of. All her life she took care of someone, everyone, and during this time, she felt the need to be taken care of. All she got was a couple who took advantage of her and Bobby. Never paying for anything, not the food, not the liquor they drank, and not even the odd utility bill. Bobby was furious with the two and told Maria in a kinder-than-should-be email. Her response to him was cold as ice and incredibly business-like. Bobby could see his lovely wife cleaning up after them and paying the bills with what little money was left, crying as she did and then cooking for the four of them, only to have to clean up after all of them. It was all too much for her, and Bobby saw it. Maybe he shouldn't have written Maria about this, but he thought it was the right thing to do.

He didn't tell her of the email. He figured he could take care of this issue on his own. It wasn't until she opened their joint email account that she found out what had gone on. She read Maria's icy email response and became immediately beyond mad. She was a volcano ready to explode, and explode she did, in the form of a phone call straight to Maria. And with that, Maria informed her that their shit would be packed by the weekend. She corrected Maria and told her that their shit would be packed by this very evening!

After Maria hung up on her, she crawled back to the safety

of her bedroom. She didn't leave from there. All she knew was that someone came home for about a half hour and they were gone. She crept out of her bedroom to see that in fact their shit was packed and had gone. She wandered her house for any sign of the two. As she opened the garage door, she saw the place stacked with all of the rest of their belongings. Being a pissed off madder than hell Mexican with the stubbornness of her German heritage, she marched into the garage, opened the big door and started to stack the rest of their things outside. After about a half hour of getting it out of there, she promptly called Maria back, but this time Maria wouldn't answer the phone; she let the office machine pick up the message.

It was short and sweet: "Maria, the rest of your belongings is on the driveway. Make arrangements to pick it up before the end of this evening." She hung up and went back to the safety of her bedroom. For the next two weeks, she never left, never went any further than her bathroom. She felt safe there. It was the safest place in the world. Unfortunately, she would not be able to stay there in her cocoon. The desperation weighed heavy on her heart. She was at odds with who she really was as a person. She had always felt like she contributed to society in some way until now. She just couldn't see the point…the point in staying alive. She had nothing to look forward to. No job, no friends and no family. After the big blow out with Maria, everything else seemed to spin more out of control, more out of control than she thought possible.

She had always seen Maria as a sister and so did her mother, maybe a little more than she should. It didn't surprise her much when Maria decided to call her mother and tell her things that just weren't true, things like "she kicked me out of the house and she threw all my stuff all over the streets," things of that nature. So, low and behold, her mother decided to side with Maria and believed all the lies that Maria had told her. Her mother called and left three terrible phone messages, things that a mother should never ever say to a daughter. She called her a used-up piece of dog meat and something about how she and her father had wanted to get rid of her but it was too late when they found out she was pregnant so they had no choice but to keep her sorry ass and that she was just jealous of Maria because she was young and she was nothing but a saggy-ass 50 year old woman with dementia, amongst a myriad of other nasty and cruel remarks. One of the

372

worst of the remarks her mother made was that she ended the last phone message with, "I hope you die in that house." What was unfortunate for her was that she believed those things her mother had said. She taped all three phone messages her mother left her, each one more depraved than the other, and she played them over and over and over, until one night she couldn't stand the thought of being alive any longer.

Chapter 16 -- "Mother Dearest"


Bobby didn't know what to do for his distraught wife. He had never seen her in such a state. He knew that she had never had so much as a blemish on her professional record, much less been fired before. He tried and tried for the whole month to help her, to get her out of the deep depression she was in, but nothing worked. He grew more and more worried, and the messages his mother-in-law left were just wrong on so many levels. He wished he had been there when they came in. He would have told that woman a thing or two. But he had gone to the 7-11 to buy his babydoll a Big Gulp Dr. Pepper. He remembered how much she loved those and hoped that his little gesture would bring at least a little spark back in her eyes. What he remembered about her big brown almond-shaped eyes was the spark that was as bright as any light you could have ever seen, the light of life in them. The light danced around all the time in there, but now all he saw was sadness--deep, agonizing, all-consuming sadness. He could kick himself in the butt for not being there when her mother called. He thought that those calls might have pushed her over the edge from just being mildly depressed to full-blown ready to kill herself depressed.

He thought before those messages the little spark came back for a minute or two when he talked about the garden to her. He reminded her of the dreams she had and how they could make them come true and now that they had all the time in the world. She perked up quite a bit at the thought of doing just that, then reality would hit and she would say, "But we have no money. We can't do anything. We barely have money to eat. We are on the verge of losing the house and the car," and slumped further into the covers of the warm bed, her sanctuary.

Bobby had to do something and something quick before he lost her for good. He told her he would be right back. Before he left, it appeared that she had fallen asleep, just that quickly. He looked for that tape recorder. He had to take that from her without her knowing. It was making things a helluva lot worse, he thought. He prayed that woman would call again. He would give her a good size piece of his mind. He knew that she had once been very close to her mother, even during all those years she spent in Germany. She'd still managed to call her once a week, every week, for years on end, and for her mother to say the things she said made him want to rip her heart out, if she had one. He found out that the problems with her mother had started last year when her mother had begged her to bring Maria out to live. For some reason, her mother doted on Maria as if she where her very own daughter.

Bobby recalled the things she had told him about what seemed to be the beginning of the end for her and her mother. She'd said that last year she had planned a surprise visit to see her mother during the 4th of July week. Maria was supposed to pick her up, but there was no sign of her at the airport. She waited for two hours, still no Maria. It had been a while since she was in San Antonio but felt that if she rented a car, she could make her way to her mother's new house. Her mother had moved into a new place closer to the military hospital about a month prior. Anyway, as the story went, she in fact found the house, surprised her mother and spent the next week helping her move in. She didn't mind all the work moving her in and getting her settled, even though it was

376

supposed to be her vacation. By the end of the visit, her mother had almost begged her to please take Maria home with her. She had met Maria's boyfriend for the first time during the visit. She neither liked nor disliked him; she made no judgment. If Maria loved him, great for her. She knew how dramatic her mother could be, so she calmed her down by saying that she would do her best to get Maria up to Maryland.

After about being home for a month, her mother would call almost daily pleading with her to bring Maria to DC. She finally told her that she would call Maria up and see if, in fact, she wanted to leave. Maria seemed to jump at the opportunity but was concerned for the costs; she had no money to speak of. She assured Maria that she would take care of everything. Then Maria said that she wanted to bring her boyfriend with her. She assured Maria that it didn't matter to her one way or the other, but her boyfriend had to pull his own weight, and that meant he should at least bring something to the table, money for the motel and for food at minimum. Maria assured her that would be no problem.

Like most things she did, she organized everything, and everything had its own list. That was just the way she was. Find

Maria a job, find a place for Maria to live, find a job for her boyfriend, rent U-haul for Maria. As the days went by, the items on the list were being whittled down. Paid Uhaul, check; found Maria and boyfriend jobs, check; found condo on the water, check; pay 1st months, last months rent and security deposit, check. During all of this her mother called and asked about progress. Maria had pleaded with her not to say anything about her boyfriend coming along, that she wanted to be the one to tell her mother. So she left nothing out but that little tidbit of information when talking to her mother. That was until the day before Maria and her boyfriend were to leave Texas.

Her mother found out and also found out that she didn't tell her about the boyfriend coming along. She told her mother that it wasn't her call to make. The anger rose in her mother in a fevered pitch as the woman slammed down the phone. Her mother called back one more time to tell her that if Maria would show up at the house that she would shoot her in the face with a gun. She knew her mother very well and knew this was just more of her dramatics. Bobby thought, *what in the hell was this woman on to say such a thing?* Little did he know that her mother would say such terrible things and even worse. That was just a little prelude to what was really lurking in her sick mind, as he later found out.

She never called again, at least until just a few days ago, and to his utter shock, she had said the worst things on the phone. These types of messages had to come from a very sick mind. No one, regardless of how they felt inside should be able to say those things without some sickness creeping in their system. The terrible thing was that she started to believe the terrible things that crazy woman said on the phone. Her mother would say things like, "You are nothing but a used-up piece of dog meat, you're nothing but a three-foot gnome with shoulders like a football player, tattooed scarred up body, you are just jealous of Maria because she is young, and you are nothing but 50 year old saggy-ass with dementia setting in." Bobby believed that it was those very things that totally snuffed out the once bright light in her eyes, especially the last comment she ever heard her mother say: "I hope you die in that house!" She would listen to those taped messages over and over and over again. It killed him to see her listen to it as the tears streamed down her cheeks. He had to find that goddamn tape recorder and destroy those terrible words. Bobby felt that would be

379

a good start at helping her climb out of the deep black abyss she was in.

*She must have it under her pillow,* he said to himself. He had to help her. He had to get her out of this agony. He tried his best every single day, more than 15 hours of being on the computer or on the phone calling one company after another. They did get a few calls, but those few calls fizzled when they found out about Lockhart Marion. They were poison now.

As she lay there pretending to be asleep, she heard Bobby walking around looking for something. She didn't want to let him know that she was awake; that would only cause conversation, and that was the last thing she wanted from anyone, even Bobby. She wanted to sit and listen to her mother's words over and over and over. She was a used-up piece of dog meat. Her mother had always been right in the past, so she must be right this time as well. This was no exception. And besides, a mother wouldn't lie to her own daughter. A mother would only tell the truth. With the last words her mother ever told her still echoing in her head, she knew what needed to be done. She first listened to the sounds in her house; nothing, not a sound. Bobby must have left; for how long, she wasn't sure. She knew what she had to do wouldn't take too long, not long at all.

She looked for her briefcase and rifled through it till she found what she was looking for. She grabbed the bottle of valium, a bottle of vicodin and a bottle of percocett. She thought the combination of all three would do the trick, and she would be able to go quietly. She would be out of everybody's way, and she wouldn't be wasting valuable oxygen. She knew her mother would be glad to finally get rid of the used-up piece of dog meat. Before taking all the medication, she made sure to grab a big glass of milk. She knew if she didn't have something in her stomach, all her effort would go to waste because she would undoubtedly throw it all up. With the tall glass of cold milk in her hand, she went back to her bedroom to prepare for her final minutes. She was glad that she was alone and could do this undisturbed and in peace.

She wondered how many she should take to do the job. She didn't want to take too many at one time and throw them up. She knew how sensitive her stomach could be. She wanted to make sure she did the job correctly. How miserable would she be if she couldn't even do this one thing right? She started with the percocett; she only had five of those. She initially thought she should take the five percocett and wait but then changed her mind and took what was left of her vicodin as well. Ok, ten of those left, plus the five percocett should do the trick. She thought that the valium wouldn't be needed so she set the bottle on her antique vanity.

She stood there in the dark tomb she now referred to as her bedroom. Facing the mirror, she saw the old woman standing right behind her, to the right. She raised her hand to her mouth to swallow; she felt a cold icy tightening feeling around her wrist but her reflection in the mirror showed no such image. Her hand started to shake uncontrollably. All the tablets scattered like leaves on a windy autumn day. She must be more afraid to do this than she thought.

Her first thought was to look under the vanity right where she was standing, then for some odd reason even to her, rummaged through the covers and tossed pillows here and there, but she could only retrieve eight of the tablets. She thought that would still do the job. Again, she lifted her hand to mouth, all the while looking at her image and at the old woman behind her. The image remained unmoved; no movement from her or from the old woman. They both stood there just staring at her, but she could see a tear roll down the old woman's face. The shaking started all over again. The eight tablets scattered to and fro. The old woman stood silent and still, still but for the lone tear rolling down her cheek. She couldn't believe what was going on. It felt like someone was grabbing her by the wrist. She shook her head in bewilderment. Where in the hell were all the pills? Again she looked under the vanity and then the bed skirt, nothing; under the nightstand, nothing. Not a pill in sight, not one single pill or bottle, empty or full. She regrouped and thought that maybe she could just take the whole bottle of valium instead. She looked to her right at her antique vanity and those were gone as well.

What in the hell was going on here? Could she be losing her mind as well? Her mother had said she thought she was going through dementia. *Maybe this is how it starts,* she thought to herself. She grabbed her briefcase again and dumped the contents on the bed…not one single pill, not even a Motrin. She knew that she was starting to lose control, but this was sheer lunacy. She knew she took out three bottles of pills, but she couldn't find any evidence that said as much. She was running all over the house looking for the pills she thought she had with her in the bedroom. She ran to the kitchen just in case she took them with her when she got the milk. She was out of breath. That was the most exercise she had done in almost a full month. Just as she was going to tackle another room, she thought she heard the front door. Bobby must be back. She wasn't ready for any talks right now, definitely not now. Not yet and maybe not ever.

She knew he deserved someone special…maybe his real true love because, after all, she was a used-up piece of dog meat, not his soul mate and definitely not "lobster" material. She wasn't going to give up this quest. She would wait for another time when she would be alone. This time, she had a different tact, one that would not be as neat and tidy as this attempt. She hated to do what she had to do, if only because Bobby would have to be the one to clean up after her. She wondered if there was another way out. As she laid her head down on her favorite pillow thinking of the alternative method she would use, she fell quickly to sleep and started dreaming just as fast. The dream was of what had *just* happened to her but this time she wasn't alone. The kind old woman from Germany was there, right there in her bedroom with her, sitting on the bed right next to her. The dream was short and sweet. She saw herself putting her hand to her mouth to swallow all the pills, but just before she did that, the old woman grabbed her wrist and said, *"Was denken Sie Sie tun, Sie dummes Mädchen? Ihr Vater würde über Sie beschämt sein; den einfachen Ausweg, anstatt Sie, zu kämpfen, nehmend haben Sie einen Mann, den Lieben Sie er die einzige Familie ist, die, Sie Sie haben alles benötigen, zum für Bezahlung zu leben keine Aufmerksamkeit zu, was Sie haben gesagt bemuttern; sie ist krank."*

And with those last words hanging there, "she is sick," she awoke just as quickly as she had fallen asleep. She sat bolt upright; wide-eyed and totally awake and surprisingly feeling refreshed. She hadn't felt that way in so very long. She jumped in the shower and put on her little Hawaiian shorts and white tank top and looked around the house for Bobby. He would be glad to see that she had finally gotten off her ass and out of bed to re-engage with him and with life in general. She stood there looking at her reflection in her antique mirror and thought back to that quick little dream she'd had only minutes before and the words the old woman had said to

385

her. The things the old woman said had made perfect sense. Her dad would be very ashamed of her for taking the easy way out and that she did in fact have a husband who loved her. She knew that Bobby was the only family she needed, would ever need. She also knew that it would take a sick mind for a mother to say those things to her own daughter. She knew she had been stupid for even listening to such crazy talk, but it still hurt her heart to the very core of her being. It felt like a million little paper cuts on her heart. One paper cut alone was insignificant as far as pain, but a million of them was unbearable.

She again looked at herself in the mirror, the words the old woman said spinning in her head, and for just a split second, she saw the old woman standing right behind her reflection in the mirror, her old frail hand resting on her shoulder; she even felt the weight and the coolness of it right there. And just barely an inch to the right of the old woman's reflection was her garden through the window behind both of their reflections, but it wasn't the way it looked now, all pathetic and sad. It looked more like the garden in her dream. She turned to the right in one quick motion, but no one was there, and the back yard looked as pitiful as always. Still, she smiled her little half-crooked smile to herself and knew in her heart that the old woman was still there and would always be there with her and that her garden would look just as she dreamed it would, someday somehow.

With that, she was out of the bedroom and yelling down the hall for Bobby. She was ready to tackle that poor excuse of a back yard and turn it into a beautiful Garden of Eden, just like in her dreams and also just as ready to tackle life with as much, if not more, enthusiasm. She finally had a plan. Thank God her good friend Susan was still interested because she now knew what to do to get them out of this mess.

Chapter 17 -- Prized Possession

Bobby had no idea what to do next. He could see that his wife was totally out of it. He had to be the grown-up this time. He knew that he counted on her strength a lot of the time instead of the other way around. *Not this time, this time she will lean on me for strength.*

Bobby knew what he had to do next. His father had given him this particular pocket watch for his 16th birthday, much like his father's father had done and his father's father's father and so on and so forth for several generations, right down the line. It was the only thing he had from his family, and he cherished it with all of his heart, but he needed to do something and something quick. He knew a guy who had envied the timepiece every single time he saw it, and Bobby knew that this individual lived in the DC area, so off he went to sell the only prized possession he had. He didn't know if it was considered an antique or not and wasn't sure how much it was worth, but he felt that they could live ok for at least a few more months. It was his only possession worth any amount of money. He loved the watch, but he loved his wife more. This would at least put her mind to ease concerning the bills. He felt confident that they wouldn't have to live necessarily modestly but more or less on a budget than either one had been on before. His wife was worth it to him, just to get her out of this place she was in.

He took the pocket watch out of its little black velvet bag. He only wore it on very special occasions. In fact, he didn't believe he had worn it since their wedding day. Even though their wedding was very casual, he in beige linen beach pants and she in a beige lace strapless sundress, he'd wanted to have the watch with him so he tucked it in his pants pocket and said his "I do's" with it close by. He gave it a once over. He really should have done at least cursory research on the internet to make sure of all the particulars. The appearance of the watch was not fancy, actually more on the plain side, and that suited him just fine. He didn't like a lot of dials and fancy gadgets that would take a masters degree in Engineering just to figure the damn thing out. The condition of the watch overall looked to be excellent; the case, excellent; the dial, very good; and movement, he thought excellent again. He then turned the watch over and saw the brand but didn't know if that was good or not. The back of the watch read "Louis Berthoud." He could tell that was a French name. His lovely wife would have loved the fact that his one prized possession was French. That would definitely make her smile that crooked little half smile he loved so much. He wasn't even sure if she knew he had it on him that day or even if he actually owned this pocket watch, but it was not the time to tell her. Maybe later, maybe when he bought it back from the dealer. He would never tell her what he did. That would only make her feel worse. He would keep this from her…for now.

As he walked towards the door, he thought he saw someone in the darkened hallway going into the bedroom. He rubbed his eyes and looked again. This time he saw what he thought to be an older woman. Boy oh boy, was he losing it. Must have been the dream he had last night. It was very strange but somehow real. He made a mental note to tell his babydoll about it later on. Lately he felt that she didn't want to see him or hear anything he had to say.

He wasn't sure if she blamed him for what had happened. Truthfully, he carried the blame deep down in his gut. He knew he didn't do anything wrong, but there the guilt stayed like a big rock in the pit of his stomach. Just to be certain, though, he walked down the darkened hallway and opened the bedroom door. All he could see was his lovely bride lying on the bed, head facing towards that dreadful back yard. He was glad that she had left the window treatments open. She'd had them closed, sealed off tight from the outside world for over three weeks now. Regardless of how the back yard looked, it was still a beautiful day. His hopes were that she would see that pitiful yard and get out of the dungeon she had created for herself out of their bedroom and do something about it. At least it was a start, he thought; she hadn't completely closed herself off to him and to the world…not yet anyway.

As he looked around the room, he thumped his head with the palm of his hand. *How dumb can you get, seeing old ladies in your dark hallway. I've really lost it now,* he said to himself. As Bobby walked down the hall, he could hear someone talking but not in English. Maybe she turned on the TV. But when he looked in on her, she looked sound asleep. So there he stood in his

391

darkened hallway just listening. It was German, someone was speaking German. He could only make out a word here and there. He shook his head and walked towards the door. *Stress, it's only stress. I'm starting to have hallucinations, for godsakes!*

Bobby got into their other beetle, this one being his lady love's Turbo S beetle. She loved to haul ass everywhere in that little car. Bobby hit the gas and zoomed out of the housing development and headed to DC to see his former colleague who was now a master jeweler. An hour and a half later, Bobby pulled up to the ritzy-looking jewelry store. He wished his lovely wife was with him. She would love this type of store. It was so over the top luxurious that it would even impress her. *Maybe when she's better,* he thought. He felt confident that by tomorrow she would be on top of the world or at least as close to the top as one could be in their situation: unemployed.

When Bobby walked into the store, he immediately saw his friend. Ron was a blond blue-eyed Ken doll replica, complete with the brightest, whitest teeth he had ever seen on anyone. They greeted and chit-chatted about this and that, then Bobby felt it was time to come to the point of his visit. Ron could tell that something was up and just asked straight out, "Ok, Bob, where is it? Where is that pocket watch I have been trying to buy from you every time I see you?"

Bobby was glad he had broken the ice in such a way. This was hard for him for a couple of reasons; one, just selling something so special and two, Bobby knew that Ron would know that they were in trouble financially, and that embarrassed the hell out of him. *No time for such nonsense,* he said to himself.

Bobby pulled out the little black velvet bag and said, "I'm glad you asked, ole buddy, ole pal." Bobby handed the timepiece over a little reluctantly.

Ron was smiling from ear to ear. He had been coveting that watch for such a long time and finally had it in his hands. He was almost beside himself with joy. He felt kinda bad for Bobby; times must be really tough if he was finally willing to sell his beloved pocket watch. He made sure that he gave him the best deal he could. He wouldn't do anything underhanded. He knew Bobby was a proud man and would only do this if he was in dire straights. He wouldn't ask him the why's, where's, or what for's. He respected Bobby and if he wanted to tell him, he would listen.

Ron eyed the timepiece and started to speak to himself, "Very fine and rare French 18K gold repeating chronometer antique pocket watch by Louis Berthoud, Paris, circa 1795. Antique pocket watch by Louis Berthoud, Paris. Very fine gilt fusee movement with Ernshaw type spring detent escapement with compensation curb, capped escapement, the balance under the dial. Quarters repeating against the plain polish consular case. White enamel dial with chips at the winding hole, edge chip at 6:00, and a crack at 9:00. A very fine example of French precision watch-making in the late 18th century by a member of an eminent family of watchmakers."

Bobby just stood and listened. It sounded like good news to him. He hoped the watch would get him at least ten thousand dollars. That would hold them until September for sure and without having to live too modestly. They could stretch the dollars a bit if need be. Ron was beside himself. He'd had his eye on that particular watch of Bob's forever and a day.

Ron looked up at Bobby and said, "I'll give you twenty thousand for it."

Bobby stared at his friend in disbelief. All he could think of to say was "What?"

Ron looked at his friend and said, "Ok, ok, twenty-five and not a penny more, and that is a great deal."

Bobby couldn't believe his luck. Ron knew that the actual value was ten to fifteen thousand but he knew something had to be terribly wrong for Bobby to do this. Besides, Ron really wanted the watch for himself. He knew he could easily sell it for thirty, but he really wanted to keep it. They both lucked out and Bobby thanked his friend and waited for the check to be written out. Ron felt like the luckiest man alive.

While Bobby walked back to her car, he couldn't help but smile to himself. He was a bit sad, but he knew this was the best possible solution. He knew this would bring her back to life, not having to worry about looking for work as someone's maid or some such craziness. He knew that both had the time to get a job they both wanted and they would be able to work on the back yard until then. No scrimping for them. As Bobby got closer and closer to home, he decided to bring home a bottle of their favorite beverage; Jose was coming home with Bobby.

He zoomed around the corner of their housing

395

development. He thought he could see her in the back yard. *How strange is that?* She hadn't left that room in over three weeks, and she was standing outside on the deck just staring at that pitiful yard. He must be really losing it, although it would tickle him pink to think that she might be out there. Bobby was smiling from ear to ear; first his good news and then his babydoll standing outside on the deck looking like she was ready to tackle the backyard. What a wonderful day, a truly wonderful day for the both of them!

He pulled up quickly to their driveway and practically bolted out of the car and ran to back of the house. *Weird,* he thought as he walked to the other side of the house. He just knew that she was standing there only seconds before. He could see her little Hawaiian shorts and little white tank top that said "the most beautiful girl in the world" on it. There was one thing that was strange though. "She was barefoot," he said out loud to no one but himself. She never was barefoot. She had shoes of any variety or socks on, never absolutely never went without something on her feet. She had the strangest way of walking when she had only her socks on. She seemed to tiptoe all over the place, all the time. Once she put shoes on though, she walked flat-footed.

In the back yard, he tried to open the screened in porch--locked up tight. He was really losing it now. He went to the front door and tried to open it, but it was locked just like he had left it. He got the keys out and unlocked the door, opened it slowly, and just as he was entering the hallway, out she came as if she was bouncing off the wall, much like her normal energizer bunny self. The couple stood there in the hallway hugging each other as tightly as they could, content in the closeness, not only physically but emotionally as well. He could feel the bond that was between the two; she felt it as well. They kissed each other all over the face. Not the deep penetrating kisses he usually liked but little butterfly kisses all over. She came back, she came back to him. He couldn't believe his good luck. He couldn't wait to tell her the news. After all the kissing died down, she started talking a hundred miles a minute about the back yard. He smiled to himself and thought, *she's back; she's come back to me.* She grabbed Bobby's arm and dragged him out the back door through the screened-in porch to the deck and right out there in that sad looking yard. She was so animated that he didn't know where to look first. He completely forgot the fact that he thought he saw her standing right out there

397

in the very clothes she had on less than five minutes ago. All of that completely slipped his mind. All he could think of was her, the magnificent light back in her big brown almond-shaped eyes. She hadn't even stopped to ask where he had been or what was in the brown paper bag he was holding. She went from tree to tree pointing out all the things that had to be done and how they had nothing but time on their hands. He wondered to himself, and he felt so bad for feeling this way, but he wondered how did she think they were going to pay for all the stuff she was talking about? She had no idea what he had done or where he had been. He was going to ask but was afraid that he would lose her again, so he let her ramble on about this and that. He took it all in and tried to "see" what she saw back there. He couldn't, but he tried anyway.

Finally after about a half hour of animated talking, she sat on the steps of the deck and wiped her brow. Boy oh boy, was she pooped just talking about the things she wanted to do. Bobby must think she was insane right about now. He was probably wondering how in the hell were they going to pay for all the stuff she wanted to do. She had a plan and had already made the appropriate calls to ensure it would be taken care of. The way she figured it, they would be able to pay the bills for at least four months or so and be able to do the things to the yard if they did everything themselves and if they didn't splurge. Of course, they couldn't do all of it right now but the little things, the things that would make a big difference. She knew she had it in her to find bargains. She would only buy the plants that they both loved and nothing short of that, even if it meant getting less done. She would rather do that than have a yard that was totally filled with flowers and plants that were just so-so.

She knew she had to get out of the house first thing in the morning and stop by where her friend Susan worked. It was a small exclusive jewelry boutique in the heart of historic Annapolis. It would only take about a half hour to get there, but Susan thought best if she came before it opened. She remembered how much Susan loved the necklace. She recalled telling Susan all about the trip to Belgium to have it custom made. She could almost hear Susan going over the stats on the diamond, "Round three carat diamond near 'D' in color with almost a VVS1 in clarity. Double check this info. This would be a wonderful coup for my store," Susan had told her over and over again. Susan didn't have the

399

jewelry store as of yet, but she was confident that one day she would.

She had to tell Bobby that she wanted to go window shopping. She knew that he would want to go with her, and under normal circumstances, she would love for him to be there as well, but this was business, and she needed to do that all by her lonesome. She didn't want him to know what she was going to do. He knew how much she loved that piece and that was the reason he couldn't go with her.

Chapter 18 -- She's Back

So there they sat, the two of them staring at the more than pathetic back yard in silence, each with their own thoughts. Then it hit her, Bobby was holding a paper bag. She looked up at him and asked, "Surprise presents for me?"

He mussed her hair and said, "Yeah, a little welcome home present for the both of us." He pulled out the glorious liquid. They looked at each other and almost in unison said, "Freezer!"

They laughed. They still had it. *Thank God,* he thought. They could still finish each other's thoughts. Bobby jumped up and popped it in the freezer, but before doing so, he took out her favorite shot glasses and poured them a couple of warm ones. She looked up, surprised by the two shots but welcomed it nevertheless.

It was warm going down but still delightful. How they

loved their tequila. She decided to tell Bobby about her window shopping trip for tomorrow. He was excited that she wanted to go out of the house. He waited to see if she would ask him to join her, but she never did. His feelings were a bit bruised, but he thought that maybe his little one needed some alone time. They had been together 24/7 since they met. It was only natural for her to want a little time apart. So there they sat, sipping on the warm liquid and talking about the back yard. She ran back into the house so quickly that it surprised the hell out of him. To be truthful, it actually scared him a little bit. He wondered if she was ok or if something happened to her, but out she came with her little sketch pad and pencils. He loved when she got so into a project that she would have to get it all on paper as quickly as she could scribble her ideas.

How he had missed her these past few weeks. It was lonely in the house without her jumping up and down and running around. She brought so much life into any situation, but these past three weeks she was "gone." He didn't know where or for how long, but he knew how very much he missed her and glad she was back. He knew that there would still be bad days but they, hopefully, would deal with them together. He knew with losing their jobs, the possibility of losing their house and their cars, then the fight with Maria and then her hateful mother for saying those terrible things on the phone didn't help matters. He would ensure she would be sheltered from any of that crap from now on.

He knew that at least he had taken care of one of the issues, and with time, the others would fall into place. He felt confident that "the" job for the both of them was right around the corner. Then there was Maria, well he just didn't know what to do about that situation. He knew that she missed Maria more than she would let on. He also knew that she tried to call her several times to say she was sorry, but Maria wouldn't have anything to do with her. It would crush her to the core each time Maria hung up or didn't even take the call. What Bobby didn't know was that it felt more like a million little paper cuts all around her heart. But he still thought that maybe with some time, they would just go over and see what happened. And as far as that mother of hers, well that was up to her to decide. He wanted no part of her mother. That woman was dead to him. He couldn't believe that a mother could say those things to her own flesh and blood, especially a daughter who had respected and doted on her. It was inexcusable and unforgivable as far as he was concerned, but he would leave that subject alone.

Bobby excused himself and walked into the kitchen, hoping that their favorite beverage would have cooled to the perfect temperature. *Mmmmm,* he thought, *just perfect!* Before pouring them another shot of the chilled liquid, he took a quick trip to the bathroom. He strolled down the darkened hallway and recalled what he had thought he saw today. Actually two different episodes. The first he'd had before he left and then right when he was coming home. Surely it had to be the stress. What else could it be? He walked into their bedroom and stood staring at the bed in shock or maybe disbelief. He didn't know what to think or do. He had never seen the bed in such a state: pillows randomly thrown all over the room, covers thrown back half off the bed, half on.

What was more disturbing was what he saw on the bed: an array of his babydoll's meds. He didn't recognize the name of the pills, but he knew she only took those when her migraines were especially bad. But there on the bed, they were all scattered about. It looked to be a handful of pills, too many to help with any type of migraine. He gathered all the pills and looked for the bottles that they belonged in. What had she done? Did she take some of these? Was she going to take all of these? Bobby was very scared. He didn't know what to think. He searched high and low and under the covers for the bottles. There should be at least two bottles somewhere here. And why would she leave them like this? Did she want him to see them? Did she want some type of reaction from him? He just didn't know. What was so totally strange about this whole picture was that when he came home, she was her usual energizer bunny self and not the zombie in a coma she had been these past few weeks.

He finally found the two *empty* bottles waaaay under the bed. Did she take some of these pills already and if so, how many? *What to do, what to do, what to do*, he kept repeating like a mantra as he went into the bathroom. Was this a test? If not, what was it? He decided the best course of action was to sit and wait. Put the pills back where she usually kept them and say nothing. She would have to tell him what she wanted him to know.

As he walked back through the bedroom, he saw something poking out from the end of the bed. It was yet another bottle of pills. This time, it was closed and full. Bobby wiped his brow.

*Phew, totally full bottle.* He didn't know why that thought made him feel better but it did. He straightened out the comforter on bed and picked up the pillows that were scattered all over the floor and fluffed them a bit. He wondered if he should tell her of his hallucinations, about the old woman or about seeing her outside just minutes before. He also wondered where in the hell was that goddamn tape recorder. He knew he had to destroy that bit of trash. He would do whatever it took to stop her mother from destroying that wonderful woman, his wife, or he would die trying.

He wondered if his babydoll would think he had totally lost his mind or would she be intrigued by his sightings? And as far as her mother was concerned, he wouldn't say another word about her.

She sat on the deck waiting for Bobby to get the lead out and bring her a nice chilled glass of nectar of the gods, otherwise called José Cuervo. She thought about her "shopping trip" tomorrow. She mentally went over her list of things to do. She hadn't realized just how much she missed being in control of her life. She never really knew how much until now. How could she have just given up control and let the black abyss swallow her whole and without much of fight? She could kick herself in the ass for doing that. "Well, that is over and done with. Enough time spent on that little pity party," she said out loud.

Back to her mental list: she would have to get up bright and early; the traffic, not to mention the parking situation would be terrible any later than 9 o'clock. Annapolis is a wonderful place to go, especially in the springtime, but it sure did get crazy busy there. She then thought about what was entailed the next day and had such mixed emotions about it. It seemed like she'd had that diamond forever. But she knew that Susan would give her a good price; she trusted her. She remembered how Susan eyed that particular piece of jewelry, even back in the days they were in both in Germany. Even knowing that Susan would treat her fairly in regards to the price she would offer didn't make it any less difficult to let go of the beautiful stone, but she knew what she had to do and she would do it to save the both of them.

It was funny but she remembered how, when and where she had first met Susan. It was her and Richard's first tour in Germany. She had just started working in civil service, working in the same building as her husband. She didn't know a soul, other than

Richard. She always hated the first few days of work where you go around feeling as if you are twisting in the wind or floundering about like a fish out of water. She hated the thought of not knowing anyone. Out of the blue, in walks this tiny woman with the reddest hair she had ever seen, who had a "make no friends take no enemies" attitude that scared the shit out of her. Susan had been one of few Army women interrogators. If Susan only knew just how shy she was, and then to have this forceful woman stare her up and down made her cringe more than just a little bit.

Susan was not that much taller than her, but she commanded the presence of someone at least six feet tall. She would say good morning and good evening each and every single day, but all Susan would do was look her up and down and simply turn around and walk away without saying word one. This happened the whole time during her in-processing and for the following month, not one single syllable from Susan. She resigned herself to thinking Susan, for whatever reason, hated her ever-loving guts! She tried to exchange pleasantries; a good morning here a good afternoon there seemed to fall on deaf ears. Susan wanted no part of her. As the days turned to weeks and weeks to months and the feeling of floundering subsided, just as she decided to stop trying to make an effort, Susan surprisingly came around to her. From that point on, they became fast friends, but as always with friends in the military, you part for a few years and then meet up again at some other exotic locale, the last particular exotic location being Washington DC.

Chapter 19 -- Susan's Story


Ever since Susan was a little girl with the wildest, brightest red curls, she absolutely loved jewelry. She would rifle through her mom's jewelry box and put on not just one piece at a time but all of the costume jewelry and prance all around the house pretending to be a very rich lady. She loved how the jewelry made her feel and how each piece just glistened as she pranced around the house. She knew that one day, when she was older, she would own a store full of this wonderful stuff.

As the years went by, Susan's love for jewelry never died. Unfortunately, Susan took a different path career-wise; she joined the Army early on in her years. Susan realized that she had the knack for talking to people and getting people not only to talk back to her but to just open up and spill their guts to her. It was almost happenstance that she became one of very few women interrogators in the Army. She had a wonderful career doing that, but when her twenty years were up, and with her money saved, she decided to open a little exclusive jewelry shop--correction, THE jewelry shop in the historic part of Annapolis. Her clientele were mostly rich tourists, but every now and again she would get one of the local retired naval officers in to shop with their ladies. She put her talents to the test as she talked and got her clients to tell her exactly what they were looking for. She also had a knack for finding and purchasing one of a kind pieces so her customers were always pleased with what they found at her shop.

That beautiful spring morning as Susan was opening her little shop, she saw her dear friend walk across the street--only at the cross walk, never would she jaywalk in her life, even if it meant walking an extra meter further; that was the German side of her friend. She wondered who the older lady was that was walking with her friend. She had never seen her before, but it seemed that her friend knew her well. Susan also noticed that her friend never looked as sad or as tired in her life. Every time Susan had ever seen her, she'd seemed to be bouncing off the walls. Well, of course, other than when they first met back in Germany, oh so many years ago.

Back then her dear little friend was shy and more than a bit timid. Susan never was one to trust people right off the bat, and she didn't trust this little woman at first glance. She was just a little too cute, and Susan knew how women like that were. It had always been Susan's experience that cute little women were usually mean, back-stabbing bitches. So Susan decided she would wait and see how this little one would be before she would give her the time of day. Susan had to admit, though, the little one did try to exchange pleasantries day after day after day, never giving up. That was up until about a month of doing that with Susan not even looking in her direction. Then she just stopped one day, not saying anything to anyone. Susan thought that maybe, just maybe, she needed a friend and maybe they could be friends. Susan recalled the first time she said good morning to her; she about dropped the stack of papers in her hand out of shock. From that point on, through tours here and there that would separate them, they would keep in touch and see each other eventually, the last place being DC.

Susan wondered what the frantic-sounding phone call was all about. Her friend wanted to sell that wonderful necklace that

412

she had been eyeballing for all of those years. Susan would make sure she gave her friend her money's worth. Susan could see that her little friend really had an eye for designing jewelry, and this particular piece was no exception. She thought that if only she could get her to work here with her, it would be a match made in jewelry heaven, but she knew her dear friend loved the world of intelligence just as she did those years back. Besides that, she knew her friend's love was interior design. She could do wonderful things with a home. It was if she had some kind of vision upon entering a room. She could see her friend's eyes dart from wall to wall with the decorating wheels spinning around a million miles a second. Well, at least she was like that with her little boutique. Susan knew that she wanted her friend to be with her while she looked at different locations for her shop. Her friend had the ability to see--a vision, if you will--promise and potential with each and every place they checked out. So when Susan finally purchased the sad little space that her friend said would be a show stopper, she was the only one Susan would call to help--correction, to do the job and do it right. She wanted to pay her for all of her hard work, but her friend simply loved doing it so much that she wouldn't hear

413

of taking a dime. She made the process seem so effortless and easy.

Susan's thought came back to that beautiful piece, the three-carat brilliant diamond smack dab in the middle of an Omega chain, which was more like a choker style necklace. It brought back a huge smile on Susan's face. The design was beautiful in its simplicity. No fuss, no muss, just big humongous diamond taking centre stage. It was designed to fit exactly on the clavicle notch of most women. Breathtaking was all one could say when one would gaze upon it. Susan had loved that necklace for ages now and was shocked when her friend called her out of the blue to let her know that she wanted to sell it. Susan didn't ask any questions, she knew that it must be something terribly wrong for her to want to sell it. If she felt the need to talk, Susan would listen, but she wouldn't ask any questions so as to avoid any embarrassing moments for her friend. The last thing she ever wanted to do was to hurt her.

Susan knew straight away that something was amiss because, first of all, she called her to say that she and Bobby were back from Iraq and that they weren't going back to Cuba; that's it, nothing more. Susan knew how much she wanted and had

414

volunteered to go to Iraq and that she absolutely loved Cuba. She had once told Susan that if there was ever a way to buy property over there, she would be first on the list. The silence from her friend worried her and now this; wanting to sell this beautiful piece of jewelry was almost more than Susan could bear. She kept tossing the idea of asking her what was going on and then not asking her. What if she needed help, what if she was too embarrassed to ask for help? The thought kept jumbling around in her red-headed head!

Susan decided first and foremost that she would give her the best price she could and then add 10 thousand on top of it. If her dear friend wanted to talk, she would make herself available and she would make sure she knew that right from the get go.

As Susan walked to the door to let her friend in, she noticed something she hadn't before: the old woman was gone. *How weird is that*, she asked herself. She couldn't recall taking her eyes off her friend as she and the old lady crossed at the crosswalk. She had to have turned off to the left immediately after they crossed the street; there would have been no other explanation to it. Didn't matter, she opened the doors and hugged her friend tight. Susan couldn't feel the spunk, her friend called it "moxy," in her little body any longer. Susan remembered her friend as the "energizer bunny," always moving, always thinking, always talking, but not now, not here. Her friend was quiet and subdued; she was here on business.

As she left Susan's shop and strolled across the street, she smiled but she could not stop the lone tear that rolled down her cheek, even if she had tried. She knew she had done what had to be done. Susan gave her more than her money's worth; she knew it and Susan knew it, and she was appreciative of Susan for not asking any potentially embarrassing questions. She still wasn't ready to talk about any of this, not to her dear old friend Susan, not to anyone; it was just too soon. She knew that the amount that Susan had given her would carry her and Bobby through at least six months worth of bills and also enough to do a nice job on their "Garden of Eden." They couldn't splurge, but they could get exactly the type of plantings they both loved; maybe not as many but at least a few of their very favorites. The idea of starting this project with Bobby made her smile that much more. She wasn't 100% sure if he liked that kinda thing; heck, she wasn't sure if she liked that kinda thing, but the dream kept coming and coming when she least expected it to, so it had to mean something. Something also told her that the yard didn't get that way by landscapers; it got that way through blood, sweat and tears--hers and Bobby's blood, sweat and tears!

As she jumped into her little punch buggy, she made a mental list of all the flowers she loved dearly; there were so many of them: Lily of the Valley, Gardenia, Casablanca Lily, white Roses, Moonflowers, Phlox (David), Cleome spider flowers, Butterfly Bush, Lilac, Hibiscus, and, oh my, vines--she loved flowering vines, all types, all colors but all with a fragrance, like honeysuckle, Madagascar Jasmine, plus the Carolina variety, bougainvillea, wisteria, Mandevilla, Morning Glory, Trumpet Vine and all the different types of Clematis.

"How to chose?" she said out loud to no one in particular. Oh my goodness, she hadn't even thought about the types that Bobby liked. He was from the south, so she thought that perhaps a magnolia tree and maybe a Peony or two, or even a Camellia.

Her next thought was, where in the hell do they start? That back yard, which was nothing but a mushy marshy area, would be

417

transformed. That would take some serious work, but how?

Then her thoughts drifted off to being unemployed. This was truly a first for her. She didn't know how to react to this, even a month later. She still didn't know what to think or how to feel about it. She only knew that her first reaction--all–consuming, dark, deep depression--wasn't it. So she thought, *how would Dad take this type of news if this had happened to him?* She couldn't answer that question. She just couldn't see her dad getting himself into this kind of predicament.

Chapter 20 -- A new beginning; like it or not

That evening the pair took it easy. They knew what the morning and the next God only knew how many mornings and days and possibly nights had in store for them. They sat looking at the pitiful back yard and drank their chilled José. Bobby was unusually quiet. She wondered what he was thinking about. Could he be wondering what she did all afternoon? That she went shopping but didn't buy a thing? She had gotten used to him being the strong one, being in control as she let her world fall apart all around her. She wondered if it was a question of money that was preoccupying his mind. Should she tell him? Would he be upset with her? Would he think what she did to be the stupidest idea she had ever come up with? So many questions and no answers. She stared at him lovingly. She loved those piercing blue eyes and wondered what was to become of them. Sure the money situation was taken care of, at least temporarily, but what if no one would hire them, ever? What would become of them? Would they become one of those crazy homeless couples you see wandering the streets of downtown DC pushing their shopping cart of what was left of their possessions? Surely the powers that be didn't ensure they made it all the way back from a goddamn Iraqi prison in the middle of a war, safe and sound, for that to be their demise. But what was in store? All she knew was she loved this man with all her heart and soul. She also knew that their time in Iraq was far from over. She felt that there was still some unsettled business between them and that country. She knew one thing and one thing for sure, she wouldn't tell Bobby her feelings on this topic; not now, not ever. That was the last thing her husband needed to hear. She knew how strong he had been for her, for the both of them, when they returned from that god awful place, and she felt that that little bit of information from her might throw him into a head spin down the abyss, much like where she had been for the past month. She couldn't, no, she wouldn't have that happen to him. Not to this wonderful caring man. The man with the piercing blue eyes yet showed so much trust. She would have her mind set on the garden

420

and only the garden from now on. No negative vibes here at their little house.

As Bobby sipped the chilled golden liquid, he wondered two things. One, what brought his wonderful woman out of the sinking black hole she'd been living in, and two, where in the world would they start on this pitiful backyard? The thought of getting started on that yard seemed a daunting task at best. Hopefully his little wife had a plan of action; she usually did. He went back to his first thought, what in the world happened to snap her out of where she had been the past few weeks? Did the scattered pills have something to do with it? She still hadn't mentioned it. He also wondered where she went and what she was up to this very morning on her supposed window shopping trip. He knew she had mentioned doing just that, but this seemed different. For one, she was back in record time, as if she had a mission to do, did it, and returned promptly. She had been on several window shopping trips in her day and never did they end earlier than five hours. Yeah, his little woman was definitely up to something, but that something he just didn't know.

With their own thoughts floating around in their respective

noggins, they looked over at each other and said, "More José!" It was more of a statement than a question. Yeah, they still had it. Sometimes, most times, they could read each others thoughts with such clarity that it was frightening, but since they had been back, neither one really knew for sure what the other was thinking. There had been much introspective thinking and feelings that neither was ready to share with each other, or anyone else for that matter. They wondered if they would ever be the same after this big blow to their egos and to their pocketbook. With time and patience they would get it all back and more. They deserved more...if only they could find jobs. Little did either of them know that they had been sitting and thinking of the exact same thing for the past half hour. They still had it; they were just too scared to see it.

The pair experienced a lot in their short period of time together, specifically the last couple of months. They both knew that war changes people. They hoped if it had changed them that it would be for the better; made them both, separately and together, stronger people who could and would take what life had to dish out, and boy, had life dished out some shit to the pair.

Tonight was for rest and relaxation before the long

laborious process of lawn duty called them into action.

As the sun started to rise in the horizon, suddenly, quite suddenly, she jumped up and out of her lawn chair and stood looking at the yard from the deck. It was not even 6:00 in the morning and she had been up, made coffee for Bobby and was sitting outside drinking her Dr Pepper, standing there, looking out at the yard.

"Time for action," she said out loud. She wondered if perhaps she should wait on Bobby, let him at least get a cup of coffee in his system before busting out the yard tools. "Hmmm, damn, speaking of yard tools," she said out loud. With those words still ringing in the cool morning air, she ran over to the garage and opened up the door. Not a single yard tool in sight – not one shovel or rake or even pruning shears. She let out a little exasperated sigh and walked back to the deck to sit back down.

Ok, shopping was in order before any manual labor was to begin. She hoped that when Bobby finally woke up he could take his coffee in a large to go cup while she thought up the plan of action for the day's festivities. She knew that he had mentioned last night that he needed to spend at least five hours of each morning working on the computer finding them THE job that would help end the madness of their current lives. She was good with that idea. She really wanted to do a big part of the yard herself. She knew the sheer manual labor would be therapeutic for her; just as she knew Bobby working on finding them jobs would be therapeutic for him.

She got up from her lawn chair again and decided to walk through the backyard amongst the monkey grass and weeds, and God only knew what else was out here waiting for her to bend down and accidentally touch it. She just knew there would be all types of snakes, spiders and whatever insect du jour waiting to greet her.

She never actually walked through the back yard before today. She had been content to view the ugly mess from the deck. This was the first time in her life that she lived out in the wilderness so speak, so she was more than comfortable viewing it from afar, but she had to get over whatever phobias she had in order to do this job right. It wasn't going to get done all on its own.

As she stepped off the deck in her flip flops and walked through the monkey grass, she felt the squishiness of what used to be marsh land that was now her backyard. She never realized just how big the actual backyard was until she walked through it totally. She felt confident that everything would fit…a lovely garden on one side and the pool /tikki bar combo on the other. She really hadn't gotten into much talk of the pool/tikki bar combo with Bobby, but she was confident he would totally love the idea.

She stood dead centre in about ankle's deep mud and realized just how daunting this was going to be. She wondered if she should seriously think of getting some help. Without a job for either one of them, she decided no for two reasons: one, she didn't want to waste any of their cash on something that they could take care of themselves, and two, she needed this. She really felt she not only had to but needed to do this. There were still parts of the day she could feel herself slipping back to the way she was last month. She could succumb easily, she thought. If she didn't occupy her mind and her body with this garden, she could easily be back in her little dungeon with the bottle of pills at the ready. Instead she would put her passion into action.

As Bobby stretched on top of the big pillow top bed and yawned, he wondered where his little woman was at. Oh yeah, he remembered; the first day of lawn duty. He wondered how long she had been up either waiting on him or just up doing all the work herself. He knew just how impatient his little wife was. He did remember telling her that it was a must for him to spend at least four to five hours every morning looking for jobs, "the job" for the both of them. He had to do this; hell, he needed it! He didn't know why but he felt responsible for what happened to the both of them over there. He knew in his heart he didn't--they didn't do anything wrong, but his head was another mater. Sometimes during the past month he wanted to crawl down that deep black hole of depression with his wife. He could feel waves of depression washing over him every single day, but he made himself think of other things. He had to be strong for her, for the both of them. He knew he had a need to find them work just as she needed the garden to work on. Bobby thought of those pills himself a time or two and felt if he didn't busy himself, really busy himself, with the computer, he could easily go that route right there with her.

Bobby sat up in bed. He could look out at that pitiful backyard and see his little woman, who looked as if she was ankle deep in mud. She had the strangest look on her face. She looked to

426

be talking to someone. He wondered if the next door neighbor John was also up and helping her with whatever she was doing. He jumped out of bed and threw on shorts and a tank top and hurried down the hallway. He could smell some wonderful gourmet coffee brewing and grabbed a cup before going outside to see his baby doll alone in the middle of the yard. Her little arms were outstretched as if she was saying, "Get me out of here, I'm stuck!" Bobby smiled broadly and asked if perhaps she could use his assistance. She groaned out loud as each movement sunk her deeper and deeper in the mud. She had no idea just how far down she could go. "HELP ME!" was all she could say.

She looked like a young child in a boatload of trouble. As he walked towards her, he could feel the squishiness himself and worried how close to her could he actually get without being knee deep in the black mud himself. He kicked off his flip flops and went for it. Bobby was able to get to her, but he too was now ankle deep in the mess. The only difference was that he could still lift his legs out of the muck. His babydoll was actually totally stuck there and couldn't move, as if she was in quicksand. As Bobby got closer, he could just barely touch her fingertips, but the strange

427

thing was that when he did actually touch them, he felt a little spark. She too felt the familiar but almost forgotten spark. That familiar little spark was back, it had been a few weeks since he had felt that, and there it was out there in the middle of that crazy pitiful yard. He looked at her and realized she had felt it as well. They stood there, smiling lovingly at each other, enjoying the moment. The next thing they both knew, in she went, one inch deeper in the mud. That made her bust out in laughter to the point she splatted in the mud, butt first, with her black "no fear" baseball cap flying off. Bobby didn't know whether to laugh or be extremely serious. When the shock of what had just happened wore off to some extent, she again busted out in a gale of laughter that sent Bobby into his own fits of laughter.

After a few seconds, Bobby got close enough to his babydoll and grabbed her by the arms and lifted her out of the muck and threw her over his shoulder, fireman style. He had not realized until he sat her little body down on the deck steps that she was barefoot. After he sat her down on the edge of the deck, he looked at her bare feet and was shocked to see no shoes, not even her flip flops. He couldn't believe what he saw or didn't see for that matter--shoes. She could tell what he was thinking. She answered his unspoken question, "My flip flops are still in the mud over there."

"Oh what a pair we are, aren't we, babydoll?"

This was only day one, hell, not even 8am. Boy oh boy, this was going to be quite the adventure. "Perhaps we wait a little before getting started. Wait for the mud to harden up a bit," he said to her.

"Great idea. We need yard tools, lil bear. We can dig out my flip flops later." She jumped up, tip-toed to the water hose and washed off her feet.

As she hosed off her feet, he watched for the very first time since they had been together, her walking around, especially outside, without shoes of any kind on. She came bouncing back ready to hit Home Depot for the much-needed yard tools. It shocked Bobby to no end that she didn't own one single yard tool. How did she live in this little house all of this time without a single yard tool? He said as much to her. She just looked at him, shrugged her shoulders and dragged his ass to the car so they could get started on this crazy crazy adventure the two of them were about to embark on.

She ran up and down aisle after aisle grabbing this and that, and he wondered where in the hell were they going to get the money. Sure, he knew that there was money to cover all of these items, but they had not had that discussion yet.

As she ran up and down the aisles grabbing everything she could see, she wondered if he was totally blown away by what she was doing. She still had not had that discussion with him concerning their cash situation. She stopped for a moment and turned to look at Bobby.

"Let's talk, lil bear."

"What about all of this stuff, hun?" he said. He was scared not to get these items right now. He feared that would make her digress back into the abyss. He had to chance it and say, "Ok, let's talk."

With that, they set aside the almost full cart and walked outdoors. They both tried to talk at the same time on the way to the car, but she finally cut him off and said, "Let's get back home and sit outside and have a little powwow!" As they drove back over the Bay Bridge, each in their own thoughts, she wondered how she should broach the subject. It was kinda strange that he said he had something to say to her as well. What could he have to say to her? She decided not even to guess but to just sit quietly until they got back to their little home.

They drove back to the little house in the woods and walked straight back to the deck, looked at each other, and they both started yammering at the same time. They laughed till their sides hurt. For the next two hours, they cleared the air and all was known by both parties. Although both of them felt a type of empathetic pain for the other at having to sell their prized possession, but when it came down to it, that was all it was…a possession. They realized that their love was what mattered and helping each other the best way they could. It was funny, how through all of what had happened to the two of them, they both still thought alike. They both sold something that was very special to them so something more special could survive.

For the next six months, she busted her ass morning noon and night on that little garden of theirs. Bob did his share but spent a good portion of his time finding just the right jobs for them both. There were so many times that she could barely get up in the morning. She was sore all the time and all over. She had even developed carpel tunnel syndrome on both wrists, but it was well worth it. She looked out one summer morning and saw all the beautiful colors that were glistening in the morning dew. She couldn't help but stare from her bed and smile so broadly that she belted out a tune for Bobby at 5:00 in the morning. All the beautiful colors were there to behold. It looked like a box of Crayola crayons, every color in the rainbow plus extras!

Bobby looked like an innocent child there. *Sleep of a child,* she thought. She couldn't help but belt out a rendition of an old Cat Stevens song called "Moon Shadow." "I'm being followed by a moon flower a moon flower, moon flower," at the top of her lungs. Bobby pretended to stay asleep, just smiled and rolled over. He wanted to see just how far this little show would go. Good God, what would she do next? She left the bed each and every single morning no later than 5:00 and never came in the house before 8:00 at night, not even stopping to eat breakfast or lunch. He tried to bring food out to her, but she wouldn't take anything, only the occasional Dr. Pepper and, of course, a bottle of beer or a wine cooler after the appropriate time of day, and that time kept getting a little earlier each day.

Bobby would start his day each and every morning scouring all the websites for intelligence jobs and applied for everything for himself just so they would have a good start and so she could continue her gardening. He never realized how much she seemed to enjoy even just puttering around back there, always in such deep thought, even when she was busting her ass. He wanted to take any job until the perfect one came along for the both of them, but for now he could see the pure unadulterated joy on his little wife's face. It looked to him that most of the work was done on the little garden in the woods, except for the other side where she had explained her ideas for a pool and tikki bar combination. They both knew they would have to wait a while before they could do anything there. She purposely left that side totally undone, at least until they went on one of their many antiquing treks when she saw the most adorable antique white wrought iron gazebo. He could see her mind racing as she did measurements with her body.

She could not believe her good luck as she eyed the antique white wrought iron gazebo. It looked exactly like the one in the dream she'd had just the other night. The dream was a beautiful

433

one, which they usually were when it was about her garden. The dream was pictured at nighttime with all the loveliest sweetest smelling white flowers and bushes all around the gazebo. It was so magical that when she woke up that morning she tried everything she could to go back to sleep, and it was already past 6:00 in the morning. As she puttered around the garden, she kept thinking of the gazebo and how beautiful that moon garden was.

She came running into the computer room to let Bobby know that she was going to take a quick trip to St. Michael's where they had some of the cutest antique shops. Bobby looked worn out and tired. She had no idea how long he had been there working on that computer or even if he had even gone to sleep in the first place. She begged Bobby to go to bed and relax the whole day. He was working his ass off trying to find just the right job. He had already been to a couple of job interviews, but he hadn't heard anything from any of those. It had been almost five months now and still nothing for either one of them. He was getting desperate and thought about what she had said about going back to Iraq. He didn't want to do that. He knew that she wanted to go in the worst way, and she knew that he wouldn't let her go to that goddamn

434

country without him going with her. He was worried what she would do next, since her gardening was almost completed, not that a gardener would ever think it complete, but complete enough where she spent most of the days puttering here and there and not the actual manual labor she'd been doing the first three months.

With her encouragement, he decided to head back to bed for just a quick little cat nap while she went off to do some antiquing. As she lay behind Bobby, rubbing his back to relax him, she could almost immediately hear his soft snoring. It was only 7:00 in the morning but she figured an hour to shower and change clothes and about hour to get to the shops, she should get there when they opened. She quietly slipped out of bed, kissing him on the back before departing for her shower.

She drove and drove and finally got there, and there was just so much to look at, shop after shop after shop with all the cutest outdoor stuff, that she could barely contain herself. Then as she was walking from one shop to another, she saw it; it stood out back close to an old dilapidated garage. It looked as if is was glowing; the most perfect white wrought iron gazebo, the same size and shape from her dream. It was everything she had hoped to

435

find. As she walked towards the octagonal structure, she saw a woman walking with the sales person towards it. She panicked and started running towards it now. What would she do if this other woman was getting ready to purchase it, the structure of her most current dreams? She couldn't let that happen.

Luckily for her, the other woman had just sold the gazebo to the salesperson. It had belonged to her great-grandmother who had had found it in an old barn in Germany. Without even asking the price, she told the both of them that she wanted it and wanted to have it delivered as quickly as possible. Both looked at her and wondered if she even had cared how much this structure would cost. She, of course, did and didn't in the same breath. She knew she had to have it; it was in the dream for god sakes, and she did care because the money was starting to dwindle, and she knew if they didn't find something quick they would be forced to take jobs doing anything and everything to keep afloat.

She thought for a second about the job offer she had to go back to Iraq. She wanted to go back in the worst way but knew Bobby was totally against the idea. The company that had been calling her told her that they would know something within the next month; it had already been five months out of work. They had some good days and some really bad ones still, but time was going by quicker than either one cared to think about.

When she returned home, she found Bobby outdoors looking over his wife's hard work. He smiled so broadly that it almost hurt his lips. She had done such a tremendous job that he thought that maybe not only interior design was her bailiwick but perhaps landscaping was one of her talents as well. He could almost see the exact dream she had described to him only seven months earlier; almost to a tee. How she did it was beyond him. See it, describe it and then make it happen. She was terribly talented, and what was sad was how she didn't see it.

## Chapter 21 -- Going Back

She ran out to the back yard hoping Bobby was there but also because she couldn't stand to spend more than an hour away from that garden; she loved it that much. As she grabbed his paw to bring him down to her level so she could kiss him, he told her the news. He looked sad as he told her that she had gotten good news today from the company that she had been talking to about going back to Iraq. She didn't know what to do. Inside she was so excited but then sad because she could see the sadness in his eyes. She thought that maybe, just maybe, if they could go together, it might make him just a little happier. He pondered the idea and then said, "But they don't want me, they want you. They don't even know I exist." She told Bobby that she had been talking to the company about him and had already sent them his resume, and that they would like him to join the team, if he was interested.

With that, he sucked up all the sadness he felt in his heart and said, "Yeah, let's do it!" The next few weeks were a flurry of activity for both of them, a quick drive down to Shaw AFB to in-process and to get some of their equipment. The company had assured them that they would both be located in the same city. It wouldn't be until they were both in Qatar that they found out that they would be 30 miles away from each other, he in Balad and she in Baghdad. No one told them that it would be the longest 30 miles of their lives.

She and Bobby sat at the kitchen table waiting on the taxi that would take them back over there. He truly hated the way he felt this morning and hated even more because he could see the sheer excitement of this new adventure on his wife's face. Why was she so happy that they were going to be in the middle of a war, especially after all the shit she went through just a short six months ago? Was it because of the paycheck that neither of them had gotten in over six months time, or was it more than that? He stared at her in wonder.

She glanced over to her "little bear" and saw pure misery on Bobby's face, a face filled with doom and gloom. How he

439

didn't see that this was another adventure was beyond her. She knew she would miss him, that was a given, but the work promised to be more than exciting and even more different that she had ever done in her long career as an intelligence analyst.

They both sat quietly waiting for their taxi to take them on yet another crazy adventure; so many adventures in their short lives together, some good and some not particularly good. Little did either of them know that a sense of de je vu washed over the both of them at the very same time. Cuba and that trip to hell, Abu Ghraib, crossed their minds and the reason they both had to go back to Iraq.

She quickly jumped out of her seat. "Bobby, I'm going out to my garden for a little while. Want to come with?"

Bobby looked at her and her enthusiastic little square face and smiled. He wanted so very much to take that walk with her but knew how much she enjoyed being out there alone in her own little world, which meant her "Garden of Eden."

"I think I'll sit here, finish my coffee and wait for our taxi. Go, enjoy, I'll give you a holler when the time comes."

She didn't walk out of the room as much as she jetted out

within a blink of an eye. She was walking amongst her beloved flowers. Bobby looked out the kitchen window and wondered what she thought while she was out there. Sometimes he would catch her talking out loud and then other times looking like the saddest little lady in the world. If he could only crawl inside her head to hear the things she thought of, to learn more and more about her. He still couldn't get enough of her.

The morning was a comfortable one, not cold, not warm; just right to be meandering about her happy place. Everything looked so beautiful. All the plants that she and Bobby planted looked and flourished so well. It surprised her since the soil out there really did suck big time. She knew their neighbor John would do his utmost to keep it beautiful.

"Babydoll, it's time!" with that she slowly and deliberately started her walk back into her little French country home. As she climbed the deck stairs, she glanced back and wasn't too surprised to see the little old woman there, but this time she was more casually attired than the other times she had seen and talked with her. This time the old woman had the same black "no fear" baseball cap on that she herself had. The old woman waved, and a tear slowly slid down her cheek as she turned and walked into her house.

When they got to Qatar Airport they couldn't believe the heat, sniffling hot heat, and it was in the evening to boot. Their point of contact in country found them and drove them to on base quarters to rest up for the evening so they could catch a flight the next day to their respective bases. As they sat in their little one room trailer, they thought of what it would be like for them to be apart for the first time in their "coupledom." Would absence make the heart grow fonder, or would it be out of sight out of mind? He told himself not to worry about the latter happening to them, but only time would tell for the pair.

While they were sitting there, each one on a different bunk bed the next morning, they wondered how long they would get to stay here in Qatar. She loved the place, with its stifling hot weather without an ounce of humidity and its bright sun that felt as if it was less than a meter away. Bobby, on the other hand, was ambivalent about being in this country or any country other than his own. Sure it was better than being in Iraq, at least they were together here, but other than that, it held nothing for him one way or the other.

They decided to take a walk around and find the chow hall to get some breakfast. She wasn't much into eating that early in the morning, but she knew Bobby needed his coffee and a quick bite to eat. She was content to have her Dr. Pepper and nothing else. They stopped at the PX and roamed around a bit before getting to the chow hall. If truth must be told, chow halls over in these parts were really unbelievably good: mass quantities of food and it was good too! It just didn't suit her tastes. She preferred a more exotic fare. She could see that she would lose quite a bit of weight with this type of food and no alcohol for a whole year! She didn't care, she was ready to get busy, although she missed her little garden terribly. She knew that she left it in good hands; John promised to do his best at keeping everything alive and hopefully still as beautiful as she left it.

Chapter 22 -- Chris, who was he really?

She didn't know what to say or do. He'd just left her office for the second time. She hated how she felt when she saw him. She didn't feel love; it was lust, plain and simple. She hadn't had those feelings since before she'd met Bobby. Bobby, her one true love. She tried hard not to eye him as he walked in and out of her office.

It had been nothing more than a chance meeting. She'd been in Baghdad for over six months now, and all she thought or could even fathom was getting back home to Bobby and their wonderful life together...until now—now her thought went to those blue/grey eyes. She sure was a sucker for piercing blue eyes, but Chris had extraordinary blue/grey eyes. His eyes were a little different than her husband's eyes. She almost couldn't explain the difference. Chris had the type of blue eyes that held a certain "I'm only here for the beer" fun time, a little mischievousness about

444

them. It was as if he was up to no good, not in a bad way but in a pure unadulterated "let's get crazy together" way. Like someone who wanted to have a good time, even in this war-torn country of Iraq. He also had this little smirk when he smiled as if he knew the world's oldest secret was the cat who swallowed the canary. The man oozed sexuality, totally oozed it. She thought over his last words to her as he left, "Give me a call if the database doesn't work. *I'll hook you up good and proper.*" It wasn't his words as much as it was the twinkle in his blue/grey eyes and the smirk on his lips, especially when he came to the part "good and proper."

She didn't know if he was being serious about her computer or about hooking her up! It had been ages and ages since anyone came on to her so blatantly. His look was intoxicating. She actually felt a little tipsy just looking at him. As he sat there at her desk downloading the software, she could actually feel his heat, the heat radiating from his skin. She knew that her face was all flushed. Surely this good-looking man with the silver hair, silver "soul patch," which is like a goatee minus most of the hair but just this little "landing strip" right below the lower lip, sly kinda smirk and the mischievous twinkle in his blue/grey eyes coming on to

445

HER? She was at least ten years his senior, she thought. She was old and this country made her feel a lot older than her 47 years. Still, she couldn't help but blatantly stare at his ass as the door closed behind him.

Then she noticed that not one of her co-workers were watching her watch him but they ALL were watching her watch him exit. Some of them looked shocked to see her show anything but the utmost professionalism. But there she sat, eyes filled with lust and longing. They all knew of Bobby. All she could do at that point was wave them off and then laughed it off because she had truly been busted big time by her co-workers. She grabbed all the paperwork around her and tried to busy herself. She had much to do, but this new software Chris had installed would cut her research time in half.

Chris, that was his first name, but everyone called him by his middle name, Edward. She didn't know a lot about him other than he worked for another one of those big contractors. He looked to be around 38 or maybe 40, but that would be a stretch, and the only thing that made him appear to be that age was the color of his hair. Silvery hair; *what a total turn on,* she thought. But then again, everything about this man was a total turn on for her--and those eyes. She couldn't stop staring at those blue/grey eyes. That twinkle scared her and enticed her at the very same time. He looked at her big brown almond-shaped eyes telling her about the software he was installing in his computer lingo, words she really didn't understand but kept nodding so he would just continue to talk so she could blatantly stare into his eyes. She wanted him to continue this dialogue, not so much for her understanding but for the opportunity to unabashedly stare into those eyes, the eyes that held so much promise, promise of fun and games, of something incredibly naughty.

She had always loved eyes, blue eyes in particular, much like her long lost fathers' had been. Eyes and accents were what she was attracted to, specifically southern, and the more of a southern drawl, the better. But Chris had a slight accent that was not southern, perhaps New York but not the typical accent like one would think. Maybe from someplace like upper state New York. His accent didn't matter to her because of those eyes; his eyes could melt her resolve, she feared. Not her love for Bobby but definitely her resolve. She knew the right thing to do and that was to stay faithful to the vows she had made to her husband.

She had no intention of doing anything wrong, but she didn't see anything wrong with fantasizing about his man, was there? Was that considered cheating? To lust in her groin and her mind for another? She knew this would have never happened if she and Bobby had been together here or even back home. She knew it was because she was truly lonely here. She had no one to talk to, no one to express her deepest darkest fears, the fear of being here alone, the fear of dying here.

She had just gotten a new team of special agents only three months prior. The last team that had been stationed here were the best. They were all much like big brothers she never had. Steve was the one who had picked her up at the terminal almost seven months ago. He too had piercing blue eyes but not the kind she was attracted to. He was the "talker" of the bunch. He was well liked by everyone. JW, Jim, was a quiet one. He seemed to be the one with the most experience. She was surprised that she had liked him as much as she did, being that he was Hispanic. Her mother had convinced her how evil Mexican men were. Anyway, she liked his quiet self assurance. She also liked and appreciated the fact that he

448

would always not only mention the help she gave him but publicly thanked her in the daily team meetings. Then there was Andy. She could tell right off the bat that this "boy scout" was the officer of the bunch. He had the carriage of one. He held himself in a way that was different than the others. He had a good look about him, like things always came easily to him. He was tall, athletic, blond, and blue-eyed. She had spent several hours talking and getting to know him one evening. She could tell that he was used to women throwing themselves at him. She wondered if he ever wondered why she had not. It was true, he did have incredible looks, but she felt closer to him in a brother/sister relationship than anything else.

She loved the old crew and it seemed as they loved and respected her right back. They spent three holidays together; Thanksgiving, Christmas, and New Year's, the three biggies to her. They felt like family, and who else would one spend the important holidays with, but family?

There was one more agent left to mention. She was her first "battle buddy" and tent mate. She recalled the first time they met. Steve had dropped her off at the tent so she could unpack and get settled. As she opened the flap on the tent, she had to take a second to re-focus her eyes. She couldn't believe how dark it was inside this old dilapidated tent. She first noticed the "sheet walls" almost the full length and width of the tent. As she walked in, she saw a cot and a dusty metal chair in one cornered-off section of the tent. The space could have not been any larger than perhaps a 6'x6' box. Surely she was not to spend the next 12 months in this little box. It was true that it was not as bad as her living conditions at the prison but not that much better either.

She dropped her bags where she stood and wandered around towards the other end of the tent. Further down on the left, she found what looked like a storage room where cots, shelving and metal chairs and other discarded crap was piled up and left. It was louder on this end of the tent, but it was a larger area, albeit filled with a bunch of garbage. She didn't know what to do with all of it. Still, she preferred this to the little box she had first seen upon entering the tent.

"First things first," she said out loud, "organize the shit." She pulled out shorts and tank top and got busy. After about five hours of seriously hard work, she managed to get the area ship shape. Before throwing herself on the bed, she thought a shower was in order. Being deployed for the second time, though the first time was only a week long experience, she knew what was needed for the trek to the women's shower tent, thanks to Bobby. She dug into her carry-on bag and pulled out shampoo, shower shoes, towel, soap and a little red bag to carry it all. As she left her tent, she stood there not quiet sure which way to go. Steven had given her a quickie tour, but she was all mixed up and it was dark out now. Everything looked different at night time. She looked to the left and to the right. She thought perhaps a quick stroll to the left would be in order. So about three blocks into her "trek" she started to worry just a bit because nothing looked familiar or even the same as this afternoon's tour. She thought maybe she should just double back and try the other side of "tent city," as her new home was fondly called. Just as she was about to turn, she saw a flap open on a tent less than a block from where she stood. "Ah ha, found it," she said out loud. Happily she scooted on her way. She opened the flap and looked into the empty tent. She had never been in a shower tent before. At the prison down the road they had shower trailers. This shower tent was altogether different. She stripped down and walked towards the showers. She looked up,

451

way up, and wondered how in the hell was she ever going to take a shower in this country. She stood up on her tip toes as far as they would stretch. The tips of her fingers could just barely touch the metal but couldn't quiet pull the lever down.

She wondered if all the shower stalls were the same height. She moved to the left a bit and, to her delight, not only could she touch the metal but pull down the lever with just the slightest little hop. "Thank goodness," she said out loud, and in she walked with her shower shoes on and towel thrown up and over one of the pipes. The shower felt great. She wondered if it would be ok to take a little longer than the three minute "battle shower" everyone was supposed to take. *No harm in taking a little longer, no one here but me.* She lathered up her hair and thought to herself, *this isn't so bad.*

## Chapter 23 -- Battle Buddies


She came out of the shower tent, freshly showered. In the next split second she got scared, very scared. She had no idea, out of all the sea of tents in front of her; she couldn't for the life of her remember which one was her tent. They all looked the same to her. All she could remember was that her tent was one on the end, but was it a left end or a right end? Her mind went totally blank. Oh God, she was about to cry. She was so afraid that she would wander this little tent city all night long. *Pull yourself together, little girl. This isn't rocket surgery here!* She wiped her tears away and walked with the self assuredness of someone who knew exactly where they were going. As she neared what she thought was her tent, fourth one down on the left, she saw the mattress that was right outside where someone had left it. She let out a large sigh and said, "Home at last."

She walked into her little bedroom that she had decorated with the "happy bunny" paraphernalia she had just bought prior to this trip. It made her smile for the first time since she had left Bobby in Qatar. She'd left him there looking at the bus that would take her on her first solo C130 flight. She and Bobby had made this flight together twice the first time they were here. But this time she was to do it all alone. He stood watching his wife board the bus to her very own destiny. This was the first time they would be apart since they first met. As she boarded the bus, she tried to suck up all the emotions she was feeling before looking back at Bobby one last time. She didn't think she could look back at him standing there all alone without having a mini breakdown right then and there, but she knew she had to be strong for herself, for him, for the both of them. They both knew that this was the best thing…considering they had no other options available to them.

In the six months they were out of work, not one offer came through for the pair but this one. This was it; this was what it was going to take to get the pair back into the employment game and back into the best financial situation for the both of them. As she sat in her little tent atop her happy bunny blanket, she pulled

454

out her little notebook where she had been jotting down notes for the book she wanted to write. She had started this little notebook on her last trip here. Out came the highest pitched sweetest little girl voice she had ever heard.

"Hello, anyone home?" In she came, this tiny blond, blue-eyed woman, the last of the special agents on the team. In came Tawney looking as fresh-faced as any 16 year old, without a stitch of makeup. She plopped herself down on the cot and gave her a quick hug and proceeded to say how completely proud she was of her for the hard work at getting her little bedroom as cute as it was. Tawney's honesty and openness made her a bit wary at first, but she seemed so incredibly sincere and honest. Tawney was such a girly girl, much like herself. The pair of battle buddies clicked automatically. As the days turned to weeks, they became closer. Maybe not really, really close, or at least not until one evening.

Back then there were only four females all living in tent number D18: a very large Air Force LT, a young Hispanic female, herself and her battle buddy, Tawney. On one particular evening when everything changed for the pair, everything was just the same as the night before, nice and quiet. Everyone doing what they normally did at this hour of the evening: LT asleep early and young Hispanic girl listening to music with her headphones on. She wondered where her battle buddy was and assumed she'd hit he rack early tonight. She was lying on her bed watching a movie on her portable DVD player with her headphones on. She was watching *The Manchurian Candidate; she was at* the part where there was some type of explosion. It was strange, but it actually startled her, even though she had seen the movie before, but this was different. She could actually feel the explosion. She quickly pulled off her headphones and poked her head out of her door to see if any of the girls knew what had just happened and what to do next. She called out Tawney's name; no answer. She called out a little louder, just in case she had been sound asleep; again, no answer. Then without any warning, it happened again. The loudest BOOM she had ever heard. She was so frightened that she just called out to anyone in the tent to find out what to do next. Finally the LT came out, and then the young Hispanic girl poked her head out of her room.

The three of them looked as frightened as anyone could imagine. Where the hell was Tawney? She asked the LT what they should do next. Should they get their gear on and get out to the concrete bunkers? LT instructed that they were to get down on the floor. They all hit the floor and waited for the next rocket to hit. As they all lay there in the dirt on the floor of their tent, in ran Tawney a little out of breath. She had been in the shower tents when the first rocket hit. She threw on her clothes as quickly as she could and made her way to the closest bunker, which happened to be the closest bunker to their tent as well.

Tawney squatted there in the bunker and started to wonder what happened to her battle buddy and why she wasn't out there as well. She waited there for her to come out and join her, but when she realized that wasn't going to happen, Tawney decided to get up and run over and get her to safety. Tawney jumped up and ran to the tent. She saw her little friend and the other two lying on the floor of the tent. Tawney instructed her friend to throw on some sweats and jacket and grab her gear as soon as possible; she was going to take her back to the bunker where it would be safe. As Tawney stood there waiting, she dressed and grabbed her stuff as quickly as she could. Tawney stood at the door for one more second and then grabbed her little friend's hand, and they both set off running to the bunker.

There they squatted side by side in the mud watching the "fireworks." It both scared and exhilarated her. In a strange way, it made her feel more alive than anything or anyone ever had. The feelings she was having right here and now worried her. She thought that there could be something wrong with her that she should feel so excited by the danger. She looked over at Tawney and noticed that she too looked excited by the danger. Then without the least bit of warning, the flash of light and sudden explosion so incredibly close to the pair that their once excited expressions turned to shock and straight-on fear.

The shock of it all and the reality of it all made her weep. Tawney took the sleeve of her sweat shirt and wiped off her little friend's tears. As she looked at Tawney, she felt a closeness for this woman that she had never felt with any man she had ever known. Tawney had actually risked her life to come back for her, to save her. She was so grateful for that one act of kindness and bravery she didn't know what to do or say or feel. She just couldn't seem to stop the flood of tears streaming from both eyes. As the tears continued to roll down her cheeks, she tried to stop the waterworks but couldn't, try as she might. Tawney opened up her arms to take in her very frightened battle buddy. She hugged her tightly and as Tawney hugged her for comfort; for the both of them, she looked up at Tawney, their faces only an inch apart. Both of their breathing came at a fast pace and faster yet. She couldn't believe how she was feeling. She couldn't stop what was about to happen right now even if she wanted to, which surprisingly she did not. Tawney continued to wipe away her tears from her tear-stained face but with her bare hand instead of her sweatshirt sleeve. She held on to Tawney's delicate soft hand against her face and started to lightly kiss her fingertips, then to the palm of her hand. The rockets were coming more quickly now but not any closer. Then without any hesitation in either one of them, they kissed so lightly that it felt more like a butterfly wing's flutter.

They had both felt a special bond, a closeness that was foreign to them both. Both women were happily married to men. Neither one had ever experienced such a closeness with another woman before. But now here in the dark muddy coldness, shivering from the cold, it seemed to be the most natural thing in the world. As they were about to kiss again, perhaps more passionately, an announcement came on the base loudspeaker instructing everyone that it was "mission essential" to make it in to work as fast as they could. All imminent danger was gone for now. She got up quickly and helped Tawney up. They stood looking at each other for a second more before Tawney told her that she would be ok and that it was all over and that she had to get to work immediately. With those words still hanging in the cold winter air, she left her standing there in the bunker alone and lost with her mixed feelings.

She loved Bobby more than she could ever say or show, but she also felt something for this woman. As she walked back to their tent, she asked herself, *what in the hell did I just do?* She found herself all alone in the tent. All the others were military and had to report for duty, everyone but her. She stripped back down to her boxers and tank top and tried to sleep, but her mind just couldn't let go of what had just happened, at what she herself had done. With thoughts of her first battle buddy in her head, she dozed off to sleep.

The days passed after that one night, neither one of them mentioning any of it. Tawney was to leave in two short days, and she wondered if she should say something, anything, but what? She left without much fanfare and just as quickly as she entered her life. Tawney's replacement came in the very next day. He was on the quiet side. He had the nickname of Scuba Steve.

She immediately took to him, not as a potential lover or boyfriend but as a friend she could talk to and, as she later found out, one she would be able to tell her deep dark secrets to. She felt he could be trusted to that extent, but for some reason it wasn't meant to be because Scuba had to go back on emergency leave that would last longer than a normal tour here in Iraq. But even after her good buddy Scuba left Iraq, they stayed in contact and would talk for hours on end on email. She never did share those deep dark secrets with him or with anyone else. You just couldn't spill that kind of information on email, you just couldn't.

The good thing was Scuba's replacement was another female. She hoped the new female agent could be someone she could talk with. Her nickname was "Doc" because she had her Doctorate in biology, on the "bug" side. It was a fitting nickname for her. Doc was not the girlie girl like herself or Tawney, but more on the athletic side. Doc looked like a marathon runner. She

461

had a natural beauty to her that required no makeup. She absolutely had the clearest skin she had ever seen. They became fast friends and would commensurate almost nightly for hours concerning the new agents coming in.

She and Doc had their own fair share of adventures. She recalled one such adventure when she and Doc where out and about at the mini "haji" mall on Camp Slayer. The mall was comprised of local nationals who worked on base at different shops such as video, clothing and rug shops. There was also a restaurant that served the most fantastic Arabic food as well as a small grocery store. She and Doc were there to question some of the vendors concerning insurgent activities in the area, when they decided to take a quick break before questioning the next vendor. As they stood out in the open, they heard small arms fire all around them. After being in this place called Baghdad for a few months, the sounds of AK47's being shot just didn't make you jump as when you first get there, strange as that may sound. So regardless of the sounds all around them, she and Doc continued their conversation there just sipping away on their cold drinks and talking about the next vendor to be questioned, when one of the big burly special forces guys that they had come with grabbed the both of them and quickly ushered them indoors.

As they rushed the both of them to safety, she turned around to see little puffs of dirt fly up off the ground at the precise location the two of them had been standing only seconds before. Only then did she realize that they, she and Doc, were the ones being shot at! That realization shook her to her core and but also made her realize just how short life is.

Unfortunately for her, Doc's tour came and went, and she was left alone with that new crew who hated her and Doc for whatever reason. It was strange exactly why they hated the both of them, but she was later told by the LT that it was because she was friends with Doc and the team thought Doc considered herself too good to associate with any of the new team, and also they thought she had been a snitch to the new Detachment Commander. Only one of those reasons was true, but still far from fair!

Chapter 24 -- All about Chris

As she sat at her desk thinking about the old crew, she heard a hard knock at the door. One of the new guys got up to answer the door. Chris strode back into her office with the cockiness of a Chippendale calendar model. She about had a heart attack as her pulse raced out of control and her pits started to drip. *Keep in control, old girl,* she told herself silently. He stood closer to her desk and stared deep into her brown eyes, and she couldn't help but stare right back into his blue/grey eyes.

"I left my notebook. Have you seen it?" Chris asked her as she boldly stared. She couldn't stop the staring; staring into those eyes. That little twinkle was really getting to her. She tried to come back with something a bit sarcastic to help belie her feelings, but it kind of backfired on her.

"You just wanted to come back and talk to me again, didn't
464

you? You don't need any excuses. Come by whenever you like to chat," was all she could come up with. It wasn't clever nor that sarcastic, but it helped stop her from gawking at the man.

What really backfired was his response to her, "Look, lady, I'm just a computer guy who accidentally left his notebook." With his comment hanging out there like some old piece of meat, he saw the notebook, grabbed it and hurriedly walked out the door, not once looking back.

She could feel the new team eyeing her. It had only been less than a half hour ago that the whole team had witnessed her blatant staring of this man's ass as he left the office. She wondered if any of them heard either hers or Chris' comments to each other. They all would have a field day with that, if they had. She had been so lonely because this new team not only didn't respect her, they didn't like her either, or that was how they acted anyway. The three new guys on the team came to this country with an agenda all their own.

The officer of the bunch, only a LT, was probably not so much the laziest person she had ever met but definitely felt he should be the one in charge and made every attempt at a coup

465

d'etat at every available opportunity and even some opportunities not so available. The other agent had been here before and wouldn't let anyone forget that little fact. He was extremely quiet. At first she thought maybe he was just shy, but even when he was ordered to talk to her, most days he just out and out refused to, but when he couldn't get out of it and had to talk to her, it actually appeared to pain him to do it. It appeared to her that he felt that he had to "dummy down" every single thing to her, as if he was the one with 20 years experience in counterterrorism and not just a few months time. Then, last but not least, the overweight comedian who went on and on and on about anything and everything. He fancied himself funny when all he ever was was caustic. He followed whatever the other two instructed much like a puppy dog would. All together, they did as they pleased. Each one as disaffected as the other. This team was prosaic in comparison to the old team, and they knew it and didn't give a damn either.a

She looked quickly up from her notes to see if anyone had paid attention to what just happened, and luckily for her, they were ignoring her per usual, thank heaven! She sat there saddened and almost relieved by his remark. How could she have actually

466

thought that this man who appeared to be at least ten years her junior, who was so very good looking with a twinkle in his blue/grey eyes, be interested in some old woman, someone like her for god sakes? Some days she was just plain ole stupid. Part of her was relieved though. She didn't want to even think about what she would have done to him had he been remotely interested. She had to email her good friend Scuba about this and get his view on the whole story. Thank God he was there for her, even though it was only by email.

Part of her was glad this happened. She really was starting to get concerned when it came to sex. She started to think she just didn't crave it any longer and simply just didn't need it, and that sure as hell wouldn't sit right with Bobby if they ever got the chance to see each other again. She had absolutely zero desire in her, at least until "he" showed up. What she and Tawney shared that one evening wasn't the same as this. That was about an intimacy. This was plain old fashion lust!

As she sat there trying to rationalize all of this in her head, up popped an email from Chris. Part of her was afraid to open his email. She had no idea what he would say next; hopefully nothing

467

too hurtful or mean, nothing like he had already said out loud in front of everyone. She thought for a second about just deleting the damn thing. That way he couldn't hurt her feelings again. Her little index finger started to reach for the delete button.

There, she did it, she hit the delete key—but she knew all to well that it was still sitting there in her delete file waiting to see just how weak she really was concerning this man. She hated this weird power he seemed to have on her. She, who was so used to being in charge of her life and of her emotions, and specifically to a stupid email.

She cursed his name under her breath as she opened the delete folder. There it was sitting there, beckoning her to just open the damn thing and read it. She decided to hit the delete button once more and get rid of the damn thing and the stupid control this man had over her. Gone, gone for good! She felt good about it; exhilarated, actually. She felt in charge again. Then, up popped yet another email from him, from Chris. She looked at it then deleted it, just that quickly. Then moved to her delete folder, and as she aimed her finger towards the delete key, she thought, *ok, what the hell,* and hit enter.

"I'm so sorry for the way I responded to you earlier. I was shocked and embarrassed by your comment, but I was also intrigued. I was so worried that your co-workers could see my obvious interest in you, so I played it off. I hope you can forgive me. Please meet me later this evening at the subway. I would love to talk. Chris." She read it over and over. She couldn't believe her eyes. The email held so much promise and also so much pain. She thought about deleting it this time for good, but she was compelled to keep re-reading the stupid thing over and over again. She thought about just responding back to him as he had done to her less than an hour ago. But she knew better; she knew she didn't want to respond in such a way. Not to someone she obviously wanted to be with, if only for one night; one night that could potentially change her entire life. She looked around towards to her co-workers to see if anyone had been paying her any mind. Of course, they were not. She was invisible to them all. At least until they needed something, then they were all buddy-buddy.

So there she sat, wondering and waiting and wondering. She couldn't believe she was even thinking about this, about him. She tried to push Chris out of her mind and replace him with thoughts of Bobby. How she truly loved him, how he loved her back. She couldn't understand why she was acting like this. What was wrong with her, for god sakes? If she continued to think of Chris, this could possibly ruin them. Was he worth it? Was any man? With those thoughts fresh in her mind, she deleted it—gone, never to be read or re-read again nor answered. As soon as she did that, she felt a weight lifted off her broad shoulders and also felt a degree of sadness.

She got back to work and busied herself with the dossier she had been reviewing. That was more like it; back to her boring little life alone in Baghdad. Boy, she had worked up quite a thirst over this predicament. So off to the break room for her second Dr Pepper of the day. She really tried to limit her intake to just two for the day, but she seemed to be supplementing that addiction with a couple of Red Bulls. She stayed on a caffeine high, not only throughout the day, but well into the evening, and most of the time, early into the morning.

She walked back to her computers and noticed something different from the distance. On both screens were emails from Chris. Oh geez, what was this man trying to do to her? Delete, don't delete, delete, don't delete. What a freaking dilemma she was facing. "What the hell," she said under her breath.

"I'm sorry!" Short, sweet and to the point. As soon as she read that email, up popped another one. This particular email said, "Please don't delete this email. Take the time to hear what I have to say, ok?" She was definitely intrigued now. What in the world was this guy up to? She scrolled down further to read the remainder of his email.

"Please, I'm sorry for sounding like an asshole to you in your office. I tried to apologize in the first email I sent you but you deleted it without reading, understandably. I was nervous. I didn't know what to say or what to do. I've never been hit on by anyone before, especially by anyone as cute as you, and on top of all of that for you to say something nice to me as you did...you made me nervous. Can you or will you meet me? Please say yes. I really would like the opportunity to get to know you. Or if you don't want to meet, can you at least email me back?"

She looked up to check the times he sent these emails. They sounded too much alike. Apparently they had been stuck in some cyber queue and were coming at her randomly. This email in particular made her blush a deep shade of red. She peered above her monitor towards the direction of all of her co-workers; still virtually ignored by them all, thank God. She thanked the heavens above for their indifference towards her for a change.

She sat upright in her chair and began her reply. Should she respond professionally, or the way he talked to her not that long ago, or maybe just a tad flirty? She still felt the sting of his first response. "Hi Chris, nice to hear from you." *Good,* she thought; professional yet not too stuffy. "I always enjoy the opportunity to meet new people. Let's say we chat on email for a while. How would that be?" She read and re-read the email over to make sure she didn't convey the wrong idea or message. Not too flirty and not altogether too professional either. She led her index finger to the send button. *Done deal—now back to work. If he writes me back, fine. If not…oh well, no biggie,* she told herself, knowing it was a lie. And with that thought not even completed, up popped another email from Chris.

She thought about doing a thorough check on Chris and also his wife to get an idea what he was all about. She knew the perfect website that would do the type of "looking into" she wanted done. It was called "Intelius." She hurried through the company's browser to find the type of check she wanted done. She felt that a quick "names check" on him wouldn't be enough. She wanted to know who he, and specifically who his wife, was and where they lived. She felt those type of details were important. What if he or even his wife had some type of police record? You just never know if you might be dealing with some type of criminal element. As she was thinking about whether to invest the time and money to do so, up popped yet another email from him. He sure was persistent; he did have that going for him. She wondered if he even had a chance to read the email she had just sent him. Surely not: open email, read, respond, and send—no way he could have done all that in two seconds.

This type of persistence made her wonder, so she decided to do the very thorough background check on him and his wife. The information she got back confirmed that he was indeed married as she had surmised and that he lived in Tampa, Florida. *Hmm*, she thought. She would find out as much as she could about him on her own and then would ask him a question here and there to find out if he would lie. You would be surprised to find out just how many men would blatantly lie about things, simple easy things for one reason or another. As the reports came fast and furious to her email address, she read through all of them. She thought to herself that he had bought his house a few years ago and it was a ranch style home just like Bobby's and her house. She also saw that he lived in an older, more established community. Then she saw that he had lived in New York and Texas and Colorado. *Interesting,* she thought. She loved to do thorough research when research needed to be done. Ok, nothing too damning. There was a bit of something in Colorado but nothing too crazy. She wanted to retain all this information so she could quiz him later on it. She knew that side of her was not one of her best qualities, but it was who she was. She had done the same to Bobby before they got too involved. It really was her. She couldn't quite trust anyone, although with Bobby, she had come to trust him more and more as the days went by.

As she fingered the enter button ever so lightly, up popped his email. Sure enough, he had not gotten to the email she had just sent which was ok by her; there was time. They both had that going for them, lots and lots of time. This email simply said

'**PLEASE SEE ME**!" all in caps and all bold letters. She opened

his next email. This one simply said "**PLEASE**!" also all in caps

and all bold letters. *Wow,* she thought. This dude was starting to

sound desperate. She liked the idea of that more than she probably

should have. As she sat there staring at her monitor to see if he

would actually read the one she did send, she couldn't help but

wonder what in the hell she was getting herself into. *It's not too*

*late to back out of all of this, out of this situation right now.* She

contemplated her thoughts and really didn't know what she was

getting into with this good-looking sensual man with the blue/grey

eyes, but for the very first time in her life, she didn't care. Sure, of

course it would and should matter what Bobby thought. She still

loved Bobby, loved him like no other man in her life. That fact had

not changed one single bit, but for some reason she wanted to

throw caution to the wind. She wanted to be able to act solely on a

whim, on impulse, to live each of her days in Baghdad as if it

could be her last, and if that meant flirting with a man who looked

totally yummy, so be it. Because when you come right down to it,

no one really ever knows which day could be their last. She would

do whatever it took not to hurt Bobby. That was paramount to this whole affair, if you will. If anything was to happen between the two of them, her and Chris, she would protect Bobby with everything she had, first and foremost! That was the conditions she placed on herself. That and not to get too close to Chris. To keep her emotional distance. She would not let him touch her heart, not even a little bit. Her whole heart was for Bobby and Bobby alone, but as days turned to weeks turned to months, he got to her; maybe not initially but eventually he was there. Chris had touched something in her heart that she couldn't understand, and worse, she didn't want to understand. She liked the way it felt for him to be there in her heart, even though she was confident that she was not in his.

Ok, third email from Chris. Surely this one was a response to the one she sent. "Thank you for responding to my email and not just deleting it. I would like very much to email you but I really would like to meet you in person but glad that you are at least willing to write me. Maybe with a little time, you and I can meet after work for some coffee and a talk."

And that was how it went for the next four weeks or so; emails that started by the normal "getting to know you" stuff to more and more provocative emails until there was nothing left to do but actually meet in person. She was glad to have gotten the time to get to know him and realized they had more in common than at first glance would have it. She was happy to find out that he was, in fact, not ten years her junior but only a year younger than her 47 years. They seemed to have read some of the same books, loved the same music, Robin Trower in particular and Led Zeppelin being their most favorite group when they were both younger; motorcycles, Harley's; tattoo's and José Cuervo. They were both married but neither said much on that topic, understandably. He lived in Florida, the place she always wanted to live again but hadn't had much luck getting back there.

They decided to actually meet one Sunday early afternoon to "watch movies." He would come by to pick her up, grab some lunch to go and some Cokes before settling down to their first movie together, the first of many movies they would watch during their time together at Camp Victory, Baghdad.

As Chris drove to them to the base where he lived, she sat silently; they both did. She was so very nervous, excited, happy and sad all at the same time. She had no idea what he was thinking,

477

nor would she, to some degree, ever find out, even as their days turned to weeks turned into months, fewer months than either one of them anticipated as it later turned out. He was never able to open up to her in that respect, not to that extent, not ever. Sure, he was more than a fantastic lover and handled her body with the know how and expertise based purely on instinct. It was as if he sensed her mood and reacted in kind. He was the only man who could coax her into her fullest expression, to assist her in evolving until her peak, then as she would begin her steady inevitable decline, he knew exactly what to do to bring her back up. How he did that, she never knew and felt comfortable not knowing. She was glad that he did it so effortlessly and so well right from the very beginning.

She would ask Chris tons of questions, all under the guise of research for a book she was writing, when in fact that was only partially true. Mostly she really wanted to know him better than he would let her know if left up to him. Of all the questions she asked Chris, he never once asked her a question in return; not once. It was almost as if he preferred not really knowing her, just the basics like her name and birthday. He never knew what her middle name

478

was or even where her people were from. It just wasn't important to him, it seemed. She was shocked one morning when he actually said to her that he was curious about what it was that she could possibly want to know about him. It really hurt her to her very core that he wasn't the least curious about her, but even with the hurt that she felt, she couldn't stop seeing this man. She tried her best to tell him things that were private or personal to her, in hopes he would do likewise—he never did.

Every once in a while, he would mention something of his past, and that would make her smile. She recalled the time she had asked him about his ethnicity. She totally radiated when he came back with information concerning where *his* people were from and what war had taken place there all those years ago. He also mentioned simple things from his past like his first job at Tastee Freeze to save up money for his first motorcycle, a Kawasaki. Or even when he spoke of the tattoos he had, the dead eagle he designed himself that was on his chest so he could see it, that had been a souvenir from a trip to Russia; to the tribal band he had around his arm but not all the way around because it was bad luck. The tribal meant "life to the fullest;" to the abstract V-twin engine with HD on his other arm that he had also designed himself.

He never talked of his past or about his wife or the future, only the here and now, but when he did let her inside a little, she simply beamed that he had opened up at least that much of himself to her...for her.

Chris knew next to nothing about her, the woman he had been "watching movies" with for weeks now. He knew nothing of her family, not even that her dad had been in the Air Force and that she grew up on air force bases all over the world or how much she missed her dad and needed him more than ever right now. Chris didn't know that she flew straight through from Germany to Texas to be there with him as he was dying or that the last time she ever watched a football game was with her dad the day before he passed: Cowboys, his team and Steelers, her team--Steelers winning, of course. Or how she was there alone for his very last breath and had closed his eyes shut right after. Or that she kept a picture of him on her desk while she was in Iraq.

He didn't know that she was the middle child with two older sisters and two younger sisters and how no one in her family gave a damn about her even while she was in that god forsaken hell hole country of Iraq. She did not receive one package from her family during Christmas or ever during her 8 month tour there. While all her teammates cheerfully opened presents from loved ones, how she cried herself to sleep because of it and that she still did, mostly out of sheer loneliness.

Chris never even asked her about the strange private email address when she had passed it on to him so he could keep in touch after she left. Why c_robins? Who was c_robins? Not once did he ask. He never found out that it stood for Christopher Robins from the Winnie the Pooh stories or why that was the least bit significant to her.

She did recall once during their time together that he did ask her a question. It was after a particularly hot Sunday afternoon of "watching movies," him behind her for several minutes, afterwards he asked about her tattoos on her back and what they symbolized. She was so shocked and elated by him wanting to know something about her that she was so totally flustered that she just wasn't sure how she answered.

There were things he did know about her; he knew she was married. She volunteered that information to him via email right

481

from the start. But he didn't know that she had been married twice before or that the second time, to a man who was not so nice to her. A man who verbally abused her at will.

She wondered if he was only interested in the sexual aspect of her. Surely he could have found another if that was the reason or was it because this was easier for him? She had practically thrown herself at him and he knew that she was totally hot for him and only him; she let him know that little fact in an email. She wondered why he didn't even ask her or even comment on a portion of the book she had written that she passed to him to read, even when it was about him in particular, or that she decided to take that part out of the book she was writing. Or even why she decided to write a book in the first place or even why she had no other choice but to write the goddamn book.

There was just so much he didn't know about her, and it appeared to at least her that he was content in not knowing. Not knowing what made her cry, what made her laugh or even why she had finally given up eating altogether there in Iraq. Or even though she loved her first husband so much but wanted children so very much and he didn't and that she decided to leave him, only to find out that she couldn't carry a child full term. Or even the fact that she had three miscarriages before she was 35 years old. Or that her first husband got her a puppy that she had now had through three marriages and 3 boyfriends which totaled to about 15 years, and that his first name was Russian.

Or even that her favorite song in the whole world was still Robin Trower's "Daydream" and how Robin's hauntingly sad guitar riffs could make her weep. Or that she had always wanted to make love while his music played in the background but never did. These things Chris was unaware of. She was sure he didn't know that he was the only person she knew who had even heard of Robin Trower.

He didn't even know that she'd started to hug her pillow at night wishing it was Chris, wishing it was him to help chase away the loneliness she felt since coming to Iraq. Or that she couldn't fall asleep before 3am unless she was with him. Or how scared she was to leave this country, to leave him, to never see him again. So afraid that she would never feel what she felt when she was with him. To never feel or experience the totally sublime lovemaking he had shown her.

Or how much she missed her little house in Maryland with its French antiques, Austrian crystal chandeliers and Persian rugs but that she was somehow comforted with being with him in his trailer that he shared with a roommate she had never seen or met.

Or even how truly sad she was every Monday morning after spending wonderful relaxing Sundays with him as close as two people can get, only to go into work and not hear from him, yet she still felt no regret.

Or even that she would be leaving this country, leaving him sooner than expected, before the end of her contract was over in October.

And that her favorite place in the whole world to be was at the beach.

Or that she pretended to be as cavalier about their whole situation as he did. Or even that she wondered where he went after he dropped her off every Sunday afternoon. That she couldn't help but wonder if he was with someone else, someone with less emotion than herself.

Or that she worried about his safety when he went on one of his many trips throughout Iraq. Worried that something would happen to him, that he might not make it back, back to Baghdad, back to her.

And lastly, he definitely didn't know, would never know that she had fallen so incredibly hard for him, even though she had promised herself to keep the same wall up that he had kept up and that try as she might, she didn't and couldn't keep the wall up. That she opened her heart and let him in willingly. Or that their last night together frightened her so very much that she had to tell him about what happened to her at the prison the year before.

And that after she left Iraq he continued to be in her thoughts daily for many years that followed, and it was usually while she was in her garden, the only place she let her mind wander back to the war, back to Iraq, back to him. She felt all of those things even knowing that it would never lead to anything, but she made special note to never let him know of these feelings for him. That promise she made and kept. She also knew that their time together was so very limited and she did not want to waste one single precious moment if it could be helped. Regardless of all of it, he had gotten under skin and inside her heart, and once he was there…he was always there, regardless of their outcome or ending.

Or how she loved her husband so completely and so deeply yet she never regretted her decision to have a relationship with Chris, even with the knowledge that it would never lead anywhere but with memories, some good, some not.

You could fill a house with all the things that Chris didn't know about her, but he was such a fun person to talk to and to be with, as long as you didn't want or need more from him in the emotional sense. He kept that wall up at all times concerning her, just as she had told herself that she would do concerning him. Unfortunately for her, her resolve on this matter was not as strong as Chris'. They enjoyed each other's company for the remainder of his months in Baghdad, which turned out to be a matter of days and not months as both had anticipated. They parted as friends, to her dismay, with no more than a kiss and a hug goodbye. But before she left, she handed Chris a little gift. He smiled at her with the same little smirk she had come to love, as he opened his going-away present. She wondered if he ever took the little six inch bendable Gumby toy home with him, back home to Florida. She had bought the pair of toys for the both of them. She proudly

486

displayed her bendable Pokey toy on her desk, and every once in a while when asked about it, she would only smile and say "no comment."

As the days turned to weeks that turned to months, she and Chris both thought that they would have at least five more months of "movie watching." She didn't find out how differently things would end for the two of them until one hot afternoon as she was leaving Chris' office. He simply blurted it out as he walked her to her car, "I'm leaving next week." It was so matter-of-fact that it made her wonder just how long he had actually known about it. How long before he broke down and told her that he was leaving? They walked silently to her car; she with her own thoughts and he, well only he knew what thoughts he was having.

He saw the overwhelming sadness in her big brown eyes. He knew that she didn't think that this was the way it should end. She was supposed to leave first. She was to leave this place, to leave him in five months time when her contract was up. Not like this, not this quick "I'm outta here next week" bullshit. All he knew was that he didn't want her to feel bad. He wanted to make it up to her somehow.

He smiled at her and said, "Babe, I've got a friend that will take me to the commercial side of the airport to get us something, and I will pick you up and we can spend the night together."

Her eyes lit up as she asked, "What time, babe?" Chris knew that she understood what that "something" would be. Their minds worked the same way when it came to things of that nature.

She loved the way his blue/grey eyes twinkled when he said "something from the airport" and the little smirk that appeared at one corner of his mouth. She knew exactly what he meant when he said that. It had been so long since either of them had any alcohol. It wasn't allowed in a war zone, but if one was resourceful enough, "something" could be found.

As she drove away from Chris and back to work, she wondered how this man would be with a little alcohol in his system. Most of the time he kept so much of himself back. The most the two of them talked was usually about each other in sexual innuendo and double entendres; that, music and motorcycles was the extent of most of their little email and talks, and every once and a while the work-related crap. She wasn't sure exactly what type of alcohol he was going to have, but she knew he knew how much she loved her José.

By the time she got to the office, she had almost forgotten about him having to leave the very next week and was only looking forward to spending the night with this man. She had spent the night with him once before and, of course, they had their Sunday "movie watching" afternoons, but never a sleepover with alcohol included. She was excited and she was scared that she would only get closer to this man, closer than she ever should, and now with him leaving in a week, she wanted to break down and start crying, but she wouldn't let herself do that. She wanted this evening to be perfect and it would be, if she had her way.

She turned on her computer so she could get busy and prayed that the three remaining hours left on the clock would go quickly before meeting up with Chris. Up popped the now familiar "Chris" email on the screen. She loved when she would see his name pop up on her screen. She opened his email—he said "Russian for me and Mexican for you. Pick you up cutie at 8." She loved all the pet names he gave her over the weeks. He started out with the pet names first. She was too scared to do so for fear she would scare him off. She recalled the first email when Chris said,

489

"hey babe, I'm leaving for the day." It seemed so very casual the way he said "babe," but it meant so much to her. Why? She had no earthly idea. She didn't know why most things he said or did excited her so. It wasn't like she wasn't used to men fawning all over her. That she was used to, but for some reason it seemed extra special when he did it. She responded in kind, "ok babe, see you tonight." It felt so good to talk to each other this way. It made her feel closer to him somehow. Almost as if he was really starting to like her. It had only been two months, but sometimes it felt as if they had always been together, but yet still strangers to each other.

She deciphered his code to mean vodka and tequila. *Nice,* she said to herself. She felt so confident that with a little alcohol in him that it would make him open up and maybe share some of himself with her. She didn't mean physically, he all too ready and willing and had shared himself, ALL of himself in that aspect with her. Anything she wanted to do to him, she had carte blanche to do so.

She sat there thinking about this man. How was it possible that this man could bring so much back into her life, all that had been missing for over a year now, since last April after the terrible situation at the prison here in Baghdad? She had totally withdrawn from everyone, even Bobby. She became more and more closed off that no one could touch her, either physically or emotionally. Sure, she still loved Bobby with all her heart, but there was something that wouldn't let herself feel totally open to him or to anyone else, at least, not until Chris. She didn't want intimacy, and she knew she lacked passion and desire for Bobby and for everyone or everything else. She had lost all of that, all of it that one evening when she was drugged and raped. She could only remember bits and pieces of it. She had blocked out most of it. After her and Bobby's return to the States and after their company had fired them both, she tried everything she could to block all of it like it was a very bad dream. She had spent more than a month locked away from everyone, including Bobby. She just kept withdrawing into herself more and more until that one day she couldn't see the point of going on.

She shook her head and wondered why in the hell did she let herself go back there, back to that place. The place she hated more than anything else in the world. She tried to think of happier things, like Chris and how he had brought passion and desire back

491

to her and brought it back by the bucket full. She shook her head and then brought herself back to the here and now. She started to wonder what she would wear this evening. She wanted to look her best since she felt that this would be their last time together. That little fact she didn't have to, didn't want to dwell on. She was going to only dwell on the here and now, much like Chris normally did, she thought. *Ok, 6pm, time to split for the day.* Her boss looked at her strangely as she said her goodnights at 6pm. Everyone watched her walk out the door in shock. Everyone knew that she never went home before 9:00 at night but usually around 10:00 or so. She didn't care. She had things to do to prepare.

She made it to her tent, grabbed her little shower bag and made her way to the shower. She knew straight away that she was not going to take no stupid three minute battle shower. Not today, not now. She would do her best to take a nice long hot relaxing shower, shave all body parts and make sure she would give her feet a good scrubbing. She wanted to make sure all of her was baby smooth for him. She wondered if he knew how much work she would do to make sure her body was "just so" for him. Probably not, probably thought she was born this soft and with this wonderful smelling body.

She didn't mind doing these blatantly girlie-girl chores. In fact, she really missed doing them. In Iraq there really wasn't any reason why one would need a pedicure, much less soft skin. All that really mattered was that you shower at least once a day. She was so glad to have a reason to do these things again. Chris brought so much of herself back in such a short few weeks. He would never know how grateful she was to have found herself again in, of all places, the place where she not only lost sight of who she was but had it taken away from her. The one thing that had changed in her was her "don't really give a shit attitude" with men; with other men but not her Bobby. All her years she had a love 'em and leave 'em attitude. She was in control, she was the boss, she directed what and when something was going to happen when it concerned relationships. She was used to men just throwing themselves at her and definitely never the other way around. To say that men around her were pussy-whipped would have been an understatement. But not this one, not this man, not Chris. He intrigued her right from the beginning because of this. Right from the first comment to her when he came back to get his forgotten notebook. This time it was he who seemed to have the 'tude and she felt that attitude towards her.

Some days it felt, at least to her, that they both wanted to be together as much as the other but sometimes, just sometimes, it felt as if she wanted to see him more than he wanted to be with her. She couldn't blame herself though. This man had brought her back, gave her life again, showed her how to live. Really, what did she give him? Did he even realize what he had given back to her?

As she showered, she took special care to make sure she was smooth in all the right places. That man loved to languish all day and night on her little body, never seeming to tire. He could recuperate faster than any man she had ever known after he climaxed. It had never taken him more than 5 minutes, 10 at the most to "re-charge." Damn, a phone took at least an hour to recharge, she thought to herself. They both could enjoy each other's bodies over and over and over again in one afternoon. She took what he gave her pretty damn good too! Of course, after he would drop her off back at her tent, she would have some difficulty sitting down or even walking. She would be so incredibly swollen for at least three days. How did he have such incredible stamina, especially for a man his age? He could come and come and come again all in one afternoon. It totally blew her mind.

After she shaved, showered and applied lotion, she made her way back to her tent to find the right outfit. Sometimes she would just say "fuck it, I'll just wear whatever" but then would spend that much more time checking and re-checking how she looked in the mirror. She didn't want to appear too put–together, but neither did she want to appear as if she just threw on some old rag.

As she sat at the "Subway," all showered, changed, smelling great and listening to her one of her favorite bands, "Audioslave," she wondered how tonight would progress. This would be the first time in over seven months that she would drink alcohol. She by no means felt like an alcoholic, but she did love her tequila, and Chris had cryptically promised her something "Mexican."

She felt the familiar flutter in her tummy when she saw his gun riddled truck come around the corner. She wondered what movie they would watch today; hell, also tonight. She was going to spend the whole goddamn night with this wild man. She had spent evenings with him in the past but never an evening with alcohol involved. She wondered if he would act differently and if so, just how so?

"Hey, babe, sorry I'm late. Damn the entry control point; ECP got hit and the traffic was backed up for miles so I decided to make my own route up here." He smiled and winked, and that small little look made her weak at the knees and he knew it.

He wondered what in the hell did this fine looking cutie with the rockin' bod actually see in him? She was classy and graceful and he was…well, he was Chris. Just a guy with his own demons to live with that he had acquired along the way. He felt like he had lived and experienced two lifetimes already. And she had such a purity about her that was until he caught a glimpse of the two tattoos that were visible, one on her ankle and one on her wrist. But even with the two tattoos, she still had an innocence about her that he just couldn't explain and he was all about helping her change all of that!

Even as the weeks turned to months of their very special friendship he realized just how deceiving looks, especially hers, could be. She was a wild little thing and she also surprisingly took everything he gave her and he gave her plenty. He gave her all of his ten inches with a six inch girth! His first thought after they got to know each other in the biblical sense was that she had to be the smallest woman he had ever been with and not only in stature. It just about took the will of God to get his big fat dick inside her tight, pink, pretty pussy.

She truly was the smallest, tightest little woman he had ever experienced, and he'd had his fair share of experiences with that particular part of the female anatomy. All things considered, his size, her size, she took it all and took it has hard as he gave it and as often he gave it to her. That was another thing that surprised him, and at his age and experience that was sometimes difficult to actually accomplish; never in his sexual life had he been able to cum then cum and cum again so quickly and so often. He rarely needed more than five minutes before he was ready to go yet again. How in the world did she have that effect on him and a man at his age as well? It was as if she was a drug and he the addict; he couldn't get enough of her. Chris knew a thing or two about being addicted and also a thing or two about drugs, but that was another lifetime, a time long ago but not so easily forgotten.

Today was going to be all about fun. They would grab some pizza, get some Red Bulls for his "something Russian" and go back to his trailer for a fun time of eating, drinking and "movie watching" as they liked to call it. It was their way to talk about it on email without raising any red flags to those who made it their careers to monitor email. They both had voracious appetites when it came to "watching movies" and when they couldn't be together to "watch movies," they loved to talk about it on email.

She loved that wink of his and he knew it. He hated to think about such things as feelings, but in the short few months that they knew each other, he felt he had perhaps had a feeling or two for this little woman. Maybe not straight-out love--that he saved for his wife and kids, but he did feel something for her. He knew that in a few emails he had told her that he adored her and she didn't quite understand what he meant by that. Hell, he didn't know what he meant, but it felt right to say it to her. He adored her!

They sat side by side in the cab of his truck as they made their way back to his place on Camp Victory without so much as a word. He couldn't help but check out that slammin' little bod of hers. She had the brownest, strongest-looking legs he had seen in a long time. He wondered what she was thinking as she sat and stared out the window. He loved that she was still quite shy with him; he didn't know why she was, but he could tell by how easily she blushed if he said something that was a little off color. One thing was for certain, the woman wasn't shy in bed; nowhere near it.

As they pulled up to the Pizza Hut on Camp Victory, he asked, "What kinda pizza would you like, babe?" The suddenness of the question broke her daydream, and she was day dreaming alright and of all things: Bobby.

She smiled at Chris and replied, "Meat, I am a total meat eater." That made him smile more broadly because he had found out just how much of a "meat eater" this woman was. She took her time on his "meat" and knew what and how to do the things he loved so very much without so much as a word of instruction from him.

"Will do, be back in a minute or two, babe, or do you want to come with?" Chris asked her.

"Sure thing, babe," she answered back.

With pizza and Red Bulls in hand, they started the trek

from parking lot to his trailer. Oh God, how hot it was walking around in the early evening sun, and she knew that it was to get much hotter, much much hotter! They walked into his ice-cold trailer, and she felt the familiar chill, not only from the temperature in the trailer, but with anticipation of what would happen next. He sat everything down and sat on his bed, grabbed the little woman by the wrist and led her to him.

The next thing that either of them knew, they were in a hot sweaty naked tangle, both exhausted and famished. He threw on his grey boxers and said, "Ready to eat, babe?"

Oh man, was she ready to eat and the pizza looked good too! After opening the box of pizza, he took two bottles from his wall locker, one for her and one for him.

The next few hours were surreal to her. They were having the time of their lives. Chris opened up and talked to her for the first time since she knew him. Then things seemed to get out of control. He was angry; he started talking about her friend Jim and how they were probably "doing it" when the both of them weren't together. Sheer madness ensued and somehow she wound up locked out of his trailer without any ID or a way to get back in. She

500

walked to the women's restroom and washed her face. She stood looking in the mirror and wondered what in the hell had just happened. She was scared; she didn't know what to do next. She didn't know why he was so mad at her and why just all of a sudden and why did he walk out so quickly? She thought that maybe he would be back at the trailer by now, so she started the walk back there. She tried to open the door, and it was still locked. She should have never walked out to try to find him, but she was so worried that something would happen to him. She didn't know the damn door automatically locked. She wasn't 100% sure, though, that he wasn't sitting in there and just pissed off at her. The thought that he could be in there and not letting her in made her so sad that she just sat there on the steps of the trailer and cried. She wasn't sure how long she had been sitting there crying, but up walked Chris smoking a cigarette. He was surprised to see her sitting there and especially surprised that she was crying. He didn't know what had gone on or why he got so pissed at her, but he knew he had to leave before he became violent. He didn't want to hurt her, hell, hurt anyone anymore, so he walked out before he lost control of his emotions. He scooped her up and pretended that nothing had happened and laid her down on the bed as he lay right behind her, and they both finally dozed off to sleep.

Sometime during the night, they both had undressed and were under the covers, him spooning her, when she felt the growth of him. She smiled to herself and knew what would happen next. He usually started out very gently with her, then he would go buck wild. This time something was different about him. He flipped her over on her tummy so quickly and tried to push his dick into her asshole. She was so shocked about it that she moved quickly, and in her quickness smacked his face with the back of her hand. His first reaction was to grab her by the shoulders and shake her. When he did this she lay there, small and scared, and looked him in the eye and started crying. What was going on with this man? He hadn't had that much to drink the night before and surely he still couldn't be drunk now. He stared back at her and let her go and looked around for his clothes, put them on and as he walked to the door, looked back and said, "Be ready in ten minutes. I've got to be at work early, and it will take us a while to get you back to Camp Sather."

With that, he closed the door and she sat there wondering

what in the hell did she do wrong. What happened? Did he want to end everything like this? Did he just hate her so much that he didn't want anything to do with her? They still had a couple more days before he had to leave, so why was he doing this, ending it like this and why now? He came back refreshed, grabbed the car keys and his badge and said, "Ready babe?"

It was as if what happened this morning never happened. Was he schizophrenic or what? She didn't know what to make of all of this, so she simply grabbed her sunglasses and her badge and followed him out the door. Now Chris was never a touchy-feely kinda guy out in public, for obvious reasons, but this was different. He walked to his truck like she wasn't even there with him. He just kept the same pace, not even turning around to see if she was there or not. As they both climbed up in the truck and buckled up, they held a painful silence until she just couldn't take it one more second. They both heard a loud explosion.

They stared at each other in shock and silence. "What the hell was that?" she asked Chris. He just sat there in silence and started up the truck and drove away. It wasn't until later that day that she found out a mortar had hit the very next trailer to his. His

503

trailer had limited damage, nothing like the one next door.

"What did I do? Was it something I said? Why are you treating me like this? Do you not want to see me anymore? Please talk to me, Chris, please. I'm sorry for whatever I did. I don't want it to end like this. Please, I'm sorry for everything."

With those words of hers stinging in his ears, all he could do was say, "It's ok. You didn't do anything wrong and of course I want to see you again. This isn't over. We are still going to spend all day Sunday together. That is only tomorrow that we will be together again. I don't leave until Monday afternoon. We will spend the whole day together, and it will fun."

Why didn't she believe him? She didn't feel 100% confident in any of his words. She couldn't take comfort from any of his words. She looked up from her lap and realized that they were already at Camp Sather, where she worked and lived. She slowly climbed out of the cab and looked at his face, and effortlessly the tears rolled down her cheeks as she said goodbye to Chris. He told her to stop all of this nonsense and that he would be here tomorrow at 10am sharp to pick her up. She walked slowly to where she worked and wrote a letter to Chris. She wanted to tell

504

him everything, every single thing. Maybe it would make him change his mind about seeing her. She didn't think she would see him again, that was why she thought email was the best way to get this to him.

She also left a note for her boss to let him know that she was calling in sick that day. She simply didn't think she could work, the way she felt. She walked back to her tent and crawled into her little cot and slept for the next several hours. She woke up around 6pm and walked to work to let her folks know that she was ok and if they wanted her to come in on her usual day off, Sunday. Her boss assured her that wasn't necessary so, before she walked back to her tent, she checked her email. There was one short email from Chris that said, "Pick you up at 10, babe. And oh, by the way, the explosion we heard this morning, the trailer down from me was hit." That was it. Nothing more, nothing about her painfully detailed email to him about the prison and what had happened to her there. Just a big fat nothing from him about her heartfelt email.

Maybe he wanted to talk to her in person about it. Yeah, that was it, she thought. She slowly walked to her tent, grabbed her shower bag and walked to the showers. She felt so bone tired and

505

old. She didn't want to think of anything this evening. She didn't want to recreate what happened last night in her mind, but she couldn't help but to do so. She got back to her tent and looked through all of her movies and tried to find a comedy. She cried and cried as she thought about the email she sent Chris. The last email she would send him from Iraq.

She woke up Sunday morning feeling nothing but dread. What in the hell was this all about, she thought to herself. She should be happy to at least some extent. Sure, Chris was leaving the next afternoon, but today was going to be good. They would spend the whole day and most of the evening together. She walked to the showers with her gear, and she came to the conclusion that Chris was gone. He had already left. She felt it strongly, but he didn't call her like he said he would in case that should happen. She felt it though. Felt it in her every pore. She showered and walked back to her tent knowing he would not be at the Subway like he had promised her he would. Nevertheless, she walked over there at quarter to 10 and waited. She didn't bring her flak vest or her helmet as she normally did; she knew she wouldn't need it to get off this base because she wasn't leaving this base today. He

506

wouldn't be there to see her. She wouldn't get the chance to see that little wink and smirk of his that she loved so much.

After waiting for about 15 more minutes, she walked to her office and called Chris' office; he in fact had left that very morning at 2 o'clock. Chris had told his co-worker to give her a call at her office to let her know so she wouldn't just be sitting there waiting on him. As she sat there at her desk, she thought back to the email she sent him.

Chapter 25 -- Last Email to Chris


Chris, I am writing this email to explain a few things to you. I know how very upset you were last night and have to tell you the truth about the one night when you saw me with my friend, Jim. I tried to tell you last night but you didn't or couldn't listen to what I had to say. I thought that maybe you would read this and at least understand where I am coming from. It is important to me that you know what really happened. I know when you saw me and the long haired guy that you thought that I was "doing" him as well. I tried very hard to tell you what was what. So here it is. This is what happened at Abu Ghraib that one night and eventually the connection between Jim and me.

It started out late one night; my roommates and their friends with benefits were going at it as usual. I grabbed my shower gear and walked down the steep steps and I could hear someone there with me but I couldn't see them. The area is pretty dark up there, but I made my way. I was walking pretty quickly towards the stairs, and I heard someone walking towards me. I started to run, and then that is when I fell all the way down the stairs and busted up my right elbow. I just got up as quickly as I could. My head was bleeding and I was pretty banged up. Someone grabbed me from behind and pushed me down on the couch that was in the day room. I was not only dizzy but bleeding badly. That didn't stop the guy from doing what he did to me. I couldn't scream; he had his hand on my mouth and he kept repeating over and over that no one would believe me and that he would take care of my husband if I said anything to anyone. After he was done with me, I ran to the showers and stayed in there for most of the rest of the night/morning. I had taken my shower and cleaned up everything. I wanted to tell someone but I was afraid "he" would do something to my husband.

Before I went back up to my room, I found a dumpster to throw out all the clothes I had on, including the towel that I used on my head to make it stop bleeding. As I was walking back to my room, I saw my husband, and he could tell by looking at me that there was something wrong. I only told him that I had fallen pretty hard down the stairs. I told him I wanted to leave right then and there. I wanted to go home. He was panicked. He went to the new NCOIC and got us on a convoy back here that very afternoon. We didn't tell our company anything, we simply left. When we got back to the States I wasn't the same. I had changed so very much. We went to the company to tell them we had left and wanted to go back to Cuba.

They fired the both of us. I was completely and utterly devastated. We didn't know what to do or say. We went home and I immediately went into a depression that I had never experienced before. My husband had to go back to Cuba to get our household goods. He came back within 3 days. He didn't know what to do; he didn't know what to say. I couldn't tell him because I was so embarrassed and ashamed and scared. I just went into myself more and more until it was too unbearable for me to even be. I tried to kill myself. I still couldn't tell him what happened. I stayed in the bedroom for over a month, not eating, not talking, and not wanting to be looked at or touched.

I couldn't get close to anyone. I didn't want to. Then I took everything that was inside of me, all the hatred and disgust and all of the bullshit I was feeling and went to my backyard and tried to transform it and me in the process. I would go out there from 5 in the morning until 8 at night; sometimes later. My husband would be on the computer to try to find us work. I told him I had to go back to Iraq. I had to finish off what I had started off doing. He didn't want me to go but knew that I would regardless of what he said. I found the company and waited on them to get the contract. My husband turned down job after job after job there in the States so he could go with me to Iraq. We finally both got hired

I was in Baghdad about two days when everyone from the office I worked with decided to go to the big PX on Camp Victory. Once we got there, everyone went their separate ways to buy stuff or to eat or whatever. I got there and made my way to the gazebo that was in front of the PX. For some reason, I just broke down right then and there. I couldn't stop crying, that's when I met the guy with the long hair, my friend Jim. He sat with me and talked to me. I had not told anyone anything before then. I had not gotten close to my husband the whole summer. I sat there with Jim telling him every single thing that happened at the prison. He wanted to

511

take me to the hospital. He told me he would come by the office later that day after I was done working and we could talk some more.

From that point on, he became my most trusted and best friend. He was the one that encouraged me to write the book in the first place, to help me get it all out. He never came on to me; he never tried to pressure me to get "close" to him in that way. I had not been "close" to anyone, ANYONE! Not until I met you.

As soon as I met you, I felt some type of bond with you. I know that sounds so incredibly stupid but I did. I trusted you immediately. I don't know why, but I did, and for the first time since last April I felt like being "close" again. I let myself get close to you physically and emotionally. It felt so good to let out all the bad shit in my head and to just be able to feel good again.

That is why I was so adamant about not sleeping with the long hair dude. I couldn't, I didn't; he was my best friend. He helped me get all the bad shit out of my head. He helped me be myself again to some extent. Without him, I would have never been able to be with you or anyone else for that matter.

Well, Chris, that is the story. That is what happened.

Believe it or not, it is what really happened. "

She emailed the story of what had happened and just hoped for the best. After he left she didn't know what to do with herself. She felt sad and empty inside. For whatever reasons, she just couldn't bear to be in this country without Chris. So instead of hanging around, she felt the urge to convince Bobby to go on an early R&R with her and go back home for a couple of weeks for the 4th of July weekend, and while there, they could check on the company that had been courting them since their last R&R in February.

Bobby was more than receptive to this idea. He had the chance to be back with his babydoll, his lobster, once again; *what's not to love,* Bobby thought. For her, although she too wanted to, needed really, to see Bobby again, she knew deep down in her heart that she just couldn't bear to be in Baghdad without him, without Chris.

Within a few hours they were able to make plans to leave Iraq, and as it looked, might even beat Chris home. He had only left less than 24 hours prior. She hoped that somewhere they would get to see each other again, but one just knew and shouldn't try to hold one's breathe until then.

To her, she felt that he was satisfied with only being her "fuck buddy" in Iraq. Would he even consider a meeting down the road? She thought not but still kept the hope alive in her heart that he may one day enjoy a visit from his little Gumby. It was her hope, anyway.

After several hours that seemed to turn to days, she and Bobby made it back home to their little house in the woods.

Chapter 26 -- Final Return Home to Bobby

She and Bobby finally got into BWI and were on their way home to the little house in the woods. Bobby's eyes gleamed with excitement. She, on the other hand, couldn't understand what was going on with her. Why did she feel so very sad? She should have been the happiest she had ever been, but there she sat in the taxi like she had just gotten a prison sentence of sorts. She felt so strange, almost as if she dreaded coming home to Bobby, their lovely home and her little garden. But why?

While she and Bobby were apart in Iraq, she knew she loved him and missed him very much. But sitting there with him at that moment, she just wasn't sure what she felt. She truly, honestly did not know what she felt about him or about being back home. Had she completely lost her mind while she was in Iraq? Is this what happens to people when they get back from a war-torn country? It was apparent to her that not everyone acts this way. Bobby looked so ecstatic, and he was talking a mile a minute while she sat there desperately sad.

Bobby started work with the new company within days of their arrival home. He was actually on two separate contracts at the same time. He didn't want to go back to Iraq, and if all of his belongings never made it back to him, he was more than fine with that. For her, for some fucked up reason even to her, she wanted to go back. She used the excuse about having all her belongings there and no one she trusted enough to pack her things, which was 100% true. This was the excuse she told the new company that was ready to hire them both, right then and there, and this is what she told Bobby as well. She told them that she would pack her belongings, give her notice and come back home to Bobby and to the new company. She knew in her heart, though, she was not going to come back. She wanted, needed really, to go back.

She tried to fit back into the scheme of things at home but couldn't. She thought that if she could at least concentrate all her efforts back on her garden that it would make all the difference in the world. The little garden had helped pull her out of some bad issues last year so there should be no reason why it wouldn't work again for her. But she knew that within a few days she would be headed back to finish out her contract then pack her bags and return, so what would be the point in concentrating all efforts on the garden until her return? It was as if she didn't want to get too involved with anything or anyone, to include Bobby, to his eventual dismay.

They had only been home less than a week, met with the new company, and Bobby was to start work in a couple of days. He was so totally ingrained with being back home that it made her head spin and there she was, stuck in Iraq in her mind and wanting to go back sooner vs. later in the worst way.

What was wrong with her? She finally had everything, a very loving husband that was all about her, jobs for the both of them to die for with salaries that were out of this world; a beautiful home with wonderful additions in the works, and all she could think of was her little cot in a tent she shared with seven other females. Boy oh boy, did she need professional help in the worst way.

Nevertheless, she wanted to go back. Bobby had simply

emailed their company and told them he wasn't going to return. She was and had already made plans to return to finish out her contract. She told her new company that she would return within the week, but secretly she knew that she would stay longer if they asked her too. She just wasn't ready to come back home for some strange reason. But as her luck would have it, when Bobby emailed their company that he wasn't returning, she received a very strange email from the company. She wanted to let them know of her intentions. Although she found the email from her company more than condescending towards her, she wanted to let the company and the customer know that her intentions had not changed in the least. That she and Bobby were two separate and distinct employees who were not joined at the hip. She knew in her heart that she was going back, unlike Bobby, who had simply quit on the spot. Her company had emailed her back on Saturday to tell her to give them a call on Monday morning; she was to leave the following Tuesday for Iraq.

It had been a tough week for her and Bobby. It was that she didn't feel at home in her home or with Bobby. She couldn't bear to get close to either one. All she knew was that she had to leave him and her once beloved home and garden to go back to Iraq, perhaps to get some type of closure.

Many nights that followed she stayed up all hours crying and worrying. She was so worried that she wouldn't feel what she had felt for Bobby before they went to Iraq this second time. She wanted the feeling of lobster love, but it just wasn't in her for some reason, and that made her so incredibly sad; sad for her and sad for the both of them. She tried many times to talk to Bobby of these strange and unwelcome feelings she was having. He said he understood and would give her the time she needed, but still she wept and wept nightly, trying hard to pull herself out of this mess.

Bobby would take her to the places that they both had once loved to try to help bring her back. All it did was make the distance between them greater. They only had a weekend left before she was to leave to go back to Baghdad, and he was to go to work at the new company.

Try as he might though, nothing appeared to work for the pair of lobsters. Not even her garden could pull her out of what she was feeling, and that feeling was to put much distance between her and her home and distance between Bobby and herself. She hated these feelings, but she couldn't lie or deny their existence or even contain them, try as she might.

At precisely 5am Bobby's alarm went off. They both groaned in unison.

Chapter 27 -- What's the Problem?

To any onlooker who saw her and Bobby back home, they would think that everything was idyllic for the pair. For Bobby it really was perfect. They were both out of Iraq alive and in one piece and no worse for the wear. And they were back at home with excellent paying jobs awaiting them. So why wasn't she as happy as he? Even taking walks in her little garden did little more than make those big brown almond shaped eyes of hers all the more sadder.

Maybe it would be a good idea for her to get away after her return from Iraq, to get away all alone. She had mentioned wanting to go to Tampa for some ungodly reason, maybe there. He hated the fact that she was going to go back without him, and worse, that she actually wanted to go back. Why? Why did she want to go back to that god forsaken hellhole of a place, Baghdad. He let that soak into his grey matter for a minute or two. Then like a bolt of lightening that came out of the blue, it hit him. *Oh my god, she wants to go back there because she left someone over there. She wants to go back to him.* Bobby tried his best not to be the jealous type, but good God, he couldn't help himself. His babydoll was a hottie with a bangin' body and he knew it and all the "rams" that circled around his little lamb knew it too!

Was that the sadness he saw in her deep brown eyes? He hoped he was way off base with this crazy thinking; he hoped he was wrong. But something in his gut told him otherwise. Bobby wasn't a real fan of gut feelings. He knew that she had always trusted her gut feelings and that hers were rarely wrong.

Did she want to go back to Iraq for him? For a lover she had left behind? Why didn't he just ask her? He would rather know that than not to, but he was afraid of the answer. He was so scared his babydoll had met and had possibly fallen in love with someone else. The thought of her being with anyone else made his blood run ice cold. He shivered at the mere thought of it, the thought of his lady love and another.

*How could she do that to me, to us,* he thought. What was

522

she thinking? She knew how much he loved her. She knew that he had cheated when he was married before and he had vowed to her with his heart and soul that part of his old life was over. There truly wasn't anyone remotely for him but her, and she had made similar disclosure to him. So what was her rationale? How could she let it happen? Boy, Bobby was really letting his imagination go wild now. He had her doing all sorts of things in his mind, and it was getting out of hand. He had to take back control of these stupid assumptions he was entertaining, but it was as if there was a movie playing in his head and there wasn't a pause button, much less a stop button. Bobby felt that he was right on the edge, and he just didn't know what was going to happen next. If he didn't stop with these all too vivid thoughts he was having of his wife and her supposed lover together in Iraq, he would just lose his mind entirely.

She was scheduled to leave within days now. He should just come out right then and there and ask her what she was up to. He couldn't or maybe he wouldn't ask her such a blatantly accusatory question. He thought that maybe she should just go back and get all of this shit out of her system once and for all. She would then come back to him, to their wonderful life and little house in the woods, wouldn't she?

To both of their dismay, it happened his first day at work. His lovely wife got more bad news. Their company had called her the day before she was to leave to return to Baghdad, only to be told to cancel the trip. The program manager apparently got upset by the email she had sent him, and he took his anger out on her by telling her that her office didn't want her back, that she had a done a shitty job over there and couldn't see the point in her returning and that they would make sure her belongings made it back to her. And with that bit of news, his wife sank further and further into an abyss, into that familiar abyss that had gotten a hold of her little body last year.

It worried Bobby the way she had calmly and with a manner of fact attitude told him on the phone right after receiving the phone call herself. No drama, no emotion, no nothing from his wife. He was scared for her. He didn't know what to do next. He still had three hours left of work before he could leave. He decided that it would be best just to come home and be with her. He felt shitty for all the crazy ideas he had been thinking about her and her "lover." He could kick himself for being so stupid to have those terrible thoughts about her.

As he drove home, he wondered if maybe this would be the closure she needed and would be back to her same ole self. Maybe that was why she was so calm on the phone. Maybe, just maybe she would feel the closeness and love she had felt for him and their little home once again. Bobby knew differently as soon as he opened the front door. Inside the house was pitch black and silent, so very deadly silent that it made his ears ache.

He called out for her, "Babydoll, are you in here?" Nothing, not a sound, not one little movement. He started to panic inside his heart but outwardly remained calm and intact. She didn't need for him to be a loose cannon right about now. She needed someone calm and reassuring; reassuring her that everything would be ok.

He slowly walked to their bedroom; nothing, not a goddamn noise anywhere. Then he walked ever so quietly to the bathroom, nothing again. He didn't know what to think or do. He switched on light after light after light and couldn't find her. Then like a light bulb going on in his own mixed up head, he decided to go out back to the screened in porch. He knew that she wouldn't be totally outside since the mosquitos were totally out of control this summer, especially this time of the year.

There she sat in the semi-darkness with only a small candle burning. He couldn't see an expression on her face yet. His eyes had not become accustomed to the darkness yet, and when they did, he saw the saddest face on the planet. No tears, just the biggest, brownest, saddest eyes in history. He didn't know what to do or say, so he just stood there waiting to take a cue from her, from those eyes.

Chapter 28 -- Much Needed Rest in Florida – alone

As she walked through the lobby of the Hilton Beach Resort Hotel in Clearwater Beach Florida, she was greeted by her new found friend, Edward. She met Edward her first day in Clearwater. He was a former fireman working in Tampa but had gotten out and was now working the front desk at the resort. He had been so friendly and nice to her upon her arrival and the subsequent days during her stay. She had told him that she had just returned from "over there" and wanted rest, relaxation and plenty of José, chilled, no lime, no salt.

He smiled broadly at her last request but said, "Will do and if there is anything, absolutely *anything* you need or *want,* I can and will make it happen." The way he emphasized those particular words in his conversation made her think. "Anything" and "want" were two of the words in particular. He knew she had been in Iraq for eight months; could he really be thinking of a sexual "anything wants"?

She really couldn't be bothered at this point. All she needed and wanted was a nice cold shower to cool her hot body in every sense of the word. She and Edward exchanged pleasantries and also talks of tattoos. She wanted to "finish off" her back, and he wanted to get his first one. He told her that he, his dad, and his granddad had been firemen in Tampa, and he was thinking about getting a Celtic cross on his back with his dad and his granddad's names as well as their fire station designation number.

She strolled to the elevators and punched in her floor number, 6. The elevator slowly climbed to the sixth floor, and she walked to her room and opened the door to the most stifling heat and humidity that actually felt like a slap in the face. She opened her room and was relieved to find that the maid service had not changed the temperature. Thank God for small favors. The temperature could still be fixed, and she wouldn't have to live in this unbearable wet heat. She loved it icy cold. No sooner had she changed the temperature than the phone rang; it was her new friend Edward. He wanted to tell her that management wanted to make sure her first meal was free if she would come down to the dining room. Luckily she was famished and practically ran down the stairs, barely putting the phone back on the hook.

After a very filling and satisfying meal, she decided to take the stairs up to her room to work off the wonderful seafood dinner she had just inhaled. She let out a very loud and audible "brrrrrrrrrr" as she entered her icy cold room and proceeded to strip down, shower, and call it an early night. As she lay there in the bed, the room and bed that she had thought she would be sharing with Chris, she wondered if perhaps she should just pack her bags and go back home to the man she loved with all of her heart, but she just couldn't do it. She was feeling so ambivalent about him and everything else in her life, to include her little house with all the projects that were in store. She actually didn't know if she loved Bobby any longer. She had gone through so much shit in the years that she had known him and wondered if all the bad things that happened to her were his fault. With the sad and, to some extent, unknowing feelings she had, she quickly dozed off.

The sun streamed in the bedroom before 6am the next morning, and she was raring to go. She thought it a bit too early to actually go lay out, so instead decided to just take a walk around the area to see what was out there. She found a place to get her nails done, a place to finish off her tattoo on her back and a convenient store to get her morning Dr Peppers. Perfect! It had been a good long walk and seemed to be the perfect time to get suited up and lay outside. She stripped off her thong and bra and inspected herself in the mirror. She had gotten amazingly much more chocolate brown than she had already been. She looked like the color of French roast coffee and just a hint of pink around the top part of her breasts. "Just a hint of pink ain't too bad for a walk around the neighborhood," she thought out loud.

As she inspected her small, trim body, her eyes gravitated to her incredibly painfully flat looking belly. Why did her skin have to be so lose in this area? She worked hard on her abs, if nothing else. She realized that she had let other body parts fall to the wayside while she worked her abs morning, noon, and night, but to no avail. The skin sagged in ripples much like a ruffles potato chip. She had a love/hate relationship with her abs. She loved the hard, flat look of them but hated the loose skin that covered all her hard work.

She had told Bobby over and over again how she wanted to "get them done" but he would look at her and say, "Your tummy looks fine, babydoll, but if you want to do something, then I support your decision to do so." She scanned her once very strong, muscular legs and wondered what happened? When had she become an old lady where every inch of her body would seem to sag?

She thought for a second about Chris and wondered what he thought. He who had a much younger wife, a wife Bobby's age for that matter. She secretly smiled to herself because she knew, instinctively knew, that she had her beat at least in one aspect. One aspect he would never ever come out and say. He knew and she knew that what she had that his wife didn't and apparently other women in his much experienced life didn't have, was a tight unstretched pussy.

She delighted in the fact that he would go on and on about her tight little pink pussy, whether it was on the phone or in an email or even in person. He couldn't get enough of it or her it seemed. The thought of him made her want to just... she stopped herself, dismissed those thoughts and climbed into a cold, cold shower, but her thoughts went back to him, back to Chris.

Why couldn't she stop this insistent thinking of this man who didn't appear to give a damn about her? After all, there she was, paid all this money to be with him and he wasn't even there, and she wasn't sure if he would be during her whole two weeks visit. Bastard!

She toweled off and thought about room service before hitting the beach. She decided against the idea and decided to just throw on her bathing suit. She made her regular stop at the check-in desk to say hi to Edward and to see how his morning was going.

As she strode into the hot Florida sun that early Saturday morning, towards the Gulf of Mexico, she noticed something very strange. The resort she had actually picked out was a very family oriented resort, so needless to say, there were families to the left and to the right of her with a plethora of kids playing and just doing what kids do: making noise.

She tried to find a bit more secluded part of this resort; i.e. get away from all the noise. She'd had enough noise in Iraq, and she was ready for some serious peace and quiet. As she walked past all the families and couples, she noticed a strange phenomenon. She started to notice how all the men started to segregate or separate themselves from their respective partners and/or families. She couldn't understand why this was happening.

She knew that it wasn't that she was a classical beauty; she definitely was not, but she was indeed different than a lot of women, and she was also alone: no kids, no husband or boyfriend or even girlfriend at her side. She thought that it could be hard-wired into men to be a predator, to go in for the kill, so to speak. For the "rams to circle the little lamb" as Bobby had mentioned to her while she was in Iraq when he found out that there had been a few "rams" interested in his "little lamb."

As she came to a more secluded part of the beach, she decided to throw down her bright day-glo orange towel on a chaise lounge and relax for the first time since she left Iraq.

She started to wonder why she had come here to Tampa, Florida, of all places. She was sure that Bobby wondered that was well. Only she knew the real reason for being here, and she would take that reason to the grave with her, much like all the other disgusting and embarrassing things of her past. There was a big part of her life that had disgusted even her, and she had to live with

533

that, with the mistakes she had made through the ages. She was hard on herself. She knew a woman her age had to have their own share of "mistakes," but it bothered her, the stupid and dumb decisions she had made. But it was what made her who she was today.

She really wasn't a bad person. She had made some bad decisions in her 47-plus years, but doesn't everyone? Don't they? She at least thought there must be others like her dumb ass making mistake after mistake. Surely there had to be.

So there she sat alone at long last. She had been with Bobby for only a week and a half after their return from Iraq before she could stand it no longer. Bobby had become completely and fully immersed in the DC way of life. She'd floundered, not knowing what was real or even what she really wanted to do with herself. She was stuck in limbo with no way to get out other than returning to Iraq or maybe just going away.

She thought for barely a nanosecond about going back home. Oh good God, that would be like going from the frying pan straight into the fire. No, she couldn't, correction, wouldn't do that to her already frail psyche. She knew where she longed to be and who she wanted to be with. She was so torn inside that it actually made her stomach turn as if it had been doing flip flops inside.

She wanted so much for things to be the same with her and Bobby, but there was a small part of her that wanted to be with someone else. Did he feel the same? Did either one of them? She was starting to wonder how Bobby felt about her. Did he still love her? She thought that at least most of the time he seemed to tolerate her at best. She knew in her heart of hearts that Chris was not her lobster but only someone she had an infatuation with. He had been so different than anyone she had been with in her adult life. He was a "bad ass," and when it came down to it all, she never picked a "bad ass" to be with. She loved the men who were all about her, men like her first husband and men like Bobby. She knew he loved her but sometimes she thought he was just interested in the physical aspect of her and not true adoration. She knew and felt that Chris adored her. He told her over and over again that he did. He also told her that being adored was infinitely better than being in love. Was that an excuse for him not to say he loved her or did he really adore her? It really didn't make a difference to her. All she knew was that she felt so conflicted.

He was supposed to be with her right here, right now in the warm Florida sun. That was what she had--correction, that was what "they" had planned. They had both planned to spend as much of those two weeks together as possible.

As life and luck would have it when it concerned her, a last minute TDY to go to GTMO, Cuba totally fucked up all their plans. He was to be gone for at least a week of her two-week stay. Before she left, she wondered if she should cancel her trip because he wasn't to be there or should she take that time to sort out her thoughts and her feelings or should she go home and be conflicted for God only knew how long?

After Chris' phone call about this unexpected trip to Cuba, she decided to go ahead and take the trip anyway. Take that week alone in Tampa to sort out her feelings about "him," Bobby, and most importantly, about how she felt about herself.

She pulled out her pad and pen that she always kept with her just in case. She had been attempting to write a book about what had happened to her and Bobby last year when they were both humiliated and fired and told to leave Iraq and of their beloved Cuba and also, to some extent, what happened to her at the

536

prison. She had the odd, random thoughts that she liked to jot down so she could use later on. The thoughts of what had happened to her made her scared. She was too scared to actually put pen to paper concerning that little incident. Could she really relive that? Could she bring out all the bad shit again?

As she lay there, she could feel the familiar tingling feeling of a burn on her already cocoa brown skin and also the tingling she felt for him. She decided that maybe it would be best to take her burnt body upstairs and take a much-needed cold shower. She simply couldn't stop thinking of him. She knew in her heart of hearts that he was not her lobster, nor could he ever be; Bobby was her only one true lobster. She knew that like she knew she was there baking her already brown ass in the Tampa sun.

She lay back down and decided to continue to bake. As she lay there tanning her body and wondering what to do with the rest of her day, she decided to take out her notepad and pen and continue on the book she started, what seemed years ago but in reality only a year and a half ago. It was true, though, that those six months being unemployed with nothing but time on her hands, she didn't write one single word. She didn't start her writing until she

537

went back to Iraq the second time. Back then the pages seemed to write themselves. Some mornings she would re-read what she had written the night before and would be completely and utterly caught offguard by the words on the page...by "her" words.

It was almost as if she was temporarily possessed as she wrote down the story of her life that she had fictionalized to some degree, to a great degree actually. It was funny how this book had taken on a life of its own. She wrote the ending, then the beginning. She seemed to be stuck in middle of her life in more ways than one, sadly enough.

She stared straight into the waters of the Gulf of Mexico and thought hard to herself and wondered how she could let her life come to this point. It was only less than two years ago that she had the perfect life and she totally blew all of that for what? For some guy that didn't love her but who had said he "adored her," whatever that was supposed to mean.

As she gazed at the water, she had the strangest feeling that someone was looking, staring really, at her. She looked to the left, nothing; she looked to the right, nothing again. She slowly turned her head around and saw two men at the tikki bar in the distance looking in her general direction. Surely they weren't looking at her, not when there was at least 100 other people in the near vicinity.

She turned back to gaze at the water to attempt to get inspiration she just didn't have or feel. She always loved the ocean and always felt like home no matter where in the world that may be as long as she was close to the water.

She decided to go ahead and go inside because she knew the little tenderness she felt on her shoulders was a sign that she could be a little burnt. So up she went to shower and towel off. She thought seriously about room service for about a second and ordered a sandwich and a shot of her beverage of choice, a shot of José, chilled no lime no salt. While she waited on room service to arrive, she decided to call Bobby to see what he was up to. They actually talked and talked and talked, more so than the week and half they had been home together, since their returned from Iraq. Bobby told her that he missed her terribly but she really had no idea how she felt other than she knew down deep that she did love him and didn't want to be with any other man.

They continued to talk for the next 20 minutes or at least

until her room service made its appearance. They exchanged their normal "I love you; no, I love you more; no, it's not possible" sayings and then hug up. As she eyed her ham and cheese sandwich and downed her José, her phone rang and rang, but she really just couldn't be bothered to pick up the damn phone. The phone just wouldn't stop ringing, so she hesitantly picked it up only to realize that is was "him." She could barely contain herself. She heard his New York accent immediately and melted. He cooed his adoration and "missing you's" to her, and she felt like she was floating on a cloud. He was still in Cuba and would be home soon, to her or so he said. He told her that she would be the first to know, even before his wife knew he would be home. He told her he wanted to be with and needed her and wanted her more than anything else in the world. Of course she knew that meant anything else besides his wife and kids, that is. She could accept that, she thought to herself.

Chapter 29 -- Her Return


After her return from Tampa, a day never went by that she did not think of her friend Chris, especially during the quiet times in her garden. The garden was the only place she would let her mind wander back to Iraq, back to the war and back to him, back to Chris and the months they'd had together, fewer months than either one expected as it happened to be. She would never let Bobby know of the thoughts she had while working in her garden. She would never hurt Bobby in that way. She kept the memories and painful longing for a man who never opened up to her emotionally and who never felt the same for her, deep inside herself at least until she was alone in her garden. That was the only place she could let it all out, all the wonderful memories, the movies they half watched, the talks, the emails, and the special love she felt for him, all of it.

She often wondered if it was possible to love two men at the same time. Sure, it was a different kind of love she had for Chris than the kind she had for Bobby, but nevertheless, she felt love for the both of them. She wondered if she would ever meet up with Chris somewhere at some time, and would things between them feel the same? In the beginning, when she had first returned, she tried her best to keep those particular thoughts at bay. It just wasn't healthy to long for a man who had moved on as soon as she left Tampa; hell, even before she left Tampa. She had given Chris her private email address in hopes that he would at least drop a line just to say how he was doing and maybe, just maybe, plan another little get together somewhere down the line.

She knew that there would always be a little bit of her heart that no one could touch or even reach, but with that there would also be a sadness that you could see when she didn't think anyone was watching, in her brown almond-shaped eyes every now and again, usually while she was in her garden. When she left her sanctuary, her garden, she was as fun-loving and crazy for Bobby as she had always been. She loved Bobby more than anything or anyone, even Chris. They had a great time back home when she

542

finally returned from the much needed rest she had in Tampa.

Bobby had gotten a lot done to their little house after his return from Iraq. Although she really wanted him to get much-needed rest before continuing his career, Bobby wanted to make sure her little house was all in order. He wanted a lot of things done before she came home from Tampa. Not the big projects she had planned, that was her thing to do, but the smaller projects. He had the house cleaned top to bottom by professionals. They did the normal cleaning to polishing the silver, cleaning all the chandeliers till they sparkled, to putting a much needed good coat of bee's wax on all the lovely antique furniture, to getting some of the other stuff fixed that had broken down in their absence. He also had some work done to the outside as well. The trees he needed to have cut down to ready the area for the pool and of course the fence that was mandatory in order to have the pool put in. She would be overjoyed to see these additions and deletions had been taken care of so she could concentrate solely on her two very big projects.

Chapter 30 -- Big Projects


As she looked over her plans for the day, her first official

day of being a "lady of leisure," she thought that his was the first

time since she was 15 that she didn't have a job, and she just

wasn't sure to do with all the time. She knew that she would cook

something wonderfully ethnic for dinner, but that wouldn't take

but an hour  to an hour and a half at the most, but right now, what

the hell to do right now? As Bobby pulled his Jag out of the

driveway, she realized that it was only 6am. She said out loud,

"What in the hell am I going to do with 12 full hours?" Ok, first

things first, shower, drive to the 7-11 to get her big gulp Dr. Pepper

then back home to sort out her "things to do list." Not THE list but

the list she made daily for stuff she wanted to accomplish

throughout whichever day she was on.

As she jumped in the shower, she had the fleeting feeling of not being alone, but what was weird was that is wasn't a scary feeling, it was a feeling of comfort. Whoever was there with her was a calming sort, a person she felt close to and one she trusted. Then the strangest thing happened next. As she turned on the warm water, a faint but very distinctive oriental yet spicy smell hit her nostrils. The lovely spicy smell was of her most favorite perfume in the whole world. As it wafted in over the shower door, the smell of the familiar oriental yet spicy scent filled her hungry nostrils. She knew instinctively what it was, "Must de Cartier" by Cartier. She recalled the very first time she ever wore the spicy scent. It was for her 26th birthday. Just the sheer smell of the perfume bought her back to a time back in 1983, her birthday, when her first husband Richard had bought her the wonderfully fragrant perfume.

As she lathered up her hair; even with a slight sting in her eye, she could see someone, the old woman, sitting on the toilet seat right in front of the shower door. What was really weird was that she wasn't scared or anything creepy like that; she was used to the visits from the old woman. The only thing that crossed her mind was why would this old woman wear her favorite perfume?

She shouted over the shower stall and asked how she was doing this fine morning. She knew if anyone else had witnessed this one-sided conversation they would quickly question her sanity, but for some reason and only to her, it just seemed the most natural thing in the world.

Apparently the old woman came to see how she was doing and to see if she was feeling ok, to see if she had been feeling a bit out of sorts.

"Wie fühlen Sie?" the old woman said over the shower stall.

Without any hesitation, she answered, "I feel pretty good." She was half lying. "Why do you ask?" There was nothing but silence on the other side of the shower door. *Oh well, much to do and not enough time to talk to people who aren't really there,* she thought to herself.

She jumped out of the shower, dried off and got into some "work clothes," which usually meant shorts, tank top and flip flops, even though before she would start working on anything garden related, those flip flops would be dumped on the side of the deck. For some reason, she loved being out there without any

546

shoes, without any gloves; she wanted to be "intimate" with her garden with nothing between the two, flesh to dirt and vice versa. All her grown-up life, she always wore something on her feet. Her pet peeve of coverage on her feet happened after a particularly nasty accident on her big toe in England when her dad was stationed there.

Ever since the doctor in England pretty much had to slice off the top layer of skin on her toes after she ripped almost all of it off by stubbing it on the curb, she kept something on her feet at all times, even inside the house. Of course that was true until she got stuck in the mud and her flip flops lay deep in the Maryland clay for God only knows how long more than two years ago, that very first day of her attempt to landscape that ugly little piece of land she called a backyard. That was back when she and Bobby first started the Garden of Eden.

She sat on the edge of the deck, kicked of the flip flops, pulled down her "No Fear" baseball cap and looked over her notes of her beloved garden.

With each passing year, that garden of hers took on a life all its own. It took her totally by surprise what would actually grow and where it would eventually pop up, sometimes not even remotely close to the location she thought she had planted it. Of course she had totally forgotten all the things she planted; some not only lived but seemed to thrive while others died almost immediately. Two years had passed since that first early morning she started her little garden.

She knew all too well that when she was outdoors she would not be able to look at that little garden from afar; she had to be in the thick of it, to be an actual part of it, to be one with the garden that she loved and cherished so very much, but no time for that now. She had other things she had to take care of.

As always, before leaving the deck, she made sure she was totally covered with bug repellant. Those nasty mosquitos loved her tender juicy brown skin. As she left the wooden deck and started to walk on the concrete slab of the pool decking, she had added so much bug spray that it stung her nose. Those bastards, as she now referred to the pool company that was building their pool, told her that the pool would be done any day now, and here it was, three months and counting. Their excuse du jour was the flagstone; couldn't find any more of the light tan with purple running through it. The pool guys searched high and low and just couldn't find the damn stone that had started both of their projects; tikki bar countertop, coping of the pool and an extended deck around the pool.

She shook her head in disgust as she walked past the still half-completed pool towards the almost completed tikki bar. The tikki bar, which was really more of an outdoor kitchen, was truly a work of art. She loved the design; hers of course, and all the high end appliances she had installed for her hubby. That man of hers loved to grill 12 months of the year, and she wanted him to be safe and dry during the bad months. The contractor who took on her projects had a very good reputation on the Eastern Shore where she and Bobby lived, but it took her keeping after them day after day to actually get this far. She thought that maybe another month or so, the tikki bar would be done, but the pool, well the pool was a totally different story. Life is much like trying to get anything done on the Eastern Shore; projects start and stop without any apparent reason.

Throughout the years, she worked very hard on that little backyard and beautiful French country home, and in fact as she took her last walk around their lovely little home, she had a quick flashback to the dream she'd had more than 50 years earlier. It indeed looked like a garden of Eden, her's and Bobby's "Garden of Eden." NOT SURE WHERE THIS ACTUALLY FITS IN.

## Chapter 31 -- His Big Mistake

As she lay there sleeping, she had never looked so peaceful and small, so very small. He knew that the years of chemo took a lot out his little lady, but here in the bed sleeping, she looked like a young child. The only difference was that her hair was now snowy white. After the chemo he remembered how she hated when it had all fallen out. She felt embarrassed and usually wore her old black "No Fear" baseball cap. That cap had seen more than a few miles, as she always said and then added, "much like myself." Bobby decided that when her hair started to fall out he would shave off what was left of his thinning white hair as well, as a show of solidarity. Little did she know he was going to do that, so when he came home one afternoon with no hair, she looked up from her book and just laughed and laughed. That was the day she stopped wearing her baseball cap. What a pair they were. She was upset at first when her hair finally started to grow back because it grew back a fluffy white color. She had been dying her hair red for so long now that she had forgotten what it looked like "natural." After it all came in, though, she decided that it just didn't look that bad for a woman her age, a woman of 92. She still looked pretty good for an old broad.

He knew what was going to happen next, but he just didn't know how to deal with it. How do you let go of someone you have spent the last 50 years with? If God makes these decisions, why doesn't he just take both of them at the same time? Why let just one go without their mate? That's all he thought about for a couple of weeks. It just wasn't fair.

It did make him glad that she wanted to be here in their home during this time instead of being hooked up to all sorts of machinery in the hospital. She had always had a living will that was added to her Last Will and Testament, to make sure that she wasn't just a shell of her former self, surviving on just the powers of electricity. She wanted to be remembered like she used to be— full of life and always on the move, the energizer bunny. The doctors weren't sure how much time she had left, but whatever it was, she wanted it to be with Bobby and him alone. As he sat there at her bedside with a book on his lap, he started to wonder about how wonderful their lives had been these past 50 years or so.

It wasn't always great times; in fact, there had been some bad times for them as well. That very thought took him back to one of the worst times. Worse than the time he almost lost her; lost his soul mate. That was the worst summer they had ever spent, but even this incident had topped even that, if that was even possible. Well, at least in Bobby's perspective. Bobby didn't know how or why it even happened. He silently cursed himself for letting that slip back into his memory. He promised himself that he would never ever think of this. But there it was, right in the forefront of his thoughts. It was during one of seldom low points for them, for their marriage. They had just returned from Iraq, the second time. For some reason she was having difficulties adjusting to being back in the real world. She seemed so distant. She couldn't talk to him like she used to. She seemed to be hundreds of miles away, perhaps back in Iraq. It always happened whenever she stepped foot in her garden, the garden that they had done together the previous summer. He never really found out where she was, not

553

even to this day, he still had no idea. He tried to reach her by going in the garden with her to help wherever she may need it, but she said she could handle everything and would go about her puttering, deep in thought. Bobby thought best to let her have some time out there on her own, but he could not help but worry so much for her. His little babydoll sometimes appeared so sad that it literally felt like his own heart was being broken in two. So much sadness in those brown almond-shaped eyes, but when she was out of the garden she would be her same crazy fun-loving self. He wished he could understand what was going on with her, but without her help, he couldn't; he simply couldn't if she didn't let him in.

After they came back, she decided to decompress from the long hours and hard work both of them had put in over there. Bobby, on the other hand, was ready to get back into the rat race of DC. Bobby wanted her to stay home and take it easy. She wanted to supervise the work that was about to start on their little home, the swimming pool and tikki bar, which was to be reminiscent of a natural pond or lake and, of course, the master retreat addition that was to be built. She felt better being there to talk to the guy in charge about anything she might see as not being the way she

554

wanted it done. Bobby loved the idea that she would stay home, and he could take care of her for a change. It always seemed she was taking care of him, and he loved it but it was time for him to do the same. So there they were for one of the few times they would be separated during the daytime hours.

The offers for jobs back in that area were coming fast and furious for the both them. It seemed like all the defense contractors wanted them for their firsthand experience, particularly their time spent in Cuba and Iraq. A particularly small company courted them both, and they decided to go with them. It was a company that she knew right from the start was THE Company for them. They courted the both of them while they were still in Iraq the second time. The company's small hand-selected staff had impeccable résumés, mostly retired "agency" folks. The job sounded more than interesting. They had not begun the procedure to take what was called the "lifestyle" polygraph. This type of poly usually meant the job was very hush-hush or at beyond a Top Secret level with accesses beyond belief.

They both were very excited, and in addition to the interesting job, it also meant a lot of foreign travel to go along with it. It was during that point that his wife decided she needed to go back to Iraq to pick up all of her personal belongings, come back home then take some time off and until the projects were done on their little home, then she would join the company after a year or so. They both passed the poly and Bobby was to start within the next two weeks. They spent every single second of the week prior to her departure back to Iraq and before he was to start his new job. She went over every detail of the plans she had drawn up to make sure he loved the ideas as much as she did. Bobby saw a couple of things he wanted to add or slightly modify and the plans were ready. Well, the day was here; the alarm went off at 5:00 in the morning. They both groaned in unison that first morning. While she got up, Bobby would shower, and she would make her way to the kitchen to make some coffee for him.

While Bobby and the coffee were getting ready, she would take her first stroll of the day in the little garden. She would grab the mosquito repellent and her little purple plastic carry all case that held all her gardening tools. She knew the guys would be coming within the week to start the work on the pool and tikki bar, then about a month later the guys would start on the little house,

the master retreat as she liked to call it. Bobby would look out
their bedroom window and watch her putter around. He was
always amazed at how much she loved doing that. He would
wonder what she thought as she puttered with this flower or that
bush. It looked to him that she was not only talking to herself as
she puttered but looked as if she was carrying on a full-blown
conversation with herself. If he could only take a trip in her head
for the day; to hear the things she had yet to say and to see what
she saw.

All he knew was that while she was out there, she would
smile her crooked little smile, but sometimes he saw incredible
sadness in those eyes, as if her heart was breaking. That garden
was her safe haven, he thought. A place she loved to come with
him or with friends but mostly alone with her thoughts. As he was
trying to find the proper tie to go with the suit she had picked out,
he would get upset over the fact that she had always helped him
with this part while she was getting ready herself. A man his age
should know how to pick out his own tie, for god sakes. He
thought about yelling out the window for help but didn't want to
disturb her while she was out there. So instead, he just grabbed one

and started to tie; she preferred the half Windsor. He could smell

the coffee brewing. She always found the best gourmet coffees for

him to try; this morning was no exception. He thought it might be

that blend from Hawaii: Kona. She loved the smell of coffee but

never acquired the taste for it.

She came in as Bobby was taking his first sip. Bobby

thought that this was the shortest period of time he had ever known

for her to be in her garden. He assumed because he was to be

leaving within minutes and wanted to be with him before he

headed out in the crazy traffic of DC.

"You like?" she asked him about the coffee.

Bobby nodded and then asked, "Do you want me to go to

the 7-11 for your big gulp Dr. Pepper?" He had done that

throughout their whole relationship, usually only on the weekends

where they would both have time to sit in bed, sip their favorite

morning drink, coffee for him and Dr. Pepper for her, and watch

their well actually HER favorite weekend morning TV shows on

HGTV. She told Bobby that she would perhaps take a drive out to

the 7-11 after her shower. They sat on their eckbank, in their little

breakfast nook with their own thoughts of how the day would

unfold for the both of them. Bobby asked her what she had planned to do on her first day as a lady of leisure. That made her laugh right out loud, as she had never in her life been a lady of leisure. She told him she just wasn't sure, that she would just kinda play it by ear. She would have her cell phone on her in case he got lonely during the day and needed to hear her voice.

With that, Bobby had to get going; traffic would be getting worse as the morning passed. With a quick kiss and a big tight hug, she walked him to the door. As Bobby made his way to the new Jag they had purchased when they returned from Iraq the second time, she took a seat right on the steps of the porch and waved him off. That was the first and last time she would wake up with him and see him off. He reminded her that she was a lady of leisure and didn't need to get up at such an ungodly hour. She was very hesitant at first but then took him up on it.

As Bobby got more and more comfortable with his work schedule and with work in general back in the real world, he felt as though his darling wife was growing further away from him again. She seemed lost in her thoughts and lost inside herself. There was that sadness in her eyes he saw sometimes when she thought no one saw her, out in that garden of hers. Sure, she seemed happy enough, and the work on the house and pool and tikki bar were going on well with her designs, but there was something he just couldn't put his finger on. He would come home, and she would be excited to see him and, of course, have a wonderful meal prepared for him, but there was just something there, something sad, something he couldn't understand, no matter how much he tried.

After his phone call to see how she was doing on her first day as a lady of leisure and his first day of work, she told him that their old company had called her and told her that she was no longer needed nor wanted back in Iraq. He was beside himself and at the same time, quite happy. He didn't want to see her go back, even to just go there and pack up her stuff and come straight back home, but he knew just how much she wanted to go. She was devastated, and he just wasn't sure what to do for her. She was so unemotional and removed during the whole phone call that it scared him. He didn't know what she would do next. He decided that maybe he should suggest a couple of weeks away, perhaps Florida. Florida used to be one of her favorite places. Perhaps a couple of weeks in the sun and with a whole lotta peace and quiet might help his little lady. As he planned this in his head, he noticed someone standing at his door.

As he sat at his desk staring off into space, one of his colleagues, Lindy popped her head in to ask him a question. She must have stood at his doorway for a good five minutes. Lindy finally cleared her throat, and that brought Bobby back.

He blushed and said, "Uhh umm yes, Lindy. Can I help you?"

She said boldly, "Maybe I can help you? Do you need or want to talk?"

At first, Bobby's thought was "absolutely not" and pretty much said as much, but as she turned to walk away, he said, "Wait, maybe... if I can just run something past you. You're a woman, right?" He groaned as he heard himself ask that dumb question. "I mean, since you are a woman, maybe I can ask you."

Lindy made herself comfortable on the couch in Bobby's office. "Spill it," she said. Lindy was glad that Bobby had picked her to talk to. She didn't care what the topic was. She'd had her eye on this man since he started working there. Lindy thought of those piercing blue eyes. She couldn't take her own blue eyes off of him. As she sat on the couch, she just looked deep into his eyes. She wasn't even sure what he was saying to her; she didn't care, she just wanted to be near him. But then all of a sudden, Bobby asked her "What do you think?"

Lindy blushed deep red because she really hadn't been listening to a word he said, and now he knew it too. Did he sense her interest? What would he think or say if he did? Oh hell, she didn't care as long as he didn't kick her out of his office or out of his life altogether.

Bobby looked at Lindy quizzically and wondered what the hell. He had just spilled his guts to this woman, and she wasn't even listening to him. He sure as hell wasn't going to do that again. She even had the gall to say "what?" After a couple of minutes, Bobby said "never mind" and went back to work. Lindy, still blushing, apologized to Bobby over and over and pleaded with him to please talk to her. She lied and told him that she was thinking about a project for work but would push all of that out of her mind so he could talk to her. Bobby paused for a minute and then decided it was best to talk to her since he had gone this far. He had to find out what was wrong with his bride. So he went through the whole story again. This time, Lindy listened. She didn't care too much what she was hearing as it seemed that this man she wanted in the worst possible way was very much in love with his wife. But Lindy thought perhaps since there appeared to be problems between the pair that maybe she would have a chance. So instead of Lindy telling him what really could be wrong, she decided to make up the worst of the worst lies.

As Lindy went on and on about how women were and what they were up to when they acted this particular way, Bobby's eyes got as big as saucers. He was in shock. Surely his wife wouldn't be up to these types of shenanigans, could she? Could it be one of the contractors that were working on her designs? Working on his woman, his little lamb? Lindy had to be dead wrong about this, and Bobby told her as much. Lindy said that she felt confident that this is the way women act when they are having affairs. *Oh God, she said that word out loud.* He refused to believe it, but Lindy had left this idea in his head, and it was enough to make him wonder. Lindy directed Bobby to come to her with any new information, and they could talk about it over lunch so they wouldn't have to cut into company time. Bobby agreed. He did feel guilty sitting here and talking to her when he should be busy working.

So for the next month or so they would meet for lunch, sometimes after work for just a quick drink and some conversation. Bobby never really knew when or how this affair started, but once it did, it got incredibly out of control. It was to the point that he was outright lying to his lovely wife. He even stopped thinking that she was having the affair because he was just too busy with his own. As the weeks turned into months, and his affair grew more and more evident to everyone at the office, Bobby knew that it was just a matter of time before Lindy would want more and that his wife would find out. He couldn't let that happen. He wouldn't let that happen. She would be devastated to find this out, that he had been lying to her all this time.

Just as Bobby was thinking of this, Lindy popped her head into Bobby's office. She said to Bobby, "We need to talk". Bobby knew that was a statement that no man ever wanted to hear. As she sat on the couch where it started over six months ago, Lindy just blurted out, "I'm pregnant. What are we going to do about it? You are going to leave her, aren't you?"

Tears started to well up in his eyes. He looked at Lindy

dead-on and told her that would never happen. He would never leave his wife, not for anything in the world and specifically not for her. That statement pissed her off so much that she wanted to scream at the top of her lungs, but she was a professional and she was at work. Lindy looked at Bobby and said, "we will just have to see about that."

She calmly walked out of his office and never walked back in. He was so panicked that he had no idea what to do next. He decided to go to his boss and ask for a couple of days off. Bobby's boss agreed and said, "Take the time you need."

With that Bobby slowly walked to his car and wondered. What would she do, his wife, the woman of his dreams, if she knew the ugly truth? How could he let this happen to them, to their perfect life? Why? His only thought was to get home to her, to talk to her, to be with her. He decided that he had to tell her everything. She would hate him. She would never trust him again, and he wouldn't blame her. Would she want him to leave, to never come back? He hoped against all hope she wouldn't do that. He wouldn't, couldn't bear it. He would rather kill himself than to let that happen. He felt so stupid.

As Bobby drove home, which took over an hour on a good day, he kept thinking of the best way to handle this. He knew it wasn't going to be easy; not on him and definitely not on her. As he pulled up to the bright yellow house with the emerald green shudders, he thought that he would just tell her straight out. As he got out of the car, she walked out the door. He knew instantly that it was too late. She knew. Her face and eyes said it all. Those big brown almond-shaped eyes filled with tears. Her little square face was streaked with tears. He wanted to go up to her and hug all the pain away...all the hurt...all of the mistrust. What would she do if he tried? Would she slap him, ignore him, or simply ask him to leave, no questions asked or answered?

As he got closer to her, she walked into the house and didn't say a word. As he closed the door, something caught the corner of his eye. It was his luggage, packed and ready for him to pick up. No questions, no answers, just bags packed and that was that. He understood how she felt, he had this coming and he knew it. She didn't say one word to him, not one. She simply picked up her little purple plastic carrier and walked into her garden. He knew there wouldn't be anything he could say to her, not right

566

now. He would wait forever if that was how long it took and hoped that at some point she would talk to him again. He knew he didn't deserve her, she deserved better but he couldn't let her go, wouldn't let her go but he would give her time to come to terms with all of this. He hoped and prayed that she could forgive him, even though he knew he didn't deserve for her to.

Bobby left the house and found a local hotel to check into. He didn't want to be too far. He had to be close to her, even though she didn't want him close. He would wait and wait and wait till the end of time for her. Until then, he had to get the situation at work resolved. As he unpacked his suitcase, the one his wife packed for him, he could tell how upset she had been when she packed it. Everything was thrown in there. His suits, his underwear, even his Monte Cristo #2's, just a big pile of his belongings stuffed into three very large suitcases. He lay on the bed and thought what his life would be like without her. He couldn't bear to even think this way. He cried and cried all night long, cried about how stupid he had been and what he could do to make it all go away so they could be the way they used to be. He knew that, even if she took him back--how he prayed that could and would happen--that things would be different. He wasn't sure if they would ever be the same. With that thought, he fell asleep and woke up promptly at 5am. He thought about getting ready when he realized that he had the day off. The boss had ok'd him taking a few days off. He was glad he had asked for that time off, he was going to need it.

He called Lindy and asked her to meet him. He thought she sounded a little too excited about this. Surely she couldn't be that stupid to believe he would voluntarily leave his wife for her, could she? No, that would be insane. Early on, they had both agreed that this was just for fun. No strings, no attachment, and definitely no kids resulting in this. She broke her part of the deal. He had brought condoms with him on their "lunch dates" but she said she had that part taken care of. There was no need. He didn't quite believe her and told her that he felt better to wear something. He didn't know her that well and wasn't sure if she had been around. As Bobby dressed in jeans and polo shirt, he had hoped that there wouldn't be a lot of drama. That was why he had picked the most crowded place he could find in the DC area. Old Ebbitt Grill. Old Ebbitt was DC's oldest and busiest restaurants around. It was located right on 15th street, not too far from their office. *Good choice,* he thought, *crowded.* He hoped no drama would ensue while they were there. He wasn't there to eat lunch, just to take care of the situation at hand. They were to meet at 1pm sharp. He would wait no longer than 15 minutes. Lindy was notoriously late, and she knew that he wouldn't wait a minute longer than need be.

So Bobby sat at the section called Grant's Bar. Boy, did he ever need a drink. He knew that a chilled Jose' would be good right about now but would not order one. Bobby had not drank this with anyone but his wife since they first met, and he wasn't about to do it now, no matter how bleak his life looked. It was precisely 1:15pm by his Rado watch, a watch she gave him one Valentine's Day. As he downed his shot of Jack Daniels, paid and got up to leave, in walked Lindy, late as usual.

What in the hell did he see in this woman in the first place? She looked nothing like his little exotic wife, nothing at all. She wasn't small, exotic or classy. His wife would glide into a room, and people would stop and look. Lindy was a big girl, not fat but Rubenesque in looks, if not what you would call downright thick. She did have the largest chest he had ever seen, but he really didn't find hers particularly attractive. They simply were too large and

569

yes, there is such a thing. Her skin was as white as skim milk and more freckly than he had ever seen on any one person. She had bright orange/red hair. He kept thinking she looked a bit like Drew Barrymore but a bit thicker, not in a bad way. He kept thinking what in the hell did I do? I lost every thing for this?

She slid in to the barstool next to him and tried to give him a kiss. He couldn't believe the gall of this woman. She had totally ruined his life, and she actually thought he would welcome a kiss from her. She ordered a white wine spritzer. He looked at her and wondered what in the hell was this woman doing drinking alcohol while she was pregnant? Lindy could see that he was wondering what was going on with her and the wine, and she didn't know how to break the news to him, so she just blurted it out, "I'm not pregnant after all. I got my period this morning."

That little bit of information both elated Bobby and infuriated him at the same time. Bobby stood up and said to her, "Then we have nothing to discuss." He left the restaurant. He never saw Lindy again after that afternoon. She apparently called in to her boss and quit. No one knew where she went or if she would be back. He couldn't have cared less where she was. He knew that it wasn't all Lindy's fault, that he had a 50-50 role in the responsibility for this. He was just mad that she had called his wife and told her of what had been going on instead of letting him do that terrible task.

As the days went by and the nights dragged on, Bobby would pass their little house just to see if she was ok, to see if she would be ready to talk to him or see him, but each time he came close to stopping, something told him to keep driving, and so he did; back to his motel room, back to his dull, boring, unloved life. The life of someone who truly fucked up his perfect world and got what he deserved. After a couple of months had passed, he decided to call her, to see how she was doing. He wouldn't try to pressure her or to ask her if he could come back home, he would wait. He just wanted to make sure she was ok. He knew in his head she wouldn't be that ok. No one that much in love with each other could be ok, especially after one of them screwed up royally. Oh, after some time passed, she would be ok, but not yet. He, on the other hand, would never be ok. Not now, not a month from now or even a lifetime from now would he be ok again. If only she would let him back into her life, he could be.

As he pulled up a little closer to the house than he had been before, he noticed that it appeared as if nothing more had been done to the new addition. He didn't know why he never noticed that before now. He wondered during those two months that they had been apart if anything else had been done. He didn't think so. He knew the pool and tikki bar was supposedly done, and this summer they were going to be able to use it for the first time…at least until his fuck-up, that is. He pulled in behind her car and knocked on the door. What a strange feeling that was, to knock on his own door.

He knocked for what seemed several minutes and still no answer. He supposed that she knew it was him and simply wouldn't answer the damn door. Then again, he thought that she would not be like that. She would answer, then possibly slam the door in his face, deservedly so. He thought that maybe she was out back on the deck. So he walked around back and opened the gate. There she was, sitting at the edge of the empty pool with her little legs dangling in, slumped over. She appeared to be talking to someone or maybe just to herself. Oh God, the way she looked brought tears to his eyes and an incredible painful ache to his heart.

She didn't even hear him come in, she just sat there, slumped over with her little "happy bunny" blanket she had gotten for her trip to Iraq the second time. He thought she had left that blanket there in Iraq.

He called over to her and she jumped. She really had not heard him come in. She looked up at him and smiled one of her little crooked half smiles. Bobby thought she looked the worst he had ever seen her, about 80 pounds soaking wet. It was cold out, and all she had on were baggy shorts, t-shirt and this pitiful little blanket. He bent down, and she gave him the biggest hug he'd ever had. He picked her up and carried her inside the house. Oh God, she barely weighed anything. He thought, if she let him, he would draw her a warm bath and wash her hair and rub her back--if she would let him.

As Bobby picked up her small body, all she could think of was how she too had fucked everything up and, to make matters worse, made Bobby feel like he was the only bad person in this situation. She had never mentioned her time with Chris or how she use to think of him every single day, every time she was in her garden. Sure she was pissed off at him initially with his affair with

573

that woman. He fucked up royally by letting her find out about it. He wasn't discreet about it. He would have thought something was amiss if she just let that go and stay together like it was business as normal. Then she would have had to tell him everything, tell him about Chris, and she wasn't ready to do that. She would never be ready to do that. That was just one more secret she would be taking to her grave. It made her so incredibly sad that they had let themselves get to this point. That was the sadness she was feeling and showing. She couldn't eat or concentrate on anything but Bobby and how to get him back home without having to discuss the whole Iraq situation. She wanted him home; she wanted to be in love like they had been before Iraq. She knew she had it in her to be that way; hell, she felt that way. She never stopped feeling very much in love with Bobby. What she felt for Chris was different and unforgettable, but she would let go, let go of Iraq, the war and most of all, Chris. She vowed as Bobby carried her into their little house that was what she was going to do!

He carried her down the hallway to the bedroom and laid her little body on the bed and asked her if it would be ok if she would let him do just that. She smiled weakly and said yes. As he

574

went to the bathroom to run the water, he couldn't help but notice that she looked sick, not just heartbroken or upset or sad but really sick, like something could be medically wrong with her. He wondered if he should ask her. He thought to himself, *not now.* She would tell me when and if she wanted to. He helped her out of her little t-shirt and shorts. Oh *my God,* he thought to himself. She was barely there; hip bones poked against her little panties. Her little ribs stuck way out, so much so that you could actually count the ribs on her back and her once very full chest was tiny…she was tiny…his wife must have lost at least 20 pounds in those two months. He tried not to look alarmed, but she caught his reaction and told him that she was ok. He knew and she knew she wasn't telling the truth on that one.

As he got her in the tub, he took the fluffy sponge and filled it with warm soapy water and started with her back. He thought for just a second he could hear the familiar little purr. After a few minutes of wetting her down, he took the shampoo and put a little bit in his hand and started the massage action of washing her hair. He heard it that time, the little purr came out. She had her eyes shut and head tilted back and was purring. He smiled a smile of sadness and of joy. She always made him feel two distinctly different emotions at the same time. She always could.

After he bathed her, he sat her down on the toilet seat and blow-dried her hair out a bit. He got her some comfy pj's and her little "clouds," as she liked to call the little soft socks she had found one day while they were shopping at the Pentagon Fashion Centre. As he walked her back to the bed, he noticed that she had not moved a thing in the house. Everything was the way it was the day he left. He laid her in their big bed, turned on the electric blanket so she could get warm and toasty. He asked her if he could lie beside her just for a little while, and she nodded yes. As they lay there in the semi darkness, he could now see her face and also noticed that her once balled up little hand had opened up a bit and she was holding something. He tried to move her fingers ever so slightly to see what she had been holding on to. It was the strangest little piece of material. It looked to be a thin strip of lace. He had seen this piece of lace off and on throughout their marriage. She never talked about it and he never asked. Some times he would see it and other times, he simply forgot about it.

It took a few minutes to adjust his own eyes to the

darkness, but once they did adjust, he could see the dark circles under her deep-set brown eyes. He wondered when the last time she slept or even ate was. He wondered if he was the one to have caused all of this or if there was something else wrong. As she lay there with her head on his shoulder, he could hear a slight snoring sound as he rubbed her little boney back with his free hand. He looked at her with a little bit of surprise. She never snored unless she had drunk quite a bit, and as far as he could tell, she had not. Perhaps it had been a long while since she last slept. Regardless, she was out like a light. He slid his now tingly arm from underneath her head and walked back to the front of the house. He looked around and noticed that, in fact, nothing more had been done to the house. It looked as if they hadn't done much of anything on their master retreat. That thought made him cry outright. He sat there on the kitchen floor crying because he knew why. He knew the reason why nothing had been done, and it was his entire fault.

As she slept, she told herself that she would not let thoughts of "him" creep in, but even in her dreams, there he was…there was Chris. She had felt so much guilt while Bobby was away sorting things out. Not guilt from what had happened between her and Chris but guilt from what happened between Bobby and Lindy. She knew she was wrong for packing his shit and having him move out, but she didn't know what else to do. If she did nothing, he would wonder why. And then all the attention would go back to her and what she had done. She just couldn't have that, none of it. She could never let him feel the hurt the way she hurt when she found out.

He stood up and decided that he had to figure out what was going to happen now. He had to be strong and ask, beg if necessary, for forgiveness. With that, Bobby was brought back to the present, back to his lovely bride almost 50 years later, lying there in their master retreat looking beautiful and peaceful. He thanked God every single day from that point on for her forgiveness.

## Chapter 32 -- Final Days

He sat by her side listening to her favorite music in the world, Rachmaninoff's 'Rhapsody on a Theme by Paganini.' Bobby thought this must be the most beautiful, saddest music he had ever heard. "I wonder why she loved this so much?" he thought out loud to himself. Bobby was reading one of his favorite Hemingway books, *Island in the Stream* as the music played on in the background. As he was getting into his book, he heard a strange sound; it wasn't the CD player. He just wasn't sure if it might be coming from the roaring fire that he had going or if it was her. It wasn't one of her purring sounds or a snore either. He thought he heard a voice, very quiet, very tiny little voice, a voice of a woman but not his woman. It was barely a whisper. He wasn't sure what it was, but he didn't like it one bit.

He put his book down on the nightstand and went to her.

579

He checked her breathing and it seemed ok, checked her pulse, which seemed normal as well. Well, maybe she was just having a dream is all. He sat back down and continued reading. He loved this book, regardless of how many times he had read it; he loved it more and more. This particular story was about an artist and adventurer, much like Hemingway himself. The book was about the experiences of Thomas Hudson when he was a painter in the Gulf Stream island of Bimini while his three sons came to visit. Then it goes on through his anti-submarine activities off the coast of Cuba during WWII. The greater part of this story took place in a Havana bar. One of the most interesting characters in the book was an aging prostitute.

He had started this evening like all evenings since she had come back home from the hospital, reading to her, but this time she quickly drifted off to sleep. He had read this book many times, but it was the first time he had read it to his partner. She enjoyed when Bobby read to her. She had him reading all sorts of stuff, magazines mostly. She especially liked when he read one of those women's magazines. Even after all these years and at his age, he still tried to act macho and pretend like he didn't enjoy those types of magazines, but she knew better. She caught him a few times looking over her *Cosmo.* With all the medication in her system, she couldn't stay awake for too long at any one time but nevertheless enjoyed him reading to her while she was awake and perhaps even as she slept.

He hated what was happening to her, especially the pain she was in, but he did enjoy taking care of her. It was a full-time job, but he loved doing it and would never think of leaving anyone else to do it. A lot of their friends thought that perhaps a part-time nurse to help would be a great idea, but he told them no way. She wanted to come home to be with him, not some stranger. He thought of what she had asked of him, but he wasn't sure he could follow through. There were two parts to her last wish. She asked, pleaded with him really, if the pain got to be too much for her that he should perhaps give her a little more medication than was prescribed. She felt he understood what she meant by that. She would let him know when it would get to be too much for her. But for now, she enjoyed being here in their home and with him, albeit, in much pain.

As she lay there listening to her favorite music in the world,

'Rhapsody,' she let her medication cover her like a warm blanket. Sergei Rachmaninoff wrote this piece; the Rhapsody was one of his most well known works. The 18th variation is especially well known. This was one of Rachmaninoff's most important works that he had written after he left Russia, because it had showed a new style for him because the work had no songlike Russian themes. She loved the lush, sweeping, delicately romantic music. The music of the piano and orchestra was hauntingly sad to her. She thought of the first time she heard this particular piece of music. She remembered renting the movie *Somewhere in Time* and cried and cried all the way through the ending. It didn't do well at the box office, but it did very well with her. The lead actor in the movie loved the lead actress so very much, so much that he had to end his own life to be with her.

She wondered how many men would do that nowadays. She wondered about Bobby. Would he do such a thing? She believed that the actors in the movie must have been soulmates as well…even on through death. She thought about death here and now and wondered what it would be like. She wondered about the old woman she had met the first time on the train to

Czechoslovakia, her guide. She still had the little piece of lace, and every now and again when she felt everything was falling apart, she would take it out and just hold onto it for a few days. She hated that period of her life. She thought of it every now and again, and she knew how her demeanor would change, but there simply wasn't anything she could do about it. The incident would just pop in her head when she least expected it. She didn't know why, she just knew that was something that she had lived with for over seventy years now. She and the old woman had talked many times since then. The old woman especially loved her little garden as much as she did and would always visit while she was out there puttering. She wondered if she would see the old woman when it was her time to go. Would she and Bobby still be husband and wife? She felt confident they would on all accounts. Her thoughts were varied and random and all mixed up. Normally that would bother her but here…at the end, she let her thoughts run wild with whatever they came up with.

Thinking of death brought her to her "Things to Do Before I Die" list. She wondered how many of the 20 items she'd actually accomplished. That was a strange thought to have at this point in her life. It had been ages since she'd thought of that list. She'd wanted to do so much in her life. She'd had plenty of time but something else always came up. She felt pretty good about that list though. Out of the 20 or so, she kept subtracting and then of course adding as the years went by, she made a healthy dent in the list. She wasn't sure if too many people ever made lists, but her German side required her to do so. She knew the last thing on the list was to talk to Bobby. He knew what to do if the pain got to be too much, and it was getting incredibly close to that time. She felt good about the decision she made concerning that and felt that Bobby would carry out his part; if the pain got to be too much, that is.

It was her second wish that she felt he would balk at. She was so sure she wanted this done. This would be her number 20 on the list. She knew how difficult it would be for him to complete but hoped with all her heart that he would do it. As she drifted off to sleep with the help of "the warm blanket," she thought of how she would broach the subject to him and, most importantly, when. Time was of the essence at this point.

Before her passing, she felt the old woman holding her hand and brushing the hair off her face with her other hand and then she was gone, just like that. She saw the woman totally disappear right before her eyes. She finally knew who she had been all these years. It felt good to finally close her eyes with that knowledge. When she closed her eyes, she saw her garden with all the beautiful colors of the rainbow; like the colors found in a box of Crayola's. She had the strangest feeling of floating. She wasn't sure what was to happen next, but she wasn't afraid and she felt more than ready to go.

She was glad that she finally had the chance to talk to him before now, to tell him of number 20. She saw his sad face as she told him what she needed to be done to finally complete the list. She wasn't ready to leave Bobby, but she was tired and was ready to rest. They say that before you go to heaven you are greeted by five people whose life you have somehow affected. They are there to teach you something before you enter heaven. She knew that each person's life affects the other and then the next. She wondered who her five would be.

After her passing, Bobby knew she had left him too soon

585

and now his memories would be his only partner instead.

## Chapter 33 -- Her Last Wish

He wasn't sure what to do next. He knew her wishes, her last wish, but could he do it? Could he carry the last wish out to completion as he promised her he would? He had promised her on her dying bed. He decided to call the boat charter company in Key West. He was to fly out of BWI the very next day and had his deep sea charter scheduled for two days later. All he could think of was whether he could actually carry this out. Could he do this to his wife? He thought for a long while and said he had no choice. She made him promise. He packed very lightly. A few toiletries and a couple of changes of clothes...and of course her. Her in her beautiful deep purple enameled urn. She designed it herself. She always thought of everything. Even though she knew she wouldn't stay in it long, she wanted to be located in a beautiful setting. That's just who she was. Heck, she even designed one for him.

Though not as grand as hers; he would never have wanted it that way, it was still beautiful. The beauty was in the details of it. She left nothing to chance in any of her designs.

With that thought, he walked out to their pool and tikki bar. A pool they had built many many years ago after a particularly long trip to Iraq during the war. It was their second trip over there. He took out his Monte Cristo #2 and swirled his cognac in its heavy baccarat crystal snifter. God, she loved beautiful things, and how he loved the beautifully wrapped rolled torpedo with its creamy texture that had a hint of nutmeg. The draw was perfection to him and was always consistently smooth. He felt this was the most gorgeous smoke, which to him was rich and delicious. It was, for him, a most elegant tobacco taste.

As he sat smoking his cigar, he looked up at the master retreat she had designed herself. She took such care when designing the whole thing, from the huge sunny master bathroom with its steam room and big soaking tub and multiple skylights to the dual walk-in closets, his and hers, to the incredible "love nest," as she called it, complete with a larger than normal fireplace. He remembered going to antique store after antique store looking for the one that was just right. They finally found it down the road in an antique store that they had always "window shopped" but never bought, at least until the fireplace. It was quite an extraordinary piece made of alabaster marble with an extraordinary price tag, but she thought it was worth it. It was grand, much like most of her ideas; over the top, really.

She had thought about the balcony over and over, drawing sketch after sketch. Finally she decided that a sunroom full of skylights and floor to ceiling windows complete with a spiral staircase down to the pool area would be better than just your average balcony. The mosquitos were terrible on the eastern shore in the summer, and they both loved being outdoors, especially in the summer. He remembered the second time they were in Iraq; she in Baghdad and he in Balad 30 miles north. She would tell him, via email, of all the furniture she had been looking at online. She couldn't decide on design. She went over it and over it in her mind until she settled on a style that was reminiscent of the British West Indies.

While they were in Iraq, they talked of taking a trip there, to the Island, but they just never made it. They had planned so many things back when they were young. They thought and felt like they had forever to do all the things they planned but they didn't. She even had designed a loft office overlooking their love nest so they would never have to be far apart from each other. For that room, they shopped together for the perfect his and hers pieces. She loved her Louis XV style furniture and he, well he loved it a bit more masculine. They found pieces that were totally different in styles but, when put together, worked; much like them. Bobby loved shopping for the paintings that they would hang. She had already furnished the rest of the house with paintings she had bought all over the world. This was to be his turn to furnish the upstairs. They had picked out one painting together already that hung prominently in the living room. It was a doozy of a painting. It was the first painting that he had ever bought. It hung floor to ceiling. They saw it and immediately fell in love with it. They had to pinch a few pennies to buy it, but in the end, it was money well spent. He loved it because he thought it looked like Italy, and she loved it because it made her think of the south of France. What was important was that they both fell in love with it! He knew the perfect place to shop for the paintings that would hang in their retreat. He had three rooms he was going to furnish. He couldn't wait. He knew that whatever he selected, she would love, even though whatever he picked she would think it to be the south of France.

He thought for just a split second that he saw someone in their sunroom. He thought he saw an old woman. The old woman he thought he saw on that morning right before he sold his pocket watch. He wondered if she was there checking on him, making sure he was ok. He wanted her to visit him often, like that movie he loved so much, *Jillian on her 37th Birthday,* he thought was the name. How she hated that movie. Nevertheless, he wished she would at least show him a sign that she was there, with him still. He missed her so much sometimes he could barely breathe, didn't want to breathe. He sat there and wondered about the days to follow. As the day drew to an end and night took over, he heard all the sounds of the woods where they had lived and had loved. He looked out at their garden, the garden that saved them both one terrible summer when he almost lost her so very long ago. It was after that fateful trip to Iraq the first time.

Everything was as beautiful as she knew it would be.

591

Everything had matured to almost a Garden of Eden look. How did she know it would look like this? The little arbors, the trellis, her little white moon garden with its fragrant smells. The big white gazebo in the centre of it all with yes, a crystal chandelier hanging in the middle of it and its little white metal picket fence, and they even had a little "smoking" gazebo that he had built himself. She dreamt about it one night, woke her out of a dead sleep about 4 in the morning. She started mentally sketching her idea in her head. That was that, they were on their way to Home Depot to get the things he needed to build it that very day. Everything was just perfect as only she would let it be; that very garden where her very best friend, Maria, had gotten married and eventually baptized her first child. Everything she picked, she picked with so much thought and care, much like she had picked him.

Night drew longer and he realized he was still outside in their lovely garden. He thought best to get to bed. This was the saddest part of every single day for him since she'd been gone.

The next morning he got up early, showered and changed and waited for his taxi outdoors. He strolled down to the mailbox and looked down at the sign she had specially made. She loved the idea of having a name for the house like the homes in Europe. He took special note to remember every single thing about the little house; the little house she had fondly named "*au-dessus du dessus*" and it was just that; "over the top" in every way possible, inside and out. As he walked towards the back yard to their Garden of Eden, thoughts drifted back to her, as they always did, but before he could get too caught up in his melancholy, the taxi honked and he was brought out of his reverie. He debated about grabbing his one overnight bag for just a second, then thought best to take it vs. leaving it there. The folks at the airport look at you strangely if you get on a flight without anything at all nowadays. He, of course, couldn't forget the beautiful deep purple enameled urn. They were off for their very last adventure together. A tear rolled down his eye as that realization hit him. No, he couldn't fall apart, not now. Not when she needed him to be the strongest possible, the strongest he had ever been in his whole life. He had to do what she wished him to do; so in the taxi they went.

## Chapter 34 -- Last Adventure

Bobby landed in Miami International Airport. He had forgotten just how hot it could be in the summertime in Florida. The humidity was stifling. He thought back to the first time they went to Miami together, what a fun time they had. They drove down to the Keys. The first stop was in Islamorada, at a little tikki bar. He had thought that was just about the coolest place in the world and didn't want to go further, but she knew he would like Key West so they continued on driving south…as far south as the road would take him, maybe further this time. He got to Key West and checked into the "Southern Most Hotel" and unpacked and set her on the night table alongside the little piece of lace that she had been carrying around for over seventy years. After she passed, he took to carrying the damn piece of lace with him in his pocket. He didn't know why but it made him feel better; it made him feel closer to her. He sat her beautiful urn in the same place he sat her at home for the past few months; his side of the bed, on the nightstand. Strange how he still slept on "his side" of the bed. When she first passed, he would wander over to her side, but he didn't feel right about it. He felt as though he was taking over her space and he didn't want to do that just in case she wanted to come to him for a visit. He wished and wished she would, just like that movie that he loved but she hated.

She wanted him to wait before making this trip. She didn't want him to take this trip any other time. She loved the summer. He called the "Relentless Fishing Charters" to make sure they were on track for the very next day. He wondered to himself why in the world he would pick a name like that. Perhaps because his little woman could be very relentless when it came to things she wanted or liked. She wouldn't stop until she had it. So subconsciously, he must have thought of her when he found them online. He would spend the very next day walking around Key West to visit the places she loved and of course, to "her sign." That was paramount to this trip. He hoped the captain would be able to depart from that location. There wasn't a dock there, but he thought that with enough cash, the captain would accommodate him, especially when he explained the reason why.

As it got later in the afternoon Bobby realized that he hadn't eaten breakfast or lunch and it was already about dinnertime. He thought, *What was her favorite place to eat here?* He racked his brain, why couldn't he remember something that important? He knew that she would remember…..Yes, it finally hit him. The South Beach Seafood and Raw Bar over on Duval Street. She loved the raw oysters with their favorite drink—chilled José Cuervo, no lime, no salt. So off he went. Why did he promise her he would do this? Why make him do this incredibly sad thing? He knew she thought it would make him feel closer to her and he did, but it hurt as well. After a very satisfying meal of surf and turf and of course, their favorite drink, he walked over to Soppy Joe's. Good for him all her favorite places were down the same street. He wasn't as young as he use to be, nor was his fading memory. Goodness, they'd had some good times here in Key West, so many years ago. And God, could that little woman drink. He remembered a few times she drank even him under the table, but he would never admit that to her.

He sat at the end of the bar, not talking to anyone or even looking at anyone. This was their time together. He didn't want any interruptions, so he kept his head bowed down. After several shots, he decided to walk back to his hotel. He hoped he wouldn't get lost walking back. It had been a while, and he had several cocktails in him at this point. As he strolled back he looked around to all the places she loved. He wondered why she loved this little town so much. Sure, he liked it as well, but this little town held a special importance to her. He remembered she had mentioned something about being here during a crazy hurricane and a high school reunion where she had reconnected with her friend Michael.

He hoped he could take her to the exact place she wanted to go, but he didn't think the captain would do that. But he would try; trying his best for the one and only woman he ever truly loved; her very last wish. He would do it if it cost him his life.

He said out loud to himself, "Thank goodness my woman seemed to like everything on the same street or else I might be wandering this little town all night long." It seemed to him that he had only been walking a minute or two, but there he was, right in front of his hotel—the Southernmost Hotel. He was glad; he was beat and tomorrow would be a hard day for him. Their last of many adventures they had shared throughout their lives together.

Sleep came quickly for him that night for some reason. He had the strangest of dreams that whole night. It was almost like a video in his head of his life with her. From the beginning of when they met to this very day. He woke up sweating and scared. Scared because he could have sworn he saw and heard her in the room with him. She had promised she would visit with him once, only once. Not like that movie that he liked where the dead woman comes to visit her husband almost nightly. She hated that movie. She said it wasn't healthy. Anyway, there he sat, upright in the bed, trying to focus. He hoped against all hope he would see her one last time. He waited and waited....nothing.

As he laid his head back down on the pillow, he started to close his eyes. When they were more than halfway shut, he saw her. She looked so beautiful, so very lovely. She looked like an angel to him. He thought best to keep his eyes almost closed so as not to scare her. He wondered if he should speak. Would that scare her away or would she answer or would he "feel" her answer? He decided to wait a little while and just gaze upon her beauty the best he could with half shut eyes. She hated to be called beautiful. She always corrected him by saying she was cute, not beautiful. To him, she was everything he ever wanted or needed. To him she was the most beautiful woman in the world. He decided to risk it and try to talk to her. At first it came out as whisper, barely audible to even himself. He saw her eyes widen. She heard him, he knew she heard him. He didn't actually have to talk, the thoughts he was having, she could "hear." She didn't leave; in fact, she came closer to him and sat on the bed next to him. He wanted to reach out to her but didn't know what to do. Why was it that she made him so nervous, even now? He asked how it is over there; what does it look like? What do you do, where do you go? Have you been with me since you've been gone? One question after another quickly coming out. She smiled her crooked half smile and tried to answer in the order he asked. He could barely hear her but instead felt her answers. She said it was the most beautiful place in the world. It looked much like their little garden at home, like the Garden of Eden.

"I've been with you every day, Bobby. I've been keeping you safe like my dad did for you while we were over there the second time." She reminded him that he shouldn't forget to eat and maybe not too many Monte Cristo #2's, she said that with a smile. She knew how he loved his Monte Cristo's.

He asked her one last question, "Do I still go on with the plans for tomorrow?" and as he waited for her answer, his eyes closed totally shut, and she heard the soft snoring that she had lived with for so many years. She kissed his forehead and he smiled gently.

When the alarm went off at 5:00 that morning, he shot straight up in bed and looked all over his hotel room. He was frantic. Where was she? Had she been there? Was it a dream? He hoped it wasn't a dream. What am I supposed to do today? Did she answer my last question? What do I do? He looked up towards the sky and said, "Please show me a sign." As he hopped out of bed, something fell to the floor. It must have been on the blankets. And there on the floor was his ticket for the day's deep sea fishing charter. He guessed this was the sign he had just asked for. So he jumped in the shower and changed and prepared for their last adventure. Thank goodness he remembered to grab a bottle of their favorite drink the day before. That was a must and could not be forgotten. His wife's words, she was adamant about that part of this trip. She picked that part of the day because that was the time of day they got married in Jamaica; almost didn't get married because they had been partying too much the night before. Right as the sun came up.

He felt ready today for some strange reason. A lot more ready than any other time. He walked over to the sign. Her sign. "90 miles to Cuba." He hoped that the captain would come and get him at this point. That's how she wanted it. She, as always, was very precise at the way things needed to be done. She was such a German in that respect. Luckily, there was the captain, looking a little worried but nonetheless there. Bobby managed to get his old bones down into the boat. Fishing poles, check; bait, check; food, check; little piece of lace shoved in his pocket, check; José Cuervo, check; music, check; and of course his wife in her beautiful deep purple enamel urn; check check and double check. Bobby made sure the captain had the right music—Jimmy Buffett, before leaving the sign, her sign. Check! How she always wished she could be a Jimmy Buffett person; a parrot head. They both wished that, wanted that and tried as they might, had to be content with

601

just loving his music and his carefree attitude. So off they went on their very last adventure.

Bobby reminded the captain where they were to go. The captain was hesitant to do this but told Bobby he would get as close as the law would allow. The captain got the full story of what Bobby and his wife wanted from this trip. They were to sail out as close to Cuba as they could legally get and spread her ashes as close to the country she loved so much. That was her last wish, anyway; number 20 on her "things to do before I die" list. With that, Bobby opened the bottle of José' and began to drink right out of the bottle. The captain, knowing his cue, put on Jimmy Buffett's, "Margaritaville."

As the captain got closer and closer to the destination, Bobby had to remind himself not to drink the whole bottle. He had a slight modification to her request. Things were going to end differently than she had specified. He hoped that she wouldn't be upset and that sooner or later, probably later, knowing her stubborn German streak, she would forgive him but he knew in his heart what he had to do. What the right thing to do was. The captain said to Bobby, "This is as far as I can go." Well, close enough, Bobby

602

guessed.

The captain was at least on the Windward Passage between Cuba and Haiti. That was as close as he was to get. With that in mind and about two fingers left of tequila, Bobby did the unexpected. He grabbed her urn, opened its little top, grabbed the rest of the tequila, doused himself with it and held the little urn over his head and emptied it. Emptied it right on top of himself and with a quick jump, he was in the water, swimming frantically in the direction of Cuba. Thank God Bobby listened to her and took swimming lessons once they got the pool in their back yard, otherwise, he would have been scared to death to just jump in.

The captain yelled and screamed and threw over the life preserver. Bobby just kept swimming and swimming. The captain didn't know what to do. At one point, the captain lost sight of Bobby so he turned the boat back on and slowly trolled the area. He couldn't be found. As Bobby swam under water so as to be undetected by the captain, he realized that he was out of breath. He was in the throes of drowning. Was this really how he wanted it to end? Would his wife be mad or would she understand? The thought of drowning scared Bobby for a second, and then he saw a strange but familiar object there in the water, a figure of an old

woman, the old woman he saw once before a long long time ago.

He had thought he saw her once walking down the hallway of their

home but it couldn't be her, it just couldn't. As he swam closer he

saw that it was her, his true one and only lobster.

So as the pair of lobsters, Bobby and Elle, made their way

down to their little lobster den deep in the azure waters of Cuba, to

toasted their final toast, with of course, Jose', chilled, no lime, no

salt.


~ Juste le commencement (*just the beginning*)~

Made in the USA
Middletown, DE
04 July 2018